SILENT TRUTH

SHERRILYN KENYON

AND

DIANNA LOVE

POCKET BOOKS
NEW YORK   LONDON   TORONTO   SYDNEY

Pocket Books
A Division of Simon & Schuster, Inc.
1230 Avenue of the Americas
New York, NY 10020

This book is a work of fiction. Names, characters, places, and incidents either are products of the author's imagination or are used fictitiously. Any resemblance to actual events or locales or persons, living or dead, is entirely coincidental.

First Pocket Books paperback edition May 2010

POCKET and colophon are registered trademarks of Simon & Schuster, Inc.

For information about special discounts for bulk purchases, please contact Simon & Schuster Special Sales at 1-866-506-1949 or business@simonandschuster.com.

The Simon & Schuster Speakers Bureau can bring authors to your live event. For more information or to book an event contact the Simon & Schuster Speakers Bureau at 1-866-248-3049 or visit our website at www.simonspeakers.com.

Design by Lisa Litwack. Illustration by Larry Rostant.

Manufactured in the United States of America

10 9 8 7 6 5 4 3 2 1

ISBN 978-1-4165-9745-2
ISBN 978-1-4165-9753-7 (ebook)

*We're dedicating this to the men and women in
the military who are away from their families
protecting us all back home.
Bless you and may God keep you safe!*

Acknowledgments

From Sherrilyn Kenyon

Thank you to Dianna for being such a good sport and always making me smile. I never thought I could co-write anything, but given that we often share a common brain—LOL—you made it not only easy, but a joy. Thank you so much for all the support.

Thank you to Kim, Jacs, Brenda, and Retta for reading all my manuscripts and making great comments. Thank you, fans, for coming back day after day. You guys rock!

To my husband for being my shelter in the storm. I'm grateful every day that I said yes when you asked me out to see a movie I couldn't stand. For my kids, who are always my comfort and my greatest source of pride. May God bless and keep you all.

From Dianna Love

A huge thank-you to Sherrilyn for being the best friend and writing partner a person could ask for. She's an amazing talent we're lucky to have in publishing and one of the most genuine people I've ever had the pleasure of knowing.

Anyone who has met me or interacted online with me knows nothing I do would be possible without the unflagging support of my wonderful husband, Karl. Everything he does nurtures my muse and makes it easy for me to indulge my second love—writing. A special thanks to all the fans who have asked for more BAD Agency books and don't hesitate to share their favorite book and characters with us. Your enthusiasm and excitement are all we need to keep expanding this series.

Thank you, Cassondra, for being the best assistant, who is making my life easier every day! Also, thank you to Tracy and the wonderful women at Shamrock Café in Tyrone, Georgia, who keep me fed when Karl is out of town. I love hearing from readers—dianna@author diannalove.com—if you want to send me an email.

From both of us

Lauren McKenna proves continuously why she's an exceptional editor. She has a gift for understanding the direction we take with each story and is always open to new ideas. Thanks also to Megan McKeever for all her help in getting the book out and to Merrilee Heifetz for her constant support.

We appreciate author Mary Buckham (so much!), who reads early drafts—quickly, no less—and makes great suggestions. Her study of interesting things like Asian culture and her husband Jim's knowledge of rare information have stimulated some fun ideas when Sherri and I brainstorm. Another talented writer, Cassondra Murray, also reads every story and comes up with subtle suggestions that make a huge difference in the final draft. We have husband Steve Doyle to thank for a limitless knowledge of weapons and military procedures from his time with Special Forces, plus his feedback from reading every story. We appreciate Annie Oortman's PAL creative reports on every book. Thanks also to Hope Williams and Manuella Robinson for their beta reads that mean so much in the final version.

Thank you to each of the following: We used information on electronic forensics shared by Keith Morgan. Westly Bowen, on staff at Fayette Community Hospital in Georgia, provided medical information. Former NBC anchor Wes Sarginson helped with research on television reporters. Thank you to James Love, Dianna's brother, who shared details about the Gulf of Mexico, and to Gail Jensen for her help with researching Chicago. Errors slip through on occasion just because we're human and if you find one, it's on our part, not the source who generously shared their time and knowledge.

An extra hug to the wild RBL Women, PW blogger Barbara Vey, and the Petit Fours & Hot Tamales bloggers—thanks for all the support, laughs, and martinis. You are too much fun!

We love our readers! You are the reason we work so hard to create a story that will take you away on an adventure for hours of entertainment. We appreciate the time you spend writing us emails and coming out to visit when we tour and sign—and the amazing gifts (you rock!). Thank you for allowing us to spend hours doing what we love most—creating a world where our characters can come out and play. Thank YOU!

If you're a paranormal fan, check out the exciting new Belador series we have coming out in fall 2010 . . . details at www.SherrilynKenyon.com and www.AuthorDiannaLove.com.

CHAPTER ONE

Four years ago off the coast of Kauai, Hawaii

Hunter Wesley Thornton-Payne III didn't believe in premonitions of doom, but now might be an optimum time to reevaluate those beliefs. That last bone-jarring shudder of the thirty-year-old fishing trawler beneath him qualified as a preemptive warning.

Salt water sprayed across the deck from each side of the wheelhouse where he stood. Wearing a wetsuit didn't mean he wanted to be blasted with water every thirty seconds. For the past forty-five minutes this floating hazard had plowed south through the Pacific Ocean toward tonight's black-ops objective.

Failure would trigger hideous deaths for unsuspecting CIA agents over the next twenty-four hours.

A simple mission . . . on paper.

Scaling a sheer rock cliff rising two thousand feet out of windswept waves, and on a moonless night, might give him pause if not for his partner Eliot Sawyer. Having him on this mission should quiet any concerns.

But a dark shadow continued to hover over Hunter's psyche, a sixth sense he trusted almost as much as he trusted Eliot.

A ferocious wave broke across the starboard side, the tip of its watery tail lashing his face with cool spray. The faded teakwood deck quaked beneath his feet.

"This piece of shit better hold together long enough to get us into position." Hunter wiped water from his eyes again. "You can bet that sack-a-shit Retter is riding around out here in something that can do more than ten knots. I should be hauling *his* ass up that cliff since this was his idea."

Eliot laughed. The bastard laughed more than any other human Hunter had ever known. Even in college, humor had balanced out his mammoth size. "Thought you agreed this was the only way to slip inside Brugmann's compound."

Hunter hitched a shoulder in a don't-remind-me response. He'd come to the same conclusion as Retter—BAD's top gun and the lead on this operation—that approaching from the north under the guise of a decrepit fishing boat offered the optimum insertion point. Ehrlich Brugmann's private residence perched on a cliff above a vertical wall of volcanic rock overlooking the northern coast of Kauai.

Brugmann had traveled alone to Hawaii this trip. Had he thought the United States wouldn't notice him selling out the CIA and national security if he didn't do it in DC at his primary residence?

Hunter suffered another whiff of fishy stench permeating the wood. He stared out over the starboard side at the last shred of light as the sun sank closer to the ocean. Twilight silhouetted a pair of fifty-footers bucking waves a mile off.

Two more boats held together with hope and slime.

Retter's doing as well.

Boats were okay in Hunter's book—the sleek half-million-dollar ocean racers he'd once piloted to trophy finishes.

But he hated the kind that tended to sink without notice.

Aging joints creaked in complaint when the deck pitched again. Hunter's grumble ended in a vicious curse.

"Good night for a swim, eh?" Even Eliot had to grab a handhold or bust his silly ass. Pale lights mounted to the wheelhouse cast a sallow glow over his wide body outfitted in an identical black wetsuit, and lit his crooked-tooth grin.

The same grin Hunter had run up against the night he bumped into Eliot while breaking into the dean's office at Harvard. Eliot had already disarmed the alarms when Hunter appeared beside him. Surprisingly, he and Eliot had broken in for the same reason—to correct the grades of a female student who had spurned the advances of a tenured professor and stood to lose her scholarship. Eliot had laughed in the dark and told Hunter to cover their butts, which he did. And was still doing.

Nothing bothered Eliot.

Not even the time the yacht they'd been on had stopped floating in the middle of the night. An explosion in the engine room had been at fault, but the reason really didn't matter when you had to tread water for the next nine hours.

"Not worried about tonight, are ya?" Eliot pushed and prodded until he got what he wanted, a part of his personality that could be annoying as hell at times.

"Worried? Be serious." Hunter ran over the mission again in his mind. His brain assured him everything was a go. His gut argued but failed to produce concrete evidence of a problem. Didn't matter either way. He and Eliot were going in. They thought as one mind and had faced missions more dangerous than this one. With an unmatched ability to breach any security and expert climbing skills, Eliot was the perfect partner.

But the deciding factor had come down to a matter of trust.

Hunter trusted no one, or at least he hadn't until Eliot took him rock climbing back in college. By the end of that first day, Hunter's life had been in Eliot's hands more times than he'd wanted to count. After that, he knew without question that Eliot had his back in any situation.

And he had Eliot's.

Of course, Eliot's heart was his greatest weakness.

"What about the CIA?" Eliot was back on track with the mission. "If they find out you've been here or seen their list of agents—"

"They won't. We're in. We're out. No one'll know. He's got two rent-a-guards. Stop worrying like an old woman. I got this," Hunter added, using their "end of discussion" phrase. With no choice but to insert, he wanted Eliot thinking only about breaching that security system. He gripped the vertical aluminum rail bolted to the wheelhouse and changed the subject. "Speaking of women, you still seeing that professor?"

"I am." Eliot's grin curved up, widened. Beamed.

Ah, hell. That silly look can't mean what I think.

"Was going to tell you this later, but . . ."

No, Eliot, we had a deal. What happened to the "no ties, no commitments, no baggage" rule they'd shaken hands on in college?

"I never could keep a secret from ya for long. Cynthia and I got married." Eliot shrugged. "I would have included ya in the wedding, but we did a quick trip to Vegas."

Married. Of all the stupid things to do. Hunter licked saltwater from his dry lips. *Open mouth and say something, dammit. This is my best friend.*

Only friend.

"Congratulations. I guess?" Hunter scratched his chin. One thing was for sure, he'd never complicate *his* life that way. Not for a woman. They all came with agendas. Like his mother, for one. "Wasn't a shotgun two-step to the altar, right?"

"No way. I'm crazy about Cynthia."

"What about what we do for BAD?" Hunter had joined the Bureau of American Defense after leaving the CIA. BAD operated as a covert agency that protected national security. They had no boundaries, no red tape, and no support if they got in trouble since their secret existence wouldn't be acknowledged. "Cynthia's another person an enemy could use against you if they found out about her."

Eliot stopped smiling and swallowed so hard his Adam's apple pulsed. "My family's never met her, doesn't know she exists. You're the only one who knows about her and I trust you with my life, so she's safe."

What could he say to that? Hunter felt the weight of Eliot's confidence press down on his shoulders, but

Eliot was right. Hunter would protect his friend—and any other BAD agent—with his life. "Have you told her what you do?"

"I told her I do investigative work for INTERPOL and that she can't say anything about my job without putting us both in danger. She's solid as a rock."

"And what about the risks we take?" With anyone else Hunter would have let it go and wished the poor sucker good luck. But he'd been friends with Eliot too long to give him the patent superficial garbage Hunter's family considered the foundation of all relationships. Showing a sincere interest in someone's personal life was paramount to asking how much a luxury car cost. Wasn't done in his family.

Eliot swayed with the rocking boat, moved his feet for balance, and wiped water that dribbled from his buzz-cut head off his face. "She thinks I'm teamed up with a guy named Leroy, which would be you. I told her you handle all the dangerous work. I'm just the on-site geek."

Like any good lie, that had a trace of truth. Eliot really had contracted to INTERPOL *after* a stint with the CIA, where he'd been trained along with Hunter. They were both proficient in electronic invasion, but in spite of looking like the bigger physical threat Eliot's natural gift was cracking a safe or violating security systems, which left Hunter to neutralize opposition. Not a problem.

Hunter didn't mind getting his hands dirty on an op.

But he had no patience for bullshit, which had gotten him in deep trouble with the CIA on one particular job.

If the director of BAD hadn't intervened, Hunter

would have disappeared like a puff of smoke in a strong wind.

The CIA had allowed him to walk away—alive—as long as he stayed clear of any agency operations. They'd never know he was at the Brugmann compound tonight . . . unless something went wrong.

The FBI thought their people were coordinating with a covert CIA team. No one knew BAD existed, except the U.S. executive branch, and no one there would admit such. Plus the CIA wouldn't confess to having a team on U.S. soil, which made it easy to step in when an order came through secure channels.

He just had to insert, confirm the list of names, and exit.

"I didn't forget our deal in college." Eliot had spoken so softly Hunter almost didn't catch it over the rumble of diesel engines beneath his feet. "But I can't live my life without Cynthia and she deserves the respect of marriage."

The time to offer unwanted advice had passed, but Hunter believed his friend would regret the move down the line. This business punished anyone foolish enough to let emotions play into decision-making. He'd just have to do what he'd always done and cover Eliot's back by researching Cynthia more deeply than Hunter's initial scan to ensure she wasn't a threat.

But he couldn't prevent her from breaking the fool's heart.

"Say what's on your mind," Eliot said. "Go ahead. Get it off your chest so we can celebrate later and get drunk."

Hunter wanted to be pissed off at Eliot, an easy feat

with anyone else but this clown. "Just think it's an unnecessary risk. I mean, what're you going to do if she
gets pregnant?"

The trawler engine's sound changed abruptly, going
from loud rumbling to silence when the captain cut
back on power.

That was the sign for Hunter and Eliot to get hump-
ing.

They had two minutes before the props rotated
again.

Hunter pulled his diving hood into place, checked
his gear, then sat on the rail next to Eliot and rolled
backward into cool water. He popped up in the inky
liquid and paddled to the stern, where BAD's latest
propulsion water sled floated.

Everything they needed was strapped in a watertight bag between two control arms. Hunter grabbed
one arm and Eliot grabbed the other, both paddling
away from the trawler while Eliot flipped on the power
switch.

A tiny vibration in the handles indicated the electric
turbo spun quietly within a cage.

The trawler engines rumbled to life and the boat
moved off.

Unable to see Eliot's face, Hunter called, "Ready."

Eliot took a second to answer. "Cynthia *is* pregnant.
I want you to be the godfather." He rolled on the accelerator before another word could be spoken.

Shit. Just like Hunter had suspected.

Another woman with an agenda.

He'd deal with this over beers later.

After thirty-eight minutes that passed with the

speed of a stiletto slicing butter, Eliot anchored the water sled close to the access spot. Currents surged, yanking Hunter back and forth, trying to draw him down into the undertow first, then bash him against jagged outcroppings of rock carved from weather and sea. He'd reconned the face of the cliff yesterday with a high-powered scope during a whale-watching cruise chartered for him and six agents.

The only dicey part would come when the wall angled out at a forty-five-degree slant two-thirds of the way up.

Once they cleared that area, the rest of the climb would come down to memory of the mapped-out route, skill, and patience.

They'd executed these maneuvers many times in low-light conditions, and night-vision monoculars with infrared illuminators would pick up every detail.

He climbed at a steady pace to reach the access point in the allotted time but slowly enough to avoid mistakes.

At the top of the cliff, he reached up until he found a handhold on the steel structure supporting the massive observation deck that shot out four feet over the cliff's edge. He silently thanked the architect of Brugmann's home for including a deck and pool in the design. Climbing up into the framework, he unclipped from the rope connecting him to Eliot.

Spider-climbing sideways, Hunter reached the corner of the deck and huddled in a pocket of space to scan for threats while Eliot tied off the rope. He slipped on gloves that were like a second skin, then pressed a button to illuminate his watch face for a brief glance. Six minutes to eight. Better time than he'd thought. Enough to reach the house before one of the two guards on duty made his hourly perimeter walk.

But when he pushed away from the deck to recon the open ground they'd have to cover, something was not right.

A heavily armed guard in black fatigues stood between the rear wall of glass defining the two-story Mediterranean-style house and the patio. He paced back and forth.

Something had changed since last night's intel.

A permanent guard on this side meant additional— unanticipated—security. Why so heavily armed?

Hunter turned back to Eliot and used hand signals to tell him the security had increased. Eliot would normally have signaled "What the hell?" right back, then grinned.

This time he hesitated, no doubt thinking of his new family.

No room for baggage in this business.

As if catching the direction of Hunter's thoughts, Eliot gave the "Let's go" signal.

Hunter moved out. They had four minutes to make the door on the pool cabana attached to the main structure before encountering the guard that *should* be circling the compound.

Plans always played out better on paper.

Hunter had just reached the corner of the cabana with Eliot tucked in close when heavy footsteps from the front of the house thudded toward them.

Damn guard was early.

The guy covering the rear of the house had reached the end of his pacing route at the opposite side and turned back in the direction of the cabana.

Either way Hunter went meant exposure to a threat.

He was supposed to insert and exit without alerting any security, a stealth op just to confirm documents were in the safe so the FBI could bust Brugmann, a CIA field coordinator, before he sold agency assets.

No noise, no sign of breach, and no blood.

Two out of three was better than dying.

Hunter put his hand up for Eliot to stay put.

When the approaching guard stepped within two feet of their narrow hiding spot Hunter came out of the black shadows, slamming a chop at the base of the guard's neck that didn't kill him but took him out of play. He lowered the limp body between a wall of thick evergreen bushes and the house. Eliot gagged and secured the guard.

If the other guards performed an hourly voice check this would go to shit in a matter of minutes. If not, he and Eliot could still get in and out without notice.

No choice. Not unless he wanted six deaths on his hands.

When the rear sentry turned his back, Hunter entered the cabana with Eliot. Once inside, he passed the bar and service area, then went on through the showers, which reeked of chlorine. An interior door opened to a black-and-white-tiled hallway, which led to an out-of-the-way servants' stairwell to the second floor.

At least *that* intel hadn't changed.

Brugmann's only nighttime staff, a housekeeper, had been called away with an FBI-induced emergency.

Hunter moved up the steps without making a sound on the thick Berber carpet. A walkway exposed on both sides and crossing over the living room area bridged the spot where he stood and the door to Brugmann's bedroom, where the safe was housed.

Lowering to his stomach, Hunter snaked his way across the bridge with Eliot right behind him. Few spotlights above were on, but shadows cast through the carved wood railing showed clearly on the white and sand-colored yellow living room below.

When he reached the far side, Hunter pushed up to his feet in a tight corner next to the door. The bedroom doorknob opened on a whisper. The home had been in Mrs. Brugmann's family for a hundred and twenty-seven years. She hadn't accompanied her husband on this trip and Brugmann had no history of seeing other women. The bedroom should be empty.

On the other hand, Brugmann wasn't supposed to have additional guards tonight either.

Eliot slithered past Hunter, into the thankfully empty bedroom with open windows welcoming the salty breeze. Voices downstairs approached the living room from the foyer.

Hunter paused. Brugmann had a guest.

The buyer for the list of CIA operatives and reason for additional guards?

This was about as much fun as a surprise birthday party, which Hunter ranked alongside boats that sank. He and Eliot had less time than expected.

He waited until the voices drifted into another room before entering the bedroom and pushing the door almost closed. Eliot had located the safe hidden behind a wall of mirrors. Documents in his gloved hand, he read quickly, then gave a thumbs-up.

Hunter released a tight breath. *One* thing had worked according to plan.

Eliot shuffled papers, pausing to read, then shook his head. He signaled he'd found something unexpected and turned his thumb down in a "bad news" sign.

What? Was it written in Egyptian or something?

Hunter leaned down to view the page under the light of the safe. The first document listed *seven* CIA agents, their posts, photographs of five men and two women, plus the codes needed to approach them as a friendly. Eliot snapped shots of all documents in case the FBI didn't contain them, but they now had evidence to convict Brugmann of treason. The minute Hunter vacated the premises he'd send Retter a signal to contact the FBI agents waiting a mile away to bust this prick.

When he reviewed the second document, Hunter realized the problem. Eliot had found a map indicating detonation points beneath a hospital to be bombed the day after tomorrow in England.

England's prime minister had just been admitted for brain surgery, to take place in *that* hospital on *that* day. One of the finest specialists in the world, Peter Wentworth, was traveling from the U.S. to perform the surgery with a full contingent of security.

The Wentworth dynasty ranked among the top ten wealthiest families in the world.

Nothing in the document indicated who was behind the bombing or specifics on the target—the politically embattled prime minister or Peter Wentworth, who supported the prime minister's unpopular economic views.

Eliot returned all documents to the safe but did not relock the safe or reset the security alarms he'd bypassed since the FBI would be alerted within two minutes of their exit.

Of course, the way Hunter's luck was running tonight, he wouldn't be surprised to meet Brugmann at the door to the bedroom. But when he checked the hallway was clear. Melting to the floor, he made efficient moves. A door across the foyer from the living room below opened. Brugmann's bald head and round body popped into view. He waddled to the living room with his guest right behind.

Hunter mentally catalogued the guest's robust physical build, straight black hair to his collar, clean-shaven face . . . and a scar running along his right cheek and jaw. He wore his off-the-rack dark-gray business suit casually with the collar of his blue shirt unbuttoned.

Nothing distinctive about the clothing or his mannerisms.

No time for more surveillance. Hunter continued inching his way across the walkway bridge to the exit steps with Eliot on his heels. At the other side, he raced silently down the stairs to the cabana entrance, checked the outside guard, then made it to the corner of the building without incident.

The guard he'd put down hadn't moved an inch. Still out.

"Jocko!" the guard at the rear of the house shouted.

Hunter froze and stuck his neck past Eliot's imitation of a statue to check the rear guard, who had stopped and faced away from the cabana. There was something familiar in the guard's posture. He cupped his earpiece, listening for a reply that wouldn't come if Jocko was the unconscious man behind Eliot.

Hunter signaled Eliot to keep moving forward slowly, but he stopped again quickly. A third guard appeared between them and the corner of the deck.

The guard blocked their exit point to where the climbing gear waited. He and Eliot would lose a firefight of two 9mms against an arsenal of HK rifles. Lights flooded the pool area and decking. Hunter sucked back deep in the shadows.

The guard near the house shouted, "Where's Jocko, Smitty?"

"Looking for him myself." Smitty stood near the edge of the cliff. His flashlight beamed on. He started sweeping the area, walking toward Hunter and Eliot.

Hunter recognized the voice of the guard at the rear of the house as belonging to Filet Bailey. Filet Bailey and Smitty were mercenaries out of the UK who took short-term work for high pay. They specialized in leaving no evidence.

Where were Brugmann's regular clean-cut security guards?

These mercs killed for relaxation.

"See anything on the lower level?" Filet Bailey called out.

Smitty swung his flashlight in a circle, washing the last bit of shadow away from where Hunter and Eliot hid.

Son of a bitch. Hunter signaled his intent to Eliot, then raced ahead and shot out of the darkness toward the guard's left side. He silently sandwiched the guy's head between his hands, wrenching hard as he brought him to the ground.

Smitty's neck snapped with a dull crunch.

"Smitty?" Filet Bailey called out, paused, listened, then yelled into his transmitter, ordering men to the rear.

Hunter waved Eliot ahead of him under the deck, then hunched down, working his way back to where they'd tied off the rope to the steel crossbeams. Eliot hooked up his climbing gear and dropped over the edge.

Hard voices shouted overhead. Boots hammered the decking.

Hunter calmly lashed his climbing gear into place, then hit a series of clicks on his radio to alert Retter he could authorize the FBI to raid the compound.

Like right fucking now would be a good time.

Filet Bailey shouted orders. Lights flashed between the wood slats overhead, glancing off Hunter.

Hunter gave Eliot a fifteen-second lead. The original plan had been for Eliot to quickly rappel down the face, followed by Hunter using the same rope.

That plan hadn't involved additional security or shooting.

Now they couldn't risk someone cutting the rope before they both made it down, which meant Eliot dropping a hundred feet to find a new anchor point for their rope.

Bullets burst from the side of the deck where Hunter had dropped Smitty. The guards had found their exit path.

Unclipping a smoke bomb from his belt, he pulled the pin, counted several beats, then lobbed it into a trough in the ground that fed the rolling grenade to the corner of the deck.

"Go." Eliot's sharp whisper came through Hunter's earpiece.

Hunter dropped past the edge. Smoke boiled over the cliff. Eliot had fed enough slack for Hunter to rappel below where Eliot hung anchored from an SLCD — spring-loaded camming device.

Bullets pinged wildly, but the guards hadn't figured out how to flood the cliff with light yet. Hunter ripped off a round, silencing the shots above for a moment. He stowed the weapon, freeing his hands for ten seconds. Snagging the rope that trailed from Eliot, Hunter hooked the free rope into his second locking karabiner so they could leapfrog going down.

Hunter dropped two hundred feet like a lead weight into the black abyss waiting to swallow him.

The eerie silence above disturbed him more than rounds of live fire. Eliot hugged the wall, waiting for the signal to drop just past Hunter and hook to his trailing rope.

What was going on at the Brugmann compound? Hunter doubted the FBI had arrived or contained the site that quickly and without more shots.

Too quiet, and Eliot was stuck exposed.

Hunter stopped just above the section of rock wall that slanted in. He had to get Eliot out of firing range. Running his fingers over the face, he found a deep cut in the rock from memory. He shoved an SLCD into the opening, then pulled up twenty feet of trailing rope to tie an anchor sling. He fed slack out the top of his karabiner so Eliot could rappel while Hunter gave cover.

He ordered, "Go," into his transmitter.

Once Eliot reached Hunter they'd use a series of

anchors Eliot had placed on the way up to now climb below the inclined face of the wall, which would protect them both from enemy fire.

Eliot started dropping fast.

Lights in the compound blazed high above him, but still no sounds filtered down. And no one looked over the edge.

A red laser light bounced on the wall above Eliot . . . on the SLCD anchor where the rope was tied off. One bullet sang out, then a second one hit the anchor . . . snapping the rope.

Hunter lunged for the wall to brace himself for the sudden yank of Eliot's weight.

If Eliot had locked his karabiner or had a knot to stop the rope from sliding out.

Rope whistled past Hunter's ear. Eliot bounced against the cliff face next to him with a sickening thud.

Bone cracked. Eliot screamed.

Bile ran up Hunter's throat.

The rope jerked taut with Eliot's dead weight. Hunter gritted against the pain wrenching his muscles. He gasped for air.

Another bullet ripped loose, the report echoing in the silence.

The rope wrenched and Eliot howled in agony. "I'm hit."

Hunter's blood turned into ice.

He twisted to look down.

Eliot's life depended on Hunter keeping his head and holding tight to this anchor. Even shot, Eliot was stronger than most men in their best condition.

Hunter *would* get him off this rock.

Men shouted above. Maybe the FBI, but no one could help him and Eliot hanging off this rock face.

"Swing. Your . . . self," Hunter shouted. If Eliot could swing a couple times and find an anchor, something to grab . . .

Doubt bombarded him. He'd reconned the wall himself and remembered no easy place to grab on to the slick surface. Eliot hung below the last anchor they'd set earlier beneath the inclined wall. Fuck it. Hunter would untie from the anchor and . . . shit, he might not be able to hold Eliot's weight. *Think!* If Eliot swung in, he could—

"No," came through Hunter's headset, thin with suffering.

"Swing yourself. Now, godammit!"

No answer. Hunter took a shuddering breath. Adrenaline flooded his body, willing him the strength to hold on as long as it took.

"Shoulder's . . . blown." Eliot's strained voice broke through Hunter's earpiece. "Leg . . . broken."

Good God. Hunter started calculating how to lower him down. Eliot had no rope.

Fuck. Fuck. *Fuck!*

"Swing in, man. Do it," Hunter pleaded. He might have been wrong. There could be one spot Eliot could grab with his good arm.

Eliot groaned. "Watch over . . . my family."

"Don't start that shit!" Hunter clung to the rope, his heart thundering with the first panic he'd ever experienced. He had no idea how he was going to get them both down, but he'd do it or die trying. "Swing, you bastard."

Eliot wheezed hard, then begged, "Let me . . . go down."

"Working on it. Just—"

"No." The next words choked from Eliot, sounding too liquid to be good. "I got this."

What the hell is he talking about? Hunter twisted around to look down.

Eliot hung backward, his body dangling. He moved as if every effort cost him greatly. His undamaged arm lifted something up from his belt—

All at once, Hunter processed what Eliot intended to do. Blood roared through his ears. *"No!* Just hold on."

Voices shouted through bullhorns up at Brugmann's house.

Hunter ignored everything but the horror that threatened to suck his heart from his chest. *"Don't. You. Do. It."*

"Can't both get down, bro." Eliot coughed. He yelped with pain. "Can't show your face. No time . . . left."

"Don't fucking care." Fear spun through Hunter's brain in a death roll. Everything slowed with sickening clarity. His throat tightened until he couldn't breathe.

"Love you both." Eliot lifted his hand, the knife visible.

Oh, God, no!

One quick slash. The blade cut clean through.

Hunter lunged, arms reaching into thin air.

Eliot plummeted out of reach, shrinking away.

Waves crashed over jagged boulders below.

His wide body stopped suddenly as though someone had pulled the plug on time.

"Nooo . . ." Hunter's scream thrashed the air. Free of weight, the rope bounced up, dangling in the wind.

Hunter stared, locked in disbelief.

Eliot hadn't just died, not that easily. Not full-of-life

Eliot . . . gone. Not the one person Hunter believed invincible.

Pain slashed deep with each breath and ripped his soul into scattered parts that had no idea how to come back together.

Bullets chattered over the rock face, a dull staccato playing backup to the macabre image of Eliot smashed against the rocks. Waves crashed in the eerie silence. The wind howled painfully in Eliot's absence.

Hunter fought for a breath from his paralyzed lungs.

A tiny red dot entered his field of view.

The laser beam danced on his arm, stealing his attention. He watched the deadly dot move down the side of his body.

Do it. Kill me now.

The dot moved on. A bullet ripped loose, striking muscle and bone in his foot. Burning pain forced him back into the world of the living.

The world where he'd find the sniper and make him pay.

The world where Hunter had to save the people Eliot had just died to protect.

He flipped his weapon out and fired mercilessly in the direction of the last shots. When he stopped, a laugh drifted to him on the breeze.

You will die, and not quickly.

Had to go. One numb movement after the next, Hunter lowered himself until he reached the water sled. He cut the anchor line and motored the propulsion craft through turbulent waves and located Eliot pinned on a jagged rock outcropping.

If there was a God, his friend had died immediately.

He removed an inflatable vest from the watertight bag, then dragged his friend's lifeless body down to the water. He held Eliot in his arms, hugging him. The ocean buffeted them.

Why hadn't he done this when Eliot was alive?

Hunter struggled for one painful breath after another until he had a grip again. He put the vest on Eliot and inflated it.

He kept waiting for Eliot to say something funny about how bad their luck sucked tonight and how good the beer would taste, but the silent face would never split with a goofy smile again.

Hunter laid his palm against Eliot's cold cheek. "You shouldn't have done it, bro. Who's going to show up at my apartment at midnight on Christmas Eve to drink beer? Or tell me when I'm being the biggest asshole on the planet? Or . . ." Hunter swallowed. "Teach your kid to ride a bike? Goddammit, Eliot. You weren't supposed to get hurt."

Why didn't the bullet hit me?

No one would have missed him if he'd died tonight. His brother would have mourned for a while, then life would have gone on.

But there'd never be another Eliot.

Hunter secured Eliot's body to the sled. When he thought he could speak without his voice breaking, he used the radio on the water sled to contact Retter. The last thing he could do was let anyone at BAD hear or see what Eliot meant to him.

Retter would sideline an agent he thought might turn rogue. Hunter wouldn't allow anyone to sideline him right now.

Not even BAD.

"They get everything?" Hunter asked when he radioed Retter.

"Got the list. Target and five security were down when they arrived."

"I only terminated one."

"The rest taken down by knife or by hand."

"What about the guy with the target?" Hunter would give Retter details on the guest with Brugmann once he debriefed.

"Nobody found with the target. Three of the security unidentified."

"They were mercs." What had happened to Brugmann's guest? Was the scar-faced guy the sniper? He turned the water sled toward the open sea. "I'm on the way in."

"What about Eliot?"

"Terminated." Hunter's chest clenched at the cold reference, but he had to start selling that image now.

Retter didn't speak for a couple seconds. "Need to pick you up quick and get you secured."

Like hell. "Why?"

"The safe had a camera at the back. Recorded your face."

Was there no end to this fucked-up op? He engaged the water sled's motor, steadying Eliot's body with his free hand. Hunter wasn't going to ground, not even to hide from the CIA.

Nothing would stop him from finding that sniper.

CHAPTER TWO

Current day, Chicago, Illinois

"You can't afford to refuse my offer."

"Mmm-hmm." Abbie Blanton kept her eyes on the jerky downtown Chicago traffic ahead of her Ford Explorer, which was slugging along in the first sunny day of March. She refused to meet Stuart Trout's eyes. How could he call exploiting her personal crisis for his own benefit an offer? She wasn't actually surprised by that, any more than by his asking for a ride back to the office after lunch. The general manager of the WCXB television station did nothing without an ulterior motive.

She was ready for him this time with her own angle.

"*If,*" Stuey continued. "You want a raise *and* to work a flex schedule, you've got to give me something to hand the board." His bulbous fish lips stayed in a perpetual pout, more like a largemouth bass than a mountain trout. No fresh outdoorsy scent to go with his looks, though. His aftershave smelled as sickeningly sweet as the French bathhouse-designer name on the bottle suggested.

"The board?" Abbie asked. "The only board member after blood is old man Vancleaver. I'm thinking the rest of our board would frown on using my investigative skills to do what boils down to snooping around like the paparazzi. Do you really think the citizens of Chicago care if one of our senators is having an affair?"

"When it's with a state judge, yes."

"She's a fair judge and you know it. Vancleaver's just PO'd because she ruled against him in a bullshit lawsuit. *And* because their politics differ." Abbie's knack for research and sniffing out corruption had launched her career investigating for news stories, but she was sorely tired of digging around in people's dirty laundry. Her soul felt as soiled as the mud-crusted piles of snow shoved up against the street curbs. One day she'd . . .

"I'm doing you a favor, Abbie. I could have offered this to someone else if I didn't want to help you."

She had a favor in mind for more than his lame offer. Not yet. She'd test his threat. "This story sounds like something Brittany could use for her weekend entertainment spotlight. Why doesn't Vancleaver want his granddaughter to get the scoop?"

"The senator's affair isn't with just some woman but a judge under consideration for a justice seat with the Illinois Supreme Court. Chicago's citizens deserve to know about her and this senator before she's voted into the highest judicial position in the state and he's up for reelection."

She shifted her gaze in time to see Stuey puff up with indignant righteousness. Over morals? Yeah, right. She knew the real Stuart, the predator who fed on interns while secretly dating a woman who could further his career. She swung the Explorer wide to pass a group of cars hugging each other's bumpers at turtle speed and let him sit on his soapbox a minute.

She hadn't hit Stu with what she really wanted—yet. First she had to decide if she'd go after the senator or not. Even if she did, WCXB would have to live with what she dug up, which might or might not point a finger at the senator and the judge.

Stuey sighed loudly. "I'll even consider asking the board about funding the documentary you want to film on abandoned children."

It took all her control not to react. He would make that offer *now* when she couldn't capitalize on it. Not with her mother's illness. She'd been trying to break into documentaries for several years in hopes of one day pursuing her true passion. Had Stuey been rattled by the recent layoffs? Did he need a ringer story to cement his position?

"Bring me a story with teeth if you want my help," Stuey pressed. "I'll get you on the air—"

"No. I work best when no one knows who I am and I have no interest in sitting in front of a camera." That would mean wearing makeup, having her bushy head of curls tamed into something chic, and wearing real clothes. Not the sweater, jeans, and boots she wore today and every other day.

She might have to sell her soul one more time, but she refused to make this easy for her manipulative, underhanded, scheming boss. That pretty much described all the men she'd had the misfortune to know in her life.

Except, of course, her father. The one who adopted her.

"Abbie?" He barked her name tersely as an order.

"Heard you, Stu. I'm *think*-ing."

"Do it while I'm still young." The forty-six-year-old general manager for Chicago's second leading news station wore his dull brown hair short and slicked forward, styled camera-ready. His squinty hazel eyes had never met hers during the lunch they'd just finished, but she felt the weight of them bearing down on her now.

Patience didn't come as part of his job description.

"I don't want to make a rash decision." Her father would have laughed at that if he was still alive. *Impulsive* had been her middle name from childhood until she went out on the town six years ago looking for some action to pay back her cheating fiancé. She'd gotten drunk and woken up in a chain hotel in South Chicago next to some guy with long scraggly hair, a ratty beard, and a buff body the following morning. She never saw him again. She'd called him Samson and he hadn't corrected her.

She'd curbed her impulsive ways that day.

But she had a stubborn streak that could kick Stuey's overbearing attitude any day. He was right to some degree. She couldn't afford much right now, like the luxury of pissing him off. Not when she desperately needed something he held within his power.

An engraved invitation to the Tuesday-night Wentworth fund-raiser for the Kore Women's Center. She had to get inside and not be marked as media.

"Your cell phone's buzzing." Stuey's pissy tone indicated how much he hated having his time imposed upon.

She dug her cell phone from the black-and-brown

leather bag next to her feet. The caller ID said it was Hannah, the only one of her two sisters Abbie would take a call from.

Driving with one hand was not a problem since the traffic was getting worse. She answered, "I'm in a meeting."

"Dr. Tatum needs to talk to you."

"What about?" Abbie didn't want to discuss their mother's situation in front of Stuey, who had enough leverage on her as it was from when she'd asked to go on flextime. She'd added the raise thinking he'd give her the relaxed scheule before he'd turn loose more money.

"How should I know? I assumed it's about Mom's condition, but when I told him to tell me he said he really needed to talk to you." Hannah's tone spewed insult between each word.

Abbie's hands tightened on the steering wheel. Tatum had shared information about her mother's condition in confidence—with Abbie only—last night and made her swear not to tell Hannah or anyone else. Information that might shed some light on why their mother had become critically ill ten days ago.

She'd rather be at the hospital with her mother right now, but Tatum's disclosure had dropped his best hope for helping her mother in Abbie's lap, which had instigated today's lunch with Stuey. "How are things today?" she asked Hannah.

"She's incoherent, in and out of it." Her sister's voice wobbled a little, then toughened up. "Her blood pressure keeps fluctuating. Skin color isn't good. Her liver's . . . worse."

"Crud." Abbie hadn't slept much in days for worrying

about her mother, but hearing the fear in Hannah's voice amplified her own stress. Hannah rarely let anyone think she didn't have the world by the balls.

"Hold on," Hannah said. "I need to move out of the way for the nurse."

"Abbie?" Stuey repeated in a low but insistent voice.

She managed not to snap at him, but her quick glance must have transmitted a bite of annoyance.

He blew out a stream of air to let her know how irritated he was at being ignored.

She wanted to tell him to stow the attitude.

Don't lose sight of the goal. She still needed that invitation from him. She needed her job, too, for all the obvious reasons, but Stuey couldn't afford to lose her either. She hoped. He'd hired a new hotshot who had potential with some training, but Abbie had handed WCXB's anchors a wall of Emmys. She hoped that played heavily in her favor. Getting into the Wentworth fund-raiser offered the only glimmer of hope for finding out what had happened to her mother.

Tatum said if he could discover why her spleen had started malfunctioning after her mother visited the Kore Women's Center ten days ago he'd have a fighting chance to cure her. But the Kore center blew him off, stating her mother had only donated blood and participated in routine tests. Nothing else.

That's when Tatum had divulged details on Kore that would rock the Wentworth Foundation, which supported the women's center, if Abbie released Tatum's disclosure as news.

And she would do just that if she didn't get to speak with Gwenyth Wentworth, who had yet to return a phone call. The Wentworth heiress hosted the fund-raiser. If Abbie could get inside the event, she'd find a way to talk to Gwen.

When Hannah came back on the line, Abbie said, "I'll call him when I get to the office."

"When are you coming to the medical center?"

"Soon as I can, but I'm busy right now—"

"Give me a break, Abbie. Just because I don't clock in somewhere doesn't mean I'm not busy, too." The real Hannah had returned, shrouded in her usual self-importance and unwilling to be one-upped by a sister who worked for a television station. "Besides, how serious can digging up dirt on our police be? Whose life are you ruining this week?"

"You want crooked cops on the streets?" Abbie snapped.

"Of course not, but you act like everyone in law enforcement is on the take. Some of them are protecting us."

"I know that and I don't think they're all bad seeds." Not really. Abbie switched lanes and pretended to ignore Stu's finger tapping on his knee. "Back to what we—"

"I have appointments, too," Hannah said, cutting her off. "But I'm not letting *mine* take priority over Mom."

Bully for Hannah that she put Mom ahead of spa treatments and having her house redecorated. "I'll come by tonight, but I gotta go now. Call you later." Abbie ended the call before Hannah forced her to say too much in front of Stuey.

"Boyfriend?" Stuey asked.

"My personal calls are just that." She threw a look of low tolerance at him. "Personal."

He twisted his fish lips, frowning as though he had a hook in his jaw. He was in his standard stewing mode, the reason her secret Stuey nickname fit so well.

She used a fingernail to scratch the middle of the thick curls she'd twisted up off her neck and secured with a plastic clip. She couldn't let temper interfere, not now when she had to get into that fund-raiser. Attending a snooty party meant wearing shoes designed by sadistic trolls and dressing to compete with women born to make fashion statements.

She'd been born to pig farming.

And had one outfit that might suffice. Her sister Hannah had given her a satin dress a half size too small for Abbie after being told dark green was not Hannah's color. The only reason Abbie might be able to wear the Saran Wrap dress now was because she'd spent so much time with her mother at the medical center, where food just wasn't appealing.

Her mother was losing weight faster.

"We'll be at the station soon." Stu's voice switched from social to superior.

Not helping his case one bit.

Abbie sighed loudly enough to ruffle the flat silence perched between them in the seven-year-old sport utility. Flipping on the turn signal, she hung a right onto Michigan Avenue, where—hallelujah—the traffic was moving. Some people considered driving through Chicago challenging, but she'd grown up in south Illinois hauling loaded livestock trailers behind a twenty-five-foot-long flatbed truck.

Guess it was time to start negotiating. Abbie lightened her tone. "How about a deal? I've earned the raise and flextime option. So what if I agree to look into the senator's affair with the judge if you'll get me an invitation to the Wentworth fund-raiser tomorrow night as a guest?" She'd found out Brittany Vancleaver had an invitation, because of her grandfather. Stuey could use that angle to get Abbie an invitation.

Stuey didn't reply, intense as a fish stalking bait.

Come on, baby, take it. Abbie wanted to steal a glance and see if he'd bite, but she kept her shoulders relaxed and her attention on the road. He might have thought their hour-and-a-half-long lunch had been about him prepping her to go after the judge, but Abbie had been luring Stu toward this moment.

"Deal?" His acidic tone surprised her. "I'm offering you what you *need*—a position with more money and flexible hours, because you've obviously got some family crisis happening. *That's* the deal."

Her heart sank. No wonder he kept going through office managers faster than water through a rusted-out pot.

Stuey had the perceptiveness of a rock. He was guessing at her having a family crisis, but if he really thought that was the case the bastard could show some understanding.

Money had never been at the core of her motivation to do anything other than survive. Something crooked officials who'd tried to pay her off had found out. She'd taken to investigative work like a duck to water when she first dug into her father's suicide, but she was sick to death of chasing shakedown cops and political weasels. Of having law enforcement treat her as if she'd sell out her grandmother for a story.

Abbie had asked Stu to allow her flexible hours for personal reasons. What did Stuey do? He saw a chance to use it against her to help his position. One day she'd have the money to call her shots and travel the world as an international journalist filming documentaries that made people feel good.

That wasn't in the cards this week.

"You know," Stu murmured slyly, his clothes rustling when he moved close to whisper, "I have better things to offer than getting into a fancy party. You could sweeten the pot on the deal . . . later tonight."

Stuey thought she was willing to, to . . . to prostitute herself for a freaking job?

That pig. *Like the one I almost married and not near as useful as the ones Dad had raised.*

Abbie wheeled her vehicle into WCXB's parking lot, slid into the first open space, and stomped her brakes.

Stu slammed his hand against the dash, stopping his forward momentum. "What the hell?"

She shifted a steel-hard gaze at him, hands gripping the wheel to keep from locking them on his throat. "Number one, I'm not sleeping with *anyone* to get anything, much less do that for a job. Number two, you flatter yourself if you think I'd sleep with *you,* and number three? You're dating Brittany."

God, but she hated men some days. Most days.

They lied, cheated, and manipulated their way through life.

Her heart thumped from a dangerous mix of adrenaline and anger. She would never let another man screw her over again.

All of them were dirtbags, especially her boss.

Boss . . . crud. She'd let her temper boil her brain senseless. She still needed the pass to the damn fundraiser.

"How'd you know—" Stu caught himself and snapped his lips shut. His face turned a deep shade of guilt.

Hmm. Maybe she could work this in her favor.

She hated having to give Hannah credit for this news scoop, but fair was fair.

"How'd *I* know you were dating Brittany?" Abbie put the car in neutral and left the engine running. She turned to face him. The possibility of impending triumph surged into her voice. "Brittany's brother went to school with my sister Hannah, who is now in a book club with Brittany. During their last book club meeting, Brittany started talking about how much she loved being a society reporter for WCXB and said that's how she met this *wonderful* guy—Stuart—she'd been seeing for the past *month.*"

Stu's face lost the cocky angles and turned pasty. Dating old man Vancleaver's granddaughter might not have been Stuey's best idea, even if they were well suited. Abbie would normally have felt it was her duty to clue in Brittany about dating the lecherous Stuart, but Brittany had a reputation for two-timing her men and bragging about it.

Who was Abbie to interfere with a perfect match?

But Brittany wouldn't overlook *his* infidelity.

Abbie added, "I'd venture to say *she* thinks you two are dating. If you're available you should let her know right away." She never thought she'd be thankful for having endured Hannah's recent rambling about her own latest conquest—a self-made millionaire with three houses in different states. But in the midst of her all-about-Hannah review, her sister had suggested that Abbie should take a tip from Brittany, who had nailed a man considered one of the most eligible bachelors at Abbie's television station.

I do not hate my sister.

Well, at least not Hannah.

Casey, her twenty-five-year-old baby sister, was another story.

Abbie rarely suffered from the green-eyed monster, but hearing how she should learn how to get a man from gorgeous Brittany or conniving Hannah hadn't made it one of her better days.

Now she pitied Brittany almost as much as she did the poor rich sucker Hannah had in her feminine crosshairs. As the middle child of three kids, and one who hated growing up on a pig farm, Hannah had started sleeping her way to an impressive investment portfolio the minute she'd turned eighteen. She'd made it clear she would not dirty her hands ever again.

As if Hannah had ever helped out on the farm.

Casey had set her sights on more attainable targets. Unfaithful men. Hard to aim much lower than that.

Abbie had loved her dad and his farm. She would one day prove he hadn't committed suicide and left her mother destitute.

Stu swallowed hard, the sound loud in the car. His fish lips narrowed and turned down at the corners. The shoulders of his navy Brooks Brothers suit slumped. "I, uh, may have given you the wrong impression about my intentions."

Nice try, Stuey, but no free deals today. "Oh, I think I understood exactly what you were saying." Abbie had an evil side that rose to the surface in the presence of assholes.

He studied her a moment, his eyes flickering with unchecked worry. "About that deal . . ."

She wanted to smile, just a little, but this was not the time to gloat. Not when she had Stuey dangling by his short hairs. "I want the raise you offered—" *Never* leave money on the table. "—and the flex schedule, and . . ."

Stu's frown deepened with each demand. He leaned forward slightly. A sign in her favor.

"I want an invitation to that fund-raiser tomorrow night."

His lips parted, some objection hanging there.

What wouldn't fly? The money? Okay, Abbie could bend on that one, but not the flextime or getting an invitation to the fund-raiser. She had to enter as a guest and not as someone connected to the media. She doubted Gwenyth Wentworth, who avoided the media, would knowingly allow an investigative reporter inside.

Brittany was of the same social class. Not a threat.

Abbie would never be one of *them* and posed one hell of a threat to the Wentworths. Every passing hour decreased her mother's chance of recovery from whatever ravaged her body.

"I'll find the money to give you a raise and approve your schedule, but there is no way I can get you into the Wentworth event," Stu said almost apologetically, as if he would dearly love to ease his balls out of Abbie's fist. "Brittany's using her grandfather's invitation. She isn't even taking me."

"Not good enough." She relaxed her grip on the steering wheel with great effort and started tapping her index finger. She wanted to give him the impression that she had her own limit on patience. She'd never considered blackmailing anyone, and this didn't constitute blackmail so much as forcing Stu to take stock of the blank pages in his moral code book.

Thanks to Dr. Tatum, who had been her mother's doctor for as long as Abbie had been alive, she now had a glimmer of hope, a chance to save her mother. Tatum had told Abbie about how her mother had made visits to the Kore Women's Center for thirty years.

Three decades of secrets. Tatum had handed Abbie a weapon to bargain with that no public relations firm could spin.

Blackmailing Stuey was the least of what she'd do.

Stuey shrunk back, staring at her with the fear of a weasel that had chased dinner into a snake hole.

Abbie stopped tapping the steering wheel. "I'd hate for our little discussion to get out in public."

"I can't, Abbie. I would, but I can't . . ."

Bullshit. Stu could make this happen. "Why not?"

"Because the only way you could go is if Brittany doesn't. Any chance of getting her invitation and giving it to you would end up with her thinking something was going on between *us*. We'd *both* lose our jobs. Can't do it."

CHAPTER THREE

‿

Could the mole inside the Fratelli de il Sovrano sending BAD intel be trusted? Or was tonight's mission at the Wentworths' annual March fund-raiser an elaborate setup to expose BAD's agents?

Out of instinctive reflex, Hunter checked for the 9mm he didn't have due to the metal detectors he'd have to pass through. He felt naked without it. The sigh he let escape sounded noisy, a testament to the whisper ride of a stretch limo.

"We'll be there soon, Mr. Thornton . . . Payne . . . the third, Your Highness, sir," came from the wiseass in the front seat driving a limousine so new the leather had a robust scent.

"Fuck. Off." Hunter was in no mood for anyone's crap tonight. He had enough on his mind without dealing with the dickhead driving. That sixth sense of his stirred to life with an antsy feeling he couldn't finger the reason for, but not from concern over executing tonight's mission. If the mole's intel was solid, trustworthy, Hunter would walk away one step closer to someone he'd hunted for four years.

The assassin who killed Eliot.

A valid reason to feel edgy.

He would have volunteered to lead this op tonight

for that reason alone, but the choice had been made for him before he entered BAD's mission room. Hunter's credentials—having been born with a silver spoon in his hand to flip Cheerios across the room—put his name at the top of the list.

A derisive chuckle rumbled from the driver's seat.

Hunter wished again for a weapon but wouldn't actually use it on the cretin playing limo driver.

Not worth ruining a tux with blood splatters.

"What're you so pissy about?" BAD agent Korbin Maximus looked more like a corporate bodyguard stuffed in a dark suit than a reserved limo driver. Mexican genes mixed with who knew what else to give him his muscular six-foot-one build and eyes that were more black than brown. He laid heavily on the barrio accent that came and went with need. "You get the cherry assignments with champagne, limos, and women . . . how tough is that?"

"Yeah, my life's a cakewalk," Hunter muttered, unwilling to engage in another round with Korbin after the argument this morning in Nashville. The muted ding of Korbin's phone followed by quietly spoken words meant Hunter might be spared any further conversation for the rest of the ten-minute ride to the Wentworth mansion. They both knew tonight's plan and their jobs, so the less said for the duration of this trip the better.

Hunter could hold the peace but doubted Korbin would.

Cherry assignment? Not from his vantage point.

The team should be thanking him for having the juice to pull an invitation to this fund-raiser with one phone call, not giving him grief over refusing to take a female BAD agent as a companion.

Some might see his assignment tonight as just another advantage of being one of only two Thornton-Payne heirs.

Hunter loathed spending an evening enduring mindless chatter from the perpetually self-consumed almost as much as dealing with the damned media that hovered with a vulture's eye for opportunistic misery.

But he'd attend fund-raisers every night for a year if it meant the chance to find Eliot's killer.

And he'd do it for Joe Q. Public, BAD's director. Joe had brought him into the organization seven years ago when they met in a complicated situation that should have ended with Hunter's death.

A male snitch in Poland, known only as Borys, had saved both Hunter and a female CIA agent from being made while deep undercover inside the Russian mob. Four months later, the CIA cut a deal with the same crime family to trade Borys for information.

When Borys disappeared before the exchange could be made, the CIA cornered Hunter. Joe pulled off a maneuver to save Hunter's neck that would have impressed a wizard.

The CIA allowed Hunter to walk away as long as he never interfered with one of their operations again.

If they ever located Borys, Hunter's life would be worth less than the snitch to the agency.

Entering the Brugmann home four years ago could have resulted in a breach of his agreement with the CIA if not for Joe's quick action. Unbeknownst to Hunter and Eliot, a camera at the back of the safe had filmed both of them. Mere hours after the FBI's raid on Brugmann's property, a team of BAD agents stole the film from an FBI evidence locker before the CIA had a chance to review the images.

Ass saved once again.

If only Eliot had survived. Hunter had gotten Cynthia into the funeral home after-hours so she could have a private moment with Eliot since his family didn't know she existed. Her anger had rivaled Hunter's. She'd railed at him for bringing Eliot home in a box. Regardless of what she thought of him, Hunter watched over Cynthia and her son. He'd put aside his feelings over how she'd trapped Eliot and do his duty to his friend forever.

But tonight he had to pay back more than one debt. If he followed his mission instructions, he would only stay long enough to recon the guests attending and pick up the USB memory stick Linette Tassone—their mole inside the Fratelli—dropped at some point during the event, then he'd eavesdrop on the Fratelli meeting if he could locate the three expected to attend.

If. Small word with too much room for autonomy.

During the mission briefing, Joe had told Hunter the CIA had tied the killer at Brugmann's in Kauai—better known as the Jackson Chameleon—to a series of linked deaths. They wanted the JC assassin.

The CIA should have made better use of the last four years while Hunter had patiently spent his time proving to Joe and Retter he would not go rogue. Waiting on his chance to find the killer who had laughed when Eliot cut his rope. And fell . . .

"Yep, Joe's right," Korbin said, interrupting the

silence. His cell phone call had obviously ended, to Hunter's chagrin. "You *are* the perfect choice for this gig." He shrugged with feigned acceptance. "Guess it's like you said about Rae. No one can play in your league if they're not born to it."

Thanks for reminding me of the low shot I had to take at Rae to keep her out of danger tonight. Hunter couldn't allow anyone to be tied to him once he walked into the Wentworth complex. Rae Graham would do anything BAD required of her, and at a level of expertise that impressed them all, Hunter included.

She deserved to know if she was walking into a dangerous situation, but Hunter could tell no one his plans. "I did Rae a favor."

Korbin's harsh laugh was vacant of humor or understanding. "Forgive me if I don't see the generosity in your argument, amigo."

Can't let it go, can you, jerk-off? "If she tried to enter as a guest, someone in tonight's crowd would nail her as a poser and lacking. Her presence would draw the kind of attention we can't afford. The minute one woman got a hint of any shortcoming the rest would turn on her faster than a pack of cougars at a frat house." Hunter cringed internally against the snick of guilt his lie triggered. His job required lying, but he hated doing it at the cost of a teammate's pride.

Rae and Korbin were fairly new to BAD, on board for just over two years now.

Both had proven to be elite agents.

At five-eight with a buff body, one hell of a brain, and sharp feminine features, Rae would have actually been the perfect companion and made Hunter's job a whole lot easier this evening. As it was, she'd still be on-site tonight, but as part of the catering staff. Any other time, Rae would have had no issue inserting as a servant, but she didn't care for being snubbed publicly.

Hunter sympathized. He didn't care to be the asshole doing the snubbing, but he had a personal agenda that would put his neck in a noose if he got caught.

And might pressure an assassin to act even if Hunter didn't get caught.

That could put Rae in a sniper's crosshairs without any warning.

Not going to happen.

And if anyone at BAD knew what he was up to he'd get yanked out of the field so fast he'd have vertigo. He could live with the team pissed off at him for openly dissing Rae, but he couldn't live with putting any agent at an unfair disadvantage in a dangerous situation.

Neither would he pass up the chance to find Eliot's killer.

Which made him the scourge of this mission.

What the hell.

Most agents at BAD didn't like him on a good day. They respected his skills and intelligence-gathering capacity, but no one would partner with him after Eliot's death.

Maybe because he told them *he* had cut Eliot's rope, using cold logic when he explained how Eliot couldn't climb so getting him down would have been impossible.

Would it have been possible?

Hunter's gut contracted. *Don't replay what-ifs again.*

His lie to Joe and Retter had been the simplest way

to prove he was still the ruthless agent BAD expected him to be. Sad to recall how easily everyone at BAD had accepted it as truth, that Hunter could cut the rope on a friend and teammate.

They'd taken an internal step back, eyes judging him as soulless. Which suited Hunter.

He'd never trust another person as much as Eliot.

Never get that close to anyone again.

Never allow someone else to sacrifice their life for him.

Korbin's dark gaze shot into the rearview mirror, the black eyes stirring with an unfinished battle. "You screwed Rae this morning."

Didn't think you'd give up yet. Hunter shrugged callously.

"She fooled everyone as the wife of an American diplomat at the queen's shindig in Great Britain last year. Rae's damn good—"

"—at handling weapons and neutralizing threats," Hunter cut in, getting tired of sounding like a bastard. "But she'd be culled the minute she walked through the door. Plus, no one would believe *I* was involved with *her*."

Let it go, Korbin.

Black eyes continued to damn him via the mirror.

Hunter drew a breath of resolve and added one final slam he was glad Rae couldn't hear and doubted Korbin would share. "She might fool world leaders attending tonight, but not those raised with old money. The Wentworth guest list is based on financial power first, political markers second. All the training in the world doesn't cover the tiny nuances these women learn from birth."

"Men bring trophy brides to these things, right? I think she could handle walking around looking gorgeous. Looking happy to be with *you* might have tested her skills."

Hunter noted the ping of irritation in Korbin's voice and the relentless defensiveness on Rae's behalf.

Big mistake, Korbin.

Dangerous to care that way about another agent.

But it was Korbin's mistake to make.

Hunter cranked his attitude wide open, determined to shut down any further discussion. "Even with Rae's extensive speech training, I still knew she came from a London gutter the first time I talked to her."

"So?"

"I'm not known for dating sewer prostitutes."

Korbin didn't say anything. Hunter noted his knuckles on the steering wheel whitened in a death grip.

Anger punched through the car from both ends.

Hunter pressed his elbow down hard on the door handle, embossing the soft leather. His finger muscles wanted to tighten, but he kept his hand open, relaxed looking to the casual observer.

Korbin would see what the world had to see—a Thornton-Payne heir who disdained anything and anyone who failed to measure up to his lofty standards.

A man whose blood ran so cold it could freeze a syringe.

Hunter had come by that blood naturally.

Only Eliot had ever known when Hunter's gut twisted with hidden anger . . . or pain. Eliot could always separate the façade Hunter showed the world from the truth.

That nothing-matters-to-me mask had been formed the night before Hunter's seventh birthday as he and his five-year-old brother Todd witnessed another argument from where they hid at the top of the stairs. His mother had taught him how to sit silent as a shadow. She backhanded him and Todd over any infraction, particularly Hunter's sharp tongue. But wife number one, better known as Mother Dearest, hit her limit when his dad ordered her to spend more time with her children.

Their gorgeous statuesque mother had marched across the marble foyer with her Mercedes keys in hand. His dad stepped into her path, telling her, "Your car's locked in the garage until you start acting like a real mother."

"*What?* Giving birth is pretty damn real, but I never agreed to be a nursemaid. I kept my end of the deal. You got the two kids *you* wanted. Heirs to the Thornton-Payne dynasty. You should be grateful as hell they favor me and didn't turn out looking like trolls."

Hunter had never looked at his dad the way he had right then, seeing the wide-set eyes, thick eyebrows, hook nose, and short stature. His father visibly shriveled in that moment, his voice sad when he said, "I thought having children would soften you, but you're just a cold gold-digging bitch. Can't you at least *act* like a mother? I keep you in jewels and cars and clothes. What else do you want?"

"My freedom. If you think I'm going to live like a prisoner with snotty kids, you're wrong. I'm over this." She squared her shoulders, looking down at her husband with evil twitching her lips. "I want a divorce . . . *and* custody of the boys, which won't be hard for me to win since you're never home. Don't look so surprised. *I'm* more of a mother than you are a father anyhow."

Even though Hunter spent most of his days assuring Todd their mother liked them, he'd had his doubts. Until that moment, he'd also suffered a child's need to know he was loved. He watched, still not sure he could trust the sincerity of her words.

"I see your game," his father said in a quiet voice shaking with fury. "You only want the boys to hold over me so you can get more money than agreed to in the prenuptial."

"Even if that was true I wouldn't wage a battle against your team of lawyers for more money." His mother had laughed sarcastically through her perfect lips. "What do you care? You're never around. Just pay me enough to hire decent help to take care of the pain-in-the-asses and neither one of us will have to deal with them, but I want my freedom."

Todd whimpered. Hunter cupped his brother's mouth to keep him from giving away their position.

His father lifted his chin. "I will not give up my sons."

That's when Hunter saw a gleam of victory in his mother's green eyes. She said, "In that case, here's my only offer, and it's good for twenty-four hours. I get everything in the prenuptial plus two million. That's a million for each kid."

She'd sold him and his brother with no more thought than she'd have given to pawning a diamond ring. Actually, she might have shed a tear over losing the jewelry.

From that day forward, Hunter held his trust close, refusing to risk letting go until Eliot forced him to take a leap of faith.

The limo slowed and turned right onto the road to the Wentworth estate.

"You've got being an arrogant, cold-hearted snob down to a science." Korbin's sarcasm cut with a razor's edge. "Doubt anyone else on the team could pull off your level of asshole—or even wants to. We're lucky to have someone who's *born* to it."

"Did you come out of the womb a dickhead or develop that jockstrap personality on your own?" Hunter considered the heat in Korbin's anger over the issue with Rae. Sounded too much like that of a sack mate instead of a teammate. Maybe he should warn Korbin only a fool would break Joe's rule of no fraternizing with a teammate.

But he didn't know if Korbin and Rae were doing the midnight tango or not.

He didn't care.

Joe and Retter's problem.

Hunter had no trouble keeping everything in a professional capacity on a mission. That way he never had to think about anything unrelated to the job.

Like the possibility of watching his only true friend fall to his death.

Korbin swung the car left, then stopped at the gate to clear Wentworth's entrance security before continuing down a one-way drive bordered with spruce trees. Tiny blue-white lights glittered along the branches. He pulled into the circular drive that encapsulated a granite fountain with a bronze fifteen-foot-tall sculpture of a fierce Poseidon battling a sea serpent.

Not what Hunter would have expected to find in front of a French Country–styled home sprawled under seductive up-lighting and custom steel-and-bronze sconces.

The wealthy called any oddity "style."

Four valets attended vehicles. Two doormen stood at an arched entrance with custom gold-plated double doors. A smattering of international luxury sports cars and sedans lined the expansive horseshoe drive, along with stretch limos. The rest of the vehicles were likely stashed in a hidden lot on the estate.

Korbin parked and hopped out, which thankfully prevented any further conversation.

The car door on Hunter's left swung open.

Shoulders straight, Korbin looked every inch a professional driver without a trace of a smirk or attitude on his face. Hunter hadn't thought he had it in him, but Korbin had proved more than once he also had ice water running through his jugular.

When Hunter stepped onto the driveway paved with stones cut in swirling designs, he paused to straighten his cuffs. The temperature had dropped with the last rays of sun, leaving the air cooled to a frosty mid-forties.

Korbin closed the door and slowed as he walked past Hunter's shoulder long enough to whisper, "Asshole or not, we've got your back." He climbed in and drove away.

Hunter pinched his silk cuff so hard the material should have turned to powder. He missed Eliot at the strangest times. Eliot would have also called him an asshole, but in a way intended to draw a smile instead of blood.

Screw it. Hunter had a package to retrieve and a killer to find.

He took several steps forward, pausing to lift his phone from the inside pocket of his tux and tilting his chin down as though to check a text message.

In truth, he used that moment to take stock of the exterior security mixed in with the valets.

A car door opened and closed behind him, offering a plausible reason to turn so he could scan the rest of the setting.

His gaze bottlenecked at the woman exiting a black corporate sedan. Age around thirty, maybe five foot five, shapely, in a soft inviting way. She'd wrapped her curvaceous body in a dark green dress with a black sash and black heels. Intriguing.

He continued pressing random digits on his cell phone so he could enjoy the delightful vision more closely while she dug around in her glittery evening bag. She wore her curly brown hair piled high, screwed into some kind of style that showed off sparkling earrings, a matching necklace, and the sweet, sweet curve of her neck. Inexpensive costume jewelry. Minimal makeup, little more than dressing up her simple face, though her lips did have a delicious appeal.

Something in her movements and face seemed familiar.

Did he know her?

Didn't look like someone he knew socially . . . or had dated.

She didn't resemble the rail-thin, self-absorbed females with a penchant for exotic jewelry and one-of-a-kind designer clothing he'd tolerate for a night.

Curly Locks didn't have a drop of blue blood in her.

A plus in his book.

But how did she know the Wentworths?

Hunter prepared to dismiss her as interesting but not significant enough to be noted when she lifted her head and glanced around as though getting her bearings.

Her gaze crashed into his and her eyes widened.

He stared into anxious turquoise-green eyes. Dark lashes framed the worried gaze that once again brought on a sense of déjà vu.

Had he met her somewhere?

Where?

She lingered a second longer, the extra look making him think she found his face familiar, too, but the moment ended abruptly. She broke eye contact and rushed up the four wide steps flanked by marble columns and disappeared inside.

Probably one of those "everyone has a twin" things.

But he'd investigate further once he had time.

Never dismiss anything unusual on an op.

He stepped forward, affecting the casual pace of the slightly bored. Passing through the arched entrance integrated into a two-story wall of glass, he paused for the doorman, who bulged with a censorious air.

Can't allow the unworthy to slip through.

Hunter withdrew the silver-and-black invitation that had been couriered to his hotel at noon. He handed the card off without waiting for a comment before walking on.

A Thornton-Payne was never denied entrance to any social event.

He strolled through a brief hallway boasting art rarely seen outside museums, likely owned for generations. If any of the Rembrandts, Monets, or Rubenses could talk about what went on inside this home the result would be a bestselling gossip book. The Wentworth family had been mired in mystique and rumors that rivaled the Kennedys'. The buzz of voices lured him ahead to a ballroom with soaring gilded ceilings that boasted hand-blown chandeliers shaped as flowers and vines. Classical notes of Bach floated from a pearl-white baby grand between quiet conversation supplied by over two hundred patrons awaiting the entrance of Gwenyth Wentworth, who sat on the board of the Kore Women's Center.

But her father, Peter Wentworth, still led the revered family.

And Peter would have died in an explosion four years ago if Eliot hadn't given his life to ensure Hunter made it off that cliff in Kauai to deliver the plans for a terrorist attack on the UK hospital.

So what was the connection between Peter Wentworth and the Fratelli de il Sovrano, a secret organization that had seriously threatened American security more than once in the past two years?

BAD disarmed an attack on the U.S. Congress last year with the help of an infamous electronic informant known only as Mirage who worked via the internet until she was captured by a fellow BAD agent and unmasked as Gabrielle Saxe. Gabrielle became involved in their mission after being contacted via a cryptic postcard by Linette, a woman she'd known as a girl when they were both teens at a private European school before Linette disappeared.

By the end of the mission to uncover the Fratelli's

plot, Linette had become a mole inside the Fratelli camp, where she remained against her will. Supposedly.

Hunter had yet to be convinced Linette was entirely trustworthy. No BAD agent had met her in person.

But that might change tonight since, according to her last missive, Linette was supposed to be in attendance at the Wentworth event along with three Fratelli superiors, each from a different country—a UK representative, a Russian spokesman, and one from the U.S. known as Fra Vestavia, who BAD had a keen interest in.

Vestavia had infiltrated the DEA, as Robert Brady, then disappeared before being exposed as a traitor and was now perched at the top of BAD's list of wanted criminals.

Hunter had his own elite wanted list, with the assassin who killed Eliot first in line to answer for his sins.

But Hunter's assignment for BAD was priority one.

After four years of patience, he could not afford the mistake of rushing.

Once he retrieved the USB memory key Linette planned to drop tonight, he did intend to review the information before passing the key to BAD. Linette indicated the key would include copies of kill photos Vestavia had received, the pictures marked with an unusual emblem as confirmation of the contractor's kill.

She described the spoon-shaped design as having a smiling skull with sunglasses in the bowl and the body of a chameleon on the handle. The same design engraved on a titanium baby spoon with a carved Jackson's chameleon for a handle found by FBI at Brugmann's home on the coast of Kauai the night Eliot had died.

The FBI had dubbed the assassin in the Jackson

Chameleon—the JC killer—and connected that death with some that went back ten years.

Why a baby spoon? A macabre calling card.

As if the shooter had taken to killing since birth.

Hunter pushed those thoughts out of the way and continued moving through scattered pods of guests, careful not to make eye contact. Most gave him a subtle double take.

They were deciding if he was who they thought he was.

BAD assets scattered throughout the party had entered as catering and additional security, filling in holes created when specific personnel on the staff came down with a case of intestinal flu.

Amazing what modern medicine can do to cure or to induce an illness.

Everything was in place for a successful mission.

BAD agent Carlos Delgado entered Hunter's field of view wearing a navy suit and a wire curling from his ear. He'd inserted as part of additional security for the event. Venezuelan by birth, Delgado's dark eyes squinted with suspicion at everything he observed.

Carlos coordinated the on-site team.

He was also the one who'd captured Gabrielle last year and understood the risk involved with trusting an informant no one at the agency had ever met or could vouch for.

Gabrielle used her amazing electronic skills for BAD now, lived with Carlos, and believed completely in her friend Linette's credibility.

All well and good, but Hunter hadn't survived this long in covert work by giving trust so easily.

Before tonight, Linette's only contact with BAD had been limited to electronic means, which made her an easy gamble to stake a bet on until now. But the Fratelli could discover her duplicity at any time. If that happened before she had a chance to alert BAD, the Fratelli could use her to flush out anyone she'd been in contact with, which would expose Hunter.

Just another reason this type of op fell squarely on the shoulders of BAD when it came to walking into situations other agencies would hesitate to touch.

BAD sometimes had to move on an opportunity with minimum intelligence and maximum gut instinct.

Heading toward him, a sultry redhead slowed her steps, intentionally trying to grab Hunter's eye when she passed. He returned polite interest.

Any more and she'd have doubted his authenticity.

The room oozed gorgeous women. Could one of them be Linette? Much simpler for her to identify Hunter than for him to pick her out. All she had to do was watch for him to pick up the memory stick inside a container the size of a lipstick tube once she gave the signal she'd dropped it outside a specific window.

Once that was done, he'd search the mansion covertly to find where the three Fras were meeting.

Every BAD agent backing him up tonight was exceptional. Lethal. But they couldn't defend against an unidentified threat.

He noted two more agents . . . then a green satin dress and twisted mop of curly hair swished into view.

The woman he'd seen outside.

She sipped a flute of champagne. No, she pretended to drink. The liquid level in the crystal glass never lowered.

One of the catering staff offered her a selection from a tray covered in canapés decorated as works of art, but she refused with an absentminded shake of her head, then asked a question.

When a couple moved out of the way, the server's face came into full view. Rae was answering the woman's question.

That works.

If Curly Locks wasn't talking to anyone else and hadn't come to enjoy free drink and food, why was she here?

Rae handled the tray with deft ability. Above her wide smile, her eyes kept track of everything in her area. The minute her gaze bounced to Hunter he lifted his chin to bring her to him.

Didn't take her long to reach him on those long legs.

She lowered the tray into view and described several palatable offerings while two elderly men he recognized as regulars at major fund-raising events passed on her left.

"What did that woman ask you?" Hunter pretended to labor over his selection.

"She wanted to know what time the guest of honor would arrive and I told her I wasn't privy to the Wentworth event schedule." An eyebrow winged in amused curiosity. "There's a woman here you don't know?"

Hunter fingered a goat cheese–encrusted canapé from Rae's tray. "Wouldn't say that."

Rae smiled as though she was thrilled to serve a guest, proving she could act with the best of them. When she moved on, Hunter searched for Curly Locks.

Green and black satin slashed through the room with quiet determination.

He might have dismissed her as unimportant if not for his training and if tonight didn't involve a mission centering around three Fratelli expected to meet with Gwenyth.

And the familiar feeling about the woman stirred his curiosity further.

Curly Locks might have an innocent reason for being here.

Then again, she might not.

If she posed an issue of any sort that might interfere with tonight's mission he'd alert Carlos, who would give the order to have her removed. Silently.

CHAPTER FOUR

∽

As if gaining entry to the Wentworth fund-raiser hadn't been difficult enough, now Abbie had to find Gwen without drawing attention to herself.

The stuffy doorman had given her invitation close scrutiny, as if she'd counterfeited the damn thing, but her name was on the guest list so he had to allow her entrance to the Wentworth fairyland. This family was old, old, old money that originated in the United Kingdom. A Vancleaver like Brittany would blend into this glam crowd like a sparkling shell in the ocean, but Abbie was going for the invisibility of being a raindrop in the ocean until she found Gwen. It should be easy when moving through a room filled with beautiful people decorated in diamonds and precious metals.

If she made a misstep and drew any attention, this bunch would boot her quicker than a cow pony from a herd of thoroughbreds.

That would give Stuey all the ammunition he'd need to get rid of her and the threat she posed to his family jewels.

Abbie smiled constantly, hoping to disarm those whose gaze slid down the ridge of their nose. She wandered about slowly, listening to the sound of classical melodies rolling off the ivory keys of a piano that

deserved to be on that knee-high pedestal. Male and female catering staff wore tuxedos. One offered Abbie a
flute of champagne she accepted before moving on past
exotic flower arrangements taller than her that were
nothing short of artistic brilliance.

She slowed next to one gigantic floral display and
leaned in to appear as though she sniffed the scent—
an aromatic cuisine for the nose—but she actually
searched the room for Gwen.

Would the Wentworth hostess use the dual stairway that anchored one end of the room for a grand
entrance?

Abbie would. She'd never wanted to own something
like this spread, but didn't every girl think about walking down a fabulous curved stairway like that?

So far, no female matched the photos she'd studied of Gwen Wentworth, with her signature mane of
natural blond hair that fell to her waist. The identifying
mark was a silvery-white stripe running through the
left side.

Strange for a woman not yet thirty.

After researching Gwen for the last forty-eight
hours, Abbie felt sad for the woman, whose little boy
had died right after birth two years ago. Under different circumstances, Abbie would have liked to film a
documentary on the Wentworths ancestry. They had
their share of dark secrets but deserved acknowledgment for all this family had donated across the world.

She hoped Gwen's loss hadn't hardened the woman,
that Gwen had some compassion for other mothers.
She didn't allow interviews so Abbie had nothing beyond news bites on the reclusive woman. Nothing that

would indicate how difficult it would be to convince Gwen to help Abbie's mother.

Didn't matter. Gwen sat at the head of the board of directors for the Kore Women's Center. She would not want the damning information Abbie possessed released to the media.

Hopefully Abbie wouldn't have to make that threat.

Stuart had rolled out a mile of warnings, starting with not annoying anyone since she wasn't even supposed to be at this party. And not telling anyone she was with WCXB. He could have saved that breath. The quickest way to shut down a conversation in this crowd would be to identify herself as being with the media. The minute someone outed Abbie as being with WCXB and Gwen found out, security would see her off the property.

Abbie wasn't after a media interview.

She wanted access to the Kore records on her mother but hadn't told Stu when he demanded to know why this was so important to her.

He'd finally gotten the invitation, with a helpful suggestion from Abbie, then laid down his rules, telling her, "I don't know why you're hell-bent on attending the Wentworth event, but know this—I won't stick my neck out to save you if you do anything that draws negative attention to the station, and God forbid you do something that reflects badly on WCXB. I told Brittany an aunt of mine wanted to go. And if Brittany finds out I'm taking her to New York for dinner and a play just so you can attend this party in her place, she'll be looking for blood. I'm not donating alone."

Stuey had reason to worry about Brittany

questioning the motive for his surprise trip to New York. He lacked the imagination to come up with a better solution to yesterday's standoff with Abbie and deserved the hit his wallet was taking, but he was right about one thing.

Abbie's head would be the first one to roll if her plan to pull out the PR hammer Dr. Tatum had given her backfired.

All the wrangling and manipulating she'd done to get inside this place would be for naught if she didn't get close enough to talk to Gwen.

What if Gwen called security on her?

Don't borrow worry, as Abbie's father would say.

She meandered around, taking pretend sips of her champagne. No drinking. Ignoring her low tolerance for alcohol six years ago had led to the most embarrassing night of her life with a guy named Samson, a hot guy even if he had looked wild with long hair and a shaggy beard.

Wild, but endearing in the way he'd only had eyes for her and . . . kissed. The embarrassing part had come the next morning.

Who could blame her for acting like a fool after the man she'd been engaged to had played her for one?

Not the time to think about that. She headed for the arched opening to a solarium where people sat and stood in clusters.

Maybe Gwen had come down quietly and was in there.

Just as Abbie neared the marble column supporting the left side of the archway she was stepping through, a woman on the other side laughed and took a step back . . . directly into Abbie's path.

They bumped.

Abbie's still-full glass of champagne sloshed over her hand and dripped on the gigantic rug she had a sick feeling would bring a record amount at a Sotheby's auction.

Long silky black hair fanned along bony shoulders of the woman she'd collided with. The scrawny twenty-something female spun to face Abbie. Her gasp of surprise exhaled on a huff of outrage as though she'd been assaulted. "Are you drunk?"

Was it Abbie's imagination or had everyone within thirty feet heard that comment and gone silent? She felt a thick wall of eyes locked on her.

"No, I'm not drunk." Abbie went for indignant, but the catch of worry in her voice might have ruined the affect. Clusters of curious faces popped into her peripheral vision. She tried to act as though her stomach wasn't having a disco party at warp speed. "You backed into me."

"I don't think so." The black-haired woman spit her words from perfectly shaped lips in plum-colored lipstick, adding plenty of how-dare-you-insult-me innuendo. The low V of her silky purple top split in a long cut to her waist, meeting the top of black bolero pants cinched with a braided gold and silver belt. She flexed her shoulders back and one of her surgically enhanced puppies came close to nosing its way out.

Abbie struggled between offering a polite apology and snapping at this witch for being so rude.

The woman sent a withering glance at the closest security guard . . . who took that as his cue to act.

Ah, crap. Abbie could stand her ground and risk a scene or walk away with her tail between her legs.

She'd never backed down from anyone.

The security guard quietly asked Abbie, "Can I be of assistance?"

That sounded like a cultured "We got a problem here, lady?"

Abbie opened her mouth to plead her case and felt someone's large fingers close around her forearm.

Was someone trying to escort her out?

Of course they'd assume *she* was at fault.

One-tenth of a second before Abbie verbally scorched the muscle daring to touch her, a deep voice connected to that hand said, "Here you are, darling. Sorry I was detained."

She turned to the man holding her arm and recognized him. The jaw-dropping blond male she'd stared at like a fool outside. He had bottomless green eyes, deep in color, as though stolen from the center of a mystical forest.

A forest that hid something dark and foreboding at the moment as his attention fixed on the woman in purple.

Abbie glanced back at Miss Uncongeniality.

Shock rode the woman's face before her cornflower-blue eyes morphed into a bored look of amusement. Her plump lips curled with a malicious smile. When she spoke, intimate undertones smoked through her voice. "Surprised to see you here, Hunter, with—" She flicked a condescending glance at Abbie. "—*her*. I had no idea your taste ran so . . . pedestrian."

Abbie's face flamed hot enough for her skin to turn tomato red. What she wouldn't give for a decent retort, anything that would extricate her from this situation with just a piece of her dignity.

Nothing popped into her mind.

She'd anticipated a potential disaster, just not this soon.

————————

"Wy taste—" Hunter chuckled, allowing a vicious undercurrent to play beneath his words "—has always run to natural rather than manmade, Lydia."

Lydia Bertelli narrowed her unnaturally bright blue eyes to the point they turned into slits between thick eyelashes fanning her cheek. "Natural? Or dull and boring?"

The arm of the female he still held flexed at the insult.

If not for offering him an opening to meet the woman next to him, Hunter would curse his luck that Lydia was in attendance tonight. She'd normally be off on her father's yacht cruising the Greek isles or working on a deeper tan to set off the sheet of black hair she wore like a queen's mantle.

He did curse his stupidity for allowing his dick to convince him to let Lydia into his hotel room—once—a couple years ago.

In fairness to his libido, that had been before Lydia turned into a cosmetic surgeon's wet dream, and she'd seemed like a perfect choice for one night. He hadn't been with a woman in months and she showed up at his door wearing a fuck-me-where-I-stand dress.

He'd been on the receiving end of Lydia's viper attitude since making it clear he wanted no repeat of their one night together.

Especially after he'd found out the next day that she leaked to the damned media that she'd spent the night with a Thornton-Payne. Lydia had used him to stir up jealousy in a rock star she hadn't been able to close the deal with.

Women and their agendas.

"Is everything all right?" the security guard, Carlos Delgado, inquired in a firm voice.

Hunter had forgotten the BAD agent was present.

"Everything's fine." He shot a hard glance at Carlos.

"No harm, no foul," the woman next to Hunter muttered, surprising him when she spoke. She drew her shoulders back and smiled with withering politeness. "Nice meeting you, Lydia. Gotta go."

She had spirit, something Lydia and most of the women he encountered at these places lacked.

He met Lydia's eyes and sharpened his with a warning that if she didn't retract her claws she'd leave licking her wounds. When Curly Locks turned to walk away, he moved his hand to her back. "More champagne?"

"No, thanks." She stepped up her pace, pulling away from his touch.

He lengthened his stride and caught up, placing his hand at the small of her back again.

She cocked her head, sending him a look that questioned his motives. "An old girlfriend?"

"Old nuisance." He saw a pocket of space with a semblance of privacy. "Let's step over there for a minute."

"Why?"

"To talk."

She slowed. "Look, thanks for your help, but you can go now."

Her apologetic tone harbored an insinuation that

she was inconveniencing him. He was stunned. Didn't she realize half this room would notice if he walked away from her now?

And the other half would hear about it by the end of the night.

"Humor me for a few minutes." Hunter continued guiding her through breaks in the crowd, lifting his chin at familiar faces and inclining his head at others.

A scent teased his nose. Something fresh and different that didn't belong here among custom-blended perfumes.

He realized he was leaning closer to inhale a deeper breath and stopped himself before he gave anyone reason to think something really *was* going on between them.

Her curls bobbed with each step. Not professional hairstyling, but he liked the natural way she'd piled up the ringlets and used a sequined clasp to tame the rowdy mass.

She'd shown backbone, manners . . . and not a clue she'd been in danger of getting clawed. This one might have held her own under Lydia's attack for a few more minutes, but she wouldn't have for long.

Not a normal, everyday woman. A nice girl.

When he reached a giant bronze planter abutting a short wall that provided some privacy, Curly Locks took an extra step, then turned on him.

"Why did you do that? Act like you knew me?" she asked in a voice so loaded with suspicion he should be ducking for cover.

Of course, he'd be asking the same question in her shoes.

Hunter lifted a hand in dismissal. "Lydia lives for

confrontation, regardless of collateral damage. She clearly stepped into your path. Once her head makes a full rotation she's hard to bring back down to earth. Just figured I could defuse the situation before it got out of hand."

"Why? You probably downgraded your social standing in the process."

He'd have laughed if she had, but she'd thrown that out in honesty. He was used to getting the "you're a snob" routine from BAD agents, but getting that attitude from a stranger—one he'd helped—pricked his temper. The point of this meeting was to get her to talk, which wouldn't happen if he let her bait him.

"I'm not concerned about what anyone here thinks." He lowered his voice to an intimate level. "Besides, it gave me a chance to get you alone."

"Why?"

He hadn't expected this much resistance. Most women would have cooed over the attention and flirtatious line he'd given her.

This one didn't coo and her gaze kept straying the whole time she talked, as if searching for someone else.

Another man?

Damned if that didn't dig at his ego.

Didn't she realize he was flirting? Or had he lost his touch?

She stopped visually canvassing the room and gave him her full attention. One soft brown eyebrow winged up in a silent reminder that she still wanted to know why he'd asked to speak to her alone.

Stick with the truth whenever possible. "Wanted to talk to you."

"Why?"

Was that the extent of her vocabulary? He couldn't remember another word that had poked a hole in his patience the way that one was doing.

Any other woman would be smiling by now.

Her lips hadn't twitched, much less curved up. She still eyed him suspiciously.

Maybe asking "why" was her way of making *him* lose interest first.

Didn't she feel the least appreciation for his help?

Hunter released a sigh. "To be honest, I think we've met somewhere before, but I can't remember where. Thought you might know."

"Nope. Don't remember meeting you." She looked away and fidgeted with her purse, both actions saying she'd just lied as much as the too-quick answer did.

Did she know him?

Maybe she was just nervous and saying anything to get out of this situation.

Not that he thought all women should fall at his feet, but he'd never seen one in such a hurry to brush him off. Ego aside, her attitude generated suspicion. What could be so pressing that it kept her glancing around and trying to end the conversation?

He pulled out a safe question she couldn't answer with "Why?" "What brings you here tonight?"

Her eyes snapped up at him and narrowed with a flash of wariness then she seemed to catch herself and shrugged. "Same thing brings you here, I would assume. An invitation."

Still not giving an inch.

Talking to Lydia would have been easier.

"Actually, I came as a favor." Even if his teammates didn't see it that way. "What's your name?"

She hesitated, considered something, then said, "Abbie."

He'd let the last name go, for now. Hunter tapped his chin and concentrated as if her name meant something when he still had no clue where they'd met or who she was. "Abbie. Abbie. Sounds familiar. What do you do?"

Panic streaked through her gaze before she checked it. "I'm a writer. Nothing you'd be impressed with."

"How do you know I wouldn't be impressed?"

She let her eyes travel up and down him in assessment. "I know. What do you do?"

The Thornton-Payne dynasty had a hand in everything from communications to finance to arms manufacturing. He could choose one and no one would question him, but claiming any credit for the family businesses would be unfair to his brother, who actually oversaw many of the operations.

Also, she had some burr under her skin about the wealthy, so the less said with regard to his family the better.

Hunter gave her what he considered a fair answer. "I solve problems for other people."

"Like . . . helping with Lydia?"

Did she make a joke?

Abbie smiled. Her eyes twinkled blue, a natural color that reminded him of the Caribbean waters under a blazing sun. "What are you, like a rent-a-white-knight?"

Hell no. But he'd finally earned a smile and kept his sarcastic retort safely behind his lips.

Now he'd make some headway.

That smile of hers and those eyes. He *had* seen them somewhere before, dammit.

"What the hell are you doing here?" A familiar male voice boomed from Hunter's left, shattering the moment.

He turned his head to see a man whose height mirrored Hunter's, with a lighter build and the same shade of blond hair. His brother.

An icon in the Chicago corporate landscape, the high-profile Thornton-Payne heir whom Hunter would like to see any time other than right now.

CHAPTER FIVE

"Long story, Todd." Hunter shook hands with his brother, surprised to see him at the Wentworth event. Hugging amounted to a public display of affection. His family would be appalled.

"Haven't seen you in what? Eight months?" Todd finished shaking, then turned to Abbie. "And you are?"

"Abbie." Hunter jumped in before Todd could blow his anonymity with this woman by giving his last name. "This is Todd. Todd, this is Abbie."

"Nice to meet you." Her smile had vanished along with the relaxed air in the few seconds since Todd arrived. She gave Hunter's brother the same assessing sweep, made some internal judgment she didn't share, and took a step away. "Sounds like you two have some catching up to do and I have to find someone." She finished the sentence, then turned and scurried into the crowd.

Dammit to hell. Hunter wasn't through with her.

"Who was that?" Todd asked. "Don't think I've seen her around."

"All I know is her name. I don't think this is her usual social circle." Talk about blowing him off without a second thought. He hadn't been hitting on her. Not really.

Abbie didn't fit his requirements for a night in the

sack, mainly because his criteria didn't demand much. A sex kitten brimming with self-importance offered just enough challenge to keep an evening sporting for two people with zero emotional investment.

Or as Abbie had aptly put it—no harm, no foul.

No heart.

And none of the women Hunter spent a few hours burning off energy with expected to hear from him again. He couldn't say the nights were memorable, but he didn't make any promises or leave anyone in tears.

Abbie looked like a woman who bubbled with emotion.

He bet she'd be a memorable night.

But she'd expect a second date, phone calls, and more.

How had he strayed this far off his mental target of figuring out how he knew her and why she was here? Remembering Todd, Hunter started to ask how the move to Chicago was going when he realized his brother had forgotten him as well.

Todd stared with longing at something or someone.

Hunter followed Todd's line of sight to Pia, his brother's ex-wife.

Engrossed in a conversation with two other women, Pia was just as stunning as she'd been on the cover of *Cosmopolitan* when Todd first showed Hunter a picture of his new squeeze three years back. Pia still wore a size two, even after giving birth to her and Todd's little boy eighteen months ago.

She erupted in laughter at something her friend said and glanced over in time to meet Hunter's gaze, which she returned with undisguised hostility.

Hunter took in Todd's pained expression, the look of a man who had been royally screwed, literally and then figuratively.

Todd and Pia had married after a whirlwind affair, because they had supposedly fallen "in love at first sight."

What a crock.

The baby showed up seven months after the wedding.

Another woman with an agenda, and like all the others, Pia lacked a conscience and a soul. The only thing he'd say in her favor was that she never fought Todd for full custody.

Hunter cleared his throat and Todd swung around with too bright a smile, working to hide where his mind had drifted. "What *are* you doing here? You hate these things."

Tell me about it. "Doing a favor for a friend."

"Must be some friend."

"Something like that." Hunter appreciated how his brother never whined about Hunter not calling to let anyone know he was coming to town. Todd had no idea how Hunter filled his daytime or nighttime hours since they both had substantial trust funds. His brother never pried.

In Hunter's family, lack of interest was considered a way of showing respect for privacy.

Hunter had a bad feeling about the answer he might get but asked anyhow. "Why are *you* here?"

"Just doing my part for charity." Todd lifted a scotch and water into view and took a drink. More like he slammed the alcohol and handed the empty glass off to a waiter before letting a wince escape in Pia's direction.

Not a good sign.

Hunter hadn't heard of Todd dating much in the past six months of freedom from that auburn-haired ball-and-chain whose laughter punched across the twenty feet separating them. But Hunter hadn't been to Chicago since his brother moved here.

Please tell me you aren't thinking about getting back with that scheming bitch even if it means the chance to live full-time with your little boy.

Todd should just take Pia to court and get custody of Barrett.

She couldn't be much of a mother.

Relationships, friendships, marriage, families—all baggage that ends up breaking apart at the seams when life hits rough pavement. *Or was nothing more than a financial arrangement to begin with if the women involved are anything like our mother.*

"*Are* you window shopping?" Hunter surely hoped so. He didn't like that I-want-her-back look hanging on his brother's face.

"Not really. Nothing new on the market." Todd hooked a hand around his neck and rubbed. "How long you in town for?"

As short a trip as possible. "Don't know. Got a little business to do."

"You get a free night, let me know. We'll grab dinner."

Guilt peeked into Hunter's mind over how long it had been since he'd shared dinner with Todd, the only member of his family who called from time to time just to see that Hunter was still alive. None of them knew how many times that status had almost changed. "Sounds like a plan. Catch you later."

"See you." Todd took the scotch a waiter delivered and chugged half the drink.

Three steps away, Hunter slowed to turn around and tell his brother he'd definitely meet him for dinner, but he had no idea if he'd be in Chicago tomorrow night or halfway around the world.

He was still considering the possibility when the profile of a man standing in the atrium with the curved double stairway just beyond this ballroom caused Hunter's pulse to vibrate. He'd seen that face with the scar running along the right cheek and jaw once before, on the night he and Eliot breached Brugmann's compound.

During the debrief a day later, Joe and Retter had considered it unlikely that the scar-faced mystery guy could have gotten in position in time to shoot Eliot's rope.

But the guy *had* been on-site the night Eliot was murdered.

Framed by the high archway opening between the rooms, the mystery man now lingered near the left base of the stairway, partially blocked by the tiered fountain in the center of the atrium.

Hunter continued moving very slowly. Standing still drew attention.

Could that guy have been the sniper or had he been only the buyer for the stolen list of names?

Either way, he'd escaped a massacre, so he had to know something about what went down after Hunter and Eliot exited Brugmann's property.

Hunter scouted the room with vigilance, listening for the damned signal. What was Linette waiting on?

He worked casually through the cluster of attendees, letting his eyes drift back and forth as though he were interested in who was here.

When he drew within fifty feet of the mystery guy, security stepped into view on each side of the arched opening, barring anyone from entering the atrium, where the mystery guy remained.

Was he waiting for someone?

Could Hunter be staring at the man who killed Eliot?

None of the security protecting this particular area included BAD agents. He couldn't move closer without attracting interest from them, but he was the only agent in position to observe without detection right now.

Years of training and a brutal determination to find the assassin was the only way he hid the shaking need to rush that scar-faced guy and grab him by the throat.

Hunter's mental gears snapped into motion. He took stock of his position. Remaining in close proximity without talking to another guest would alert security, if they were on their toes.

For what the Wentworths probably paid, they should be.

Hunter did a fast assessment of everyone surrounding him, searching for one person who wouldn't be so intent on talking they'd interfere with his surveillance.

His gaze skidded to a halt when he found Abbie again.

She stood off by herself, leaning back against a wall, studying the room almost as closely as he had.

She sure as hell wouldn't talk to him.

He had an idea. Hunter walked over and approached from a blind side, then whispered near Abbie's ear. "I know why you're here."

She froze, her hand in midair, lifting another full glass of champagne to her lips.

Damned if that reaction didn't send his guilt meter into the red zone. He hadn't meant to terrify her, just raise her curiosity.

"What do you want?" she said in a barely civil tone, but he heard more. Surprise, disbelief . . . then alarm. As though she faced dire consequences for being found out.

He had an idea why she sounded guilty. "Ten minutes."

She licked her lips, thinking, then carefully placed the untouched champagne glass on the corner of a table and lifted away from the wall on unsteady feet.

Taking her elbow in a polite hold, he guided her to the best vantage spot for observing the mystery man, who had moved almost out of view around the corner. He turned Abbie to face him, leaving her back to the scene he watched unfold as Gwen Wentworth stepped up to the mystery guy.

Definitely a scene Hunter needed to observe, if Abbie would just play along.

She stared at the second button on his chest when she wasn't casting a surreptitious look from side to side. "My purpose for coming has nothing to do with you, so why are you bothering me?"

"Bothering you? Just want to talk for a few minutes, and think I can help you out." He cut his eyes up every couple seconds, keeping track of Gwen's position. Three men descended the left side of the stairway to join her.

"I don't need any help, but I *am* curious to know what you're offering." Abbie raised eyes full of challenge.

His ten minutes were going to disappear if he didn't find something to get her talking. He had an idea that she wanted to meet someone since Abbie had been asking when the guest of honor would arrive. Hunter had heard that the mayor and her new husband, who'd just sold movie options on his book, were attending. They weren't the most important celebrities in attendance, but Gwen had used a fund-raiser more than once to celebrate a political ally's good news. Abbie had said she was a writer. Didn't take a big leap to figure out she might want to meet the mayor's husband.

Or possibly someone else Abbie considered notable.

Obviously not a Thornton-Payne, but anonymity with even one person was a welcome break at these events.

She'd most likely gotten into the party through a friend or a corporate invitation. If she'd stand with him for ten minutes so he could observe the meeting going on in the atrium, he'd introduce Abbie to anyone here.

Except, of course, Gwen, since that would interfere with tonight's mission.

Hunter turned on his you're-so-interesting tone, which brought out the best in most women. "You said you don't know many people here and I'm familiar with a majority of this crowd. I could introduce you around."

He kept Gwen in his peripheral vision. She made introductions between mystery guy and the three men, but if Hunter correctly read the unenthusiastic look in her eyes, the way she didn't shake hands and the way her lips remained flat, he'd have to guess she was not a happy hostess.

"Why?" Abbie finally asked.

He hated that question. "Do I have to have a reason to help you?"

"Yes."

Unbelievable.

"Fine. I've got an ulterior motive." Hunter tilted his chin down to the top of Abbie's head, which served two purposes. He appeared intent on whatever she was saying and leaning this close allowed him to watch Gwen's group without Abbie realizing something else held his focus.

Her piled hair played into his view, distracting him. He'd like to see those curls sprung loose.

She crossed her arms. "What's your ulterior motive?"

Give me a minute to think of one. Hunter was trying to get a clear look at all three men who came down the stairs to determine which one might be the American known as Vestavia. "Make you a deal."

"I don't make deals with men I don't know."

"It's not that big a deal." Especially since he hadn't thought of something else to offer her. Hunter got a better visual of the dark-haired man from the trio. Could he be the one BAD knew as Brady, the former DEA agent who disappeared, then surfaced later as Fra Vestavia? His face didn't match the image BAD had on file, but that was from almost a year ago, which allowed enough time for plastic surgery. The tallest guy with pale brown hair and stern lips could have been British. Next to him stood a rigid example of Russian features with a stern jaw line, wide forehead, and thick gray hair.

"Okay. What deal?" she asked.

Hunter lifted his chin up enough to draw Abbie's gaze to his. "Why do you sound like I'm trying to sell you snake oil? Is it that much of a strain to spend a few minutes with me?"

That silenced her.

"Here's the deal. You want to meet people and I want ten minutes with someone nice." Hunter caught a movement near Gwen's group. Another woman emerged from the shadows to stand discreetly to the side of the American male. Thick black hair waved along her shoulders.

She could be anywhere from midtwenties to midthirties. A stunning creature and tense as a stretched violin string.

Italian.

Linette was Italian. *Could that be . . .*

"You know what?" she said quietly, and grasped the lapel of his tux, leaning closer to him. Perfect. He just needed her to stand here another five minutes. He could flirt with her for five minutes.

"What, sweetheart?" he answered, trying to keep his eyes fixed on Gwen's meeting, but Abbie's soft scent climbed inside his head with every breath. He added, "I'm at a loss for what to offer you. What would make you happy?"

When Abbie didn't answer, he dropped his gaze to find her closer, but she'd bent her neck back, clearly seeing that his attention was not on her.

Abbie's lips tightened with a smile born of irritation. Her quiet words were deceptively calm when she said, "What would make me happy? To meet one man who isn't a jerk. Why don't you go screw whoever it is you're so fixated on and stay the hell away from me?" She swung around to leave.

CHAPTER SIX

Abbie didn't have all night to find Gwen or to play twenty questions with a playboy looking for an hour of mindless entertainment.

That Hunter jerk had been watching someone else while he pretended to talk to her, probably another Lydia clone.

All men were liars and . . . liars.

She'd taken two steps when hands locked on each of her shoulders, stopping her forward progress.

Had to be Hunter.

She kept a leash on her temper, reminding herself he'd been the only person to step forward the last time she'd gotten into a confrontation. From the way no one challenged him then, she doubted anyone would speak up on her behalf this time.

His warm breath swirled the fine hairs along her neck when he said, "I wasn't treating you like a joke or screwing with you."

His hands were strong but held her carefully. The strength surprised her since she'd already tagged him as soft and worthless, but what else did a rich kid have to do all day besides go to the gym or play tennis?

"Admit it," she whispered. "You *were* using me to snoop on someone. Another old nuisance?"

"Yes, I *was* watching a woman, but not an old girl-friend. I saw a woman who is engaged to a friend of mine kissing another man and wanted to be sure about what I'd observed. I didn't realize she was there until I saw her behind you. I'd point her out if not for needing to protect my friend's private life." He squeezed her shoulders, a silent request for her to give him a chance. "I thought you wanted to meet some people and I *do* know practically everyone here. Now that you under-stand why I was distracted, will you help me? No one should have to marry a person who can't even start off faithful."

Those were the magic words.

Hunter had redeemed himself enough for her to give him a few minutes of her time.

Plus he could introduce her around and she would bet he knew Gwen. Everyone here—except Abbie—probably had some sort of connection to the heiress.

She nodded her head. "Fine. I'm game."

He drew her around, then gently eased her to his side and walked companionably back to their prior spot. When he turned her to face him, he latched his hands on her shoulders again.

"I apologize for allowing my distraction to result in poor manners." His eyes warmed with sincerity she wanted to believe. "I'll strive to be better company while you help me."

The way this Hunter guy soaked her up with his eyes scattered nervous prickling along her skin. He just needed her for camouflage, so ignore the sexy glint in that deep green gaze.

"Apology accepted."

"Thanks for understanding," Hunter murmured, his undivided attention spinning a cocoon of heat around her body.

What would it be like to have a man like that really interested in her.

Probably short-lived, and untrustworthy as her ex, Harry the jeweler.

She tried to shrug to break the spell trapping her mind, but his hands didn't allow much shoulder movement. "Not a problem," she finally mumbled. "Especially if it means exposing a faithless, conniving, untrustworthy . . . sack of pig manure who—" *Deserves to be horsewhipped,* she finished silently.

Harry's face blurred through her scorching thoughts. Forget about lying, cheating Harry.

Tonight's cheating female was Hunter's problem, not hers. Abbie peeked up at him, assuming his silence meant he was busy doing the snoop thing and might have missed her semi-rant.

Not even.

His gaze was still settled on her in quiet observation. "'Sack of pig manure'? You're really attractive when you're in a snit."

She couldn't come up with a reply.

Couldn't remember the last time a man had told her she was attractive.

Hunter's lips shifted. He . . . almost smiled. The muscles in his face moved stiffly, as if he hadn't used them to smile in a long time.

His fingers relaxed.

The backhanded compliment had disconnected the neurons between her brain and body. There could be no other reason she stood perfectly still as his warm hands slid down her exposed arms, waking excited nerves everywhere he touched bare skin.

When he took her hands in his, she wasn't sure what she expected. Maybe just an obligatory soft clasp of his fingers over hers, but his grasp was firm, his fingers closing with care. Strength hovered beneath the skin, warning there was more to this man than she'd initially assumed.

Something familiar about him bubbled in her mind again.

Did she know him?

In her dreams maybe. She had to tie this up and move on before she allowed herself to be flattered by his attention. "Can you see your friend's fiancée yet?"

"If you stood a little closer, as if we're whispering, I could get a better look." He didn't act on his statement until she nodded mutely. With a gentle tug, he had her chest-to-chest with him, too close for her to see his face.

But she could feel him.

Her hands went to his arms out of automatic response for somewhere to grasp. She curved her fingers around the black sleeves of his tuxedo, holding roped muscle that rippled with imperturbable confidence.

Time skipped by.

Her skin tingled where his hands touched her.

Her skin *never* tingled around other guys. She never reacted this way to anyone from celebrity land, so why was this guy pressing all her female buttons?

Had to be hormones combined with her long dating dry spell. Self-inflicted, to be sure, but better alone than lied to and betrayed by men.

Men like this Hunter.

No problem. She'd keep her end of the deal and provide a few minutes' cover in trade for meeting Gwen. Abbie hadn't missed the way most of the room noticed when he'd walked her away from Lydia.

If she watched Brittany's weekend show on celebrity affairs she might have an idea who Hunter was, but why should anyone care about how people with more money than God spent their time?

She should be glad she didn't recognize him. That meant Hunter wasn't a member of Chicago law enforcement or involved in Illinois politics.

But many of Chicago's elite knew him. Hunter had to be somebody important.

He smelled like somebody important. Like he wore cologne sold by the teaspoon.

She could taste him with each inhale.

Her ears were becoming tuned to the smooth blend of cultured voice and sexy undertones.

But he wasn't saying a word, which was starting to feel weird. She didn't know this guy well enough to stand this near him and not talk. To be honest, she didn't like standing still and not talking period.

Hunter whispered, "You smell intriguing."

Her heart thumped. "Thanks." *Thanks?* Talk about sounding stupid, but she was not in her element and he embodied this element. Stop worrying about what he thinks and act like a trained investigator. Get to the point of all this. She had to meet Gwen. "Um, so let's talk about introducing me around."

"Make you a deal."

"What? I thought we *had* a deal."

"We do. You agreed to help me catch a cheating fiancée. This is a new agreement."

Technically, he was right, since she'd bailed on the first deal to stand with him for ten minutes. She hated when her sense of fair play got in the way.

She typed her fingers against his forearm, getting exasperated by yet another game. "What's in this *new* agreement for me?"

"You want to meet people, right?"

"Maybe. Depends on what you want in exchange."

"Are you always so suspicious?"

Yes. She'd believed another man once without question and he'd stomped on that trust. "Let's just say I've been on the losing end of a proposition before and didn't like it. Don't make an offer you can't back up."

Hunter's chest expanded with a slow breath. "Didn't expect this to be quite so serious a negotiation, but I can meet that requirement. I don't like unsolved riddles. If you figure out how we know each other I'll introduce you around—"

"You already agreed to that," she pointed out, hoping he wouldn't call her on having walked off earlier.

"—as a friend of mine."

That could carry more weight to help her convince Gwen to speak in private without using the hardball card Dr. Tatum had given her. "I'm game. Just who are you?"

His next breath ruffled fine hairs along her forehead. "Hunter."

"I heard your old nuisance call you that. No last name?"

"Is it really important?" He'd asked that as if the wrong answer would somehow judge her.

She couldn't think of a way to say, "Just how rich and important are you?" and he clearly didn't want to share more than he had about his identity.

She should have set some guidelines before agreeing so quickly.

He really thought they'd met before now?

As if she'd forget meeting a man who looked like *him?*

"If I knew your last name it might help . . ." She paused. A waste of time asking since he didn't respond. "But either way you still owe me for helping with this fiancée snooping."

He stopped staring over her head and lowered his gaze to meet hers, not acknowledging or denying her point. Just giving her a scorching look that brought her dormant hormones to life.

His lips were cut like a man's should be, not too smooth or too thin. A mouth that invited speculation.

If he rattled her that much with one long look, what would happen if he kissed her?

What was she doing even thinking something so ridiculous?

He gave *all* women that look. He probably couldn't turn off his sexiness without medical intervention.

His hand smoothed upward along her spine when he glanced away, as though keeping a connection to her even when something else held his gaze.

Her skin moved toward his hand. *Don't shiver.*

Where could she have possibly run into this guy? At a function she'd attended? "Been to any weddings in Chicago in the past couple years?"

He leaned back and raked her with a curious look,

shaking his head. A lock of golden hair brushed his brow. His rugged chin fit with the relentless cut of his smooth jaw and cheeks. Professional grooming? No doubt.

Too perfect. Sort of like Harry the jeweler, that rotten low-life, cheating bastard. He'd screwed around on her the whole time she'd starved herself thin to drop two dress sizes and struggled with heating irons to straighten her hair.

She'd looked like *his* image of sexy, a total physical overhaul that never felt right.

No more starving or hair straightening.

All gone back to natural now.

Good thing. Six years ago, she'd stared into the mirror the day after catching Harry in the wrong sister's bed—Casey's.

Abbie hadn't spoken to Casey since then.

She'd made a life-altering decision that morning. The next man she got seriously involved with would have to take her the way God made her, with curly hair and a few extra pounds.

And she'd walk the minute she caught him in a lie.

"What kind of writing do you do?" Hunter asked, reminding her she was supposed to be figuring out where they might have met.

"Nonfiction." Abbie chewed on the inside of her lip, avoiding any discussion of how they met that might involve bringing up her employment with WCXB. "You do any volunteering with Greenpeace or the animal shelter?"

"No."

Another strike against this guy. Everyone should donate time to something.

An idea popped up. Her dad had collected antique farm equipment, storing treasures in his barns. She used to hunt for additions to his private museum during her travels. Before he died. "Do you own a farm of some sort?"

"A farm? Like a *working* farm?"

Why'd Hunter sound so incredulous? Some very influential people had grown up on farms and they were proud of their background. She was proud of hers. "Yes, a real live farm that produces things like crops, livestock, pigs, whatever."

"*Pigs?* No."

His insulted tone underlined how they were lifetimes apart in so many ways, the way they grew up only being one difference.

Keep that foremost in her thoughts to counteract any renegade tingling or stray hormones. She gave up. "*You* could help. How do *you* think we met?"

"No idea." He leaned back. His indolent gaze floated down to hers. "But I did meet you somewhere."

She couldn't be expected to figure this out with no reciprocal information. "What do *you* do?"

"I don't exactly have a job." He said that in a slow that-I-exist-should-be-enough voice.

She really hated men who did nothing. Harry thought selling diamonds was hard work.

Where were the real men in this country?

"We *could* get to know each other again," he said in a tone more suggestive than his words. "Might jog our memories."

Now *that* sounded like a line if she'd ever heard one.

Logic kicked in. Sure, he was hot, but underneath all

that window dressing slept another lazy pretty boy who didn't lift a hand to do serious work and would never get involved with a woman like her. A woman who'd grown up with dirt under her nails and calluses on her hands.

Hunter used a finger to toy with an errant curl dangling above her eye.

All the logic in the world didn't stop the stampede inside her chest at his touch.

Did he know the effect he was having on her?

Of course he did. He was a man, one with lots of Lydias dying to climb into bed with him.

So why is he flirting with me? Because he considered her an easy target who would be thrilled over his attention?

She *was* pretty flattered, but not enough to feed an ego with an insatiable appetite.

Hadn't she learned anything six years ago?

All men were jerks.

Never, ever, forget that.

Within an instant, all playfulness vanished from his posture. His gaze flashed up and past her shoulder, alert, at something behind Abbie. The cheating female?

A rumble of excited voices vibrated the room.

She broke away from Hunter and swung around to find out what had everyone buzzing.

Gwen Wentworth had entered the main ballroom. Finally.

Abbie had played "how did we meet" long enough. The way the crowd was flooding in around Gwen, she doubted Hunter could even see his friend's fiancée any longer. Gwen would disappear into a gulf of humans in the next minute. Gaining her ear for more than ten seconds would be tough at this point.

Hunter owed Abbie an introduction for allowing him to use her as cover. That whole bit about knowing her had probably been a big fat lie just to keep her talking.

Her conscience argued that she'd had a moment of déjà vu, too, when she'd first seen Hunter outside.

Didn't matter.

She wasn't asking for much in return and Gwen would be out of reach quickly. "That's who I want to meet."

When she didn't hear a reply, Abbie swung around.

Hunter was gone.

CHAPTER SEVEN

Hunter passed through a sea of faces more intent on being recognized by a Wentworth than noticing his retreat from Abbie. When he made it to the next salon, he whipped around the opposite side of a replica of an Elgin marble statue to observe the excited guests.

And one disappointed Abbie.

Dammit.

She *would* want to meet Gwen. An innocent enough request any other time, but not tonight.

At least his suspicion of Abbie had abated. If she had some ulterior motive for attending beyond stargazing and rubbing elbows with celebrities she'd have dressed to blend in with the other women and wouldn't have played along so easily with him.

"Regretting your decision to come alone?" Rae had approached quiet as a thought.

"No." Hunter kept watch so that no one—Abbie in particular—walked up on his conversation. But the entire room had migrated toward Gwenyth, who shimmered in gold and white like a billion-dollar magnet.

Rae offered him the humble smile of a staff member that he wouldn't trust right now to turn his back on. "I'm okay with you coming solo, too."

He sent her a look that said he knew better.

"I'm serious." Rae's smile took on life in a sly way. "If I'd been assigned to accompany you I wouldn't have had the pleasure of watching *her* walk away from you earlier. Must be a new experience for you to get shot down by a mere mortal."

"I needed a cover to observe someone. Don't make it out to be more than it was."

"That's right." Rae handed him a napkin and a flute of champagne. "She couldn't possibly meet your high standards."

He didn't want to discuss anything specific to the mission so he ended the conversation by refusing to engage further. Rae knew nothing about him. Bloodline and family ranking were rock-bottom on his give-a-shit list.

Rae started to move away, paused, then swung around and asked, "Excuse me? What did you need?"

He caught the signal. Something she had to share with him was being transmitted between agents. "Couple napkins. Sloshed my drink."

"Absolutely." With perfunctory motions, Rae sat her tray on the nearest available surface and strode back to him with a handful of napkins she used to dab at his untouched tuxedo lapel. She spoke softly. "Your new friend just shoved up close to Gwen, made some comment, then stepped away. Gwen looked shocked, then recovered and excused herself. She walked away but told one of her security something he relayed to the woman you were standing with. Who is she?"

Damned if he knew. "Don't know. That's what I was trying to figure out."

"Head of catering's walking this way," Rae whispered, then backed up and spoke louder. "Think that got it. Please, excuse me." She took a couple strides, grabbed her tray, and hurried over to where a gray-haired man in a black suit spoke to several of the staff. Immediate head-bobbing indicated they understood his instructions before the servers dispersed.

Hunter turned back to search for Abbie in the crowd Gwen had abandoned.

Maybe he'd dismissed her too quickly.

His gaze climbed the grand staircase to the upper landing, where the three men Gwen had been meeting with earlier now stood talking. The Italian-looking woman with the wavy shoulder-length black hair wore a demure royal-blue dress with a jacket and stood a step behind the men again. She moved forward and spoke to the man Hunter thought might be Vestavia, who nodded before she descended the staircase on the far side and blended into the crowd.

Could those men be the three Fratelli Linette had indicated would attend?

What of the Italian woman's identity? Linette?

Hunter couldn't go up the stairs to investigate until he had the damned package. The signal would be given on the main floor. He had plenty to keep him busy down here until Linette made the drop and sent the signal.

Like finding out why Gwen had disappeared after talking to Abbie.

Abbie clearly hadn't come to rub elbows with celebrities.

That niggling worry about tonight's mission crawled

up his neck again. He discarded his champagne flute and headed for the throng of people ebbing back into private fissures within the mansion now that Gwen had vanished.

He and Abbie were going to have another chat. One wrong answer and she'd finish the conversation in shackles. He'd taken three steps when someone on the Wentworth serving staff politely inquired, "Have you seen an emerald-and-diamond earring? A guest is missing one of hers."

Talk about suck timing.

That was Linette's signal to retrieve the USB memory stick.

———✦———

Abbie's heart raced ahead of her feet. She turned sideways, sliding like a flexible knife through the humans cluttering the Wentworth mansion.

Please don't let her be rushing into a security ambush that would hand her over to law enforcement.

When she reached the far end of the ballroom only a few people littered the hallway. None noticed her. At the next corner, she slowed to move through a hall broken up by four white doors trimmed with intricate gold designs.

One door opened. Abbie's blood pressure skyrocketed.

The young woman exiting the powder room wore a deep blue knee-length dress better suited to a boardroom than a party.

As they met, Abbie glanced over to take in the exotic female with lush black hair that fell to her shoulders and a petite face that resembled some Italian actress Abbie couldn't identify. But the curiosity wasn't returned.

Invisibility had its perks.

As Abbie reached the bathroom entrance, she paused just long enough to check behind her to ensure the Italian beauty had disappeared. She scampered ahead, following the directions Gwen's security guard had issued in the harsh tone of an order.

Probably because Gwen hadn't been happy when she'd spoken to him, which would be Abbie's fault for shocking the color from Gwen's face.

Two more turns and Abbie located the thick double doors crafted of varnished hickory she'd been told were not locked.

She placed her shaking fingers on a cool bronze handle and pressed her thumb on the lever, which moved smoothly.

Please don't let an alarm go off.

A small snick sounded then, hallelujah, the door opened.

Gwen hadn't tricked her. Yet.

A little too late to worry about being arrested for trespassing in a secured area of the mansion.

Still following instructions, Abbie crossed a paneled library that smelled of history and ink, then passed through a set of open glass doors into a sunroom twenty by forty feet. She kept walking across hand-painted tiles and through another set of open doors to a pool and patio area enclosed by a vine-covered stone wall that was chest high and appeared to be more an architectural decoration than a security measure. The fortress-looking wall a hundred feet away and partially hidden by trees should intimidate most of the population out of trespassing.

Armed security took care of the rest.

When Abbie stepped farther onto the patio, heat wafting from the walls warmed her, balancing the chilly evening temperature to a tolerable one. She watched for any sign of alarm or men with radios charging forward.

Nothing moved, not even the tiny candles hung on a stained glass screen. The tea lights offered just enough visibility for her to move around without falling into the pool, the surface of which lay still as a sheet of glass illuminated from below. Burgundy and yellow wicker furniture with bloated cushions covered in a sunflower pattern sat around the pool as if posed for a magazine shoot.

"You arrrived here faster than I expected."

Abbie whirled, hand on her chest. "You scared me to death."

Gwen stood in a shadowed corner. "Seems only fair since you weren't exactly subtle in the ballroom."

"I don't have time to be subtle."

"So you say." Gwen continued in a rich voice Abbie recognized as cultivated to sound both exquisitely feminine and professional. Her creamy skin and smooth cheeks were taut with stress lines, her eyes searching everywhere.

Abbie waited in silence.

Gwen had to make the next move, before Abbie said another incriminating word.

When the heiress lowered herself to a wicker chair next to a glass table, Abbie took the chair that faced

Gwen and the grounds beyond the patio. She drew a breath, preparing to gamble her future and very likely her freedom.

Gwen held up a finger. "First, I want the truth about why you're here."

"I told you. I found out the real reason my mother has been going to the Kore Women's Center every year and about the experiments going on there." Abbie's heart pounded loud as an angry fist on a door.

Dr. Tatum had warned her not to speak to Gwen inside the house where her conversation might be caught by electronic listening devices. She had to make Gwen believe they had to meet somewhere private outside.

Gwen sat back and crossed her arms over her chest. "Any facility like Kore has a research division."

"Not like Kore's. I know about what happened to women like my mother. Fertile women with rare blood."

Gwen didn't say anything for several seconds. "What do you think you know?"

"I know about the scam," Abbie started. "The Kore Women's Center convinces unsuspecting women to come in for free tests and lab work, then they use that information to vet potential candidates to be black-mailed into their secret program."

Gwen's eyes widened with each word. Her skin rivaled her white dress for lack of color. She visibly struggled for control, then regained it quickly. "You do realize how absurd that sounds."

"You think I'd be stupid enough to come here without evidence?" Abbie had bluffed her way into a lot of situations, such as getting her first chance in the news business, but the line of hooey she'd just handed Gwen took the prize. She didn't have anything more than a belief in the doctor who had cared for all the women in her family for over twenty years. Time to start negotiations. "If you help me, I won't incriminate you in any way. But if you don't help me, I'm going to expose everything I have on the Kore Women's Center—*and* the Wentworths—to the world and let the chips fall where they will."

Gwen sat so still she seemed mummified, then she shook her head, speaking in a whisper. "You can't do that."

"I can and will do that. My mother was perfectly healthy until she entered your clinic ten days ago. Now she's dying. You help me or I'll find a way to shut down the clinic. I don't care how much propaganda you put out about helping other women."

"We *do* help women. We—"

"Save it for someone who believes you." Abbie figured she had very little time before someone came hunting for Gwen and ended her meeting. "I have years of documentation for her visits and blood donations. My mother's doctor may have believed the bogus medical records Kore sent in response to his inquiries, but I now have proof of what you're hiding and I'll use it if that's the only way to find out what happened to my mother."

"You don't have any idea of the repercussions of what you're threatening."

True, but that had never stopped Abbie before once she had her mind made up.

Dr. Tatum had shared everything he knew, but he didn't know what had compelled Abbie's mother to make annual trips to give blood at the Kore clinic for the past thirty-two years—starting two years before Abbie was born. She planned to find out. Her mother's rare H-1 blood had to be part of the reason, but whatever test—or treatment—they did during the last visit had caused her mother's spleen to fail.

Other doctors had concurred with Tatum, who said he'd never heard of a healthy spleen deteriorating so quickly with no clear reason. It had damaged her mother's liver. At the rate she was going, she'd need a liver transplant soon. An unrealistic expectation with her rare genetic profile.

Abbie had the same rare blood but the RH didn't match. Her sisters both had normal type-O blood. If she could determine the root of her mother's illness Dr. Tatum might have a chance at slowing the progression until he figured out a cure.

"I have people willing to back me, so I won't be alone in dealing with repercussions," Abbie added. Did the lies get any bigger than that one? If Gwen called her bluff Abbie would find herself fighting a Wentworth lawsuit alone.

"You shouldn't have involved anyone else." Gwen's eyes took in everything around them, jumping as fast as her short breaths. She swallowed hard and leaned forward, grasping the chair arms with finely shaped fingers. What would terrify an heiress of a family as powerful as the Wentworths? Gwen lowered her voice. "Listen to me. Leave here and promise not to mention a word of this conversation and I won't say a word either."

Not a chance in hell. "And if I don't?"

"They'll kill you . . . and me."

CHAPTER EIGHT

Hunter signaled Carlos on his way to the front entrance then waited while Carlos diverted the exterior security force to one side to inspect a suspicious duffel bag. The one Korbin had planted earlier after parking the limo.

With security diverted, Hunter slipped soundlessly around the dark corner of the mansion. Cold penetrated his tux, but he welcomed the fresh air after being inside with so many people.

He lifted a night-vision monocular from inside his coat pocket and slipped it on.

If Linette made the drop where she'd indicated in her last message, he'd find a faux lipstick tube containing the USB key outside a bathroom window on the west side. The tube had a tiny infrared LED light on one end.

The latest in female accessories for the discerning spy.

BAD believed she'd created the device herself. Pretty sharp even for a genius since she had little freedom of movement.

Guess he'd find out soon enough if she could be trusted.

There it was in the middle of a bush, glowing bright

as a hundred-watt bulb through the monocular. The poor placement—dangling in the bush—actually gave Hunter a measure of relief. Linette wasn't a trained operative or she'd have made sure the unit reached the ground when she shoved it through the slit in the screen covering the window.

Hunter flattened his palm, fingers straight, and slid his hand into the center of the evergreen bush.

Out of habit, he made a scan of the grounds. A maze of gardens and walkways led through clusters of yew trees that partially hid the twelve-foot-tall brick-and-stone wall surrounding the premises.

BAD's intelligence indicated sensors covered the top ledge.

No reason for security to guard the wall since the sensors were linked into a continual loop. Any break in the signal would send an alarm. Sensors detected movement up to twenty feet above the wall, allowing for animals up to the size of a hawk to cross over.

But the body moving through the sprawling limbs of a tree on this side of the wall was no bird.

Security?

No. Carlos would have alerted him to anything like that.

Hunching down so he could move through deep-shadowed spots, Hunter shuffled farther around the house to determine what the intruder was after. He'd covered a hundred feet when he spotted a waist-high stone enclosure for a patio lined with bushes.

Staying close to the house in the deep shadow until he reached the wall, he peeked over the ledge to find two women talking.

One had a head of curly hair. Abbie.

The other was Gwen.

Someone who actually knew Gwen Wentworth had to wait months to get on her calendar. What had Abbie said to gain a private meeting when they'd never met?

Hunter kept track of the figure in the tree, who moved another branch higher. In a series of crab-shuffling steps, he moved close enough to listen to Abbie and Gwen. They sat on opposite sides of a small table facing each other.

Neither one looked happy.

"Are you threatening me?" Abbie asked Gwen.

What the hell had they been discussing? Hunter kept an eye on the figure in the tree. Paparazzi?

"No. Not me." Gwen's fingers gripped the wicker chair arms so tightly the fine bones on the back of her hand threatened to break the pale skin.

"Who?"

"I can't tell you."

Abbie pointed a threatening finger at Gwen. "I told you what I would do. Did you think I was kidding?"

"No, I don't. Ask your mother. If she tells you—" Gwen shook her head. Her fingers tugged nervously at her lips.

Keeping track of the conversation, Hunter eyed the figure in the tree, who had stopped moving.

"She did." Abbie dropped her hand. "Not intentionally. I found my mother's diary. I know the players and I'm going after all of them."

"Are you crazy?" Gwen asked with panic shaking her voice. "The Fras will—"

The Fras? That snatched Hunter's gaze back to

Gwen, who'd frozen and covered her mouth as if she'd said a forbidden word. Her chest jumped with panicked breaths.

Hunter took in the tree climber again, who seemed to be leaning forward in a—

"The who?" Abbie asked.

—shooting pose.

Gwen uncovered her mouth. "What? I thought . . . you don't know? You said—" She jumped up, hands fisted.

A bright explosion of light burst from where the figure stood in the branches, then the *boom* followed.

The bullet struck Gwen high in the back, slamming her forward at Abbie, who screamed.

Hunter leaped over the wall.

Abbie's wild gaze whipped around to him.

If he could get them to the ground the wall would block the shooter.

A second rifle explosion blasted the air.

CHAPTER NINE

Hunter landed on Gwen's patio and kicked over the stained glass wall of candles, killing the closest light. He dove for Gwen, who had fallen on top of a screeching Abbie. Wrapping up both women, he rolled, his momentum taking them with him.

All three bodies hit the tile-covered patio. Hard.

Abbie's next scream died in a pained *umph*.

No more shots rang out. Darkness fell over him with the comfort of a safety blanket.

But security would be everywhere within minutes if they recognized that noise as a gunshot.

His BAD teammates would.

The smell of fresh blood soaked the air. Hunter lifted up on an elbow and turned Gwen over onto her back, gauging her wound through his night vision. A dark stain spread across one shoulder of her designer dress. He checked her pulse. Steady. Reaching for the closest chair cushion, he unzipped the cover and folded the soft material into a thick pad he shoved beneath her gown.

Would that stop the blood flow long enough for medical care to reach her?

He pressed the heel of his hand on the padding. Seconds were disintegrating quicker than his chance of walking away from this mess clean.

What had Abbie gotten into?

She lay facedown on the cold tile. Not moving.

Hunter used his free hand to ease her over on her back.

She'd landed with her fist between the ground and her diaphragm, which had probably knocked the wind out of her.

Emotional stress interfered with her resuming normal breathing again. Abbie might be unconscious, but even her subconscious would be in a state of terror.

"Breathe, Abbie," he whispered, gently rubbing her shoulder. "Everything's okay. You're safe."

Footsteps pounded toward the pool from the grounds. The shooter?

Hunter couldn't leave these women unprotected, even for the mission. He pulled Gwen's dress strap over the wound padding to hold it in place and shoved to his feet. He wheeled to face the figure coming fast, ready to attack, but pulled up short at the sound of a familiar, "Fuck," as Carlos jumped across the wall.

"What the hell's going on?" Carlos was seconds ahead of everyone else only because the rest of the security hadn't thought to head the way Hunter had gone.

His jolt of relief at Carlos showing up first vanished with impending discovery of Hunter's presence. "Shooter in the second tallest tree at eleven o'clock, seventy yards from the outer wall of the patio, took out Gwen. Shoulder's bleeding."

Carlos dropped down next to Gwen, took one look, and pressed on the folded material to staunch the blood flow. He tucked his chin to his lapel and spoke low into a button that transmitted only to other BAD agents.

Hunter removed his monocular, his eyes now adjusted

to the dim light filtering out from a lamp in the sunroom.

Abbie started wheezing like a squeak toy sucking air. Her chest heaved with strangled breaths. She struggled, jerking with spasms.

Fear would make every breath harder to draw.

He lowered his face close to her and whispered, "You're safe now. No one's going to hurt you."

She gasped once, then again, eyes opening wild with panic. She raised her arms to attack.

He grabbed her wrists, gently pushing her hands to her chest and shushing her. "Take it easy. Just breathe."

"They're coming," Carlos warned. "You gotta go."

Hunter moved his mouth next to Abbie's ear so only she could hear. "Don't tell anyone I was here. I saved you from that second shot. We're even."

He needed ten minutes alone with her to find out what she knew about how the Fras, Eliot's sniper, and the attack on Gwen were related.

And how Abbie fit into all this.

"She conscious?" Carlos asked, indicating Abbie.

Hunter stared into her eyes. Answering "yes" would pull her into BAD's network, where she might not surface again any time soon, or at all, and way out of Hunter's reach.

Decisions, decisions.

"Not yet." Hunter held his breath. His fingers gripped her arms gently, thumbs caressing her cold skin.

Her eyes flared, then her chest expanded sharply. She finally drew a hard-earned breath and exhaled. Her eyelids fluttered closed.

Had she even been lucid when he spoke to her?

"I called Puzzle Queen," Carlos told him, indicating

Rae, which meant he'd instituted an improvised backup plan. "She's headed to the laundry room. Back through the sunroom and library—"

"I know the way." Hunter took one last look at Abbie, wishing he could stay long enough to be sure she was safe, but the shooter had likely left and Carlos would protect her.

Security would pour into this private sanctuary in seconds.

Hunter shoved up and rushed into the library. Navigating by a memorized floor plan, he located a door hidden in one section of the mahogany paneled walls. The invisible doorway provided the household staff access without any need for them to travel through the mansion's family areas.

Hopefully, the majority of the staff would be dealing with the party and not passing through this area. If anyone did, they'd wake up in here tomorrow morning with a headache.

He flipped the light switch off in every hallway he entered, wending his way to the central corridor that led to the kitchen, laundry, and service areas. After the third turn, a slice of light beamed into the dark from a door ajar at the end of the hall.

When he reached for the handle the door opened all the way into a laundry room.

Rae swept one look up and down him. "That's going to be a bugger to get out."

Hunter dropped his chin to take in the blood-smeared front of his tuxedo. "Shit."

"No worries." Rae stepped over to clothes hanging on an electric track. She flipped several dark outfits out of the way, took a look at Hunter with an eye for sizing up a man, then selected a tuxedo she handed him. "If anyone looks closely, they'll realize you're not wearing Armani or whatever overpriced designer you patronize, but this will get you off the premises."

He ignored the dig and started shedding clothes while she stepped over to peek through the door that exited into the public areas of the house.

Closing it quietly and turning the lock first, Rae returned with a laundry bag she stuffed his discarded clothes into, then tossed the bag aside and wet a towel at the sink.

He'd expected another slam over peeling down to his underwear. She proved him wrong by silently cleaning blood off his face and neck while he buttoned his fresh shirt and inserted cufflinks. He took the clean half of the towel to wipe his hands.

She touched the earpiece wired to her clustered earrings, listening, then raised her chin to Hunter. "Korbin scoped the area around the tree while security's scrambling to get medical help for Gwen and secure the patio. He saw a JC baby spoon stabbed in the trunk by the pointed Chameleon's horns on the spoon handle. Couldn't retrieve it. The space fifty feet inside the wall is covered in cameras. Security will find the spoon when they sweep, but we know who took the shot."

Hunter nodded. "You packing?"

In answer, she leaned down and fished a Browning BDA .380 from her boot that she then handed to him.

He started to ask if that was her only weapon out of instinctive need to ensure he didn't leave a woman unprotected.

Rae was *not* defenseless and would *not* appreciate his concern. Questioning her on anything right now would be taken as yet another attack on her ability as an agent.

Her slim weapon wouldn't fit inside the snug boots he wore. He shoved it inside the back of his pants. The poorly cut tuxedo jacket would cover the weapon.

"Thanks." He started for the door and paused, owing her something more for tonight. "You're an exceptional agent, Rae."

"I know."

He swung around to find a burning glare teamed up with her sharp tone. "I— Never mind."

Her face shifted from tense to curious.

That was as close to an apology as she'd get from him. He opened the door and checked the hallway leading back to the main ballroom before striding confidently toward the mayhem that was gathering volume. Everyone he passed literally frothed with macabre excitement over the shooting, ignoring him as just another forgotten guest or Wentworth staff.

He needed them all to forget him.

What about Abbie?

Had she been coherent when he told her not to identify him? If she admitted to seeing him on the patio with Gwen the media would go crazy searching out pictures of his face to plaster in every news report.

The last pictures of him had been taken before he became an adult and stopped allowing photos. He was of no use to BAD if the media exposed Hunter Wesley Thornton-Payne III as anything more than a worthless playboy. He'd be yanked out of the field. Maybe forever.

And Abbie? She'd disappear from her world.

CHAPTER TEN

Last to exit the elevator car that had descended forty feet below the Wentworth complex, Vestavia girded himself for the upcoming battle.

Ahead of him, Fra Ostrovsky from Russia and Fra Bardaric from the UK followed Linette Tassone's clicking steps through a corridor of travertine walls lit by blown-glass sconces shaped like tulips. When she reached the end of the hall, Linette opened a door and stepped inside a carpeted reception area that was empty save for a plush gray sofa-and-chair combo.

She crossed the room and opened another door, then stepped aside.

Vestavia followed the other two Fras, who passed Linette into the windowless room, where more wall sconces provided understated lighting. With that and the hand-buffed cherry paneling, the room offered a hospitable feel to the uninformed.

Those who had been inside this soundproof room, as Vestavia had, knew better than to be taken in by the inviting feel.

Vestavia turned to Linette. "Don't let anyone disturb us."

"Of course, Fra Vestavia." She had the demure voice of a sophisticated angel. More black hair than a man could hold in two fists and sex spilling out of every pore.

But she wasn't Josephine.

His gut still twisted in a knot when he thought of the woman with waist-length blond hair and an erotic body created for loving. Josephine Silversteen had worshipped him and made his world a place worth saving.

His bed a welcome place worth visiting.

But her cold body would never warm his bed again. She slept in a coffin and he blamed a mole in Fratelli de il Sovrano for her death.

When he found the mole, death would be a blessing compared to what he had in mind for betraying him.

"This room secure?" Fra Ostrovsky's wild gray and brown eyebrows dropped low over withered eyes that inspected the walls and ceiling as though the subterranean structure could hear and see. Short of stature and hardly filling out the black tuxedo, the Russian Fratelli representative suspected anything and everything.

Vestavia couldn't really fault him since Ostrovsky probably didn't have to deal with moles in the Russian Fratelli division.

"Gwen would not risk sending us to a location that wasn't secure." Vestavia closed the door on Linette, who had seated herself at the farthest point from the room.

She'd been with him since he lost Josephine and needed a personal assistant. He'd first seen Linette in the possession of Fra Bacchus, a sixty-two-year-old Fratelli who departed this world not long after. She'd been given to the old buzzard eleven years earlier at the age of sixteen because of her beauty and superior intelligence. If not for one small glitch in her family ancestry, she'd have been handed over to the Kore Women's Center for breeding. Her concise moves, quiet manners, and carefully thought-out answers were all a product of the old Fra's method of breaking and disciplining.

Linette had proven to be a model assistant, but she hadn't truly been tested. Not by Vestavia's standards.

He placed his briefcase at the base of a twelve-foot-long oval glass conference table that provided a clear view of the base, where a pair of snarling lions had been carved from burled wood. "And I am as much at risk of being exposed as you are."

Ostrovsky grunted acknowledgment.

Bardaric said nothing right away. The UK representative hummed with impatience. Bardaric had changed significantly since his youth and was now built surprisingly sturdier than he'd been in his late teens. Unlike most pale and slight Brits Vestavia dealt with, Bardaric's body structure hinted of Viking genetics. Wavy sandy-brown hair fell to the collar of his tux. The rough-cut locks complemented the aggression shining in his chilling gray eyes.

"Please have a seat, gentlemen." Before taking his, Vestavia strode over to the bar integrated into the wall of built-in bookcases. He pressed a panel and the doors opened to reveal anything they required for drinks. He filled a crystal glass two fingers deep with forty-year-old Macallan whisky, inhaling the sweet toffee and woodsy scent of the rare blend. He poured Bardaric a glass as well only to show Ostrovsky he came ready to bury the proverbial hatchet . . . preferably in Bardaric's neck.

A shame to waste fine whisky on that British bastard.

After pouring a chilled glass of Stolichnaya Elit, Vestavia passed it to Ostrovsky, who sat at the head of the table. Handing the whisky to Bardaric, Vestavia sat down where he could face both men.

"We must move ahead with our plans." Bardaric wasted no time in opening the discussion. "The U.S. has not been weakened sufficiently to allow for further damage to the UK or China."

Vestavia had enjoyed unquestioned control over all Fratelli missions on United States soil until someone undermined him this past year by ruining his plan to seat a Fratelli in the White House.

The fucking mole.

And now this UK wharf rat wanted to rip the United States apart before the UK tumbled. Vestavia kept his tone pleasant but firm. "Now is not the time to draw undue attention to our movement. I'm not willing to support a plan that serves no purpose but to ravage this country before we're ready for it to fall."

"We tried it your way, Vestavia, and you failed last year." Bardaric smoothed his fingertips over the table as though clearing space for a battle. "Your plans are lagging behind. My people can help escalate your time frame to put us all back on track."

"I don't need any help." Vestavia gave Bardaric an acidic smile. "As for failing last year, that was a setback we're already recovering from, but the UK lost momentum four years ago that hasn't been recovered. Or have you forgotten your failure to gain the list of CIA names *I* set up the buy on and the failed mission to kill your prime minister?"

Bardaric's eyes bulged red. "We have a new prime minister in place in spite of Wentworth keeping our last one alive. Someone in *your* country interfered in the Brugmann deal four years ago. Want to tell me who?"

"Are you accusing *me* of interfering?" Vestavia asked softly.

Ostrovsky took a drink of his vodka and slammed the glass down. "Gentlemen! I did not come for school-yard arguments. I may be only Angeli mediator for this meeting, but that does not preclude sharing my opinion. Of all the continents, yours are the two strongest. You must come to agreement on which one falls first and work together. This is crucial for all seven continents."

Vestavia caught himself leaning toward Bardaric, his muscles tight with the need to fight. He'd buried his pain over the failed mission so deep no one knew how much losing Josephine had cost him. How hard it had been to order her death when she'd been captured. To watch her beautiful head explode.

He had a mole, yes, but this UK prick was causing him just as much trouble. Smoothing his face to appear unconcerned, Vestavia willed his body to relax. He straightened away from the table.

Ostrovsky was correct. They were Angeli first and foremost.

The seven Angeli—one from each continent—called themselves the Council of Seven as a security measure so no one slipped around the Fratelli de il Sovrano.

The Fratelli thought they were the highest order on each continent in charge of preparing the world for the Renaissance, but the Council would eventually wield the true power. Like Vestavia, each of the other six had infiltrated the Fratelli groups on their respective continents. The Council would surface in due time, but for now they were letting the Fratelli do the heavy lifting.

The Fratelli wouldn't fold easily when the time came to hand over control of the world, but the Council of Seven Angeli held one powerful key to the future.

Until the day to reveal that key arrived, Vestavia refused to see North America pummeled just to make this UK fuck feel better about his position.

Vestavia and his six counterparts on the council were secretly accelerating the Fratelli's plans so that the Renaissance would happen in their lifetime, not another sixty years from now as currently expected.

"The U.S. must fall first to complete the parity phase," Bardaric argued, not addressing the part about working together.

Of course that horse's ass would say the U.S. had to fall first. Vestavia didn't react. He had the backing of the Wentworths, who carried the purest blood of the North American and European Fratelli. Their power trumped Bardaric's royal bloodline in Britain, so he allowed, "You have a valid point."

Bardaric's eyes thinned in suspicion. "Then you agree the Wentworth family is growing too quickly."

"Perhaps." Vestavia had to give up something so that Ostrovsky would report his compliance to the other Angeli. "However, I would point out that there is only one fertile Wentworth being put into service at this time."

Bardaric seethed quietly. "There must be *no* new Wentworth babies until the UK has three more births with the genetic markers. We all agreed to limit births—"

"No," Vestavia said, cutting in. "We agreed to maintain a balance of pure DNA breeding. These babies are our future leaders and our genetic stock. With only four descendants of the original seven women who birthed our civilization—and Wentworth holding the purest blood, I might add—we can't afford to limit a breeder who is on schedule because yours is behind."

"I am well aware of our limited DNA resources. I will call for a vote to allow multiple births from the three women in Europe's bloodline when I return home tomorrow so that all three can be inseminated immediately."

"I'm not comfortable with multiple births at one time in the UK." Vestavia looked over at Ostrovsky, who made a noncommittal shoulder movement. "I don't think any of us want to see a replay of your grandfather's mistake, Bardaric."

"Hitler was *not* my grandfather's mistake." Bardaric hit the table with his fist. "Hitler climbed his way into the Fratelli just as you did. My family cannot be held accountable for his insanity, only for the actions of those within our direct bloodline."

"I'm not saying your family is specifically at fault for anything, only that Hitler was allowed to breed genetic offspring like rats during your grandfather's era. The Angeli two generations back failed to contain Hitler. Our job is to ensure no Fratelli abuses the power to create life." Vestavia slid another look at Ostrovsky, who weighed in with a nod, so he continued. "Our generation has technological advantages over prior ones, but allowing any generation to breed at too fast a rate is just as irresponsible as our forefathers who experimented with plagues they couldn't control."

Bardaric's anger fingered through the pristine air that smelled so clean it seemed manufactured. "I have maintained an equivalent pace, but the last three babies did not survive."

"Can't help it if our sperm is more powerful." Vestavia spoke without emotion, as though just stating facts, but hit his mark with the verbal strike.

Bardaric's shoulders flexed, tense with hostility.

Ostrovsky shot a warning glare at both sides of the table.

Vestavia lifted his hands to stem the argument brewing. He needed Ostrovsky, the one Angeli council member most trusted for over a decade to play mediator, to report to the other four that Vestavia continued to be capable of ruling over North America. "I thought we were going to hear about your new plan, Bardaric. *If* your plan is sound and *if* the majority of the council votes yes, I'll put all my resources behind it."

That lit a glow in the Brit's eyes. "At the heart, this is a conservative plan that will serve us all well."

That was the first sign of danger from Bardaric. He liked to sell the Angeli on his *conservative* actions to cover lies and covert plans.

"I'm listening." Vestavia fingered the lip of his glass.

"This would affect only three major cities in the U.S.," Bardaric said, as though wiping out three U.S. cities would be minor damage. "We've been experimenting with a new material, something so small it can be easily transported, yet once it is constructed as a bomb and linked with more than one, the results are cataclysmic."

"What new material?" Ostrovsky asked.

Bardaric's eyes moved slyly, not meeting the Russian's. "Something a resource found quite by accident. I'm sure you don't share all *your* resources with the Council."

Ostrovsky's thick eyebrows twitched, the only sign he was annoyed. "What I do is of no consequence in this meeting. My role is merely to assure the Council you two are capable of working together."

"That's up to Vestavia." Bardaric pushed his empty drink glass away and sat back.

"I've always supported our phases. I just want to know this isn't going to be some half-assed bombing that leaves me with nothing more than a mess to clean up."

Bardaric lounged back in his chair arrogantly. "My system utilizes minimal explosives for maximum impact to take down a significant section of a city as though it was built of matchsticks. Once we hit the first city, we send a message from a new underworld organization that can't be traced to any country. We'll demand U.S. withdrawal from any occupied country, regardless of whether it is an ally. We'll give the U.S. three days to start making moves. If the government fails to react, a second city is hit, then a third city in three more days."

"This country does not negotiate with terrorists," Ostrovsky pointed out.

Bardaric leaned forward, smiling. "Make the destruction significant enough and after three cities any country will fold under the pressure of the people. We'll create a group that claims credit. They'll give the U.S. a list of demands any citizen would consent to out of fear of their city being next. Who wouldn't want to see the end of war? We will have proven we can move these bombs anywhere and destroy as much as we want."

"If all the U.S. troops come home at one time the economic impact will be devastating—" Vestavia paused at Bardaric's grin of anticipation, then continued. "—to every country associated with the U.S. Even the UK and certainly Russia."

"I disagree." Baradaric pretended a smug confidence, but he wasn't convincing Vestavia.

Ostrovsky's gaze moved between the two men during the silence, then he said, "Finish discussing plan, but know that anything this size must be put to full vote by the Council, then sold to North American Fratelli."

"What cities?" Vestavia asked in a soft tone that belied his sudden spike in blood pressure.

"Not sure yet, have to figure out the most advantageous locations." Bardaric studied his hands when he gave that lie.

The bastard had already picked out targets. Vestavia now realized why Bardaric had offered to meet here in the US. The prick probably used the trip as a cover to bring the material in if it was that small.

No fucking way was Vestavia going to destroy that much of North America yet. He'd make Bardaric bleed if he made an unauthorized move of that scope here. The best way to divert this plan would be to come up with another one.

A more ambitious plan.

Bardaric's three best breeders hadn't carried a baby to term for the past eighteen months.

Gwenyth Wentworth was already pregnant with another baby, her second one. She had sixteen days to go until she reached her second trimester.

If Vestavia could prevent Bardaric from implementing his plan before then and keep her pregnancy a secret until that time, Vestavia would hold the highest number of genetic chips, which determined voting power within the Council.

If that wasn't enough to sway opinion, Peter Wentworth's support would be the deciding factor. No one on the Council wanted to lose the Wentworth backing with so many significant projects coming up that required financial and political support.

Bardaric would push for a vote in the next twenty-four hours.

Maybe Vestavia's scientists could evaluate the impact a major disturbance in North America would have on global warming in the meantime. Something to use as leverage if the vote came up that fast.

Three generations of the Angeli council had spent the last seventy years manipulating industry and governments to reach this point environmentally. After all the effort they'd gone through to put global warming on a schedule and to manipulate green awareness when necessary to control its speed, no one wanted to cause a major shift in the environment prematurely.

"I'm all for a Council vote on this." Vestavia maintained a slow breathing rhythm. No one would know he seethed inside.

A quick rap at the door swung his anger from

Bardaric to Linette. The woman might not be as bright as he hoped.

"Give me a minute." He walked to the door and wrenched it open, trying to decide what would be the best punishment for her insubordination.

"There's a problem, Fra," Linette whispered. She looked over her shoulder.

He followed her gaze to four grim-faced men in dark suits armed with automatic weapons. He cut his eyes back at her. "What happened?"

Linette turned back to him. "Gwen Wentworth has been shot and they don't know if she'll make it or not. Peter Wentworth is . . . upset. He sent these men to escort us all to another location."

CHAPTER ELEVEN

~~

Someone dropped a blanket around Abbie's shoulders. She murmured her thanks.

Emergency personnel and security staff choked the narrow patio area around Gwen's pool. Abbie told her brain to keep sniffing the chlorinated water and not the sick odor of coagulating blood.

One team worked on Gwen, who had been placed on the gurney, her face covered with an oxygen mask. A female EMT connected a tube to her limp body and lifted a saline bag into place.

Another EMT spoke into a radio, then turned to his team. "We're taking her to Kore. Her father said they have her blood stored there. He's coordinating a surgeon." The entire emergency team kicked up their pace a notch, wheeling her away in the next fifteen seconds.

Police officers filled in spots vacated by the EMT team. One burly cop with wavy brown hair and square shoulders spoke to the Hispanic security guy who had held the makeshift compression bandage on Gwen's shoulder until the EMTs arrived.

The wide-body cop zeroed in on Abbie. He walked away from the security guy, heading straight for where she sat on a fallen chair cushion with her legs tucked.

"I'm Detective Flint," he told her, then squatted

down. "I understand you were with Ms. Wentworth when she was shot."

Abbie nodded.

"What exactly were you doing out here?"

She swallowed. "We were talking about the Kore Women's Center. Ways to bring more funding into the Wentworth Foundation, the reason for the party tonight." Her stomach already churned with the fallout from an adrenaline charge and blood on her clothes. If he pressed her very hard she might toss her cookies on his shoes.

"Did you see anything unusual out here?"

"No." Abbie paused when she noticed the Hispanic security guard had stepped over to another guard standing close by but wasn't talking. Had he moved over to eavesdrop on her conversation? She took a breath and met the pudgy-faced detective's flat gaze. "We couldn't talk with so many people trying to capture her attention inside so she said to meet her here. We'd just sat down when she got up to call for tea and—"

The vision of a hole exploding from Gwen's body burst into her mind. Abbie covered her mouth. Her stomach lurched.

For a big guy, the detective jumped up and moved out of barf range really fast.

The Hispanic guard brought her a drink. "This is seltzer water. Should settle your stomach."

She drank it and thanked him with a nod.

"You have ID?" the detective asked.

In answer, Abbie reached for her purse that had ended up next to her on the ground. This probably wouldn't go well. She pulled out her driver's license and handed it to the detective, who jotted the info on his pad. He looked at her, then the license again. "You here as a guest or working?"

She ignored the disgust in his voice. She'd been the driving force behind the story that had turned his department upside down last year. "I'm a guest."

He finished taking her statement with cool reserve, then handed back her license. "That's it . . . for now."

"I understand." When Abbie unfolded her legs to get up, the Hispanic guy was there again, offering her a hand and saying, "I'll have someone take you home."

"No, thank you. I have a car waiting." She took her handbag and wobbled her way through the house, past gaping guests taking in the blood smeared across her dress and skin.

Probably wondering if she'd attacked Gwen.

She put one foot ahead of the other and finally reached the front door, where Wentworth staff rushed up, offering her a car.

"I have a car," she repeated. "My driver should be here . . . uh, somewhere." She gave him the name of the car service she'd made Stuey hire for her.

"Right away, ma'am." A male valet full of youth and vigor dashed out to the sea of black sedans and limos, pausing at one, then pointing in her direction. The car's headlights powered up and the vehicle pulled alongside where she stood. One of the staff opened her car door.

She sank into the backseat, wishing the leather would wrap her into a safe cocoon for a few hours until her brain caught up with what had happened tonight. "Take me home."

The driver didn't ask for her address, but he'd picked

her up from home and surely still had the location in his GPS since he'd been hired for a round trip. The car moved away as if floating on air, or maybe her body had lost touch with the earth.

Gwen said a "Fra" would try to kill them if they found out. What in the world was a Fra?

And what was worth killing people for?

Once Dr. Tatum had started sharing her mother's history two days ago, he'd prattled on with endless details. Abbie had never known her mother underwent tests at the Kore Women's Center prior to getting pregnant and after each baby.

Hearing the EMTs talk about Gwen reminded Abbie that Dr. Tatum said the Kore Women's Center banked her mother's blood, which they might need if her mother got the chance to go through surgery for a transplant.

Was rare blood at the center of this?

What had been important enough to shoot Gwen for, or was that even the reason someone tried to kill her?

Something else important pressed on Abbie, but warm air flooding the car turned her tight muscles to jelly and lulled her to sleep. She nodded off . . . safe. For now.

<hr />

Hunter ignored the cold air piercing his tux and took in the area up and down Cornelia Avenue, watching for any hint of threat in the areas that were vaguely lit and not dark as a bottomless well.

The address for the modest four-story brick

apartment building across the street had been loaded in the hired sedan's GPS system as tonight's pickup and return point for A. Blanton.

That would be the woman passed out in the backseat.

He opened the passenger door directly behind the driver's seat and leaned in to shake Abbie gently. Her pale face glowed in the dark, stirring a desire to pull her into his arms so he could soothe away the fear. A ringlet fell to the bridge of her nose.

He hooked the strand of hair and it curled around his finger.

Why couldn't he recall where he'd met her? He remembered her eyes and face, sort of, but something didn't match enough to raise a clear memory. What he did remember was a sense of innocence about her, but that didn't fit with the woman he'd heard threatening Gwen tonight.

What had Abbie said to Gwen just before the shooting? Hell of thing to watch someone get shot.

He lightly rubbed the back of his hand over her cheek. Smooth skin sprinkled with a few tiny freckles.

Her cheeks had more color now. The only color before had been in those rosy lips, kissable lips. Her teeth weren't chattering anymore. Even with the heat on high, she'd still shivered from shock on the drive to her apartment.

Maybe he should have stopped to cover her with his jacket. She looked small coiled up on her side with her legs tucked . . .

Hunter stood up quickly and took a step back. What was he doing? He shouldn't think about her as anything but a lead on this mission. He shrugged off the moment of concern.

She had information he needed, but he had to be careful. He'd taken a risk by telling Carlos she wasn't conscious when she was lying by the pool, but Hunter would not give her up until he gained the information he needed.

She couldn't be an undercover operative. Nothing about Abbie fit, but the very best agents were hard to identify.

Like Tee, the codirector of BAD, a tiny, perfect beauty who had to be one of the most lethal female agents in the world.

Until he confirmed Abbie's stake in all this, what she'd been after with Gwen and why someone wanted to kill Gwen, she was an unknown entity. He leaned into the car. "Come on, Abbie. Let's go."

She murmured something and squirmed. Her eyelids moved up slowly as though made of lead. She blinked, squinted, rubbed her eyes, then blinked again. "What are *you* doing here?"

"I drove you home."

She lifted her head, studying the front seat, then slumped against the seat again. "What'd you do with my driver?"

"Paid him plenty to find his own way home."

"Back to my first question. What're you doing here?" She moved with lethargic care, slow as her sleep-dulled words. Keeping her eyes on him, she reached blindly to the seat beside her and grabbed her purse.

"Heard about what happened with Gwen and you. I owed you for helping me with my friend's fiancée and didn't get a chance to introduce you around. Besides, I wanted to make sure you were okay." He also needed to know if she'd actually recognized him at the pool or not.

She lifted her legs and moved around to get out of the car.

He backed up, extending his hand.

She accepted his offer and let him pull her to her feet, then stepped to the side out of his grasp. She wrapped her arms around herself against the cold. "Thanks, but I'm fine."

Hunter had pulled his shirt loose to cover his weapon so he could take off his jacket. "Put this on."

She tried to refuse his jacket, but he draped it over her shoulders. When she didn't say anything else, he added, "I'll just see you to your door."

Abbie lifted her fingers in a perturbed "okay" sign and walked around the car, wobbling.

He stepped up beside her and put his hand to her back as she started to cross Cornelia Avenue.

She sent him a look that said she would not be civil if he didn't remove his hand. He allowed his finger to linger three seconds against her dress, then pulled away and kept pace.

Not another word was spoken until they reached the entrance to her building. She dug out a key card from her purse for the electronic lock and paused, eyebrows drawn tight. "What exactly did you hear happened?"

"That Gwen was shot and you saw it. I was thinking—"

"So you thought driving me home would make up for disappearing on me at the party?"

He had a bad feeling he'd miscalculated something. "About that, I need to explain—"

"Because that's not the way *I* remember it," Abbie continued as if he hadn't spoken. She inserted the key card, opened the door, and stepped inside. Swinging around, she shrugged out of the coat and tossed it to him. "See, I thought you said saving me from that second gunshot paid your debt to me."

The door closed on a distinctive click. Locked.

Well, shit. *Smash the door with my fist or kick hell out of it with my boots?*

CHAPTER TWELVE

A bbie made it to the elevator without her knees folding.

Hunter—a man who probably had a car and full-time driver at his disposal—had driven her home. Why? Who the hell was he?

She still saw him jumping over the wall and kicking the glass tower of candles into the pool. Where had he come from?

Had he been following her when she met with Gwen? Why?

Back to him driving her home.

He had to be concerned she'd blab his name to security and the media, but she hadn't given him a chance to broach that topic. She'd have to go public at some point when either the police came to ask more questions or someone in WCXB's news department pressed for an eyewitness story.

Stuey would have a hemorrhage the minute he found out she'd been in the middle of this mess, then he'd go ballistic when she didn't turn in a report tonight. He'd want it both ways—to kill her and to get the news scoop. Wentworth security had managed to keep media contained outside, but names and details would leak by tomorrow morning.

The elevator door whooshed opened on the third floor of her apartment building. The carpet in the hallway always smelled of every human who had ever lived here.

But it was home, safe, home.

Gwen's face, the bullet tearing through her shoulder, ripped skin, the blood, the . . .

Abbie covered her mouth to cut off a sob before it broke her control. Her chest still hurt from sucking air in, but at least she was breathing regularly again after having the wind knocked out of her.

She fumbled with her keys and stared at her lock, hearing Hunter's calm voice reassuring her she was safe after hitting the concrete so hard. He'd calmed the panic fisting her lungs when she couldn't breathe. His whispers had soothed her terror for those few seconds.

Then the Hispanic guy told Hunter to leave before anyone showed up. Why? That same security guy failed to mention Hunter's presence at the crime scene to the police later.

She'd kept her mouth shut and hadn't shared a thing, because she was in enough trouble without starting more with some rich guy. But why hadn't the security guy said something?

Money? Someone in Hunter's position probably paid to keep his name out of the media.

But nothing was discussed while they were on the patio. Had he made that arrangement with security earlier?

She unlocked the door and turned the deadbolt when she closed it.

Better already. She flipped on the table lamp in the foyer and walked into the dark living room, where she tossed her purse on her funky grape-colored sofa. Leaving the lights off, she moved over to the window and pushed the blinds apart to see if Hunter had left yet.

The black sedan pulled away from the front of her building.

Should she have let him come up to talk? That's what he'd been after when she shut the door in his face.

No chance he'd call her after tonight, especially when all this hit the news.

Call her? He didn't have her number, her last name, nothing. He could come back to her apartment, but what would be the point? Not like she was going to hold any special place in his little black book.

He was a mystery for sure, but she still saw him jumping over the wall around Gwen's patio and covering them with his body. Shielding them in darkness. Whispering that she was safe.

He'd charged into danger. Like a real man.

She sighed out loud since no one could hear the blind adoration escape with her exhale.

Defying her earlier uncharitable judgment of him, he had turned out to be something far different than she'd imagined. Not your run-of-the-mill playboy.

She didn't know what he was exactly, but she had enough sense to keep him outside her apartment if she didn't want to do something stupid like let him end up in her bed. Enduring a close encounter with death acted like an aphrodisiac.

Climbing into the sack with *him* wouldn't have taken a lot of inducement.

Her body wanted to be held and loved in the worst way right now, and only by one man. Hunter had sparked a fire in her libido that had lain dormant for so long she wouldn't have thought a private night with the Chippendales could stir an ember of interest.

That's why she could not face anyone, especially Hunter, until tomorrow, after a shower, chocolate, and some sleep.

Chocolate might come first.

On the way to her bedroom, she slowed next to her philodendron plant that drooped over the side of the bowl, acting like this was its last day on earth. "That's not good."

Reaching around to unbutton the top of her dress, she headed for the kitchen, pulling the dress off. Her body sighed. She flung the dress over her arm. One advantage of living alone was being able to walk around in her bra and panties or less. Light blared in her face when she opened the refrigerator door, searching, searching . . .

There was the half-eaten box of Godiva chocolates.

"I am so ready for you," she murmured, snatching up a truffle that turned into mocha pleasure in her mouth. She felt her stomach moan.

I am so ready for bed. She should have a cat to round out the image of a single woman with no life. But she could barely keep a plant alive, and if having a life meant getting shot at she'd take boring any day.

Poor Gwen. Had she survived? Who wanted to hurt her?

Abbie said a prayer for the young woman, then one for her mother, who was getting worse by the day.

Where would she and Dr. Tatum find help now? The minute Kore found out she was with the media they'd shuffle her off with some watered-down press release.

If she contacted Peter Wentworth about talking to Gwen again they'd probably have her arrested.

Tomorrow, she'd figure out something.

She licked her lips and headed to the bedroom, flipping the wall switch for her lamp when she stepped inside. Nothing happened. Flipped it up and down, up and down. Nothing.

She walked over to try the lamp switch.

"Stop."

Abbie froze at the sound of a disembodied male voice in the dark room. He stood right behind her. She wrapped her arms protectively around her exposed body and tried to speak. Nothing came out. The shaking started at her knees, traveled up her spine.

Cold metal poked her back. A gun? "Get down on your knees."

Terror razored through her, but she pushed her mind past it to think defense. "Who are you?"

"Now."

The second she bent her knees they buckled. She landed hard on the floor and pushed her legs beneath her so that she knelt, trying to follow his orders until she could figure out what to do next.

Icy fingers touched her neck.

She flinched, huddling the dress protectively against her front. "Please, don't."

His fingers moved down her back. He must have squatted down. She could feel his breath on her neck.

"You did a good job tonight, Abigail."

Tonight? What was he talking about? How did he know her name?

Her heart pounded with violent thumps. She covered her breasts. This couldn't be happening.

His finger slid beneath her bra strap and moved along her back. She pressed her hands over her breasts, praying for the strength to fight him.

"Nice bra."

Her lip trembled.

He jerked the dress from her hands. The material slapped the wall.

She squeezed her eyes against a flood of tears. Don't break down now. Not when she needed to be ready for any chance to get away.

"Who's the guy that brought you home?" he said.

"I—" She coughed and tried to swallow but didn't have a drop of spit in her throat. "I don't know." Hunter?

His harsh laugh blew the loose curls along her neck.

Was he angry? What would he do to her now? "He was just a driver—"

"That's a lie."

She shook from bone-chilling fear. Oh, God. Her heart hurt from beating so fast. *What do you want?*

"His name." His voice came from above her. He grabbed a wad of her hair and jerked up.

She cried out, standing. Stars shot through her vision. Tears rolled down her face. She shoved her elbow into his chest, which felt like a metal plate, and tried to stomp on his foot.

Missed.

He yanked her head back, sending stars past her eyes.

"Keep that up and I'll pull out my knife." Cold metal touched her back again. He ran the gun muzzle down her spine and slipped the barrel inside the elastic of her panties. "You *will* tell me the truth."

That warning sent her way beyond terror. To a point of realizing what did she have to lose if she fought him? The minute he gave her an opening she was attacking this bastard and screaming at the top of her lungs.

He pulled the muzzle out of her panties and shoved the cold steel under her chin. Yanking her against him, he whispered, "Give me any more trouble or scream, I'll kill your mother."

Hunter unlocked the deadbolt, then turned the knob slowly and entered Abbie's apartment. He heard everything being said in her bedroom through the tiny round transmitter he'd pressed over one of her dress buttons.

The .380 he'd gotten from Rae was lightweight, but it felt better than an empty hand right now. He hadn't expected to need a gun when he parked the car down the road and returned. His plan had been to bypass the security and knock on her door so they could talk.

He'd ask questions and she'd answer.

That changed when he got close to Abbie's door and he picked up the intruder's voice in his earpiece.

He could still hear them, the low keening sound she made. Like an animal caught in a trap. Her raw fear reached out from the dark bedroom and clawed his spine.

He eased along the wall of her living room until he reached the bedroom doorway and peered inside.

Light from the foyer around the corner offered just enough illumination for Hunter to make out the intruder in a black stocking mask with a white smiling skull face. The head cover was thick. Reinforced? Bulletproof head cover? That would mean he might be wearing body armor of some sort, too.

Skull face had a fist of Abbie's hair and a .44 Magnum Smith & Wesson shoved beneath her chin. She clutched her half-naked body, her skin so bloodless she looked like a ghost in the dark. "Still don't know his name?" the intruder asked Abbie.

"Looking for me?" Hunter stepped into the room, his weapon aimed at the bastard's head, but he wouldn't risk that shot with an unfamiliar weapon and Abbie so close to the target. "You can have me if you let her go."

"Might want to keep you both." He twisted her hair and muscles in her neck flexed against the pain. "She could prove entertaining if nothing else."

"Hurt her and you'll meet me in hell," Hunter warned him. "I'll be the one tying your dick in a knot. You'll be the one bleeding out your eyeballs."

Abbie trembled, but her eyes brimmed with hope.

Hunter couldn't look at her and keep his focus on this maniac. What the hell was all this about? "Thought you were looking for me. What do you want?"

"Who do you work for?"

"Myself."

"No, I'm thinking CIA . . . but I would have known about any agents on the premises tonight." The intruder spoke in a melodic voice, smooth and calm. No ranting or demanding. "What were you doing at the Wentworth estate?"

Adrenaline spiked in Hunter at the realization of who might be holding Abbie at gunpoint. The JC sniper responsible for Eliot's death. He had to know. "You're the one who tried to kill Gwenyth."

"I never *try* to kill anyone. I don't miss an *authorized* target."

Hunter took shallow breaths, telling himself not to go for the head shot he wanted to take. If the armor stopped the bullet, the sniper would kill Abbie. "Why'd you shoot Gwen if you didn't want to kill her?"

"What I want isn't part of the equation. I'm only a weapon." The JC killer laughed. "Much like you."

The same laugh Hunter had heard right after Eliot had died and every night when he closed his eyes. But Eliot would expect him to use his head and not put Abbie at risk, not even to kill this fuck.

"What do you want with her?" Hunter nodded at Abbie.

"Just a means to an end. Wanted to see you." The killer released her hair, stroking softly across her head.

Abbie cringed but didn't fold. She sent Hunter a wide-eyed gaze that said she was alert and a tiny nod he read as "ready to fight."

"You got your look. Let her go and we'll talk." *Then I'll kill you with my bare hands if I can't get a shot.*

"I doubt you'll give me any more information. Abigail, however, was most helpful tonight. Going to be a shame for her to die."

Before Hunter had a chance to negotiate further or take a step, the killer used his free arm to flip a small canister up in the air past her shoulder.

Hunter recognized the canister, covered his eyes, and opened his mouth a second before the flash-bang exploded.

Abbie screamed. Thank God. If she hadn't, her eardrums would have blown.

Tear gas flooded the air next.

The silence that followed filled him with hollow fear.

Hunter plunged forward through smoke filling the room, trying to see and breathe.

Abbie wasn't making a sound, not a whimper. Shoving his shirt up to slow the hideous stink and burn of the tear gas, he fought his way in the dark. His feet bumped a pair of legs draped over the bed. She was out cold.

He scooped her up and over his shoulder, coughing his way back through the room and blind with tears. Outside the door to the hallway outside, he kicked the apartment door closed and slid to the ground. He'd turned her as he'd dropped down until he cradled her in his arms.

Searing heat raked his lungs.

But his mind burned hotter with questions. Why hadn't the guy tried to kill one or both of them? What had he wanted?

Hunter couldn't believe after four years he'd stood within a few feet of the JC killer.

And let him walk away.

He looked down at Abbie, limp in his arms and a swelling knot on her head where the bastard had hit her. Who had she pissed off and how was she connected to all of this?

Tonight changed everything.

He'd have to get answers another way, dammit.

She had to vanish. Now.

———

Jackson moved carefully along the streets. He did everything carefully.

He'd pulled off his stocking cap and shoved the reinforced headgear into the backpack he'd retrieved at the rear of Abigail Blanton's apartment building.

His black clothing and gloves, also reinforced with bulletproof Kevlar armor, protected the only flaw in his honed body. Something the operative who had come to Abbie's defense would have liked to know.

There'd been a hint of something personal in the threat her rescuer had leveled. The cocky guy had no idea he'd been facing the Jackson Chameleon. How he'd gambled his mortality.

Most people figured that out a nanosecond before they died, which reminded Jackson he needed to request authorization to dispatch Abbie's protector.

He sent a brief text to his superior that another player had entered the game. And asked for authorization to engage.

The Fratelli allowed no unnecessary deaths or he'd have dropped both Abbie and her guard dog where they stood.

He got a text back that read, "Not yet. Determine whose interest he represents."

Jackson pressed the "K" text button and sent confirmation he'd received the reply. He huddled his coat close against the chill and kept to the dark side of the street.

He hadn't planned on allowing Abbie's friend to walk around alive even if the guy hadn't seen Jackson's face, but neither could he make an unsanctioned hit.

That just meant Abbie's friend couldn't literally die by Jackson's hand, but people died everyday that he didn't touch. All it took to have that happen was to first know enough about what mattered most to a person, then provide that person with choices.

CHAPTER THIRTEEN

~~

Abbie's throat ached when she swallowed.

But not as much as the stabbing pain in her head.

She didn't want to wake up yet, hadn't rested well with the interruptions. Who had kept bothering her?

No chance of sleeping longer with this aching . . . When she reached up to touch her head her fingers bumped something cold. She pushed an ice pack aside and felt carefully, finding a lump.

What happened to her?

Blinking her eyes open in the dark, she looked around. Where was she? Recall came slowly, but the pieces began to link up, offering splattered images of how she got hurt. The last thing she remembered was being held in her apartment by a maniac with a gun and Hunter—also with a gun—showing up to rescue her.

For the second time in one night.

Who the hell was that Hunter?

When her eyes adjusted, pale blue lights glowing along the baseboards of the room offered enough visibility to make out the bedroom's boundaries. A small space, but nice. She pushed up on her elbows and had to swallow against nausea from the sudden dizziness.

Take a deep breath, exhale, and focus.

Her gaze strayed beyond the queen-size bed she was on to a lacquered-aluminum four-drawer chest on the wall opposite the foot of the bed. On the right of the chest a door opened into a bathroom—one positive discovery—and the short hall to the left of the chest ended with another door.

The exit?

She glanced up without moving her head. The low ceiling was curved from the baseboard on one side to the other across the top of the bed. No windows.

Everything smelled pristine or new, as if unused. The linens felt crisp. What kind of place was she in and who had her?

The crazy guy in her apartment. Who else?

What had he done to Hunter? Her heart squeezed. She'd reconciled herself to fighting the bastard, but knowing deep in her heart she'd lose the battle and suffer a hideous foreplay to death.

Then Hunter had appeared like an avenging angel.

Nothing in that picture made sense.

A rich guy who chauffeured people and handled a gun like James-Freaking-Bond.

Had she hallucinated the whole thing?

A gentle vibration seeped through the mattress. Listening closely, she detected the soft hum of a motor.

That felt too real to be hallucinating.

Abbie sat up and swung her legs out of bed. The room lurched along with her stomach. She clamped her teeth together and breathed through her nose until the possibility of throwing up passed. When had she hit her head? The intruder had held her by her hair, then let go . . . then a flash exploded . . . and something hit her head.

Probably the butt of his gun.

She hoped the thing backfired and blew his head off the next time he tried to shoot it.

Pushing the white coverlet aside, she got to her feet. . . . and realized she had on a filmy iridescent nightgown. She still wore her bra and panties. Nothing felt different physically, other than her headache and raw throat. She scanned the bed and found a matching robe had been draped across the other side. Donning the robe, she made her way to the bathroom, where the toilet flushed so loud she expected someone to rush in and catch her, but no one came.

She took a quick look in the mirror before leaving. Even the subtle lighting meant to enhance one's appearance didn't improve the angry red welt on her head. Her hair had been up for the party but now fell in stormy curls past her shoulders.

Party. Had Gwen lived?

Staying in here wasn't answering questions. Abbie padded out of the bathroom and over to the other door. When she reached for the handle the room moved.

"Dammit." Another movement like that and someone would have a mess to clean up. Was she on an airplane?

She opened the door to a badass-looking private ride.

Not like any small jet she'd ever flown in. The area beyond the bedroom resembled a long living room with bone-colored leather couches on the right and two captain's-seat-type reclining chairs on the left. Luxury scented the air. The aircraft moved forward along a tarmac strip she believed belonged to Chicago's Midway Airport.

She stood still, taking in slow breaths to fight off the panic attack rising from her abdomen.

Where were they taking her?

Her gaze skipped ahead to what appeared to be a meeting or dining space, where two mauve-and-tan thick-cushioned chairs anchored each end of a white-lacquered table.

Was this how killers traveled?

Screaming for help seemed stupid considering whoever had kidnapped her controlled the pilot. She couldn't jump out at this speed even if she figured out how to open the emergency door before they lifted off.

How had she gotten into this much trouble?

Where were they taking her?

Who were "they"?

As if in answer to her last question, the door at the opposite end of the cabin opened and . . . Hunter appeared. He'd changed from his tux into jeans and a navy sweater.

He frowned briefly at the sight of her and walked toward her. "What are you doing up?"

"What am *I* doing . . . are you serious?" She charged toward him, but he met her before she took three steps. Her head punished her for the quick movement. She clamped her hands on her head to stop her brain from sloshing.

He caught her by the waist, hands holding her carefully, as if she were an irritated egg. "You should lie back down."

Good advice, since her body trembled with fatigue and her stomach was making plans to decorate anything within projectile range. "What's . . . going on?" she demanded quietly.

The airplane started moving faster.

Hunter pulled her against his chest, holding her steady, his hand cupping her head. "You need to get strapped in. Think you're going to get sick?"

She pushed a hand up and made a puny attempt at shoving him back. "Stop this plane."

"No."

"I'll scream."

"That won't stop the plane and might make you throw up." Hunter heaved a labored sigh. "You've got ten seconds to move to that chair." He pointed to the side of him. "Or I'll put you there."

She didn't move.

"Five seconds."

"Oh, all right, dammit." She pushed away from him. Between the movement of the airplane and her wavering equilibrium she stumbled sideways.

He caught her around the waist again and pulled her back to his chest. She groped at his arms, clutching for balance and furious at the weak-kneed feeling she fought.

"Shhh." Hunter stood unmoving as a steel beam, rubbing his hand up and down her arm. He held her steady and soothed her with whispered words when she wanted to rail at him.

When he asked, "Ready to sit down?" she gave in. For now.

She hated to feel meek. Had never been meek in her life, but she'd never been attacked and kidnapped either. Or shot at, even though she technically hadn't been the target.

So far.

Hunter carefully turned her around and lowered her into one of the recliners facing the sofa. He snapped her seat belt into place and flipped a lever that turned the chair to face forward. "This is the best position for takeoff."

She wanted to ignore his consideration, but the recliner supported her head, which liked being stable.

Not quite as nice as being held in Hunter's arms, but the next best thing.

Nice if not for that whole kidnapping part.

He dropped into the other recliner, but instead of spinning it forward he turned to face her and strapped in, then rested his elbow on the chair arm. He leaned his head over, supporting it with two fingers, his eyes taking her in with clinical interest.

Once the airplane lifted off and leveled out, she said, "Okay, now I want answers."

"That makes two of us. But I want ice on your head first." Hunter pressed a button on the side of his chair arm, then spoke into some hidden microphone. "Bring the ice pack and . . ." He paused to look at Abbie. "Anything else?"

She cocked an eyebrow at him that she hoped suggested she'd like his family jewels served on a silver platter.

He gave her a mildly amused look that added another black mark. "How about hot tea?"

"How about a shot of Jack Daniel's?"

Both of his eyebrows lifted at that, but he called in the order to whomever was delivering.

He might have saved her twice, but kidnapping wiped out his brownie points. Before she could press

him again, a twentyish woman with short black hair
entered the cabin from the same forward door Hunter
had used.

He must have hit another button hidden on his
chair. The doors of the dark wood cabinet affixed to the
wall between their chairs opened and a table with cup
holders slid sideways and up into place at arm's reach.

Abbie felt severely underdressed next to this woman's black pantsuit, pristine makeup, and ruby-lipped
smile. But the young lady—their flight attendant?—
acted as though all Hunter's guests wore filmy lingerie
while traveling.

Maybe they did.

The flight attendant carried a sterling tray with an
ice pack, a bottle of Jack, a glass with ice, and a white
dish edged in gold filled with small sandwiches and
crackers.

"Does she know you kidnapped me?" Abbie asked
Hunter when the flight attendant served her drink.

The woman smiled at Hunter and walked away without a word, acting as though Abbie hadn't spoken.

Hunter gave her an indulgent glance. "Want anything else?"

"Do you really expect me to sit here and act perfectly okay with all this? I don't even know who you
are."

He sat back and draped his arms along the chair,
studying her for a moment. "I recognized something
about *you*."

She hadn't expected that. Did they really know each
other? "What?"

"The small mole on the inside of your left thigh."

———∞———

That comment about the mole on her thigh shut Abbie up.

Hunter hoped he hadn't terrified her. Surely she realized he hadn't touched her. Well, other than carrying her from her apartment building to the car he'd parked down the street and putting the nightgown on her when he reached the jet. It was either the nightgown or put her in the bed half-naked. The only other clothes in the bedroom had been Todd's, which Hunter wore.

No way to avoid catching sight of the tiny mole on her thigh while handling her, which kick-started images flipping through his mind. And the killer had called her Abigail.

Abbie was Abigail.

He might have realized who she was sooner if he'd spent more than a few hours with her that night six years ago in Chicago. She'd been skinnier back when they met as well.

An unhealthy thin. And her hair had been straight and blond, not curly chestnut brown.

Everywhere he went women wore their hair straight, miles of silken strands that fell like a rushing waterfall.

But curls were interesting. Different. Soft. Pretty.

"I don't remember you." She shook her head and winced in pain.

He unclipped his seat buckle, picked up the icepack, and handed it to her. "You going to be sick?"

"Not if you stop asking me that." She snatched the pack and placed it against her forehead. "How do you know me, or are you just screwing with my mind?" She propped her elbow on the chair arm to support her head and closed her eyes.

"I'm not screwing with you. We met a long time ago."

She squinted at him, taking in his face and shoulders, down to his boots.

He could see why she hadn't recognized him either. He'd been at the end of a mission just outside of Chicago that required him to grow a beard and color it to match the dark brown dyed hair hanging to his shoulders.

A bloody mission that had resulted in losing a thread they were following on a string of "accidental" deaths of prominent citizens, one of which had close ties to the sitting president at that time. That was the first time BAD found one of the JC killer's titanium baby spoons. With three carved-up bodies, one of them a child. Hunter had debriefed in a local safe house, then went looking for something else to think about, to whitewash the pictures in his mind.

Abbie had walked into the bar where he'd decided to drink away the night. She strutted in wearing just enough screaming red dress to prevent an indecent-exposure arrest and cut loose a laugh he'd never forgotten.

He'd needed her smile and the tinkle of feminine laughter. Needed to look into turquoise eyes that weren't terrified of dying.

Those eyes were unforgettable, but he'd buried the memory somewhere safe, away from the hideous ones.

The more she drank that night, the funnier she got, even though he'd sensed something troubling her. She shielded her pain well, like now, when she tried to hide her trepidation and confusion. He didn't think she had a concussion, but he'd shaken her awake several times while she slept just to be sure. She still looked too damn pale.

"I'm not up for games." She took a sip of her drink, fixing him with a look of stubborn determination.

"Me either. I'll answer your questions after you answer mine," Hunter started. "How do you know Gwenyth Wentworth?"

"I don't know her."

"Then how did you end up in a private conversation with her when others wait three months to get on her calendar?"

"I told her I wanted to discuss the Kore Women's Center." Abbie took a longer drink of the whiskey. "What were you doing so close to her private patio when she got shot?"

"Not yet."

"Then I'm through talking." She lifted her legs and tucked them beneath her, looking like an abused fairy in all that iridescent material.

He'd have to come up with clothes before he handed her over to BAD. He couldn't take her into a room full of male agents wearing *that*. "How'd the guy in your apartment know your name?"

"I have no idea. I didn't recognize his voice and I didn't know what he was talking about."

Every move in her face, eyes, and body said she was telling the truth. Or was one hell of a liar. She'd been terrified at Gwen's shooting and again in her apartment. Both had seemed like true responses. He'd give her the benefit of the doubt for now.

"You're in some kind of trouble, Abbie. If you let me, I'll help you. If not . . ." He opened his hands in a show of "what will be, will be." The JC killer had made the comment twice about Abbie being helpful tonight, but she hadn't acknowledged the statement. Hunter didn't think she knew what the killer meant, but she played some role in this and had to explain.

"I have *no* idea who that man was tonight. I have *no* idea why anyone would shoot Gwen. And I have *no* idea who you are or why you kidnapped me. That pretty much sums up what I know about all of this."

Hunter believed her on those points, but Abbie was still hiding why she'd met with Gwen. "Why did you threaten Gwen?"

Her eyes shifted away, looking past him at the floor and her glass, then she let the ice pack slide down to shield one eye. "I don't know what you're talking about."

She got the Worst Liar award.

Most women he knew had an inherent gift for re-shaping the truth, but Abbie sucked at it.

He didn't have much time before they reached Nashville and he still had to alert Joe that he was bringing someone into headquarters. When Hunter drove Abbie home, he'd sent Carlos a text saying he was following the woman who had been with Gwen during the shooting. Carlos sent back that he'd forwarded her identification information to Gotthard, who would research her.

Joe would be pissed at Hunter for not informing Carlos that he was of transporting Abbie to headquarters, but Carlos might have wanted to send another team member with Hunter. This was the only chance Hunter had to get information out of her. Handing her over to Joe when they landed might negate some of the backlash. That plus delivering the USB memory stick from Linette, which was supposed to explain the Fratelli network and details on tonight's meeting. Hunter was to deliver the memory stick to headquarters by tomorrow morning, so arriving this far ahead of schedule would be a plus.

"Abbie, I need to know what you and Gwen were talking about. I can't explain why, but it's important to national security."

"National security?" Her smile was loaded with skepticism. "Why should I believe you or tell you anything? How do I know you aren't going to kill me, too?"

"Because I'm the best bet you've got for staying alive."

She tossed the ice pack to the table and sat her glass in the cup holder, then leaned forward with hands on her knees. "Explain what you mean. Who was that guy in my apartment, since he seemed to know you?"

"He's a trained assassin. The best way to keep you safe is to put you in the WITSEC program, which I can arrange. I can't tell you what I do, but I have the connections to get you in there. That's where we're headed now." Sort of. Once Joe and Tee got what *they* wanted, she'd end up in WITSEC.

"*No!* You can't do that."

Hunter rolled out the let's-be-intelligent-about-this tone he saved for reality-challenged individuals who couldn't size up their options quickly. "I can understand how frightening it seems to leave your life and identity, but it's not as scary as someone trying to kill you. We have people who can help you transition."

"No, no, no! I will not go into WITSEC." She jumped up, looking around as if she could find a way out.

He stood and grabbed her arms to steady her. "Sit down before you fall."

"I can't just disappear. I have responsibilities. Everyone will be looking for me."

"We'll get a message that you've been called away on a family issue, then let you write a letter to your family we'll deliver."

Her lips parted, eyes wide in disbelief. "First, the police will not believe that after what happened tonight. Second, my family needs me now."

"My people will keep your name out of the media—"

"That'll be some trick since I work for a local television station."

His jaw snapped shut. She was with the damn media? "You told me—"

"—that I was a writer, which I am," she snapped, then added, "Don't look at me like that. *You* lied to me the whole night, too."

"You're a reporter." He didn't back off the disgust in his voice. "What did you tell your station about tonight?"

"Nothing. I haven't had a chance to talk to anyone between giving police reports and walking in on a killer in my apartment." She leaned forward and stabbed a finger at him, ordering, "Take me home. *Now.*"

Not in this lifetime. Hunter shook his head.

Her anger died down, but her stiff profile said she was not giving up.

He needed one of BAD's damn transition specialists.

"Have a seat and we'll talk calmly." Hunter would rather deal with an insane terrorist than an upset female. The women he normally encountered on an op usually fit into one of two categories—an enemy who would gut him without a second thought or a civilian who had to be rescued and would readily jump at a chance to be in a protective environment.

Someone should have shared the black-ops handbook with Abbie. He gave it another try. "It's too dangerous to return to your life."

"I *have* to go home." She backed out of his grasp, grabbed her head, and shuffled drunkenly until she latched a hand on the headrest of her chair.

He rubbed his eyes, recalling how Eliot had always been better at dealing with irrational or upset women than him. But Eliot was gone and Hunter had to get Abbie to talk before they landed since BAD would be waiting at the airstrip once he alerted them. "You don't have a choice about going into WITSEC. Your life's in danger."

She straightened her shoulders, but terror spilled out with every short breath. Color faded from her face. She turned a dull shade of grayish white that made him think she might lose her struggle with nausea even though her eyes blazed, battle-ready. "I don't care."

That just pissed him off. "You don't *care* that someone is trying to kill you?" he shouted.

"Of course, I care about that," she shouted right back, then took a breath. "But I still have to go home. My mother's sick. She needs me."

The agony and worry in her voice struck him in the chest. "We'll get your mother help."

"You don't understand. I have to be there myself."

"Is going home worth getting killed for?"

She jerked her head back at his words. "Yes, she's worth dying for."

"You won't be much help to your mother dead," he argued coldly. Why couldn't she see the reality of her situation?

"I won't be *any* help to my mother if I leave. In fact, I am the *only* person who can help her." She raked a handful of curls off her face and muttered, "You just don't get it."

"Then make me understand." He knew she couldn't.

Abbie curved her chin up. Tears shined in her eyes but stayed put because of the sheer determination flooding her stance. "You want to know if I'm afraid of dying? Hell yes. Who wouldn't be? But my mother needs me. I'm the only one who could have gotten to Gwen and now Gwen can't even help me, but I can't hide somewhere safe knowing my mother—"

This was going nowhere. He cut in with, "I get that you're worried about your mother, but we have resources. Just tell me what's wrong with her and I'll see what I can do while we put you somewhere safe in the meantime."

She shook her head.

Didn't the aggravating woman realize this was not a game? That she was in real danger of dying?

He pressed on. "So you don't want to see if our doctors could help her?" He sounded like a heartless bastard snapping at her, but his options were exhausted. "You want to negotiate? Tell me the truth about why you were meeting with Gwen and I'll discuss options."

Abbie folded her arms. Icy thoughts crossed her gaze. "My perfectly healthy mother went to the Kore Women's Center ten days ago to donate blood they store for her and to have standard tests performed. The day after she came home her spleen started shutting down, which is causing major internal problems. She may need a liver transplant soon. Kore refuses to admit they treated her with anything, but my mother's doctor told me the truth about Kore. That they do secret testing on childbearing women with rare blood, which my mother was when she first walked into Kore over thirty years ago. She has very rare H-1 blood. Our doctor said Kore had to have given my mother something that damaged the spleen, but he's run every conceivable test. No one knows what's wrong with her, but she's getting worse every day." Tears bubbled at her eyelashes.

Oh. Shit.

"I'm her only hope," Abbie said, forcing strength into her voice. "My mother's dying and may not live through the week. So, yes, I'd rather die trying to save her than live with the guilt of wondering if I could have. If you can't understand caring that much for someone you love then you're one coldhearted bastard."

CHAPTER FOURTEEN

H unter generally had an answer for everyone on any topic, but not this time. Brittle silence competed with the rush of air outside the fuselage.

Abbie waited quietly for him to give her an answer, worry and anticipation glowing in her eyes.

He *was* a coldhearted bastard, but taking her away from her dying mother would put him in a category of humans lower on the food chain than those he'd helped put into prison.

If he handed her over to BAD's witness protection handlers they'd make sympathetic noises while processing her and she'd have no chance to get to her mother. Not any time soon.

She'd have to live with her mother's death hanging over her forever.

Few people knew the torment of living with the death of an innocent person, a loved one, on your conscience.

Like Eliot.

Eliot's face, strained with agonizing pain, bloomed in Hunter's mind. The crashing waves and last seconds when his friend said goodbye, then cut the rope . . . and fell silently to his death. Nothing would ever erase that.

"Hunter?" Abbie called to him, concern seeping into her voice.

He blinked back the dark fog always waiting to blind him. He didn't want her concern or for anyone to worry about his well-being ever again. "What?"

Abbie flinched at his sharp answer.

Dammit. He rubbed his neck and waited a couple beats to calm his voice before speaking. "Sit down before you fall."

"Not until you agree to take me back." She'd spread her feet, stabilizing her body, and crossed her arms, prepared to wait him out.

Did she really think he could let her go anywhere she could talk to the media?

He hadn't called Joe yet, but he could only put that off so long. If he didn't turn her over now, he might not be able to take her in himself later.

Joe watched all his agents for any sign of going rogue or chasing a personal agenda after losing someone close. BAD was unforgiving if an agent broke ranks and bucked the agency. Hunter had proven to all of them that he carried no baggage from Eliot's death, but he didn't want a new partner either.

Not a problem. No one wanted to partner with a son of a bitch so cold they believed he blew off his friend's death as collateral damage.

Hunter hadn't blown off anything.

He'd bided his time, shielded his grief, and now he had a chance to catch the killer.

If he forced Abbie into the WITSEC program, she'd never see her mother again and would clearly withhold information in retaliation.

If he didn't force her, she'd end up in worse trouble than she was in now, since BAD would assign their best assets to track and neutralize Hunter.

Fuck.

Talk about sorry choices. "I can't take you home—"

"Then screw anything you want from me!" She slapped the top of the chair.

"Let. Me. Finish." He would not lose his patience with her again. She was injured, scared, and afraid for her mother. He had no idea how he was going to fix this, but he wouldn't make life any more difficult for her while he came up with a plan. "I won't put you in the WITSEC program, yet, but neither can you go home until I find out who the guy in your apartment is and why he's trying to kill you."

Her face fell. "What about my mother?"

"I meant it when I said if you help me, I'll help you. You could start by explaining how Gwen could help your mother."

She nibbled on her lip, putting as much thought into her answer as someone negotiating for her life, which she probably figured she was.

"Okay. I'll work with you if you're straight with me." She held her hand out. "Let's shake."

Was she serious? "You want to shake?" He wanted to smile at her naïveté but didn't when he realized she was serious.

She thought he wouldn't lie to her if they shook hands?

He'd only accepted a handshake deal from one person before. Eliot.

Her gaze didn't waver when she said, "My father

taught me a man is only as good as his word. If you shake then I'm willing to accept your word and trust you."

He lied with skill that surprised even him sometimes and never lost a minute's sleep over sidestepping the truth on a mission. But he and Eliot would never have broken a deal they shook on. He wanted to pretend this wasn't the same, but guilt invaded his thoughts at the idea of looking Abbie in the eye and lying to her about something she considered a matter of life and death. Breaking his word on this would rip out another chunk of his ravaged soul.

Hunter took her hand. Her fingers were cold as ice and trembling.

Hell, he had to be the cause for some of that.

She gripped his hand with resolve and strength. But she was not strong enough to stop a killer.

His heart thumped. How could she place trust in a man she didn't know based on a handshake? She still hadn't figured out how they'd met. He wouldn't put good odds on her being happy once she did.

His palm warmed against her dainty one. His fingers refused to open and release his hold, forcing his compliance.

Abbie lifted her shoulders, making the most of her five and a half feet. The tiny pulse in her neck gave away her fear. Fear of the future, fear of losing her mother, or fear of him? The urge to pull her into his arms and assure her this would all work out pressed on his chest.

But he couldn't.

Joe might send a team after him by midnight.

A man was only as good as his word. Eliot would have agreed.

Well, hell. Hunter shook. He'd back his word for as long as he had the power to do so.

The only way he'd relinquish that power would be by dying.

She tugged her hand to withdraw it from his, making him feel as though he'd held on too long. He didn't know what to do with his hands now so he crossed his arms.

"Where do you want to start?" She hooked her hands behind her. But she listed to the left and had to take a half step to keep from losing her balance.

"Sit down and we'll talk. Please." He softened his directive and reached for her arm.

She surprised him by not jerking away.

Had she really decided so quickly to trust him?

Just by shaking hands?

She moved toward the sofa instead of the chair. Once she was settled again, the energy drained from her taut shoulders. She curled up on the leather, folding her legs and feet—was that purple toenail polish?—under the bottom of her nightgown.

Her gaze took in the cabin. Wrapping her arms around herself didn't stop her from shivering. The see-through material probably offered little warmth. "What is this thing? A Learjet?"

"Gulfstream IV." A Trans Exec SP-3, but he doubted that would make any difference to her. He sunk into the cushy recliner and pressed the call button on the side.

Felicia's voice came over the intercom. *"Yes, sir?"*

Abbie looked up at the speaker in the ceiling.

"Tell the pilot to change course. Use the return coordinates."

"*Right away,*" Felicia answered. "*Anything else?*"

"Where's a blanket in the cabin?" He eyed the bed-room, a likely place to store one.

"*Beneath the forward seats,*" Felicia answered. "*Would you like me to retrieve one?*"

"No, thanks." Hunter flipped off the intercom, then got up and found the blanket stash. He pulled out a lightweight gray one and draped the wool cover over Abbie.

She had her chin propped on her hand and her elbow leaned against the end of the sofa, staring out at the black night that swallowed the jet. When he bent down to tuck the blanket around her, she swiveled her head until they faced each other.

Her eyes were more blue than green now. A lingering trace of tear gas clung to her hair, but standing so close to her filled him with the scent of her skin.

Some women smelled like a perfume ad.

Abbie had a pure feminine smell that infiltrated his brain and his groin at the same time.

Why was it a man's brain never won that battle?

Her eyes shifted, flaring bright as a blue flame and wide with awareness. She nibbled on her upper lip.

Hunter closed his eyes to keep from kissing her. He straightened away from her before opening his eyes again. That was strange. He never confused work and play.

This sure as hell wasn't the time to start.

Not with a television reporter. How could he contain someone with the media who had seen his face and seen him in action?

One problem at a time.

"Thanks." Abbie folded the top of her blanket over and pulled her knees up, propping her arms across them. She gave him a nervous smile. "You don't know where things are on your own airplane?"

"Not my airplane."

"So this gown doesn't belong to an old nuisance?"

No, the jet came stocked with everything imaginable since it belonged to his father's fleet of leased crafts. His brother kept this aircraft at Midway Airport and had loaned the Gulfstream to Hunter without a question.

His brother had a heart of gold.

At least he'd had one until that conniving Pia mined the organ dry.

"Not from an old nuisance." Hunter sat down on the other half of the sofa. With the change in course for the plane, he might be able to finish this conversation before they landed. If not, he had more time now that he wasn't handing her over to Joe. "Now, about tonight with Gwen."

"First I want to know who you are and why you were sneaking around the party and how you got into my apartment . . ." She stopped talking and cocked her head at him in a cute way if not for the stubborn set of her jaw. "How did you know what was happening in my apartment?"

There was no real benefit in trying to fool her further after what she'd witnessed in her apartment now that he'd made the choice to keep her, but there was a limit to what he could share. That choice meant protecting her, which wouldn't be easy since he needed unrestrained mobility to function. "I can't tell you what I do or who I work with, but I'm with the good guys, for lack of a more specific explanation, and I have training for what I did tonight. I stuck a transmitter over a button on your dress so I could hear you."

⚮

Abbie couldn't decide if she was thrilled he'd heard the killer or appalled he'd invaded her privacy so callously. "Did your thingamabob transmit pictures or just sound?"

"Just sound."

"So when did you see the mole on my thigh?"

"Before you jump to an unsupported conclusion, I did not take advantage of your being passed out. I covered you with my jacket at your apartment, which protected half of your modesty. Figured you'd want to have more on when you came to. That nightgown was the only thing I found."

"Where's my—" Abbie cut herself off when she saw the flight attendant enter the cabin. The woman stopped next to Hunter's chair and said, "The pilot wanted to let you know we have turbulence ahead. He'd like to take a quick break before that."

"Tell him I'll be right up."

She nodded and left as quietly as she'd arrived.

Abbie processed the brief conversation and added another worry bead to her mental string. "Are you going to fly the airplane?"

"Yes." Hunter sat forward, preparing to stand.

"Are you qualified?"

"Yes." But this "yes" was drawn out with a tail of exasperation.

Tough.

"Where's my cell phone, ID, purse . . . ?" She wanted to add "dignity" to the list. Heat crept up her neck at the idea of being exposed to Hunter and God knows who else while he toted her around, but she had to admit he hadn't said anything to make her feel uncomfortable or embarrassed about her seminudity.

"What?" He shook his head at her change of subject. "I didn't have time to do anything but get you out of there after the flash bomb and tear gas were released."

So that's what the flash and blur had been right before she got knocked out.

She took it all in, replaying what came easily to her. Hunter had walked into a volatile situation he knew would be dangerous for him and managed to get her out of there alive, plus arranged for this airplane.

Hard not to overlook his obvious ulterior motives for taking her with him or that he hadn't explained squat, but she didn't know another man who would put his life at risk for her now that her father was dead.

On the other hand, she still didn't know who Hunter was or how he knew her.

He stood to leave.

"Wait. Back to the mole." She spun her index finger in a rolling motion for him to continue. "You were explaining?"

His eyes took her in from her head to where her toes were hidden under the blanket. He hooked his thumbs in his pants pockets. When he met her gaze again his green eyes crinkled with a sly glint powered by a thought she wasn't sure she wanted to hear. "I saw the mole when I laid you on the bed. That's when it all came back to me."

"What came back to you?"

"How we originally met . . . when I saw your mole. I remember what you asked me to do."

The Jack Daniel's sloshing around in her stomach threatened to whip into a sour tornado. Her mind jumped to the first thought any woman would have about a guy insinuating he'd seen the inside of her thigh before, but she'd remember sleeping with someone like Hunter.

She'd remember just kissing a man like him.

None of the three men she'd been intimate with in her life looked anything like him. If they had she'd still be in bed with one of them.

Maybe he was just jerking her chain and had seen her on a beach or at a pool where she might have been in a bathing suit. Been a long time since she'd worn anything skimpy. What would she have asked him to do? Put sun lotion on her?

The airplane jostled. A streak of bright light fingered through the darkness outside. Lightning.

Hunter didn't budge from the motion, solid as a mountain standing there. "You can stay on the sofa, but buckle up. We're headed into turbulence."

"When are you coming back?"

"When I can." He started toward the front of the airplane.

"Wait."

He stopped short of the door leading to the cockpit and turned back with raised eyebrows.

"What did I ask you to do?" The question came out a little more tense than she'd intended.

"You *begged* me to take you home with me." He opened the door, stepped through, and snapped it shut.

———— ⊗ ————

Vestavia instructed Linette to climb into the backseat of a black Range Rover. One of six matching vehicles lined up across the seventy-foot-wide garage. Tinted windows meant they'd escape the media camped in the dark outside the Wentworth fortress.

He spoke quietly with Ostrovsky before they separated. "I want to know who was behind that strike tonight. Peter Wentworth does not make idle threats. He will not continue to support the movement if his daughter dies. The Fratelli would suffer a financial blow from loss of his support that could set our Council back ten years or more."

"That would not be a setback." Ostrovsky's stoic mouth turned harder. "That would be failure. I will report to the others—" He turned at the sound of approaching footsteps.

Bardaric joined them. "Peter has no reason to suspect a Fratelli," he whispered. His eyes cut back and forth, checking, but no one stood close enough to hear them.

"Who *should* he suspect?" Vestavia couldn't read the British prick. Bardaric appeared genuinely shocked by the attack on Gwen, but her death would benefit him the most.

Bardaric's nostrils flared. "What are you insinuating?"

Ostrovsky stepped forward. "Enough. It is in all our best interests to find the killer and appease Wentworth."

Was it? Vestavia had yet to be convinced of that.

If Peter Wentworth found out a British Fratelli follower shot his daughter, he'd pull his resources until he received satisfaction in the form of Bardaric's head.

Literally.

Vestavia would hand him the machete.

But if Peter received evidence that pointed a guilty finger at someone within the North American Fratelli, losing Wentworth's financial support would be nothing compared to the fallout within Fratelli.

Sitting atop the North American Fratelli pinnacle, Vestavia would be the immediate target. He took Bardaric's measure once more. Could the Brit be trying to take out the Wentworth breeder *and* implode the North American Fratelli?

Or is he just trying to kill me?

Vestavia saw a moment of opportunity with Ostrovsky still in attendance. He told Bardaric, "If your plan is approved, you can choose the targets, but I choose the detonation time." Otherwise, Bardaric would escalate the schedule and blame it on a communication glitch.

"You can't do that," Bardaric argued.

"Why not? I thought we were working together on this."

Bardaric lifted a finger toward Vestavia's face.

Ostrovsky stepped between them. "A reasonable request."

"Not a request," Vestavia said, earning a glare from Ostrovsky.

"I need to know the timing immediately," Bardaric demanded.

"When you have the targets," Vestavia said, indicating

the U.S. cities Bardaric wanted to take down, "we'll discuss the details by teleconference with all seven."

Ostrovsky nodded.

Bardaric shifted his shoulders in a dismissive motion. "Beats jet lag."

The prick had every reason to be confident. The Council of Seven would very likely approve the destruction of three U.S. cities since the plan to put a Fratelli in the White House last year had busted. The mole behind that failure was racking up a debt their death wouldn't pay.

"Fra Vestavia?" Cayle Seabrooke, the young man Gwen had introduced Vestavia to before the meeting, came walking up.

"Yes?"

"I'm sorry we didn't get the chance to talk more tonight." Cayle handed him a card. "Here's my contact information. I'd like to work with you."

Wentworth and several Fratelli had highly recommended the guy. Cayle had gray eyes that reminded Vestavia of a wolf on the hunt, always watching for prey or a threat to his territory. The scar slashed across his right cheek fit the lethal edge waiting beneath his veneer of civility.

Vestavia took the card. "Be in Miami tomorrow. I'll call." He walked to the Range Rover where Linette sat quiet as a mute and climbed in next to her. Once the door was shut, he pressed the button to raise the privacy glass behind the driver and told her, "Set up a meeting in Miami for tomorrow morning."

She reached into the briefcase at her feet and pulled out a laptop she booted up. "Who is to attend, Fra?"

"My two southeast lieutenants and you."

She stopped typing. "Am I to actually be *in* the meeting?"

"Yes. It's time we put another female lieutenant in the field. You'll be a part of our next mission."

Having a new lieutenant in the field would be instrumental in helping him locate the mole.

CHAPTER FIFTEEN

"Do you have some aversion to traveling like a normal person?" Abbie shouted at Hunter over the sound of the retreating helicopter, which was turning into a speck of light in the moonless night. Didn't the pilot wonder about dropping two people in the middle of nowhere?

In the middle of freezing-ass nowhere.

Really. This place might not have a zip code for another decade.

They were in mountains and she'd seen snow-tufted trees all around this open patch when the spotlight under the helicopter had swept the frozen terrain right before they landed. The temperature had to be in the low thirties or upper twenties.

"Move over here." Hunter's voice came through the dark quiet as a spirit but with the bite of a general's order.

"Like I can see where you're talking about?" She couldn't see the frost that had to be coming out her mouth. "Don't you have some kind of light and hand warmers and—"

His fingers cupped her arm.

She jumped. And screeched.

"Who'd you think had touched you?" He held on to her arm but didn't try to move her.

Did he have to make her feel like an idiot? She was in the dark, pitch dark. Blacker than a bottomless pit.

Like the night she got lost in the dark and cried until her dad found her.

Tears were justified at six years old.

Not at twenty-nine.

She would not let him know how close she was to losing it. There were scarier things in life, like not ever seeing her mother again. "Can I call my mother's doctor *now*?"

"No tower out here either. We'll try as soon as we find one. I told you it might be tomorrow before you could call again. That's why I let you talk to the hospital while we were landing."

He sounded so reasonable at times she wanted to scream. He'd only let her talk for a minute when the call went through. The hospital staff had said her mother was resting comfortably tonight. Abbie trusted Dr. Tatum to take good care of her.

Hannah wouldn't leave their mom alone, but Abbie would never hear the end of it if she didn't call Hannah soon.

And Dr. Tatum. He might have an idea of someone else for Abbie to talk to at the Kore Women's Center. She wished he'd been at the hospital when she'd called. Even if Dr. Tatum picked up the voice mail Hunter allowed her to leave, he had no way to reach her. She didn't have a phone and Hunter wouldn't share his number.

Hunter tugged a little to get her stepping forward, then hooked his arm around her waist to guide her several more steps. How could he see anything? "Be careful. Don't move or you could fall and hurt yourself. I'll be right back."

"Wait." Maybe she *should* let him know she had a limit when it came to terror and she had been pushed over the top too many times in the last twelve hours. "Don't leave me in the middle of the woods in the dark. Something might attack me."

"Not unless it's deaf. Could you hold it down some?"

"Who could possibly be *here*?" she shouted. Was he serious?

The quick shush of air that blew past her ear sounded like a fiery sigh. Maybe a tired sigh.

She'd never been a nag and didn't care for coming across like one now, but it was damn cold and pitch-freakin'-black. "Sorry, I just can't see anything."

"That's why I told you not to move." He said each word carefully, as though she had stepped on his last good nerve.

Her patience had been ground to bits over the past hour and a half, too.

She'd fallen asleep on the jet's sofa while waiting on him to return from the cockpit so she could demand he tell her the truth about having met her.

She had *never* begged a man to take her home for a night.

How would any woman not remember sleeping with Hunter?

Besides, even if she was the kind of woman who habitually jumped into the beds of strange men, Hunter might fit her physical criteria, but he was cold as a stone inside.

He hadn't even come back to finish their conversation before landing, just sent the flight attendant with this gargantuan flight suit and orders from Hunter to put it on.

When Abbie hesitated, the flight attendant had given her the last of his message. "This is your ten-minute warning to get dressed. You're leaving in whatever you're wearing when we land."

The jet touched down at a small airport with one hangar, a single-level brick building and a barely lit runway. Less than a minute after landing, Hunter rushed her from the cozy jet to a waiting helicopter that was one degree warmer than a refrigerator.

The same helicopter that dumped her in this godforsaken hole.

"Abbie?"

She might be cranky, but who wouldn't be at this point? "*What?*"

"Are you going to stand still when I leave you?"

"What country am I in?"

He muttered something that sounded four-letter short. "United States."

"What city?"

"TMI for now. The sooner you let go of me the sooner we'll get out of here."

She didn't realize she'd been clutching his arm. She let go and tried to stick her hands in her pockets, but those were somewhere around her knees. "Why can't I go with you? Where are you going?"

"To. Get. Our. Vehicle."

If his face looked anything like his voice sounded he was grinding his jaw muscles.

Transportation. That raised her comfort level. "Okay, I'll wait . . . maybe. Unless I hear something."

He didn't say a word.

"Do you have matches or something that lights up,

like maybe a key light . . . or . . . something?" she asked, her voice trailing off in the silence. She *hated* to feel afraid. Just pissed her off.

"Where'd you grow up?"

"Southern Illinois."

"On a farm, right?"

"Yes. What of it?" She hadn't forgotten his snobbish "no" when she'd asked him if he owned a farm.

"Isn't that out in the country?"

She saw where he was going with this and cut him off. "A farm is not in the wilderness with bears or mountain lions or whatever lives here that has teeth big enough to rip a person to shreds."

Another sigh. This one parted her hair.

They were getting nowhere arguing. Someone had to make peace.

"I'm sorry, I'm just . . ." Her teeth chattered. Her head felt like an explosion waiting for a fuse. She hugged her middle, ready to make another stab at convincing him to take her with him.

His fingers curled around her arm again, but this time he pulled her to him and wrapped her up against his chest.

Yes, yes, and oh hell yes.

She didn't care right then if he'd seen a mole on her thigh. That argument could wait for tomorrow. Life had sent a curveball flying at her and she didn't know if she could dodge it.

She needed to be held and feel safe, if only just for a minute.

His hand rubbed along her back, up and down, soothing her.

Hunter might not be as coldhearted as she'd thought. She pressed her face to his chest, feeling his heat through the shirt. He tightened his hold and cupped her head to his chest. She hadn't realized how wide his shoulders were until now.

Not exactly the wastrel she'd pegged him for at the party.

She had a feeling he hadn't earned this body through tennis or swinging by the gym once a week to chew the fat with the guys. He had to have a kicking metabolism to be so hot without an outdoor jacket in this temperature.

Little by little, the anxiety knotted in her shoulders seeped out until she stopped shivering and drew a long breath.

He smelled rugged and male. Not cold at all.

Inviting.

She felt his shoulders move, then his lips touched her hair. He kissed her on top of her head.

With anyone else she would think the act nice and assume it was no big deal. But she had a feeling Hunter didn't show much affection.

The simple kiss was endearing.

If she acknowledged it in any way he'd probably turn into a bear again. Best to act like she hadn't noticed the kiss.

"Better now?" His voice came out rough but tender.

She didn't want to end the moment, but they couldn't stand here all night. "Yes. I won't freak out."

When he chuckled his chest moved. His hand brushed over her hair and down her shoulder.

She shivered. Not from cold this time, but he must have felt it.

He rubbed her arms briskly in a warming motion. "I'll take you with me, but I have to carry you until you get shoes."

Her feet hadn't been cold until he said that, but now she felt the icy ground through two layers of socks. "Okay."

He hoisted her fireman-style and carried her over ground that went up and down. She was starting to wonder about this vehicle ten minutes into the walk when he stopped and pulled a car door open. He dropped her on a vinyl seat and flicked on an overhead light. She was in a Jeep truck, an early 1980s model that had been refurbished. The inside smelled worn and manly.

When Hunter slid in behind the steering wheel, he pulled the keys from somewhere under the dash and tried to start the Jeep. The engine ground over and over in a slow roll, trying to catch. He cursed softly, pumped the gas and tried again.

"Pop the hood." She looked over at him.

He gave her a you-can't-be-serious look.

She arched an eyebrow at him. "Pop. The. Hood."

"Why?"

"I did grow up on a farm. This is a Jeep CJ-8 Scrambler. I have an idea what's wrong with it."

They faced off for several seconds then he made a sound she interpreted as tolerating her fantasy of having any idea what to do. He got out and opened the hood, laying it back on the windshield, then climbed behind the wheel again.

She jumped out before he could say a word about her shoeless feet, but damn, the ground was cold and her socks were getting wet. She stomped her feet while she felt around until she found the butterfly valve and covered it with her palm, shouting, "Try it now."

The engine rolled a couple times, then caught with a growl of power. He must have pulled the choke out. The motor ran steadily with a high pitch.

Hunter appeared next to her. "What'd you do?"

"Covered the butterfly valve." She stepped back while he closed and secured the hood. "The butterfly valve won't close all the way when it's cold, which affects the fuel-to-air mixture—"

He scooped her off her feet before she could finish explaining.

"I can walk four steps," she complained.

Dropping her on the seat, he drew her legs around to face him and pulled her socks off. "I'll give you a towel in a minute you can wrap your feet with."

"I'm not one of your fragile playmates, Hunter."

He pushed her legs inside, turning her toward the dash, but she still faced him. When he lifted his head, the interior lights picked up the creases at his eyes.

She had no idea what he'd been doing in the past twenty-four hours, but she doubted sleeping had been involved.

Before he could move away, she caught his arm.

He was eye-level with her. "What?"

The sharp tone didn't make her jump this time. She'd figured out this man would not harm her. He may irritate the hell out of her at times, but he would not hurt her. "Thanks for holding me."

"You're welcome. Truck'll be warm soon." He rattled that off quickly, clearly not wanting to put this on any personal level.

Why did he turn into a grouchy beast? To keep her off balance or intimidate her into following orders? Maybe if he realized he was wasting his time, he'd warm up to the point where she could find some middle ground he'd meet her on so that she could convince him to take her back to be with her mother.

"You know what?" She didn't wait for an answer. "You don't scare me anymore."

"If you had a lick of survival sense you'd rethink that statement."

"All that posturing doesn't work on me." She smiled at getting under his skin with that one. "And I'm not buying any of your baloney about having met me before."

He didn't say anything at first, but she could see him calculating something.

She probably should have stopped there, but she wanted him to know she wasn't going to just fold and follow his rules. "I'd have remembered at least kissing you . . . *if* kissing you was memorable. Then again, you're really attractive, almost too good looking. You might not even like girls—"

Hunter leaned in, cupped her face, and kissed her.

His mouth fit the man, hard and hot.

He liked females and she could see why they would like him.

She considered pushing him away for a nanosecond, just on general principles, to let him know he couldn't do as he pleased when it came to her, then realized something. He wasn't serious about the kiss.

Just letting her know he *was* in control.

That she had better toe the line when *he* said so.

Hunter didn't like being told he'd lost his edge over her. Thought he was being sly, huh?

She'd fix that. Abbie lifted her hands to his shoulders and slid them up his neck and into his hair. She leaned into the kiss, opening her lips to sweep her tongue into his mouth.

He hesitated for a heartbeat, just enough to confirm she'd surprised him. His hands moved around her hips, his fingers molding to her body when he reached up to clasp her waist and pull her to him.

She wrapped her arms around his broad shoulders, holding on in the middle of a torrential kiss he took control of, demanding more. His fingers slid up her neck, behind her ear, driving into her hair.

At some point he'd turned her into his arms. She tucked her legs closer, twisting against the urgent heat building low. Just when things were getting so hot she was sure ice was melting on the truck, he broke the kiss, muttering something low in unintelligible words.

Like he'd cursed at himself.

She didn't say a thing, couldn't quite catch her breath.

When he released her she was shifted back onto the seat. He reached over and snapped her seat belt buckle. "That answer your questions?"

"I suppose." She shouldn't antagonize him further, but if he thought that kiss had put her off, he'd used the wrong ploy. Whether he wanted to admit it or not, that hadn't been about teaching her a lesson. He wanted to kiss her.

Damn if that didn't make her feel hot.

Hunter placed an arm against the top of the cab and

slipped two fingers under her chin, tilting her face to his. "Never let your guard down around anyone."

"Even you?"

"What do you think?"

"I'll remember that *if* I find myself in a compromising position again."

"If?"

The snot. She refused to let him goad her over what just happened. She was an adult, capable of kissing men whenever she wanted. Not that the opportunity presented itself often. Hunter was not getting away with insinuating she was prone to being in situations like this or naïve. "You're still going to have to convince me that we met or cop to checking out my body while I was unconscious. I want to know that I can trust you to tell me the truth."

"We met years ago." He sounded positive.

"Where? At the beach?"

"What do I get if I do convince you?"

"I'm not making any more deals with you."

"Then you don't really want to know."

Yes, she did, because a weird sense of "maybe" still poked at her. "You are so annoying—"

"So I'm told."

"Can't you just tell me where we met?"

"Nothing's free in this world." His lips twitched, another almost smile. His tone dropped a level to sensuous. "What're you going to give me if I prove we had a memorable meeting?"

"I don't have anything to trade."

He quirked an eyebrow.

"I am *not* trading sex and I *never* begged you for sex."

"That's not what I said." He stepped back and shut her door.

When Hunter climbed in on the other side, he handed her a towel for her feet and a blanket, both from behind her seat.

She wasn't done with him. "Yes, you did say that."

He revved the engine. "No, I said you begged me to take you home with me, but you did beg me to sleep with you, too. So what's it going to be? I won't play if the stakes aren't high enough."

She had a feeling that said a lot about Hunter.

There was no way she begged him to sleep with her and no way he could prove it. And she *knew*—without a doubt—they had never met like that before. Not even amnesia would have wiped out spending a night with Hunter. "Tell you what. If you can convince me I said that to you, I *will* sleep with you. But you only get one chance and have to prove to me we met." *And I mean sleep, not anything else, just as a safety valve.* "But if you don't convince me, I get to go home tomorrow and see my mother."

She'd never gambled in her life but desperately wanted to get back to her mother. Based on logical analysis, this bet was loaded in her favor. Another woman might have had so many trysts she'd have to hesitate. There was something to be said for a mostly celibate life.

She crossed her arms and smiled at him.

His thumb bumped the steering wheel slowly while he thought. The silence dragged out. Victory stirred in her heart.

Now she'd find out if he backed his bets with honesty.

"We met six years ago in a bar," he said, giving her a second to think on that before he continued. "You came in wearing a red dress that screamed 'do me' and tried to drink me under the table. Later that night, you told me you sneak Godiva chocolates you keep hidden in the refrigerator and you had a crush on your tenth-grade math teacher, before you begged me to take you home." He angled back into his seat and put the truck into gear. "There's no road out of here. Sit back and be quiet so I can concentrate or we'll end up rolling down a ravine."

She yanked the blanket up and stared straight ahead.

He *could* still scare her.

She'd never told anyone, not even her sisters, about her crush on her math teacher.

Holy crap. Hunter was that buff shaggy guy she'd met in a bar? He was the naked stranger she'd spent a night with and had lusted after for six years?

And here she'd thought being shot at had been the scariest thing to happen in her life.

What the hell was she going to do now?

CHAPTER SIXTEEN

Dr. Don Tatum paced in the dark, pausing long enough to glance out his living room windows, where Chicago's last snow clung to spots the sun didn't reach during the day. He squinted, checking the street.

No dangerous figures moved around, but his neighborhood was supposed to be quiet during the first hours of a new day.

Standing inside this much glass gave him a nervous life-in-a-fishbowl feeling. Not good for high blood pressure.

He'd loved this house from the first minute he walked in, happy with all the windows for natural light and to have his entire living space on one level. He'd wanted simple and convenient.

No stairs to carry his bulk up and down.

No attic to shove junk in that should be thrown away.

No basement with leaks.

He'd gladly trade the entire house for a safe room in a basement right now. He smoothed his hand over the bald spot on the back of his head and it came back covered in perspiration. The heat was down low since his girls weren't at home. Sweat pooled under the arm of the blue cotton shirt he still wore, but now it was untucked from his dress pants.

Streetlight glow from outside stretched from the palladium window over to the blue sofa, and fingered the middle of the rosewood coffee table.

The light gave him some measure of security, a defense against buried childhood fears of the infamous bogeyman, but Don worried about a real bogeyman.

He glanced at the square sandwich-size panel on the wall. Two tiny red LED lights peeked through the dark, assuring him the security system was on and ready should an intruder try to enter.

His two little girls were safe with his sister, who thought he was having the house exterminated. She lived in Alabama on a farm with no mailbox, no visitors. Good place to hide his children. She'd been the one person he could turn to after his wife died three months ago.

Tears stung his eyes. He missed his wife every day. Missed his best friend and only true love.

What would she think of him now?

If she was watching over them, she had to know he was doing whatever it took to keep their two girls safe.

Don had no idea why this strange guy had targeted him.

He had never crossed the law. Never drank or gambled, not even a lottery ticket. Why was this guy threatening him?

Don lifted a trembling hand to cover his mouth.

What about Abbie Blanton? She was Meredith's daughter. Didn't Abbie's safety matter?

Maybe she was okay. The guy hadn't said—

A floor creak spiked the silence.

Don stopped pacing next to the coffee table and swung his head to check the security panel.

No red lights. No green lights. No lights period.

"Hello, Dr. Don." The dark figure he'd watched for outside walked across the middle of the living room toward Don, wearing all black, a skull's face covering the stocking-cap front.

"How'd you get in here?" Don fought the urge to scream for help. He couldn't. He'd been warned.

Calm down. His children couldn't lose another parent.

"Let's not waste time on ridiculous questions, shall we?"

Don detected a hint of a British accent in the man's speech. He didn't care where this wacko was from. "Who are you?"

"Jackson, like I told you last time we met."

"I don't understand any of this." Don had never been in any financial trouble or had an enemy he knew of, no reason to be blackmailed into this if not for his children's welfare. This guy hadn't asked him to do anything really bad, just convince Abbie to go to the fundraiser and talk to Gwen Wentworth. Don thought the guy was helping at first, supplying information about the Kore Women's Center Abbie's mother had visited and come home sick from.

Then this guy's tone had changed. He'd warned Don to tell Abbie his exact words, to give her details he bullet-pointed verbally about the Kore center and make her believe Don was speaking from personal knowledge.

Don hadn't seen any real danger in telling Abbie and

even thought with Gwen's help they might figure out what was wrong with Abbie's mother.

But why had this wacko Jackson come to him and not Abbie?

Don bumped the coffee table with the back of his leg. He froze, nowhere to go. "I did what you said. I told Abbie exactly what you told me to say. She went to the party. She called on her way and asked a couple more questions so I know she went."

"Yes, she did. I saw her at the Wentworth house."

Relief charged through Don. He put a hand to his heart. "Thank God. So you'll leave me alone now?"

"I promise to never come back here again."

"Good. Good. I promise not to say a word, I swear it." Don wiped a line of sweat off his forehead.

"I have no doubt you won't say a word." Jackson sliced across the room, stopping in front of Don. "Open your hand."

Don complied, lifting his hand palm-up. "Why?"

"Take these." The intruder dropped two pills in his hand.

When he realized what they were, Don looked up, shaking his head. "No, these will put me in cardiac arrest."

"Precisely."

"I did what you asked. You can't do this. My kids just lost their mother. They need me." His hand shook. The pills rolled back and forth.

"You have a choice. Take the pills or I'll bring you the hearts of both your girls in a jar so you can remember them."

Don started crying. "No, I did what you wanted. I did it. You can't do this."

"So is that a yes? You do want souvenirs of your children?" Jackson continued musing. "As long as I'm at your sister's house, shall I bring her heart as well? I haven't worked with my surgical blades in a while. Didn't need them for your wife. You'll be happy to know she died immediately in the collision. Boring, but efficient."

CHAPTER SEVENTEEN

Hunter watched the second hand on his antique brass desk clock, each tick drawing him closer to decision time.

The videoconference in twelve minutes with BAD would go one of two ways. Couldn't be put off. Not after what he'd found on the memory stick from Linette.

Joe might threaten to put him in leg irons or release a termination contract on him.

Or a third way. Something worse.

No matter what, worse always waited just around the corner.

But first they'd have to find him.

Toeing his leather chair back from the onyx desk, Hunter sat back and stared at the view beyond the ten-foot-tall windows lining one wall of his office. Eliot had worshipped that view. An endless wash of Montana blue sky interrupted only by snow-dusted tips of ponderosa trees and white bark pines covering this remote mountain ridge.

Eliot would hike for days across the one hundred and twenty-eight acres of undisturbed wilderness surrounding the cabin, climbing every vertical surface cut from the volcanic rock and hiking the granite slopes.

Forever in search of a physical challenge.

Then he'd do his damnedest to drink up all the expensive liquor he could find in the bar downstairs, until he finally realized this house could operate two years without a serious supply drop.

Eliot would scoff at the pricey labels.

"Two-hundred-year-old scotch pisses out the same color as cheap whisky," he'd say the next day, then grin and add, "But I find I like it better on the front end."

A tap at the door shook Hunter from thoughts he normally kept locked away with an iron determination.

He glanced across the wide room to find his five-foot-eight permanent resident parked in the doorway leading to the foyer.

Borys could have been a ferret if he grew a black pelt and dropped down on all fours. "Compact" and "wiry" described everything about the fifty-two-year-old man who kept the household running in Hunter's absence. Short black hair stuck out in all directions, none with any plan. Whiskers tried to match his hair. He had a wadded-up face that had been left out in the sun too long until the creases were permanent, but thick lashes and hawk-like hazel eyes saved him from being butt-ugly.

Best-dressed ferret on this mountain.

He wore black suits with starched and pressed white cotton shirts, determined to match some stereotypical role he'd seen in too many movies.

Nothing had ever been said about Borys being a butler or valet or any other position of servitude.

He'd decided that all on his own.

In Poland, he'd played many roles to gain the

information he bartered to stay alive. He had a knack for languages and mimicry, which he practiced by drawing from the extensive movie library Hunter had supplied.

When in residence, Hunter wore jeans and T-shirts. He suggested Borys do the same since Eliot had been their only guest and favored jeans over any other clothing.

Borys refused to move from the basement, where he'd hidden for the first three months he'd lived here, to an upstairs bedroom unless Hunter agreed to a trade of labor for somewhere to live.

Once that deal was struck, Borys decided to dress the part.

Hunter gave up.

Seven identical eight-year-old suits hung in the walk-in closet off Borys's bedroom suite, none of which he'd allow Hunter to replace with more current styles. "Who cares about style if we have no company?" Borys would point out, turning Hunter's logic back on him.

Borys cleared his throat.

"What?" Hunter sighed at the silver platter his self-appointed butler carried.

"Thought you and the missus might like some coffee." Today Borys sounded like a cowpoke from a John Wayne movie.

"She's not the missus and this isn't a social event." By the time Hunter had put Abbie in a room last night she wouldn't speak to him. He probably shouldn't have been quite so honest when she pressed him about when she'd see her mother again, but he figured an honest answer would save days of arguing.

Telling her not to expect to get back for another week had ended all conversation. She'd withdrawn into herself. He'd have kidded her about losing the bet if she hadn't looked so forlorn. He checked the wall security monitor for the orange light that indicated the front door remained secure.

"Treat a lady nice, you might see her again." Borys's wide lips twisted with a frown.

"She's not staying long and I don't expect to see her again once she leaves." Hunter hadn't figured out exactly what he was going to do with Abbie, but she couldn't go back to reporting for a television station and she couldn't stay here.

Especially not after that kiss had backfired last night.

He'd remembered Abigail Blanton all over again when her lips touched his.

He hadn't met the real Abbie six years ago.

That one had strutted her stuff, looking and acting like every other woman he'd known to date.

The Abbie he'd met at Wentworth's party hadn't teased or flirted, and she'd filled out nicely. Unavoidable as it had been, he couldn't wipe away the vision of all that creamy skin in nothing but underwear when he'd removed his coat from her on the airplane.

He got hard just thinking about holding her again.

And that's why he had to figure out what to do with her.

Walking past the butter-yellow leather chair and sofa arrangement near the window, Borys muttered under his breath, then set the tray on the low table, a four-foot-wide slice of red oak polished to a shine. He poured coffee, grumbling, "No decent woman's gonna put up with an asshole."

Hunter ground his back teeth. Did everyone have the same mediocre vocabulary of insults?

You get what you pay for.

Hunter *would* pay Borys if he'd accept more than room and board.

No chance.

This had been the only place to hide the former snitch from Poland seven years ago when the CIA went after Borys, who had been the European connection between a Los Angeles crime family and a Russian mob they supplied with black-market weapons. If Borys hadn't tipped off Hunter that he and his female partner had been made, the Russians would have tortured Hunter, slowly removing body parts for days while interrogating him. His female counterpart would have faced worse.

Hunter couldn't let the CIA hand Borys over to the Russians when they conveniently forgot how Borys had helped their agents.

But right now he needed Borys to get the hell out of the room so he could contact BAD.

"I take it black," Hunter told the ornery cuss still fussing over a coffee mug.

"I know what you drink, dammit." Borys brought a thick white ceramic coffee mug with RUBY'S DINER printed in blue ink on the side. The one Hunter had used for over ten years after Eliot lost one of their famous "high-stakes" bets on a Texas firing range.

The loser had to produce a worn diner mug with blue ink that couldn't be bought and couldn't come from a state bordering Texas. Eliot rode his classic Triumph Bonneville motorcycle sixteen hundred miles over three days, searching for the mug.

Compared to what they both did for a living, the only high stakes worth betting on were creative ones.

Hunter smiled at the memory until a fist squeezed his heart.

"You want breakfast?" Borys asked.

"Do I ever eat breakfast?"

"Hell if I know what you do when you're gone." Borys walked away, mumbling, "Guess you don't bring women here either, but that's better'n seeing you with a man."

Hunter shook his head and waited until Borys reached the door. "I don't want to be disturbed. Would you close—"

The door slammed shut.

He glanced at the front-door security light once more, then dismissed his concern over Abbie trying to leave. She'd been rattled in the woods last night. She wouldn't face the wilderness alone.

Turning back to the computer, Hunter scooted up to the table and tapped keys to boot up the videoconferencing software. He reached over to a control box that resembled a low-profile stereo receiver and pressed buttons to close blinds inside the double-paned glass windows to darken the room. The only thing anyone at BAD would see when they came online was Hunter with a blank wall behind him.

Eliot had set up this computer system that routed to a different location every time Hunter had to make direct contact, which he rarely did from his safe house in Montana. No one, not even BAD, knew about this location. Until now, he'd never had a reason to keep his distance from BAD. Today's feed went to a location in Canada. The minute he ended communication, he would dial a number by phone that would trigger a minimal explosive, destroying the computer hidden in the basement of a telemarketing center and ending the satellite link to the site.

His forty-eight-inch monitor flashed with the image of a retro-looking video countdown like the old television sets used to have in the sixties. The number 1 appeared, indicating the link was secure.

Joe's bold face and broad shoulders filled the screen, his gray-blue eyes as hard as his tone. "Start explaining."

Hunter hadn't expected pleasantries from BAD's director, but he had thought Joe would ask for his current location first. "I followed the Blanton woman to her apartment and tagged her with an audio transmitter. An intruder grabbed her before I could get inside."

He couldn't very well tell the head of BAD he had Abbie with him at a location he wouldn't share the coordinates on. If he did, Joe would end the conversation and order them both to headquarters. He had the information Joe wanted and with a little luck he'd pull even more out of Abbie, then worry about what to do with her.

"Where is she?" The quieter Joe spoke the more an agent should worry.

"Don't know. Her apartment was hit with tear gas. When I left, I picked up a tail I couldn't shake. Protecting the memory stick I retrieved at the Wentworth estate came first so I took a jet out of Midway. I'm at a safe house. Didn't want to risk coming into headquarters in case I didn't lose the tail." Hunter paused for more feedback from Joe to test the strength of his lies.

"What safe house?"

"Belongs to a friend."

Joe didn't ask what friend. In their line of work everyone had "friends," and no one gave up a name with trust at stake.

To deflect attention from that subject, Hunter asked, "What happened to Gwen Wentworth?"

"In ICU at the Kore Women's Center, stable but not promising. She's pregnant."

Another surprise, only because Hunter remembered her losing a baby during childbirth two years ago, then her husband dying not long afterward . . . a sailing accident. "What about the three men suspected of being Fratelli? What happened to them?"

"Gone." Joe's voice dropped with disgust. "Seven matching Land Rovers exited the estate at the same time and split up in different directions in a matter of minutes. We didn't have enough resources on-site to cover them all and the three we followed each entered a parking lot, then exited with an additional matching vehicle on its tail before they took separate routes."

That meant all seven had contingency plans. It would have taken an army of agents in separate vehicles to track them.

"I need that memory stick now," Joe interjected.

"I can bring it in." Risky. Joe might use that to lure Hunter back to headquarters only to put him in lockdown if Joe silently suspected anything. "But in the interest of saving time I reviewed everything on the USB key and downloaded the data into one of our secure electronic vaults. Our informant explained the Fratelli hierarchy as twelve Fras who operate as a ruling unit on each continent but said little about their identities."

"Give Gotthard the vault code in a minute," Joe said. "He received an electronic missive two hours ago from our informant about the Fratelli in North America gearing up for an operation on U.S. soil in conjunction with a product developed by a UK Fra who's supposed to be noted on the memory stick."

"He is," Hunter said. "Here's the short version of what I downloaded. Vestavia is at odds with Fra Bardaric from the UK. Last night at the Wentworth event, I got a look at the man I think was Vestavia, but he was too far away to render a decent sketch. There may be a connection between the JC killer and this Bardaric."

Hunter continued, careful not to show any change in his voice rhythm when revealing what he'd learned about that murdering JC bastard from Linette's memory stick. "Peter Wentworth told Vestavia about ten male babies born thirty-two years ago in North America. All ten were taken as a group and raised in China to be disciplined killers completely loyal to the Fratelli. Five proved to be incapable and were terminated. Three died on missions. Of the two that remained, one was training the next generation, but he committed suicide. The tenth one entered MI6, spent four years in the organization, then disappeared five years ago. He's known only as the Jackson Chameleon, because of the titanium baby spoons he leaves when he completes a mission and the spoon image he stamps on confirmation kill photos."

"He could be MI6 or a double agent for them and

the Fratelli or just plain rogue." Joe let his opinion of "rogue" come through clearly on a note of disgust.

"What's the chance of getting MI6 to admit they have a rogue agent?" Hunter doubted the possibility, but Joe had contacts everywhere.

Joe's eyes turned the dark shade of honed steel. "About as good as getting me to tell them anything on one of mine."

Hunter didn't miss the warning. "We have a motive for shooting Gwen?"

"No. Another reason we need this Blanton woman. I'll let Gotthard explain what he has," Joe said, looking to his left before the video blinked and Gotthard Heinrich's wide face popped into view. Hair slicked back in a ponytail, overemphasizing the wide forehead and bold jawline, his bulk filled much more of the screen than Joe and Joe was no slouch in size.

"Tell me the code for the vault files and what else is in the file while I download everything, Hunter." Gotthard had phenomenal computer skills and an ability to multi-multitask.

"Peter wouldn't give Vestavia any significant details on the ten babies. The Wentworths have been Fratelli supporters for many generations, with roots in England, so Peter refuses to take sides in a dispute or in sharing breeding information. He provides financial support and political clout to the North American contingency since this is now his home. The Wentworths are one of only three families in the world that protect genetic records of the Fratelli. Vestavia believes this killer works for Bardaric since the hits that have occurred benefit Bardaric's agenda."

Gotthard stopped typing. "The meeting during the fund-raiser had to do with Gwen's baby and some other babies being bred."

"What do you mean by 'bred'?" Hunter pulled a writing pad and pen from the corner of his desk to jot notes.

"Remember the genetic markers you and I located on the students from France last fall?"

"Yes." Hunter had tapped genealogy specialists he knew in the UK who traced the heritage of royalty and world leaders. Those particular specialists spent their days inputting and analyzing ancient DNA taken from clothing, personal items, anything that might carry a specimen. Their computers weren't capable of processing that much information in a timely manner, so Hunter arranged for Gotthard to offer secure computer services as a contractor. BAD possessed a supercomputer called the Monster that Gotthard had been running the information through for the genealogy specialists . . . and BAD.

Gotthard explained, "Our informant says there's a power struggle going on within the Fratelli that has to do with these bred children. We're hoping the information you picked up will explain more. I've got the Monster cross-referencing some of the world's most influential families, like the Wentworths' group, but some have no readily available medical records."

"I have a thought on that to do with the Kore center I'll share in a minute. You think if we find the people connected by genetics that will lead us to the Fratelli?"

"That's where we hit a wall." Gotthard's attention moved to something offscreen and tapping sounds came through the speakers. "Got the download." His eyes moved back and forth, reading. "There's our start point."

"What?" Hunter had scanned Linette's information, including photos of the three Fras who met at the Wentworth home, but he hadn't put together anything linked to genetic markers.

Gotthard continued typing and reading something, then his eyes stared forward again. "The genetic markers I've found started disappearing around thirty years ago. I just entered seventeen dates of birth listed by our contact in a file on the memory stick for people Vestavia calls genetic assets for North America. The contact says there are more, but this is what was accessible. The computer is matching them to . . . yes. The birth dates our contact supplied match seventeen of the UK genealogy specialists' records and all seventeen have similar but rare blood types. And I don't mean AB blood but some form of HH. All seventeen are listed as being born at Kore during the past thirty-five years."

"I'm not following you. It's not like all the people with that rare blood type and similar DNA markers just decided to go to Kore." Hunter scribbled notes on the pad about the Kore Women's Center, Gwen and Abbie plus her mother's H-1 blood, connecting them with a line, then drew a question mark in the center. "Maybe they didn't go willingly. With this being a premier center for rare blood are any men admitted?"

"No men. We're dealing with women only. And I've been keeping a list of women with similar rare blood types popping up in our database search who did not enter the Kore Women's Center. Every one I've found ended up terminated."

Hunter stopped drawing. "What? Explain."

"We have more data to process, but we have enough to show a pattern of women dying by accident—drowning, traffic accidents, muggings, a bad fall hiking, anything but a natural cause."

"So *none* of the women had a disease or cancer or something? Hard to believe in this day and age."

"Some did, but we haven't found a female with this genetic profile from outside the center who died of a natural medical issue. And the ones who *did* go into the Kore center who died later committed suicide or succumbed to a fast-paced illness."

Hunter crunched on that. He was first to argue that anything coincidental in this business deserved a closer look. Few could surpass him when it came to electronics and processing intel, but he'd defer to Gotthard's electronic capabilities any day and frankly preferred action over studying intelligence reports. "About the Kore center. Before Gwen was shot, I overheard her tell Abigail she couldn't share something about the center or the Fras would kill both her and Abigail. I did find out Abigail's mother has rare H-1 blood and she visited the Kore center recently. Abigail was trying to press Gwen for information, because her mother was healthy when she went in ten days ago and came out sick. The Kore center claims they only took a blood donation to bank for her mother and performed routine tests."

"When'd you find all that out?" Gotthard asked with a tiny lift of his eyebrows.

Hunter understood Gotthard's sign that he was asking the question for Joe's benefit. His teammate was trying to help him. "Heard it while they were talking right before Gwen was shot."

Gotthard grunted, then continued. "Our informant inside Fratelli believes the JC killer is linked to the prime minister's death two months ago, was behind Gwen's shooting—which we've confirmed as true—and will be playing a role in the upcoming attack. The informant says Vestavia believes Bardaric's directing the killer. Based on a series of kill photos Vestavia received with the JC killer's signature stamp, Vestavia believes Bardaric is going to hit a political leader. He speculates that our president may be in danger when he meets with the new UK prime minister in DC next week over a United Nations issue coming up."

"UN issue my ass." Hunter scoffed. "Everyone knows the president is trying to smooth over tension between him and the prime minister. Hell, half the world suspects this prime minister of having a hand in assassinating the last one." A plan started forming in Hunter's mind. "Did the informant have any idea what type of attack the Fratelli were planning?"

"Possibly an explosive. Something new, not on the market."

"Time frame?"

"Nothing definitive. The prime minister is meeting with the president on Tuesday in DC, but he's arriving in Colorado Saturday to visit a friend and speak at a college on Monday. We can't dismiss someone killing the prime minister as an unwilling martyr. We're using Saturday as an early time frame."

Hunter's next move would determine if Joe suspected his actions. "That means we have anywhere from three to five days. And the informant warned us to be prepared for quick changes in the schedule. Vestavia has switched plans and escalated time frames in the past to keep anyone from outmaneuvering him. He trusts no one. Until the informant can supply a time frame, locations, and what the explosive is, our best bet is to get inside the Kore center. We locate records on those ten male babies and we'll have a shot at finding the JC killer before he strikes. He might be the loose thread to unravel this whole scheme."

Hunter forced his fingers to unfold from gripping the pen he held in view of the monitor. Opening the jaws of an alligator in the middle of a kill would have been easier.

Gotthard's eyes shifted left. He nodded, then faced the monitor again. The big guy showed wear around the edges, his eyes more tired looking than usual. Could be the job or his rocky marriage taking a toll, or both. "Joe plans to have teams stationed in different parts of the country ready to go at a minute's notice. He can't send an alert through channels to other government security branches of the possible strike with nothing to hand them as hard intelligence. If someone shows our hand too soon, we risk alerting the Fratelli. Then they'd just find the leak, reset their plans, and strike at a later date."

Gotthard's point was clear. The Fratelli would find their informant, kill her, and move forward.

Hunter had observed the long hours Gotthard spent trying to connect with this informant online last year and his friend's excitement when she responded. Gotthard didn't hide the fact that he was protective of Linette's safety. What the others probably hadn't noticed, since few had spent the intensive time Hunter had working with Gotthard in intelligence research in the past year, was that Gotthard also seemed possessive when dealing with her.

He began mentally listing what this B&E would require. "It'll be tight, but I can insert into Kore in forty-eight hours."

"A female agent has to insert," Gotthard said. "Only men in the facility are Wentworth doctors everyone knows."

Hunter sat up. "The staff is *all* women?" Of course, that would make sense for a women's center.

"Pretty much. Joe has a team searching for those three Fras. Carlos and his team are hunting the sniper and Korbin's tracking the Blanton woman."

Carlos could search all he wanted for the sniper, but so would Hunter. Korbin wouldn't pose a problem as long as Hunter kept Abbie out of sight.

That would mean locking her up here or she'd try to leave. He glanced at the orange security light still shining to let him know the front door had not been opened. How could he tell her she couldn't be with her mother any time soon and might have to stop making phone calls? He'd figure out something, some way to help her mother, too.

And if her mother died while he held Abbie hostage? *Fuck.* Moving back to his plan, Hunter said, "I can figure out a cover to access the Kore Women's Center."

"I hear ze female vaxing is vorst form of torture. Only for real men," Gotthard deadpanned, eyes creasing with mirth. He allowed his German accent to surface when he relaxed.

"You need a humor makeover. Tell Joe to give me some time to come up with a plan. If he doesn't like my plan then send a female, but if the Kore security is as tight as I think, it's going to take more than inserting as staff."

Eliot could bypass anything. Could have.

Gotthard's eyes thinned, sending Hunter a visual message to heed him. "This may not be something one agent can do alone." When Hunter didn't reply, Gotthard turned to his right, clearly listening to Joe, who would have heard everything, then Gotthard faced the screen. "You have two hours to hand Joe a plan."

Hunter signed off and shut down the computer. Time for Abbie to tell him everything she knew. He strode over to his office door, opening it to shout into the foyer. "Borys?"

Boot heels clicked across the buffed cherrywood floors. Borys appeared at the door that led to the kitchen. "I'm busy."

"Tell Abbie I want to talk to her."

"She's not with you?"

Hunter walked over to the stairs and shouted up, "Abbie!"

"I coulda done that." Borys crossed his arms. "I just looked everywhere for her. She's not in the house."

CHAPTER EIGHTEEN

"Where the hell is she?" Hunter yelled at Borys, who stomped to the front door of the cabin.

Like Abbie would be sitting on the cabin's front steps?

"Front door alarm is still active," Hunter told him, and swung around to the coat closet.

"Door's still locked, too, but if she ain't in here, she has to be outside." Borys punched the wall monitor, clearing the alarm system, then ran up the stairs. "I only stuck my head in her bedroom earlier. I'll search it, but she ain't here."

"Goddammit!" Hunter slammed his fist inside the closet and hit a panel in the only spot that would make the hidden shelf drop down to reveal a Kahr K9 9mm. He shoved the stainless steel weapon inside his waistband at the small of his back.

"Climbed out the window with sheets," Borys yelled, pounding back down the stairs.

"Who turned off the upstairs security?" Hunter roared, snatching a down jacket from the closet.

"Me! I like to crack the damn windows sometimes." Veins stuck out on the sides of Borys's neck, pulsing. "We never set the upstairs goddamn security! She couldn't've gone far."

"I activated the traps on the way in last night."

"Ah, shit. What the hell were you thinking? You never do that when you have a guest. She could be laying out there with a broke neck."

"She's not a guest!" Hunter snapped. Borys was lucky he didn't have time to strangle him. He wanted to kill something right now. "Stay here in case she comes back and don't fucking let her out if she does."

"How about fucking telling me what the deal is next time you bring a woman home so I can keep her hemmed up? You must've really pissed her off—"

Hunter slammed the door and stared at the frozen landscape. Miles of treacherous terrain so chewed-up a bear would be tough to track. He narrowed his choices down to the least-steep direction leaving the cabin. She couldn't have hiking boots . . . unless she stole some from Borys that fit. Would she take the sharp downhill incline ahead?

No. She was going for the Jeep.

He rounded the cabin to where the land sloped away less aggressively with breaks that might look like paths squiggling between swatches of pines that stair-stepped down the mountain.

An innocent-looking route.

Except for several narrow chasms where loose rocks and land would break away unexpectedly.

A fall out here could be fatal.

If she didn't fall on her own she wouldn't know to sidestep traps he'd set to stop anyone who made it past his outer security perimeter undetected.

If that didn't worry him enough, the trails down this side led to where he'd found a mule deer killed by mountain lions.

———

J oe waited on Gotthard to finish at the computer terminal, wishing this private room, which connected to the electronic surveillance and research division for BAD, had more than fifteen feet square of open area so he could pace. But the room had been constructed specifically for small groups and private meetings within their mission headquarters beneath downtown Nashville, Tennessee. The building affectionately known as the Bat Tower housed an insurance company front for Bureau of American Defense, connected to the underground operations center by a warren of tunnels.

Gotthard finished closing a file he'd opened while videoconferencing with Hunter and swung around. He propped his meaty elbow on the edge of his desk and rested his chin on his thumb. "Opinions?"

Joe had several but preferred to hear his men out first. He turned to Retter, his most dangerous agent and the only other person Joe had allowed to listen in on the videoconference.

Retter's chest barely moved with a breath. Black hair hung to his shoulders, still damp from showering. He scratched his freshly shaven chin, his guarded gaze studying the floor. The decision weighed on all of them, but Retter had taken the lead on watching Hunter. He leaned his butt against the edge of a stainless steel table adjacent to the one Gotthard sat at where monitors and electronic equipment lined one wall. Retter finally shook his head. "I never saw any change in his normal demeanor all the time I've shadowed him on ops for the past four years. Same hard-ass attitude, proficient as he is lethal. He had me convinced he'd moved past Eliot's death . . . until now."

"Me too," Gotthard agreed. Disappointment slumping his shoulders said even more.

Joe rubbed his temple, willing the headache not to turn into a migraine. "Shit, I believed he was over Eliot's death, too. But I can't be sure. Hunter didn't exactly take the bait about the connection between the JC killer and the attack in Kauai. Hard to say for sure what he's up to right now."

"If you could have read him that easily over a video monitor, he wouldn't be working for BAD," Retter pointed out.

"I know." Joe gave up on his aching temple and pushed his hand into his front jeans pocket. "We need him if he comes up with a viable plan to get inside the Kore Women's Center."

"I'll second that," Gotthard interjected. "We don't have the time to build a profile to get someone in the front door and any agent we sent in wouldn't have backup."

Joe asked Retter, "Korbin's sure he saw Hunter leave with Blanton from her apartment? He's not letting his dick talk after Hunter punked out Rae in the mission room, right?"

"No." Retter gave a quick shake of his head. "I questioned Korbin myself. He's solid. Besides, no one on this team would put a target on an agent who didn't deserve it."

"Didn't say they would." Joe didn't pull punches and wouldn't now, but there was no reason to take the head off one of the men helping him sort through this mess. "We still have to confirm Hunter's tracking the killer on his own. In the meantime, we'll give him two hours." He took in the grim faces of both men. Not a thing any of them could do yet. Not until Hunter made a clear move across the line Joe drew for every agent the day they entered BAD. Elite operatives couldn't use their skills and intelligence access to fulfill vows of vengeance. "If Hunter has a viable plan, we let him go through with it."

"If not?" Gotthard asked.

Joe never minced his words. "Then I'll give him one chance to bring in the girl and turn himself in before I send a team after him." He never wanted to take down one of his own, but he would give the order to drop a rogue and every agent knew it.

CHAPTER NINETEEN

Abbie picked her way carefully between snow-crusted evergreen bushes and scattered boulders blocking the easiest route off this frozen mountain. She'd traded in her oversized flight suit from last night for a less oversized pair of worn-but-clean jeans, two long-sleeved T-shirts, a dark green cotton sweater, thick socks, and boots a size too large she'd found in a bedroom down the hall from the one she'd slept in.

The bedroom Hunter had shown her to early this morning when they arrived and ordered her to stay put until he came to get her.

Yeah, that always worked well with her.

Did he really think she'd just sit there for a week or more? He might have all kinds of time, but she didn't.

First, her mother was dying, dammit.

Second, what about her job? Stuart would be foaming at the mouth by now, fielding questions from other media outlets, and the board and slow-but-not-stupid Brittany wouldn't be far behind wondering why he'd given Abbie an invitation to the Wentworth event.

Third, what if the police wanted to ask more questions about Gwen's shooting? Would they think Abbie had skipped out or would they think she'd left against her will?

Fourth, fifth, sixth . . . her mother was dying, dying, dying.

She kicked a loose rock that disappeared in a snow-drift. A beautiful but desolate landscape she could better appreciate with a down coat. She might have hunted for one before leaving if the sun hadn't been shining outside and she hadn't been worried over getting caught sneaking around downstairs. If she'd gone to that trouble she'd have left by the front door instead of climbing down a knotted-sheet rope like a teen on a hormone adventure.

No alarm went off when she opened her bedroom window on the second floor. Landing in a pile of snow had been fortunate, except for ending up with wet jeans.

And if she didn't get out from under these ever-greens and back into the sun she was going to turn into a Popsicle.

Suck it up and keep moving before Hunter found her missing.

He wouldn't be happy, but that was his fault.

When she arrived at his cabin last night, she'd asked when she could get back to her mother. Hunter's blunt "Not any time soon" had severed her last patient nerve. But, not to go off half-cocked, as her dad would have warned, she'd asked what he intended to do with her. He'd answered, "Depends on how much information you give me."

She kept coming back to one thing.

He was a trained operative of some sort. He could have been lying to her about everything last night and manipulating her by pretending not to hand her over to

WITSEC. She had little information left to trade, so the minute Hunter figured that out, what would he do with her?

He couldn't let her just walk away after what she'd seen.

Her best bet was to locate the Jeep. Soon.

Pushing a branch out of the way, she dodged the clump of snow that smacked the ground, then she carefully moved forward, stepping on dirt patches and testing snow-covered areas for a hard bottom or ice before she put her weight on her foot.

If Hunter had been reasonable she wouldn't be out here freezing her bottom off.

She wanted to be angry with him for everything that had happened and blame him for the crazy guy in her apartment, but that guy had called her Abigail. He'd said she did a good job and admitted shooting Gwen, so was he thanking her for getting Gwen outside? That might have been coincidental if he hadn't known her name. He hadn't known Hunter by name, though.

She couldn't figure it all out and Hunter wasn't sharing a thing. She still couldn't reconcile this man with the one she'd met six years ago.

He'd looked different back then, but the animal attraction she'd felt for the hairy version of Hunter had been the same as what hit her last night at the Wentworth party. Her first impression of Hunter back then had been rugged and earthy with thick coffee-brown hair to his shoulders, clean but unkempt. He'd reminded her of men she'd grown up around in flannel shirts, brogan boots, and work gloves softened by hard labor.

And God help her, she sort of remembered asking—not begging—him to take her home with him years back. A pathetic memory she'd like to erase. He'd been exactly what she'd gone hunting for when she strutted into the bar looking for a man. Sweet, attentive, sexy in a scruffy way, and so very human. But the somber green eyes hadn't changed.

She should have realized at the Wentworth party why she recognized Hunter's eyes.

He'd seemed so free of cares that night long ago.

She couldn't reconcile today's suave Hunter with the hairy guy who hadn't appeared capable of affording a decent hotel.

He'd said very little about himself back then, only that he'd just finished a job she'd assumed was some type of manual labor—*hah!*—given his beefed-up size and that he wouldn't be staying a second night in Chicago.

One night. No ties. Perfect.

She'd thought.

She hadn't been quite so thrilled with her rash decision the next morning when she woke up in a hotel room hungover and lying next to a bohemian wearing Brad Pitt's naked body from *Troy.*

Based on waking up in her bra and panties with no indication of any physical activity, she had passed out on him.

She'd slinked from the bed and shimmied into the hooker-red slut dress that had looked sexy hanging in a store twelve hours before when she bought it during a moment of shopping rage. After pulling herself together, she'd tried to sneak out but made the mistake of taking one last look at all that buff body.

He'd been watching her the whole time, not saying a word.

They'd stared at each other silently for a while until he asked in a sleep-rusty voice, "Need money for a cab?"

She'd shaken her head, her iron-straightened hair swishing against her arms.

When he hadn't said anything else, like "What's your last name or phone number?" she'd backed out of the bedroom and fled the hotel, mortified to her curly roots.

She'd never gone home with a stranger before . . . or after.

Would Hunter believe her if she told him that?

Why did she care?

Because he'd surprised her last night when she'd been close to panic in the dark. He'd soothed her when he could have ordered her around. He hadn't handed her over to a bunch of strangers. Somewhere hidden inside that emotionally isolated operative was a man capable of tenderness even if he kept it well hidden.

She remembered being kissed, but alcohol had wiped out one amazing memory if he'd kissed her like that six years ago.

Inside that lethal package was a Hunter she wished she'd met under different circumstances.

And, yes, as long as she was out here alone with her thoughts, she'd admit one more truth. She'd like another shot at getting her hands on all that naked male for one night.

But if he'd been interested in her that way, he'd have taken advantage of what she'd offered six years ago.

Talk about a washout in bed. The charming and

funny "Samson" hadn't jumped on what she'd offered, but the gun-toting, private-jet-flying, too-sexy-for-her-sanity Hunter sure as hell had kissed her.

She slapped a low-hanging pine branch out of her way. Melting snow sprinkled her head. When would this romantic hookup happen with everything she had on her plate, not to mention some lunatic who might be trying to kill her?

Oh, and she was currently heading away from Hunter, which would make any interlude a bit hard to orchestrate.

Besides, she had a higher priority than finding out what it would be like to peel Hunter down to that buff body again. Such as finding a way off this freezing-ass mountain.

Had to be a neighbor somewhere or hikers or a fire tower. Didn't they have radios in fire towers? She hadn't seen anything in the dark last night, but she was fairly certain this was the direction they'd come from after leaving the Jeep. The minute she found the truck, she was so gone. Her dad had taught her a lot about old trucks, like how to hot-wire the ignition.

Wind ruffled pine-needle fingers on branches behind her and cut through the layers of cotton shirts she wore. So damn cold.

She rubbed her hands and picked up her pace, squeezing through the next thicket of bushes, and picked her way six steps to the left before she could turn downhill again.

How far was she from the cabin now?

She took a step down. Something made a *snap* sound. Loose sand and gravel fell away from beneath her foot. She jumped sideways to grab a swooping branch on a tree. The one-inch-thick limb bent with the strain and swatted her hands and face with pine needles.

Ground disintegrated under her backpedaling boot heels.

The branch creaked with strain, wood fibers separating.

"Don't you dare break," she worried aloud.

She flailed one hand for another branch just out of her reach and twisted her body. Her knee bounced against the ground. Pain shot up her leg. She snarled at the worthless piece of vegetation and lunged for the waving branch again.

And missed.

Blood pumped loud through her ears. She tried not to breathe hard for fear of disturbing her tenuous position, but hyperventilating required some amount of priming.

The wind cried her name.

She paused, listening, her heart thundering with hope.

Hunter might be pissed off, but he wouldn't let her fall to her death. Screw it. She couldn't help her mother if she ended up in a body cast . . . or worse.

Licking her dry lips, she opened her mouth to call out.

The limb snapped.

She took off down the hill like a bobsled.

CHAPTER TWENTY

A bbie grabbed at anything to slow her down. She slid over snow, then hit rock and sand patches. The world barreled by at lightning speed. Momentum flipped her onto her back. All three shirts climbed up her body, letting the scrub-board-rough mountain scrape a streak of pain along one side of her back.

She spun sideways, then slammed into a snow-bank . . . hiding a boulder. The world wobbled unevenly, trying to level out. She gasped cold breaths that burned her lungs and groaned, but damn, what a good sound. Meant she was alive.

She lay there, gulping for air.

Talk about a huge flaw in her escape plan. She took mental stock of her body and considered sitting up, but not just yet.

"Abbie!" a voice roared from way up above her.

She covered her eyes to look up against the glare of sunlight. Hunter charged down that incline like an enraged bull, almost as quickly as she had, but he wasn't bodysurfing.

She took stock of the damage now that every raw nerve wanted to report in, screaming with pain. One patch on her side felt seared, but the layers of clothes had protected the rest of her skin. Her knee throbbed.

She wiggled her feet, lifted her legs, and stretched her shoulders.

Hallelujah. Nothing broken.

Branches snapped above her. Boot heels pounded against rock-hard ground toward her. Interspersed with cursing.

Better get ready to face Hunter.

Using the hem of her shirt, she wiped her face, hands, and clothes. Blood seeped from the scratches on her palms and wrists, but not so badly.

She pushed up to a sitting position and tugged her shirts down, gritting her teeth when cloth touched that one abrasion on her back.

Hunter jumped the last six feet, landing in a skid close to her. "Did you break anything?" He sounded panicked, which sort of surprised her since he'd been so calm with the killer. He squatted down next to her and examined the tear in her stolen jeans, then gently touched her leg above and below the rip.

If he kept acting so concerned and careful with her, she'd lose her grip on her shaky control.

"I don't think I broke anything. Help me up." She meant for him to give her a hand, but he hooked his hands under her arms and lifted her to her feet. When she pushed his arms away to prove she could stand, she hissed at the ache in her knee.

"You hurt your knee," he accused.

"No worse than getting knocked around in a pen full of sows," she muttered.

"What the hell did you think you were doing?" Muscles along his neck flexed with each breath he shoved in and out.

She jutted her chin up at him, in no freakin' mood to be criticized. Especially when she noticed *he'd* made it down the same incline without even getting his jeans dirty. "Don't yell at me when I just survived a near-death experience."

That might have been the wrong thing to say.

The brown chamois shirt practically vibrated with energy rippling off his body. He lifted his hands to touch her, then pulled back and crossed his arms. "I told you last night to stay in that bedroom until I came for you."

She'd had enough of this. "I don't give a damn about your orders. When will you get it through your thick skull that I have my own set of problems?"

His lips pressed tight, caging the fury riding his shoulders. "Do you realize you could have been killed?"

"No, that was just a practice run. I'm thinking about trying it again because it was so. Much. Fun!" she shouted, now shaking with anger. "What the hell do you think?"

His eyes had widened with each octave her voice jumped until he just shook his head. A vein pumped in his temple. He stood there all intimidating, which was a waste of time.

She was too damn hurt, tired, and spent to be intimidated.

"I never thought a pissed-off woman could be hot until I met you." He blew out a stream of air and unfolded his arms to reach for her hands.

Hot? He thought she was hot when she was ticked off? Why did he have to say things that knocked the legs out from under her anger?

He took her hands in his and studied the scratches

across her wrist. And a cut on her palm. That didn't improve his mood one bit. He scowled. "Sure you didn't break anything?"

"Yes. So don't start in on me." She would have added some heat to that order if not for the way he gingerly handled her damaged hands, carefully wiping off dirt and barely touching the cut that trickled blood.

"We'll get you cleaned up back at the cabin." He looked up, eyes searching the terrain.

"Aren't you listening to me?"

"Tough to avoid." He released her hands and fixed her with a green stare hard as malachite. "Did you *really* think you could escape?"

"I *did* escape," she pointed out, sure that had to rub on his James Bond ego. "In case you forgot I'm in a bit of a time crunch. I mean, what's going on? Am I a prisoner or what?"

His lips moved with unspoken words. He cupped a hand over his eyes, his fingers rubbing his temple for a second before he lowered his hand. "Where did you think you were going?"

She was out of patience. "Answer my questions first."

Hunter took her in from head to toe and back with a wry frown. "The idea of gagging and hobbling you is tempting, but, no, you're not technically a prisoner."

"'Technically'? What kind of crap is that?" She crossed her arms at her waist. "You kidnapped me. I thought you were some kind of law enforcement. Was that a scam? Who the hell are you?"

"I'm with a branch of law enforcement you've never heard of and I can't disclose. I have not kidnapped you or taken you prisoner, but you're connected to Gwen

Wentworth's shooting so technically you're in protective custody."

"I want my lawyer." Shock from the scare had settled in to foster a serious chill she couldn't hide when her teeth chattered.

"Do you even have a lawyer?" He shrugged out of his jacket. "Put this on."

She opened her arms to put on the jacket, because warm beat cold any day. Her fingers didn't appear. The bottom of the coat hit her midthigh. She looked up with a begrudging "Thanks," then added, "I'm still not through discussing this."

He zipped the front of her jacket, jerking the tab up with a quick flick that telegraphed his waning tolerance. "You're not getting a lawyer and if you try another unauthorized attempt to leave here I *will* consider handcuffing you. You can't get off this mountain without me. *Where* did you think you were going?"

No point in lying since she didn't have any other answer. "To find the truck, then I was hoping to find a neighbor. I was going to tell them I got lost hiking and ask them to help me get to Chicago."

His eyebrows dropped severely in what she saw as a prelude to lecture mode, so she added, "I wasn't going to say anything about you or that you'd brought me to your cabin . . . against my will."

She waited for him to say something, to give her any indication they were back on speaking terms. But no. He just stood there pulsating with unspent words. "I am not going to sit here doing nothing, Hunter. I'm tired of waiting for you . . . to . . ." She lost her thought when he leaned forward, cramping her space.

His voice dropped to a dangerous decibel. "Listen closely. The truck is so well hidden you'd never find it. The nearest structure is a fire tower that isn't manned. The first residence is twenty-six miles away through country that would test the best outdoorsman. You triggered a security device from the wrong side that could have caused you to break your reckless neck. And—" his voice had started to climb, reaching for a shout "—*if* by some unimaginable chance the next booby trap hadn't stopped you, there's a mountain lion den on this path. They'd have been thrilled at lunch showing up."

She swallowed. Mountain lions?

What he'd said before that sank in. "You set *booby traps* out here? When I asked you where we were going last night you said you couldn't tell me, that *no one* knows about this place. Not like you should have unexpected company."

"It's to prevent *unwanted* company, like the kind you had yesterday in your apartment."

Point taken. She tried to push hair out of her eyes and only managed to swat a sleeve at her face.

"Lift your hands." He rolled one sleeve until her fingertips stuck out.

"Aren't booby traps illegal, or don't you care?"

"The traps are meant to detain, not kill," he muttered, and worked on the second sleeve. "But they were never tested for going downhill from the cabin."

Her gaze fell to his worn jeans, where a banged-up silver karabiner hung from a belt loop. The thing looked professional quality but bent, which would render it useless, right?

Couldn't someone with Hunter's money buy a good one?

He took her hand, careful of the scratches, and waited until she looked up at him. "I'm trying to keep you safe. Don't go outside the cabin without me. Got it?"

"Got it, but you should have told me this place was booby-trapped."

"Now you know." He turned, surveying the area as though choosing their direction. "I'll take us back on an easier trail—"

"I don't think so." She planted her foot, unwilling to move another step until she got some answers.

What now?

"Stop snapping at me. I haven't done anything to be stuck here in the first place. What's got your jockstrap in a wad?"

⸺◆⸺

Hunter wished counting to ten really worked.

Abbie glared at him in silent defiance. Hair wet and tangled from the fall. A scratch on her chin marred her creamy skin. She could have died.

Hell, he could count to a thousand and still not calm down. She'd fallen like a rag doll bouncing along the mountain. He hadn't been that scared in a long time and didn't like the feel of it one bit. Now that he knew she was going to be okay his body was screaming for her in a primal way.

The need to feel her alive beneath his hands.

More than just assuring himself she was safe. He fought a rush of lust that burned through his veins.

Every whiff of her drove that lust like oxygen feeding a fire.

If she caught a hint of what he had on his mind she'd go racing away again like a crazy woman. Didn't she have any survival instincts? What had she been thinking to strike out on her own with no map, no weapon, no supplies . . .

She'd been rattled in the woods last night.

Had she thought the threat of animal attack was any less in daylight?

He had to stop thinking about all the ways she could have been severely hurt or killed. Every one of them would have been his fault.

"Hunter?"

"We'll talk back at the cabin." If she didn't like the surly edge in his voice she needed to stay put in the safety of the cabin and follow directions.

"Do you have any other tone than pissed-off?"

"I used to." *Before I ran into Abigail Blanton again and she turned me into one big frustrated dick.* Drawing a long breath he hoped transmitted his short patience, he said, "Make it quick."

She crossed her arms again and lifted two soft eyebrows, giving him a to-hell-with-you look. "I am done with blindly following you. I want answers."

"I already told you there are a lot of things I can't share. You're just going to have to trust me."

"Trust you? The last man I trusted shared my bed with another woman *after* he put a ring on my finger. Taught me just how naïve I had been to believe in words alone."

How could he argue with logic he shared? He'd heard

his mother say, "I love you," to him and his brother many times, but she'd proven him naïve for believing those words the day she sold her children for bonus money.

Maybe he could use that topic to get Abbie on his side again. "Your fiancé sleep with someone you know?"

"Yep. Someone much younger and prettier."

"What was she? A teenager? She sure as hell couldn't have been prettier." He meant that. Young and cute was fun but not hot. Not in his book. Abbie was definitely hot.

Her eyes turned buttery soft for a moment, then she shook off whatever she'd thought. "See, that's the kind of sweet-talkin' trash that got me in trouble before. I believed what he said and let him humiliate me. Then I made it worse by demeaning myself with you. I was on a roll that week."

So that's what had sent Abbie into the bar the night he met her.

His anger lost its sizzle.

She had a gift for pissing him off with quicksilver speed, but watching hurt replace the hellion spark curbed his irritation.

Six years ago she'd charmed him with her laughter.

If he didn't take care, she'd charm him all over again with her spirit this time.

But six years ago she'd been looking for a man to spend the night with to pay someone back and Hunter had been more than willing at the time. Until he realized she wasn't the cavalier bar hopper she'd pretended to be.

He shouldn't have let that golden opportunity pass

when they first met, because this sure as hell wasn't the time to find out what it would feel like to make love to all that fire.

But damn, he wanted to and couldn't believe some moron screwed her over for a kid, because she had to be early twenties when he met her. "You didn't demean yourself that night."

"Easy for you to say, but I don't remember much." The admission cost her a chunk of pride. "And it's not like you'd tell me the truth if I asked."

She didn't remember telling him she wanted to lick him up one side and down the other, no strings attached? Shit. Wrong thing to think about right now if he didn't want to limp back to the cabin.

She was showing him a vulnerability he could use to manipulate her, which was what he'd been trained to do.

What he did naturally.

But could he play with those emotions and hint that they'd been intimate, knowing another man had used intimacy to break her heart? He needed information fast—sixty-two minutes left on Joe's deadline—but using her that way would be cruel.

His job required being cruel, dangerous, manipulative . . . whatever it took to succeed regardless of the toll his soul paid.

The breeze picked up, spiraling loose curls around her forehead and face.

He stepped forward, closing the distance between them to inches. He ran a finger along the side of her cheek and under her chin, tilting it up until their eyes met. He gave her the only answer he could. The truth.

"You showed up at the bar without a car, clearly planning on drinking and not driving. By the time I realized you were too drunk to make it home on your own I tried to send you home in a cab, but you wouldn't give me your address and you were determined to have someone in that bar take you home. That's when you asked me, firmly, to take you home with me."

Embarrassment tinted her cheeks pink over the careless image that painted. Her eyes locked on something beyond his shoulder. "I stand corrected. That sounds about right."

He could see the play of thoughts on her face. How after she'd thrown herself at a stranger she believed he probably judged her as a tramp, jumping from bed to bed.

But any man with experience would have seen through her façade that night.

"And then?" she asked in a whisper, as though afraid to hear what they'd done.

Yes, he could use this to his advantage, but he couldn't bring himself to hurt her. He'd find another way to get what he needed. "I didn't touch you, because you were too intoxicated to meet my criteria for consensual sex."

Instead, he'd held her all night until he felt her start to wake the next morning. He hadn't held a woman all night before that. Or ever again.

She opened her eyes. An ocean of worry and mortification washed through them before she pulled her defenses back into place. Her words came out stinging with self-recrimination. "A truly *un*memorable night, huh?"

Not memorable?

He couldn't count how many times he'd wake in a strange bed in some godforsaken location, alone and thinking of that night with her. She'd smelled of bath powder and sweet wine. Her laughter had eased his dark soul for a few hours. He'd climbed into bed next to her, intending to ignore the warm body in spite of how much he wanted her.

She'd rolled over and curled up against him tight as a kitten looking for heat. He'd cursed her sweetness, the blatant lack of experience that prevented him from stroking her into a night of rousing sex he knew she'd regret in the morning.

That hadn't meant he'd intended to let her off without something in trade, so he'd wrapped her up in his arms and stolen a night with an angel.

"You're a very memorable woman," he whispered, his hand cupping her face. One kiss would soothe the insecurity that had crept into her voice. But if he kissed her like he had last night, he'd have her flat against the boulder behind her in seconds. He was supposed to be earning her trust. Stripping her naked on the side of a mountain wouldn't aid his cause. Instead, he pointed out, "Don't you think not touching you that night proves I'm trustworthy?"

"It proves you didn't want to make love to me any more than my ex-fiancé did." She frowned at herself, clearly not happy about that admission either.

"The hell I didn't." He still wanted her. So badly he was starting to ache.

She glanced up at him with surprise, studied his face, then gave a little shake of her head as though refusing to let herself accept some thought. Skepticism flashed in those turquoise beauties. Strong eyes that had suffered but survived. "You expect me to believe that? You forgot me the minute I walked out the door."

Forget her?

He remembered how the moonlight had fingered through the window to dance across her pale skin when she slept.

He remembered how her walking out of the hotel room had left him in an unusual state of mind. Lonely.

She might look different now with the spiraling hair and a lusher body, but she'd been memorable six years ago.

His fingers twitched with indecision. Pull her into his arms and show her just how much she had affected him—and still did—or turn away and keep a distance between them for the sake of the mission?

"Abbie, I—"

"Give it up, Hunter." She offered him a tough look, but he still saw the shimmer of hurt hanging deep in her eyes. "I saw the women at the Wentworths' that night. I'm not a sex kitten guys like you go for. I know I'm not Lydia—"

That did it. He pulled her into his arms and lowered his mouth, covering her upturned lips.

She gasped, a soft sound of surprise.

He cupped her head, kissing her deeper, savoring the taste and feel. Just enough of a kiss to let her know she was not Lydia. She was so much more.

Her arms hooked around his back. She opened her mouth, slipping her tongue in to dance with his. Not a sex kitten?

He'd argue that point.

What man—with a normal life—had been stupid enough to walk away from someone this soft and inviting?

A fool.

When she moaned, he decided to let the kiss go on a minute longer to send her a message. Last night's kiss had been a dare to make her think twice about challenging him or trusting him.

This kiss was an apology for letting her leave his hotel room six years ago thinking so little of herself.

He slowed the kiss, preparing to end it.

She must have felt the change. All hesitation gone. Her fingers dug into his back. She kissed deeper and deeper, her mouth burned with pure sex.

Desire flared across his skin. He wanted to feel her naked and damp. She went up on her toes, the motion rubbing her against his ready and willing erection. His body tightened at her response. Heat coiled inside him fast as a snake ready to attack. He held the target. His heartbeat tripled with craving her touch on his skin.

He fingered the jacket zipper and ripped downward, slipping his hand inside and under the pile of shirts. He unclipped the front of her bra.

Zeroing in on her sweet breast.

"Ohhh," she groaned in pleasure. She turned to her right, giving him better access he made good use of by cupping the soft mound. He brushed his thumb across her beaded nipple.

She made a high sound of want that pressed him for more.

He leaned her back across his free arm, exposing

the curve of her beautiful neck. Burrowing his face between the jacket and her neck, he kissed his way down the curve.

Her breathing hitched. She rubbed her hips against his stretched-so-full-he-ached erection. He sucked in hard, wanting to free the surge of heat dammed up inside, waiting to explode.

He wanted all of her. Naked and ready.

Not out here on dirt and rocks.

Back at the cabin . . . where something waited on him. Something important. He lifted his head from kissing her, forcing his mind back on task with brutal strength.

Joe's decision. Probably less than an hour to go.

Shit. How had he let *this* happen? He had better control than this.

Operative word there appeared to be "had."

He eased his hand away from Abbie's breast and pulled her shirts down to cover her breasts as he lifted her up until she stood on her feet.

She stared at him through glazed eyes as though she still spun with the world and he lagged behind, falling out of orbit.

"We've got to get back to the cabin." Where he still had to convince her to tell him everything she knew.

She blinked, glanced down between them to where his hands no longer held her. When she looked back up, the fire in her eyes had nothing to do with lust. "What was *that* all about?"

Stupid decision-making, thanks to letting the wrong head take over. "Just a kiss, Abbie."

"Why did you kiss me?" Frustration burred her voice.

Toying with her hadn't been his intention, any more than torturing himself in the process. "We've got more important things to talk about than kissing. I need you to tell me about your conversation with Gwen."

"You kiss me like *that* and act like it was just another kiss?" She could freeze a hot coal with the look she was giving him now that said he was every bit the bastard she'd thought. "I am sick to death of you jerking me around, doing whatever you want—"

He cupped her face between his hands, kissing her silent again. She clutched his shirt in two fists, pushing . . . then pulling. Her lips melted against his.

Damn, she was something, but if he kept this up he'd get them both killed. He lifted his head away.

"Why'd you do that again?" she sputtered, mad as a dunked cat. She shoved away from him.

"Listen to me." He latched on to each side of her jacket and pulled her back to him, close enough to see each fine hair in her eyebrows when he leaned his head down. "I kissed you because I wanted to, just like I wanted to six years ago and didn't get to do enough of. But if I did everything I wanted, you'd be naked right now and we'd be out here for hours."

That quieted her to the point where she was listening.

"I checked on your mother early this morning while you slept and left word at the nurse's desk that you were out of town, working on locating additional medical care so your sisters wouldn't worry. Your mother's condition is stable. Her doctor hasn't checked in, but doctors tend to work on their own schedule. Okay?" When she nodded, he continued. "I can't help your mother unless you help me, and that means trusting me. If I don't make a phone call in the next—" He glanced over at his watch. "—forty-three minutes I'll have to find a safe place for you. I don't want to do that. I'd rather keep you where I can protect you myself."

She listened intently, processing what he said, then pushed her hands up to each side of his face. Her touch was like sunshine on his cheeks after a long cold night. "Why? What happens in forty-three minutes?"

When he hesitated to answer she said, "If you want trust, you're going to have to give it in return."

Hunter had heard those same words from Eliot the first time they'd climbed together. Abbie deserved to know something.

"I should have turned you over to my people last night instead of bringing you to my safe house," he explained. "They're looking for you. I don't think they've figured out that you're with me and they don't know where this is, but that won't stop them from finding this house or us. If I don't call in time with a plan for me to enter Kore to retrieve data files, they'll send a team after me."

"A team? To like . . . bring you in?"

He didn't care for worrying her this way, but she had to know what was at stake since her life was at risk, too. "Not alive."

The rosy shade in her cheeks faded. "Oh, God. Okay, I can tell you how to access the data, but I want your promise I can get the information on what they did to my mother."

She only wanted information. Done. "Fair enough. I have a plan for getting inside, but I have to find out how to access the data files. Once I break into the files, I'll get you all the information I can find on your mother."

Abbie's eyes sparked, anxious. "Deal. It's a complicated system that requires something important to unlock the system."

"What's that?"

"Me."

CHAPTER TWENTY-ONE

~~

As promotions went, this one had all the potential of being a life-or-death decision. Literally.

Linette stood at attention, next to the brass Remington sculpture on a marble pedestal in Fra Vestavia's Miami office that looked out over Brickell Avenue. The meeting would start as soon as the two male Fratelli lieutenants arrived in a few minutes at 11:00 A.M. Not 11:01.

Vestavia sat behind his polished desk toiling over a document lying on the immaculate surface. A slim computer monitor that had risen from the surface of the desk in a space-age design faced his left side.

Silence clung with an unnatural patience, more at home in this room than the sound of voices.

Her arms hung loose at her sides, rigid fingers pointing down at the deep-green carpet that contrasted with her rose-colored pumps and matching pantsuit. Navy blue or black would have been a more suitable color for the crisp linen outfit, but Vestavia had dictated office attire guidelines when he'd brought her into his personal detail nine months ago. He expected the women in his offices to dress in professional designs but with a South Florida look, thus the cheerful suit color.

She'd followed his instructions to the letter and

shown the appropriate humble appreciation when he allowed her to include some pants in her new wardrobe.

The sixty-eight-year-old Fra she'd been handed to twelve years ago on her birthday had given her a closet full of clothes. He'd smiled magnanimously and told her it wasn't every day a girl turned sweet sixteen.

After that, he ordered her to wear only dresses . . . whenever he allowed her to wear anything.

Her chest hitched with a quick intake of air at the chilling memory. The stiff pants material crackled when her fingers shook against her leg.

He'd been dead almost two years and she still clawed her sheets when she slept, trying to get away from his ghost.

Vestavia glanced up from the document. He didn't say a word, but his eyes questioned the rustling noise she'd made.

She squeezed the hideous memory out of her mind and gave him a timid smile. "Thought I was going to sneeze. My apologies for disturbing you."

"No problem." His face relaxed, eyes returning to his document.

She'd prayed for death every day until that old bastard had a heart attack. For the first time since this nightmare began, she saw a tiny light of hope flickering at the end of a tunnel lined with years of despair.

Now she prayed to survive long enough to escape. It might take years. She had the patience to plan and wait for her chance.

She'd only get one.

Vestavia had unknowingly offered her a small step toward that goal with this promotion, which permitted her occasional freedom of movement. Even better? He'd shown no sexual interest in her, a true blessing after a decade of rape at the hands of a disgusting old pervert.

She had to use this opportunity to prove to Vestavia he could trust her, to convince him she was one hundred percent Fratelli. She'd been pretending for so long she sometimes feared how much of her was the real Linette anymore and how much she'd lost to survive.

But she would survive and watch every step she took. Vestavia allowed no room for error.

Compared to him, the old Fra had been a fairy godfather.

After a failed mission last year, Vestavia was rumored to have given the order for the sniper shot that killed Josephine Silversteen, Vestavia's assistant and paramour for many years.

Linette tensed her body against the shiver along her spine.

That mission had failed because of details she'd leaked secretly to her friend Gabrielle.

Since then, Linette had met someone online from the group Gabrielle had trusted who called himself the Bear. Linette now passed intelligence on Fratelli actions to him through coded bulletin-board posts.

Missions like the one she was waiting to participate in.

If Vestavia ever found out . . .

She couldn't think in terms of what he'd do or the worry would paralyze her. One day at a time, and today she'd find out about her first mission.

Where were the two lieutenants?

Would Vestavia blame her if they were late? She cleared her throat. "Excuse me, Fra."

He put the papers down. "Yes?"

"I did send out a text reminder an hour ago, but I'll be happy to contact both men if you would like."

"Basil and Frederick are taking care of something for me this morning, but they'll be on time."

She relaxed her mask to unconcerned. Never show an inordinate amount of interest in anyone or anything.

A knock rapped against the door with the sharp report of a gun firing.

"Come in." Vestavia stood.

When the door opened, Basil swaggered in, a scarecrow-thin Mediterranean man with an oversized nose that matched his ego.

He needed something oversized to make up for lacking in height at several inches short of six feet. "Morning, Fra."

His eggshell-white sports coat, open-collared black shirt, and khaki pants were a bad imitation of South Beach chic. He strutted his bony body as if women fell down to worship greased black hair three fingers past the collar, thin malicious lips, and a weak chin. When he finished his cock walk he stopped too close to Linette for her comfort. The stench of cigarettes and beer rolled off him.

Basil's empty eyes slithered over her. "Linette."

She gave him the barest acknowledgment, deftly hiding the disgust souring her throat. Allowing her gaze to linger on any man's face would risk encouraging him.

"Job completed, Fra Vestavia." Frederick entered quickly, speaking on a rush of breath that reminded her of a terrier hurrying to return a bone for the obligatory pat. A forehead taller than Basil and thicker in the chest, he dressed the part of a midlevel business manager in a simple brown suit and boring tie. He swung around, took one look at Linette and nodded hello, then stationed himself in the middle of the room, hands hooked behind his back.

"Good." Vestavia turned to his desk and lifted three manila files. He walked to each of them, handing out the file folders. "You're each going to be independently responsible for a specific part of an upcoming mission."

"May I speak, Fra?" Frederick asked as he took his file.

"Yes."

"Are we a team?"

"You're all responsible for the success of this mission," Vestavia answered in a noncommittal way that raised an alert with Linette.

Frederick's eyes bounced to Linette and Basil. She gave no indication of noticing. He asked, "Does that mean we're sharing information with each other?"

"No. You're each responsible for your packet of information."

Linette held her file with both hands, waiting to be told to open it even though Basil and Frederick were already reviewing their documents. She took nothing for granted, risked no chance of alerting Vestavia to be suspicious of her on his missions. She asked, "With your permission, Fra?"

The other two missed the nod he gave her. She saw that she'd impressed him by waiting. When she opened the file, she started scanning the text quickly, but it didn't take her genius IQ to figure out that she held operational plans for something that would affect a group of metropolitan cities pinpointed on a map across the continental U.S. Nothing really jumped out about the pinpoints that indicated a purpose, but this had to be some attack being planned based on the meeting at the Wentworth party.

Vestavia stood in front of his desk, eyes calm, patient, and deadly. "This plan originates with our UK brethren but will be implemented in three locations of this country. We don't have the final locations yet. You each have areas of the country you'll be responsible for, which are indicated on your maps. You will oversee the task on our behalf and coordinate any resources needed at your final target location once that is determined. Study your plans and I'll discuss them with each of you this afternoon."

His desk phone hummed and a blue light flashed. No one spoke while he picked up the receiver, listened, then said, "Send him up."

"May I speak, Fra?" Basil's attempt at humility sounded as though he chewed lemons.

Vestavia put the receiver down and swung around. "Go ahead."

"Linette's pretty new to this . . ."

She cringed at the intent driving Basil's voice, sure of where he was heading.

"I could give her a little instruction on fieldwork."

She didn't look at Basil or Vestavia, careful not to show any reaction. She'd suffered old Fra Bacchus for eleven years of hell. No more. If Vestavia gave this greasy lizard a green light to squeeze her into a corner, the stranglehold she kept on her control might snap.

"No." Vestavia turned his back on them and walked toward his desk. They were dismissed.

Swallowing her relief, she waited for Basil to make a move to leave. He did, but not before his eyes warned her not to celebrate so quickly.

Frederick had crossed the room and opened the door, then backed up to let a man enter.

Vestavia's guest had flint-gray eyes that took in her and the other two minions leaving. He passed a brief assessing gaze over Basil and Frederick, then paused on Linette.

She got a better look at him now than she had during the Wentworth fund-raiser last night. He wore another custom-cut dark suit that spanned his wide shoulders. The unbuttoned collar of his pearl-white shirt revealed the kind of thick neck that came from punishing weights. Tanned skin pulled taut over brutally attractive features . . . marred only by the scar running along his right cheek to his jaw.

He hadn't spoken to her at the fund-raiser when Gwen introduced him to Linette and the three Fras in attendance. The ensuing conversation between this man and the Fras had been beyond Linette's hearing.

"Come in, Cayle." Vestavia waved him forward.

Cayle Seabrooke shifted his attention to Vestavia, an easy smile springing to his lips that Linette didn't believe. With her next step she passed him on the way out, noticing how he'd already forgotten she existed.

She closed the door softly on Vestavia's greeting to Cayle. "You come highly recommended."

Basil and Frederick were nowhere in sight as she hurried down three doors to her office, a simple but pleasant space she'd made her own with little things like a silk plant, since the office had no windows. Vestavia had allowed her to choose the walnut desk, credenza, and matching bookcase. Volumes of business manuals and several literary tomes filled a couple shelves, but one section held children's books she'd had when she was with Fra Bacchus. The pages were worn from her turning them when she read for children of the staff.

This was her sanctuary. Somewhere she called her own.

The voice mail light on her desk phone was surprisingly dark. Thank heavens. She spread her file notes over the glossy desktop. One sheet listed each city, then the names of three individuals with specific abilities — "explosives specialist," "communications" and "defense coordinator."

This supported the last missive she'd sent to her online contact, the Bear. She was pretty sure he was a man. His word choices sounded male.

Linette stood up quickly and looked around, on alert. She'd developed a strange sixth sense for knowing when a threat approached after years of tuning her hearing to the old Fra's soft shuffle.

But he was dead. She'd been at his graveside, pleaded to attend the funeral. The other Fras had been touched by her grief. She'd only wanted to be sure he was not coming back.

Why was the hair on her arms lifting?

She pushed away from the desk and walked around to the front, studying everything. Air vents. Floor. Door.

A tiny click reached her ears.

The shiny chrome doorknob rotated slowly clockwise, then the door opened.

Basil swaggered in and shut the door.

She couldn't raise an alarm without drawing unwanted attention to herself. That would likely end with her being blamed, which would result in her being demoted, or worse.

"You didn't think a little lock would keep an experienced field operative out, did you?" He chuckled.

"No, I thought it would deter unwanted visitors from invading my privacy."

"You think that haughty attitude is going to play with me?" He stepped away from the door. Toward her.

The room started shrinking.

"What do you want, Basil?" She backed up until the desk prevented further retreat.

"To work together. That's what we're expected to do in the Fratelli organization." He smiled the smooth grin of a poisonous snake. "You want the Fras to think we aren't capable of working together?"

She sat back against the desk and let the heels of her palms rest casually. Her insides could flail around and scream all they wanted but these men only understood strength.

They respected nothing born with breasts.

"Fra Vestavia would not have selected me to be his *personal* assistant—" Let Basil assume whatever he wanted by that comment. "—if he doubted my ability to perform my duties and interact with everyone. Even you."

Basil stepped all over her personal space,

face-to-face, daring her to break eye contact first and show her fear.

She'd suffered far worse with more stoicism at sixteen.

He'd eaten a caramel candy, the old Fra's favorite. She'd never be able to taste one without risk of vomiting. Just the smell of his breath turned her stomach.

He put his hands on her desk, past where hers rested, and leaned close, his cheek next to hers. "This organization rewards excellence and commitment. More so than the other Fras, Vestavia understands the power of motivation. I intend to make my mark with this mission and move up. I *will* prove to Vestavia that nothing is beyond his grasp with me."

Her body had turned into a rigid clutch of nerves. "Good for you." *Now leave.*

"And when I do?" he whispered. "I'll get my reward. He'll give you to me and choose another woman. With Josie gone, the rest of you women are all the same. I noticed how he's not hot for you. He'll just pick a new assistant. That's how the Fratelli works."

She'd mistakenly judged Basil a nuisance.

She should have recognized his malignant ego wouldn't suffer rejection.

"Here's a tip. I suggest you keep this meeting private since I hold an important part of this project in my file. You'll only put yourself in a bind if you go tattling." He stepped away from her and licked his lips, grinning as he turned for the door. "Study hard. I can't afford for you or Frederick to drop the ball."

When the door swooshed shut behind him she tried one leg at a time to see if she could stand. Shaky but mobile, she took steadying breaths and moved around the desk, where . . . two of her papers with locations and names had been moved.

That despicable pig had read *her* notes. The ones Vestavia had told them not to share with each other.

Her fists clenched into tight wads of anger and frustration. Male humans had to be the worst mistake God ever made, right down to her father, who had given his only child to the Fratelli.

Vestavia at least treated her professionally and without any hint of improper intentions. So far. Hopefully, he wouldn't feel the need to rut one night just for a release.

But Basil had been right about one thing.

Vestavia did not tolerate failure.

Those who let him down did not die peacefully.

If she risked passing along information this time to thwart his plans, she laid her life at Vestavia's feet.

If she didn't pass the information along, she had a multitude of problems, Basil's threat to claim her only being one.

She pushed a couple papers aside to locate the last one, which stated, "successful completion of this phase of the mission will ensure casualties numbering no less than six figures."

The clock had to be male as well. It worked against her, refusing her time to think. She had to send an electronic message to the Bear now or miss her window.

How much should she tell him?

Chapter Twenty-two

Abbie limped into Hunter's cabin, ready to use the first thing she could find as a weapon to beat some sense into him.

Hunter closed the front door, cutting off the drafty air. "Go to my office. On your left."

If he gave her one more order she might show him what it means to push a woman to her limit. But he had asked if she could make it under her own power. Her pride said, "Of course."

Hunter shouted, "Borys! Bring an ice pack."

She grimaced with each step into his office, where one wall of glass windows framed the spectacular sky and mountain-range view. Sit on the gooey-soft-looking leather couch or in one of the two side chairs? She dropped her tired buns into a chair that felt like being held by a cloud.

Her head was splitting and her knee hurt.

No more escaping for today.

She had weighed Hunter's words out on the mountain and decided to believe him. The worry she'd heard in his voice hadn't been for himself. He would face his own destiny without question, but he didn't like leaving her unprotected.

That knocked down the last of her resistance to sharing what she knew.

"Borys is bringing hot chocolate unless you want something else." Hunter entered his office, crossed the space to the chair facing her, and sat down. "We'll get you cleaned up as soon as we finish talking."

They hadn't been able to discuss much on the way, because she hadn't been able to hike uphill at this altitude and talk at the same time. "You think I want hot chocolate?"

"Course you do, 'cause I make da best in da west, babee. I'm Borys with a 'Y.' Nice to meet you." Borys was a compact man with a spring in his step. He sat a tray on the coffee table made from a thick slice of a giant tree. "I make thees with Ghirardelli chocolate and hazelnut liqueur. Figured you'd need a little shot of sometheeng after your walk, *ma petite.*"

She took the ice pack he handed her and placed it on her knee.

"That's good, Borys." Hunter didn't sound appreciative. More like he was trying to hurry his man out of the room.

Her stomach growled at the rich smell of food cooking. "I hope whatever is cooking tastes half as good as it smells."

Borys poured her a large mug full and scooped two spoons of marshmallows on top. His outdated business suit seemed a bit formal with Hunter in jeans.

"What say we have jambalaya for lunch, eh?" Borys sniffed the air. "Ees ready."

"Borys." The warning in Hunter's tone should have

been enough to draw immediate compliance, but Borys ignored him.

"Sounds wonderful. I'd love that," she cooed, smiling her appreciation.

"Gude." Borys had an infectious grin and thick lashes most women would kill for. "Tell you what—"

"Tell *you* what," Hunter said, standing up. "Get the hell out now if you hope to live long enough to cook the rice."

Borys tossed the napkin on the coffee table and headed for the exit. "Good thing you don't like women—"

"I *like* women," Hunter shot back with the power of a rifle blast.

"Didn't let me finish." Borys walked out, but sound traveled easily in a house with wood floors and ceilings. His parting shot came through loud and clear. "You don't like 'em to stick around for longer than a night."

"You're consistent if nothing else," she quipped, drawing the edge of Hunter's terminal patience her way. "Is he Cajun?"

He rolled his eyes. "About as much as I am."

"Is he Texan?"

Hunter sat down again. "Hell no."

"Well, what *is* he?"

"A pain in the ass on a good day."

She lifted her mug of oh-my-God-tasting hot chocolate. "Thought you were in a hurry to talk."

"I am." He settled his arms along the chair arms, more tolerant than she'd expected. "Start with the conversation you had with Gwen."

She reran the conversation quickly, but she was not letting him think he'd won the argument they'd had on the mountain about how to gain access to Kore's records. "I have to go back for my mother, then try to save my job. I have seven years invested at that television station."

Walking away from that wouldn't mean starting over in the television business. It would mean starting over with a new career and forgetting any chance of filming documentaries.

If things turned ugly after the Gwen shooting, she might not have a career to start over. Her dad's voice chimed in with "Don't borrow trouble." *Got it.*

Hunter calmly said, "You can't go anywhere near Chicago if you want to stay alive. Once the authorities realize a male left that message I gave the nurses, and you can't be found, they'll probably think you've been kidnapped."

"I have." She offered a smile that matched her sarcasm.

"I mean by the guy who held you at gunpoint."

The hot chocolate sloshed in her stomach at that reminder. "He won't be at the Kore center."

"What makes you so sure?"

She'd done her homework on the women's center. "Except for a few Wentworth doctors, all the other staff are women. Unless you think Peter Wentworth took a sniper shot at his own daughter, I'm safe walking in there."

Eyeing his watch, Hunter clenched his fingers at what he saw, then shoved a restless gaze at her. "*I* can get the information you want once you tell me what you need, but I need to know everything on how to get into the database. If I took you to Chicago with me you'd be vulnerable to the killer. I'm not willing to risk that."

"It's not your risk to take."

"You became my responsibility the minute I took you on that airplane. And if you don't end up in WITSEC very soon . . . your other choices won't be as nice."

She hadn't considered a yet worse scenario. "Like what?"

"If you just return to Chicago with no explanation for disappearing, the police are going to question why you left regardless of what happened in your apartment. If Gwen dies, the questions will become more intense. The chances are very good law enforcement tried to contact you again today."

"That's why I *have* to make some calls today. To my sister, who's probably freaking out at the hospital. And my boss will be looking for me." *And not to congratulate me on dragging WCXB into the incident at the Wentworth party.*

He lifted a hand, stalling her. "You can't talk to the media. I'll try to put you in touch with your sister. When I called the hospital this morning, both of your sisters had been with your mother individually and together."

Abbie could just hear the verbal beating she was taking in her absence. Hannah would cut her some slack, but Casey would pounce on the opening to point out Abbie's lack of support.

She had more important issues to spend her energy on than wasting time gnashing her teeth about Casey.

Dr. Tatum was convinced the answers to her mother's illness were inside the Kore Women's Center. Abbie held the ace on accessing that information, but she needed Hunter's help to even get close.

"I'm going out on a limb trusting you," she warned.

The tense edge around Hunter's face relaxed, as if he'd been waiting for those words. "I know it and I won't screw you over."

"Tell me one more thing."

"I will if I can."

"Are you really protecting national security?"

He tapped his finger on the armchair, thinking. Debating. Not wanting to say more. But in the end, he had to know she would give only if he did. "We believe there's information inside Kore that might lead us to a terrorist planning an attack on the U.S."

She hadn't seen that one coming.

Everything crashed in on her—terror from the day before, last night, and this morning, plus bone-deep fear of losing her mother. A part of her still vacillated over believing him, but she had a feeling he might be telling the truth since he'd faced down a crazy guy with a gun who had wanted to see Hunter's face. She couldn't in good conscience risk anyone else getting harmed while she waited to find out.

Abbie drew a breath and hurried to share what she knew. "You know my mom's history with Kore. I understand banking her own blood, but I wonder about the tests they ran."

"What type of tests?"

"Blood tests? Female tests? I have no idea. The Kore center has an extensive research wing used to study female growth and development issues. They donate a significant amount of resources to programs across the country but only accept women with rare blood issues at the center in West Chicago. They offer a lot of free medical care to women with rare blood in exchange for studying them. That's what Dr. Tatum told me."

"How sure are you about him?"

"He's been our family doctor since delivering my sisters."

"He didn't deliver you?"

"No." She cupped the warm mug, a slim defense against the chill invading her bones. "I've been over this a hundred times in my head, but it doesn't make sense. Dr. Tatum had just seen my mother three weeks back and gave her a clean bill of health. He said she was a great physical example of a fifty-six-year-old woman. Then she goes to the Kore center, comes home, and ends up in the hospital the next day with spleen failure. If her liver continues to deteriorate she'll need a transplant. Dr. Tatum registered her, but the odds are not good."

"I've got resources—"

"I doubt you'll find a donor who will match her rare blood. My sisters have normal blood types."

"What about yours?" He'd leaned forward, elbows on his knees and hands clasped. The serious clip of concern in his voice washed over her like a warm breeze.

She needed someone to understand how hopeless everything felt. "I have HH, but I have a negative component that would seriously harm her. Tatum finally broke patient confidentiality this week and told me about her visits to Kore. He said he'd heard rumors through the medical community about questionable procedures the center ran in secret, but no one had ever produced evidence."

"But Tatum said he has evidence?"

"He told me that while my mother was still lucid she broke down and told him what she knew about Kore. She was terrified of dying and started telling him how on several visits she'd been taken to a special section housed in the genetic research wing where they put her under a local to be tested, but she never thought they would do anything to make her sick. Now she's not so sure. She also told Tatum she didn't think Gwen lost her baby in the way we all assumed."

Hunter's head lifted at that. "What do you mean?"

Abbie worked the lump down her throat, recalling how she'd planned to give that information to Gwen in exchange for Gwen helping her mother. "Mom told Tatum when she was coming awake in recovery from a procedure two years ago at Kore she could hear a woman scream, 'No, you can't take my baby, I won't let you . . . my father is Peter—' then silence."

"That's not conclusive."

She agreed but noted that Hunter hadn't scoffed either. "But Dr. Tatum says he has some kind of evidence that will support what Mom had told him."

"Such as?"

"Don't know. He said if I got the information on Mom and that information corroborated what he had in hand on the Wentworths he'd give me the evidence and tell me the rest of the story so I could blow it wide open. I could help other women in the same situation."

"What exactly would that situation be?"

"Tatum believes Kore is holding something over my mother, some kind of blackmail. He thinks they have the same power over Gwen." She sat back, zapped of energy. "I've told you what I know—"

"Not all of it. What was Gwen saying to you right before she was shot?"

Abbie squinted in thought. She rubbed her forehead, replaying those last tense seconds leading up to Gwen's shooting, which she'd tried to forget. "Let's see . . . told her I knew about secret tests . . . and I'd release the information if I didn't get what I needed for my mother. She said if I did they'd kill me and her—"

"Who would?"

"The Fras . . . or maybe she said *friars*." She replayed the words again in her head. "No, Gwen said *Fras*. I have no idea who or what that is."

Hunter kept his thoughts hidden, not letting on that he knew what a Fra was. Abbie had walked into the middle of a pit of vipers and shown them her jugular. The original target might have been Gwen, but if Gwen shared her and Abbie's conversation with anyone connected to the Fratelli the crosshairs would adjust to target Abbie's head.

His thoughts jumped back to Gwen being shot.

Why hadn't the sniper taken a head shot? The shooter hadn't missed and knew she'd be outside. And why had Gwen left the safety of her house without a guard? "Whose idea was it for you to meet Gwen outside to talk? Yours or Gwen's?"

Abbie cocked her head at the change in the direction of his questions. "Mine. Dr. Tatum told me I had to get Gwen outside to talk, that the house would be so wired with security and listening devices she wouldn't be honest with me inside."

That didn't track. He doubted the entire Wentworth house would be wired that way, and Gwen would know where she could talk privately indoors.

Hunter's suspicion swung to Tatum now.

Had the doctor been in on the shooting? Why else would the sniper have known to expect Gwen outside? She had a private patio with heating. If he knew she would be drawn outside to talk her private patio would be an easy guess on a chilly night.

"That's all I know." Abbie slumped in the chair, the down jacket billowing around her. As warm as it was inside, she still had to be cold not to have shed that. "I did my part, now you have to get me inside the Kore center."

Like hell. The last place she needed to go would be out in public anywhere. "Can't do it, Abbie. I'll pull everything I can find on your mother and bring it to you."

"I told you that you can't get a thing without me."

"Yes, I can." He had six minutes left to contact Joe, and the good news? He'd come up with a viable plan for entering the complex that didn't require covert insertion, but once he was inside he'd have to find a way to access the files. That would be one of those make-it-up-as-he-went plans he hated.

That had been Eliot's area of expertise.

Abbie wasn't arguing.

That should worry Hunter. He didn't want this conversation popping up again, so he finished with,

"I'm trained to do this. You aren't. In fact, you'd be a liability."

"You're not listening. You *can* get inside the center, but *I* am the key to getting the information."

He didn't like the sound of that. "You've got thirty seconds to convince me."

She frowned but didn't waste time scrapping with him. "Dr. Tatum said the only way to access family records was by having a prior patient checked into the facility. On top of that, a staff member has to enter a code that changes daily."

"I'm not willing to involve your mother in her condition."

"Me either, but I'm not talking about her. I was born at Kore. *I'm* a prior patient of the clinic and I have rare blood. All qualifications to be admitted for testing." She took a steady breath, but the vein in her neck jumped with her rapid pulse. "You obviously need something from the Kore center and must have skills to hack through computer files. You get me in there and I can gain you access to the database. There's one more step to accessing the database that requires my presence, but I'm not sharing why or how until you agree. Get me inside, then you can do your James Bond impression."

Good God. Hunter checked his watch. Less than two minutes to contact Joe.

And he hadn't thought this could get any more fucked up.

CHAPTER TWENTY-THREE

Hunter waited for Abbie to go upstairs to take a bath, then made sure the house was locked and *all* alarms were on.

He'd figure a way around taking her with him.

She *would* tell him the last part of how to access the database by tonight.

Borys shoved a bowl of jambalaya at Hunter with a bottle of water, grumbling that he had no appreciation for his talents in the kitchen when he stalked off. Hunter locked the office door before setting up the videoconference connection with BAD again.

This time, Gotthard came on and had him wait until he'd routed Joe and Retter's computers into the conference since the other two were off-site.

All three faces appeared in boxes on Hunter's monitor.

"I have a solid plan for inserting into the Kore center and accessing the records by Friday morning," Hunter stated, opening the conference. "I'll offer a sizeable donation to the Kore Women's Center based on reviewing the facility in person. It's good timing after having just attended the fund-raiser. Let them think the donation is motivated by sympathy for Gwen. Once I've toured the facility I'll find a way to insert later that night."

"What about getting into the database?" Joe asked.

"The quickest access is through patient files, but that's only available while the patient is physically on the premises and checked into the system," Hunter explained. "It's a dual access that requires a staff member's code, and that changes daily. I'll breach the employee files to find out how they receive their individual daily code, then locate a current patient to tap their information."

That sounded so simple. It wasn't. Gotthard was the only one who might question Hunter for more specifics, but he didn't.

"How you going to get around after hours?" Gotthard had asked the question, but Hunter knew his friend was voicing what he'd expect Joe or Retter to be thinking.

"There are men in the genetic testing center." Hunter caught a whisper of surprise in Retter and Joe's faces.

Surprise or suspicion?

Hunter had no idea if there was an area for men or not, but Abbie had said a former patient could come in. Why couldn't a former male patient come in? The Fratelli were a male-dominated organization. Seemed highly possible that Wentworth would have a private area where no one would see the men come and go. Would Joe go for his plan? Depended on how much time they had. "Any word from our contact?"

"Yes," Gotthard answered. "Vestavia passed out packages to three operatives with maps noting major cities that could possibly be attacked, at least sixty, but only one will be the actual target. The contact thinks

Vestavia is preparing in a defensive manner because Fra Bardaric in the UK is driving this mission. The three packages included contact information for explosives experts Vestavia's team would coordinate with, so we're dealing with a bomb situation. The contact was told to be ready to act as early as Saturday, coinciding with our speculations. We don't have as much time as we thought."

Hunter considered that good and bad news. Good, because it might push Joe to work with his plan, and bad because less time never favored defending against threats to a major population center.

Retter spoke up. "Might be wiser for Hunter to tour the Kore facility and gather intel, then let us send in a female agent to access the equipment. A woman would be less conspicuous if she had to move through the facility beyond where they keep males."

Joe nodded. "I like that better."

Hunter had hoped to convince Joe, in particular, that he was still a valuable asset, but in the past Joe would have gone with his plan. He would have trusted Hunter's assessment.

Joe and Retter weren't buying any of this.

What about Gotthard?

Hunter couldn't find out without putting Gotthard in a tough position, which he wouldn't do. He had to sound hesitant—or they wouldn't believe him—and still agree. "I think my plan would work better since I've got the computer skills and I'll be familiar with the layout . . . but if that's what you want to do that's what we'll do. I'll contact you when I leave the center."

"Call when you reach Chicago and I'll let you know

my decision," Joe said, finishing up, then the monitor went blank.

If BAD had no better option for inserting, Joe would let Hunter go forward. But that last order to call when he reached Chicago made it sound like Joe wasn't on board with Hunter's idea.

If Joe had an alternate plan for a female to insert, for sure he'd send a team of agents to find Hunter before he could walk in on a mission in progress.

Hunter considered that for a few minutes, then decided Joe didn't have the time or resources to send anyone after him right now. By the time BAD could come after him, Hunter would have new arrangements in place.

He ate the cold jambalaya and finished off the bottle of water. Then he lifted a tube of antibiotic ointment off the desk and stood up. He headed for her bedroom.

Abbie should be coming out of the shower soon.

Naked.

Perfect.

CHAPTER TWENTY-FOUR

*W*ould *the mole take the bait or let a hundred thousand innocent people die?*

Vestavia wouldn't know until he had the real mission details and a time frame. But he'd put enough into motion today with his three lieutenants to start worrying the person working against him.

He entered his soundproof conference room, where the sweet odor of high-quality tobacco lingered in the air. He had no time to enjoy a cigar right now. The space had been designed at only a hundred square feet intentionally, with a custom-built Swedish recliner covered in sandstone-white leather in the center of the room. The one-foot-thick walls had an integrated security grid system impossible to breach.

Any change, even a picture-frame nail in the wall, would set off the alarm.

One side of the room was finished in matte black, and panels on the top half moved at the touch of a button to reveal a control center that looked like something from NASA. The lower cabinet opened by pressing another button to reveal a full bar with a built-in ice maker.

He typed in the series of codes, which changed hourly, that would engage the communication system, then prepared a scotch on the rocks and settled into the leather chair. Setting his drink on the obsidian-colored marble table at his right, he lifted the remote control and pressed buttons. That activated the computer to project onto six poster-sized screens mounted on an eye-level semicircular frame in front of him.

Faces started emerging on the two screens, older versions of the young men he'd known in an exclusive college in France where they'd formed this generation's Council of Seven Angeli.

Bardaric from the UK and Ostrovsky from Russia appeared first. A green light glowed above their screens. Chike's blue-black face came to life next from somewhere in Africa. Who knew what city? Gray had started invading his inch-long bush of frizzled black hair.

Renaldo's side profile from Venezuela took shape on another screen before he angled around to push a droll look forward. A smart-mouth in college once told Renaldo his thick black lashes, high Latin cheekbones, and rosy lips were "so gay." The student never made that mistake again. Just disappeared.

A pair of black eyes, a wide nose, and skin the color of cocoa with tiny dots around one eye showed up next. Derain wore his Aboriginal genes proudly as a peacock when manipulating politics, but he was as Western-educated and groomed as the rest of them.

Where was Stoke? Damn Antarctican had little to do beyond press for more green initiatives. No government, no wars, no ambition. Stoke's oddly simple face with dull-witted blue eyes crystallized. He was looking down, fumbling with something, then sat up, hands on top of each other in front of him. That whole goofy shtick played well for someone who'd made his first kill at thirteen. The light above his screen finally brightened.

Ostrovsky had assumed the role of mediator years ago and ran the meetings, keeping everyone on track. "Floor is open to discuss the general business first."

"We have—" Stoke started.

Renaldo sent a withering look in Stoke's direction. "No, no. Last time took half hour to hear your list. *We* know your continent will be affected most severely first. World pays no attention to Antarctica. Unless your Fratelli group has actually discovered something under all that ice and snow?"

Stoke made a motion with his hand as if he were shoving papers aside and sat back, arms crossed. Half of the twelve Antarctican Fratelli were spread across the world as scholars, and the other half worked in many of the research facilities in Antarctica that corporations and study groups funded.

Vestavia interjected. "Our global-warming phase is gaining strength. The warming effect is taking shape here. The ocean temperature off Maine has risen to a record high. Aquatic life is shifting. Higher numbers of Orca and schools of whale sharks have been sighted in the Gulf of Mexico than ever before. Even the most skeptical are starting to notice the changes."

"Here and in Asia, too," Ostrovsky said, picking up the thread.

Vestavia sipped his scotch while Derain and Ostrovsky listed environmental changes in Australia and Russia. Ostrovsky finished with, "Likewise, the 'green' initiative continues to grow at a rapid pace that will peak as we intended, well ahead of the next phase. We quickly approach the time when every decision, from corporations to governments to individual households, will be based on being green, which will only make our task that much easier to accomplish in this era."

"We better hit our timeline after what we've spent developing global warming *and* the green organizations," Vestavia added. "If our ancestors hadn't screwed up so badly—"

Ostrovsky interjected. "Our ancestors had right idea but poor execution."

"They didn't have our resources," Stoke said in defense of their Angeli ancestors.

Bardaric finally weighed in. "Oh, please. Even in the Dark Ages they should have anticipated the extent of the damage. The Black Plague was impossible to control. Look what happened with AIDS. We lost valuable assets we might not have if our fathers and grandfathers had strategized better."

Chike lifted his wide chin and spoke with a deep voice. "Perhaps they thought they could see the future, just as we believe we can. We have the most advanced team of physicists, environmentalists, scientists, doctors, engineers ever created, but *no one* can predict the outcome of what we have put into motion."

Bardaric scowled and leaned forward. "I disagree."

Vestavia let Bardaric and Chike go at it, just as they used to in college. Ostrovsky would rein them in soon before testosterone levels red-zoned. Everyone on this Council had been raised by a ruthless father, men who instilled in their sons the passion necessary to lead the world into the final Renaissance phase.

Their fathers had not anticipated reaching the Renaissance prior to passing the baton of power over when all seven boys had celebrated their sixtieth birthday. Their fathers missed the ambitious glint in each son's eyes and underestimated the downside of putting seven future Angeli together at a young age so they would bond quickly.

Unwilling to wait until they were too old to plunder a new world order, this Council of Seven had used their collective genius to draft a plan of their own while in college. Their fathers all held strong positions in the Fratelli. Having been taught patience as a skill from the crib, the sons waited two years until their fathers traveled to a meeting in Switzerland where three Fratelli de il Sovrano representatives from each continent were expected to attend.

No family members were allowed to join the fathers on those trips, which was a saving grace when everyone in the luxury hotel in the Swiss Alps became ill and died within a week.

Including twenty-one international figures loyal to the Fratelli.

The boys mourned their loss publicly and buried their fathers, then set about taking over their respective family businesses and following in their fathers' political footsteps.

All seven had found their way into a Fratelli group on their respective continents during the past ten years.

Vestavia would never trust any of these six, but they all needed each other.

"It's time to move on." Ostrovsky ended the battle between Bardaric and Chike too soon.

Bardaric's face had a deep flush Vestavia hoped signaled a stroke or heart attack.

Leaning back and sniffing indignantly, Bardaric regained his composure immediately. "I'm proposing a mission on North American soil, which would benefit all of us. The Americans have not been sufficiently weakened."

"I have no problem with planning an attack," Vestavia countered before Bardaric could say more. "But I think we should perform testing, just as we've been doing with the viral weapons." He had to take care in arguing against this plan. No one expected North America, specifically the U.S., to fall easily, but the Council would not tolerate unchecked ambition.

They'd back Bardaric's plan to bring the U.S. to heel unless Vestavia could convince the Council to delay for testing. If he couldn't win that vote today, he'd need Peter Wentworth's support to force a second vote before the attack. But Peter wouldn't lift a finger until he found out who had shot his daughter, and Gwen hadn't regained consciousness yet.

"I've conducted sufficient tests," Bardaric started to argue.

Vestavia cut him off. "On a city of any significant size? I'm sure we'd all like to see the results. If the destruction is not significant enough the first time there will be no reason to continue, and every mission carries a certain degree of risk of exposure for the Fratelli and us."

"I see your point," Ostrovsky agreed.

"The destruction will be significant. My people located a strain of Uranium in the Ukraine quite by accident that is more compact in density. When they tested a microscopic amount the results were not that significant, but the next test left the scientists awe-struck. They prepared a bomb with a teaspoon-size amount of uranium X, or UX as we call it. That unit alone caused significant damage to the corner of a four-story building, as seen here." In place of Bardaric's face, an image appeared of a brick building that went from standing to having one-fourth of it fall as though an earthquake had struck. "But when the bombs were detonated in each corner in the presence of UX, the chain-reaction result compounded the damage by twenty times."

Shit. Vestavia maintained a calm face. He hadn't ac-tually believed the bastard, but the rest of the council did. "Impressive, but I'd still like to see a live demon-stration since I'll be the one handling the cleanup."

"That's fair." Stoke rarely spoke up, but he'd never liked Bardaric either.

"Unless you have good reason to not demonstrate," Ostrovsky said.

Vestavia wanted to choke Ostrovsky for giving Bardaric any help.

Bardaric's sullen face reappeared on his screen. "We can't waste the material on testing . . . we have a limited amount of the raw material. It appears to have been an anomaly of nature I doubt we'll find again."

"How much do you have?" Renaldo asked.

"Five linked bombs will take nine square blocks in any metropolitan city," Bardaric answered, then went on to explain his plan for attacking one city first and making demands on behalf of a faux extremist group that couldn't be connected to any country. "If the U.S. does not immediately follow specific instructions to pull out of occupied areas by the third day we hit the second city. In another three days we hit the third city. By then they will fold because the administration will not be able to give an acceptable reason to their citizens for why they shouldn't comply."

"Once they do comply those who have demanded the troops be brought home will find the doors to the U.S. wide open for terrorists, who will make our job much easier," Derain said enthusiastically. "How soon can we do this?"

"I took the liberty of delivering materials to North America while I had the opportunity this past week."

Just as Vestavia had thought.

Bardaric continued, his voice failing to hide the smug satisfaction he enjoyed. "I can have the units in place in twelve hours. That's how simple and mobile this device is. I suggest we detonate before my prime minister meets with the U.S. president on Tuesday. Having two of the most powerful leaders together should facilitate the decision to act. I have chosen three locations I will relate to Vestavia once everything is in place."

Vestavia couldn't stop the vote, but before it was called he made sure of one point. "I want to be the only person to authorize the detonation when it's time."

"Wait a minute," Bardaric shouted.

"No!" Ostrovsky cut him off. "That is Vestavia's right as this is a major mission on his continent. It is time we vote."

Once the vote was over, Vestavia walked over to the

control panel to terminate all connections and activate a triple-cleaning measure on the computer. He poured another scotch and walked around a moment, thinking. Bardaric was proving more resourceful than expected and could destroy the U.S. with this one move.

Not without a fight.

But he'd underestimated Bardaric. What else would the Brit do if Gwen didn't die?

Vestavia settled into his chair and pressed a button on the marble table that raised a voice-activated communications panel he instructed to connect him via phone to Peter Wentworth's secure line.

After a six-minute wait, Peter came on the line sounding haggard. "I don't have long. I just arrived for surgery."

"This won't take long," Vestavia said to reassure him. "You have to know Bardaric was behind Gwen's shooting."

"That's a dangerous charge to level."

Vestavia knew all too well. The council governed itself with a set of unbendable rules that would result in extreme measures when anyone made a false accusation of this nature. That was the only way they could function with a degree of cooperation. Vestavia rarely gambled unless the odds were in his favor, which he believed was the case.

"I believe you and Gwen are in danger. Work with me and I'll help you disappear before Bardaric terminates both of you."

"I can't just leave," Peter argued. "The Kore center holds all the genetic records to date for this continent and for the Council's long-term projects."

"Either you and Gwen disappear willingly or on his terms, Peter. We've been friends a long time. I know you don't take sides, but Bardaric is determined to prevent any more babies from our sperm. Figure a way to move the records and not leave a trail."

Vestavia disconnected the call. He closed his eyes, thinking. He had to find Bardaric's stockpile of UX. To possess that would be like holding the key to everyone's future.

Hell, he might even let Bardaric take down one city if that was what Vestavia had to do to track the Brit's people and find the trail to the source of the UX.

CHAPTER TWENTY-FIVE

Hunter had said "if."

Abbie hated vague answers. She shed her shirt and jeans in the bedroom, which might as well be a prison cell since she was sure Hunter had set all kinds of alarms on the cabin to ensure she didn't take off again.

She walked into the three-sided glass shower to face hot water blasting from nine spigots.

Nine showerheads, actually. Water came out of spigots where *she* grew up.

The luxurious bathroom attached to her suite came right out of a designer magazine. The gleaming gold-and-pewter faucet shaped in a swooping design that could be a miniature version of an Olympic luge deserved to be signed and numbered.

She should feel guilty taking snarky shots at the upscale appointments since she'd happily pilfered a brass basket filled with luxury bath products someone had left on the marble counter. Probably Borys.

Bless Borys for delivering a bowl of jambalaya and rice with fresh bread and more hot chocolate to her bedroom a minute after she'd dragged herself up the stairs. The smell of Cajun cooking was gone. She'd all but licked the bowl clean.

Then fell back on the bed and slept three hours.

That had been the only thing stopping her from indulging in the shower sooner.

Inside the shower stall, she squirted a washcloth full of a peach-smelling soap from a glass wall dispenser. The scalding water pounded stress and anxiety from her muscles while she gingerly scrubbed grit from her scratches.

Every inch of her ached from the fall.

But her mother could be in more pain and had worse problems, so enough whining.

Think more. Complain less. Even if no one could hear her thoughts.

Her next move hung on Hunter's *if.*

If he got the answer he wanted from headquarters—wherever that was—then he could possibly help her.

Not many options when she was imprisoned on a mountain with no cell phone, no Internet access, no money, no car . . .

She did think Hunter believed her when she'd said he needed her *in person* to gain entry to the Kore center database.

One point in her favor.

If she was dealing with law enforcement. Another stinking *if.*

Why hadn't Hunter shown her a badge or ID of some sort? She could ask, but he would have produced one by now if he intended to do so. Maybe he was deep undercover or doing something where he couldn't give his official ID. He could be with any agency from the cops to the FBI to the CIA to national security divisions she'd never heard of.

Had to be layers upon layers of new law enforcement operations in all areas of government these days that no one knew about.

But Hunter was obviously wealthy, or relying on someone who was, for him to have access to private jets and secluded mountain homes.

He'd been at the Wentworth party. People recognized him. Did *they* know he was some kind of James Bond guy?

Well, crap. She stopped washing and let the water batter her head. Maybe that would shake loose a few cramped brain cells.

This was the second time she'd spent a night at Hunter's place and still didn't know the man's last name.

She growled at yet more gray areas. For now, she'd have to go with believing Hunter *was* in law enforcement until she had reason to doubt him.

I hate the mountains. And Hunter.

She wouldn't be hurt right now if he hadn't brought her to a place with no roads and stuck in the middle of a booby-trapped field and failed to give her phone access and . . .

But he'd also flown her away from danger. He *had* held her when she'd been terrified last night and he *had* soothed her this morning. He'd only yelled at her out on the ridge because he thought she'd been hurt.

And he hadn't liked that one bit.

Didn't like to worry about someone.

Or the fact that he'd been turned on. That searing kiss and erection were undeniable evidence. Good thing she didn't have body parts that could poke out when she was aroused. If she did he'd have figured out just how bad she had the screaming hots for him every time his internal pendulum swung toward being sweet and caught her by surprise.

One minute he snarled at her until she wanted to go for his throat, then he'd do something completely unexpected, like hold her or kiss her.

Sort of ruined that I'm-cold-as-an-iceberg attitude he wanted to project.

She smiled.

Did others realize that underneath all that arrogance and do-it-my-way attitude Hunter had a heart? If she'd only known him as a guest at the Wentworth party and never met him six years ago or spent the last twenty-four hours around him, she'd have written Hunter off as another rich uncaring jerk.

But he'd listened to her when she begged him to not hand her over to WITSEC when dumping her in someone else's lap would have been easier for him. He hadn't demanded she tell him the last key to getting inside the Kore center records. Yet.

That actually surprised her and earned him another high mark when she knew he could have browbeaten her.

But Hunter had secrets. Lots of them. Like what he was doing at the Wentworth party.

He knew the Latin security guy at the Wentworth estate. A teammate? And if she was going to believe him, she had to accept that keeping her here at the cabin was putting Hunter at risk.

Would they really send assassins out to get him if he didn't convince them he could get into Kore? Or if they found out she was with Hunter? Again, who were *they*?

Her heart thumped erratically. He was constantly putting himself in danger to keep her safe. If he needed her help to get whatever he wanted from the Kore Women's Center, why wasn't he jumping at her offer to go there and help him?

Because he believed the killer could find her. She believed showing up with little advance notice combined with Kore's security would prevent someone from just walking in . . . which begged the question of how Hunter intended to get in.

Neither of them could wait for a better opportunity. Wasn't like she could escape again. That hadn't done her any good . . . except for that kiss.

He'd kissed her like a man possessed.

Fire rushed across her skin at the memory of how he'd touched her. She'd never been kissed like that, as if he wanted her right then and right there.

He could have had her, too.

She couldn't remember a time in the past six years that she'd wanted a man the way she'd wanted Hunter to finish what he'd started on the mountain.

Six years? She hadn't ever wanted a man that much.

Hadn't trusted a man enough to consider more than heavy petting since walking in on the pig and Casey.

Hunter might be just as untrustworthy.

She groused at the way she was thinking of him. He had her prisoner. She made a suck-bad prisoner of war wanting to sleep with the enemy.

He might have just been playing her since she proved to be putty in his sexy hands that could slide between . . .

She ran the washcloth between her legs and shivered.

Enough of that. She squeezed out the rag and hung it over the faucet. Half her body suffered from the beating she'd taken and the other was one big knot of frustration.

Turning off the water jets, she stepped out of the glass shower and snagged a bath sheet to wrap around her body. The thing fell to her knees. Did Hunter have humongous guests?

Did he even have guests?

She found a smaller towel for her hair, then dug through the basket on the counter for lotion. Staring at eyes she'd never lied to, her conscience worked overtime ticking off points in his favor.

Look at this place. Hunter could have taken her somewhere she'd be in lockdown.

As long as she was being honest with herself, she might as well face the fact that he'd surprised her when he told her about their meeting six years ago. If he'd made her feel small and cheap, she'd have folded her heart into a smaller shape and forced it farther down her throat.

But he'd let her know just how much he'd wanted her. Still wanted her, if that bulge in his pants had been evidence.

She knew without a doubt Hunter left an impression on every woman he encountered, because she remembered how he'd listened to her that night so many years ago. Considering his covert work that was understandable, but he'd really listened.

And made her smile.

And taken her home rather than leave her vulnerable to someone else jumping on her drunken offer.

He was such an unusual man. She could feel him when he was near. Feel the battle he fought to remain distant. And still he'd wrapped her in the safety of his arms more times than she could count. He was the kind of man a woman listened to with her heart. If she did that, her freedom might not be the only thing in jeopardy by the end of this.

She put the lotion on the counter and headed to the bedroom.

Someone tapped at the door.

"You'll have to wait. I'm in a towel," she called out, searching the room for a robe.

The door opened.

She shrieked, "Get out. I'm not dressed!"

Hunter didn't slow down. "Doesn't matter. That towel's coming off anyhow."

CHAPTER TWENTY-SIX

One towel between me and Abbie's wet body.

     Hunter didn't know if he could do this or not. He'd been all set to put antibiotic on her scrapes earlier, but she'd been sound asleep when he came up to her bedroom the first time.

He couldn't bring himself to wake her.

So he'd stood there like an idiot and watched her sleep for a while. He'd been tempted to pull her clothes off just so she'd be comfortable until he realized he wouldn't stop there.

By the time he walked back down to his office, he'd gotten his head straight about how to handle Abbie so he could move ahead with his next step on this mission when she woke up.

That was downstairs, before he walked in here and found her not just in a towel, but wet from the shower.

Smelling like fresh rainfall.

Water trickled down her collarbone, then turned south to dive between her breasts.

His tongue got hard thinking about following that path.

And he wouldn't stop there.

He could spend hours tracing her body with his hands and mouth.

But some other guy got the life with lazy afternoons making love to the same woman day after day. He had a job to do. The sooner he got this done, the better. "Get on the bed."

"Are you crazy?" Abbie backed up until her legs bumped the bed, realized where she was, and side-stepped toward the dresser. "Get out of here."

Good suggestion, even if it had been flung at him like the sharp point of a knife at a target, but her wounds needed tending and he was the only one who could do it.

The only one he'd allow to touch her.

Borys had volunteered to save Hunter the trouble.

Hunter had threatened to save Borys the trouble of breathing if got near Abbie when she had no clothes on.

And smelled fresh as a new day.

But blue lightning flashed in those eyes right now, warning him a storm was building.

"Just going to put ointment on your cuts so they don't get infected." He lifted the tube of ointment in his hand. "You get all your wounds cleaned?"

Her mouth puckered open then closed like a confused guppy. Wet curls dangled from where she'd failed to capture the entire mass in the towel wrapped around her head.

The bath sheet covered a lot, but wrapping her arms around her waist shoved her breasts high, threatening towel control.

Just put the damn ointment on and keep your hands to yourself.

Don't think about her naked on the bed.

Or the floor. Or the bathroom sink. Or . . .

Hell, he'd almost stripped her on the side of a mountain.

"I can put the salve on." She didn't move from the dresser, as if that was the only safe place in the room.

"You can't reach all of your back." Once he made sure her cuts were clean and disinfected, he'd exit. Immediately. But that had to happen soon. He knew one way to get her moving. "What're you afraid of?"

Her shoulders clicked back at that.

The little termagant didn't like having her courage challenged. He didn't doubt her courage. She had too much for his peace of mind. She'd put herself at risk for others without a second thought for her own safety.

"Just do it with me standing up," she suggested.

"It'll be easier if you're lying down." He hoped. Less chance of gravity taking that towel off her body.

One slip and it would be all over. Even he had his limits.

She relented, heading for the bed, where she yanked the towel off her head and dropped it on the floor, then climbed on the blue corduroy bedspread facedown.

Curls tumbled wildly.

His fingers itched to touch the soft twists.

She grumbled to herself and lifted up. Then she shoved the pillows to the side and loosened her bath sheet, pulling each side out from under her body until none of the towel was caught between her and the bed.

She scooted over, taking the towel with her and leaving him room on the edge. "Well? What else do you want me to do?"

Peel the rest of that towel off, kiss me like you did earlier outdoors, and lock your legs around my waist.

His jeans were getting tighter by the minute. If he stood there any longer and she got a look at his growing erection she wouldn't let him touch her. Not after what had happened on the mountain. If he did that again he *should* be decked for teasing her. He moved over and sat on the bed next to her hip so she couldn't see the bulge in his jeans without twisting around.

The huff she released sounded like a whispered curse.

He pinched the top edge of the towel and rolled it down off her shoulders. Then he cursed.

"What?" she asked.

"You've got one nasty scratch on your back."

"What are you angry about? My fault. Not like you pushed me down the hill." She turned her head, facing the window, and settled herself again.

But it *was* his fault. He should have anticipated anything she might have done, even trying to leave the cabin. He opened the tube of antibiotic cream with a topical painkiller he'd gotten a while back from Mako—a BAD agent with an MD who could patch up just about anything long enough to keep an agent alive until they made it to the hospital.

Rubbing the salve between his hands to warm it, he opened his palms and placed one hand on her back.

She flinched. "I'm okay."

He slowly started smoothing the medicine across her shoulders and down the sides of her arms.

She sucked in a breath.

"Sorry. Those spots need the most attention."

"It's okay." Her bottom wiggled, settling again.

Don't move, Abbie. He finished spreading the cream

on her back and slid the towel down a little more, exposing a few scratches on one cheek. He continued wiping the cream across the gentle rise.

She flexed her bottom.

Don't stare at her pert butt. Don't think about anything but clinical application of the cream.

Tell that to his loins getting heavier by the minute.

He ran his hand back and forth over her right cheek. Sweat beaded along his neck. She had a few scratches on her front, but he was done. "Think that's all the tough areas to reach."

"I'm over my modesty attack," she murmured. "Go ahead and finish. Not like you haven't seen most of my backside by now and I'm too stiff to move."

He was too stiff, too, but he doubted sharing that would draw any sympathy from her. His hand shook at the thought of touching her any longer and restraining himself.

Unbelievable. His hand had never shaken while handling a woman.

But he wanted to touch Abbie everywhere. Slide his fingers down between her legs and brush over the tender skin, tease her until she moaned his name.

She'd have let him on the mountain, before he practically stroked her, then walked away.

He peeled the towel all the way off her backside, sure he was opening a door he couldn't slam shut again.

She flexed her legs that had small scrapes.

After drawing a deep breath of resolution, he reloaded cream on each palm and walked to the end of the bed. Leaning over, he started at the back of her calves, rubbing up and down.

Moving higher to reach the top of her thighs, he massaged her muscles with his thumbs all the way back down.

He paused. Had she moaned? He kept massaging her thighs and unintentionally brushed the juncture between her legs when he stretched forward.

A shiver raced along her lower body.

The beads of sweat on his neck joined forces and trickled down his back.

He couldn't do this.

He *could* do this, but it would end with him turning her over to spread her legs and start kissing there.

If her earlier response was any indication, she had a hair trigger. He'd love to see her face when his finger brushed over and over and over that trigger until she exploded.

The only thing stopping him?

He couldn't seduce her the way he would another woman.

Because she wasn't like any of the others.

Abbie's emotions made her vulnerable. She cared too deeply. She wasn't like the ice maidens he'd taken to bed who burned off pent-up energy the same as him, then forgot the encounter a day later.

Lifting the edge of the towel, he wiped his hands until he felt certain no cream was left and put the cap back on the tube.

"You done?" she asked.

"Yes." *Stick a fork in me.* He started for the door.

"Hunter?"

When he turned back, she'd leaned up on one elbow and had a fisted handful of the towel in front of her breasts.

"What?"

"You are so cranky." She studied him, her eyes taking his full measure from top to bottom, pausing at the bulge in his jeans.

"Anything else?" He was snarling like a wounded beast, but goddammit, did the woman have to drag this out any longer?

"Just one thing." She pushed hair off her face, but the more her thick curls dried the less direction they accepted. "I'm not sure I can still reach all the spots that need . . . attention."

He told his feet not to take a step forward and informed his dick she did *not* mean that the way it sounded. She was exhausted and hurting. She was shy. She probably wanted him to massage her legs some more, or her back.

She was too damned nice to be lying there in his bed with no clothes on.

"Do the best you can." Now his feet had to move. Walk out.

"You mean *handle* this myself." A shapely eyebrow quirked.

No, she was not inviting him to climb into bed with her. He had to keep telling himself that even though he'd dearly love to have this one time with her.

Especially since the plan he just gave Joe had so many holes he expected to fall through one and never be found again.

"Do I have to spell it out for you?" she asked, getting a bit cranky herself.

Dick to brain: *She does want what we thought.*

"Well, hell." She slapped her hand on the bed and

flipped over on her side. "Guess I just made a fool of myself yet again. What's that, like . . . three times? You're clearly not interested."

"Abbie—"

"Go away."

He wished he could. But she'd been under his skin for six years and if he didn't scratch that itch soon his skin was going to burst from stretching too tight.

"Thought you'd at least wonder what *we* would have been like."

He smiled at her snippy tone, and damn his unsupportive feet, they took a step toward the bed. And another, until he stood beside the bed.

"Next time I go looking for a man—"

That did it. She was not going looking for a man. He straddled her legs. He slipped his hands under her middle, lifting her up and back against his chest, silencing her.

He cupped her breasts, using the tips of his fingers to lightly scrape her nipples, which immediately peaked.

She rewarded him with a gasp of pleasure. He kissed her neck, her skin was warm and smelled of peaches. She arched her head back. His conscience reminded him she'd been hurt once already.

"Abbie, I'm not—"

She growled at him. "Let me guess. You have no idea what's going to happen and may not be around after this. I get it. I'm not really naïve."

He smiled and whispered, "You're really something, sweetheart." He moved a hand down her stomach, slowly, lightly touching her.

"Oh, yes. That's . . . nice." Her body shook.

His muscles tightened with the effort of waiting to get inside her. He nuzzled her throat and raised his hand up, rubbing his open palm across her beaded nipples.

She gasped again and whimpered, her hips moving. Her soft bottom brushed against the front of his jeans. Electricity bolted through him.

He took a breath and filled his hand with her breast. Heaven. Lifting a finger, he traced the outline of her nipple, then skipped back and forth across the tip.

Her fingers gripped his thighs. She trembled, holding tight until he moved his fingers down to the juncture of her legs and slipped inside.

One touch and a hard shudder ran through her. The woman was amazing. He flipped her around, unwilling to have this over so quickly. The minute she faced him, her hands clasped his cheeks and she kissed him with lips made of fire and honey. He ran his fingers into her gossamer curls and let his tongue meet hers in playful battle. Fingers scrambled down his chest to his pants . . . unzipped . . . then dove inside to curl around him.

He sucked in a sharp breath at the contact and growled into the next kiss, the need to feel himself inside her roaring through his veins. She kissed his neck and stroked him.

The world would disintegrate before his eyes if she did that one more time. He lifted her until her legs went around him and reached beneath her to finger the damp folds.

The high-pitched noise that escaped her sounded strangled.

Stroking his middle finger slowly in and out, he brushed his thumb over her tender skin in sync. She dug her nails into his back, shaking with strain.

Whispering to her what he wanted to do to her, he changed the rhythm of his fingers, moving faster.

She bowed up and back, muscles taut. "Don't . . . don't . . . stop."

Mesmerized watching her, he didn't stop. She cried out, panting, then fell against him in a boneless heap. Tears hung on her lashes. He kissed the mouth that had started this brushfire. Her hands cupped his face in so tender a gesture he kissed her deeper.

When he lifted his head to look at her she smiled at him.

God, what a gift.

Her eyes fluttered shut. He reached for her breast.

A high beeping alarm went off, freezing his hand.

His pulse jumped, but not to high alert. That alarm was just a warning someone had crossed the first line of defense half a mile down the mountain.

Borys would check it and notify him immediately of any—

A second alarm sounded, bells chiming throughout the house.

Abbie's eyes flew open. She grabbed him. "What's that?"

"Trouble. Get dressed."

CHAPTER TWENTY-SEVEN

"What kind of trouble?" Abbie fought through the sexual haze that had swamped her.

"Don't talk. Get moving." Hunter ordered so calmly she'd have thought he was discussing going down to dinner and not preparing to run for their lives, which was how this sounded.

She glanced at the window. Had to be late in the day, maybe close to sunset. She needed clothes.

"You have sixty seconds to get dressed." Hunter was looking at a small electronic unit that looked almost like a black iPhone.

"Dressed with what?" She turned around, frantically searching for clothes.

"In the dresser. Borys's clothes."

She raced over and yanked open the top drawer. Pulling out a dark blue T-shirt, she whipped it over her head and shoved her arms through.

Borys's voice came through the overhead intercom system. "East, west, and south quadrants breached."

Hunter cursed low but continued working his electronic unit with the patience of someone tinkering with a crossword puzzle as he moved around the room.

She pulled out the first pair of pants she found, loose khakis with pockets down each side. She'd spent enough time around Hunter to know that when he said sixty seconds he meant he'd take her out of there in whatever form of dress or undress she was in when time ran out.

"Put on a sweater, too." Hunter hadn't even looked up to see what she had on.

She found a burgundy cable-knit sweater and wiggled it over her head. Whatever cream he'd put on her skin had dulled the pain of her scrapes.

A pair of boots bounced on the floor in front of her.

She grabbed wool socks from another drawer and sat back on the end of the bed, fumbling to pull the tubes over her feet.

Hunter dropped down on one knee in front of her, putting her boots on and tying them while she buttoned her pants. She rushed into the bathroom.

"Let's go!"

She made two turns with a rubber band to pull her hair back into a ponytail so she could see when she ran. He grabbed her hand and hauled her out of the room.

She didn't say a word, not when he was in warrior mode.

"North quadrant breached," Borys's voice announced. "All systems set to blow in two minutes. Go bags in position."

Hunter ate up the distance to the stairs with long strides. She ran to keep up with him. He lifted his phone device to his mouth, still talking in an even tone. "Go. We're right behind you." He shoved the device into his front jeans pocket.

At the bottom of the stairs, a huge beige-and-green camo-colored backpack sat next to the open front door.

Borys was gone.

Hunter reached inside the hall closet and slapped something. When he stepped out he was wearing dark shades and stuffing a mega automatic pistol into the front waistband of his jeans. He stuck his arm back into the closet and pulled out a down jacket he handed her.

"Sunglasses in the front left pocket. Do exactly as I say. Don't speak for any reason unless I tell you to."

She nodded, zipping up the front of the jacket and digging out the shades while he hooked the backpack on his shoulders. Her terror or hesitation must have peeked through the strong front she was trying hard to put up.

He grabbed the front of her jacket and pulled her to him, crushing his mouth to hers. It seemed like he kissed her forever when she knew it could only have been seconds then released her. "Just listen to me and trust me. I'm not going to let anyone hurt you."

She changed her mind about Hunter.

He wasn't James Bond.

He was Superman. A badass Superman.

She nodded and squared her shoulders, ready for whatever they had to do. "I'm good."

He took her hand, squeezed it once, and towed her down the steps across what might be the front yard if anything had been shaped and groomed. He angled toward the back of the house, heading in the area of the path she'd taken earlier but more westerly, toward the setting sun.

But *he* knew where the booby traps were.

A hundred feet in every direction around the cabin had been cleared, probably for the explicit purpose of seeing someone approach. She kept her head down, paying attention in the fading light, careful of where she put her feet.

Using logic, if all four quadrants had been breached, weren't they heading toward at least one of the enemy?

He'd said to stay quiet and to trust him.

She intended to do both.

The temperature was dropping with the sun. Darkness would take over the land in another twenty minutes.

When they reached the tree line, Hunter led her down a gentle descent for about fifty feet, then he cut left, weaving through low-drooping branches with stiff pine needles.

Pain shot through her knee. She slipped once and tensed against reinjuring it.

Hunter caught her upper arm so quickly she never felt his hand move. He slowed his pace, tediously working their path one way, then back the other way.

They were heading down with every step, but in a wide zigzag.

Where were these people who were coming up the mountain? How far away were they? It was a big honkin' mountain. Hunter must have an idea of how to get past them.

He paused, then cupped her mouth with his hand and grabbed her around the waist. Lifting her off the ground, he backed into a dark cut between two boulders taller than Hunter. The space was four feet wide and at least ten feet deep.

Not a hint of light in here. All she could see from inside this dark pit was whatever crossed the opening to the space.

Her chest constricted with the effort of breathing.

Now that he had her tucked deep in this hole, she could hear rocks moving outside.

And footsteps.

Whoever approached must not have realized they'd tripped a silent alarm system.

She hung perfectly still in his arms, frozen with fear, while he angled around, moving silently as a ghost. He deposited her and his backpack softly on the ground.

When he turned back around she was behind him and in total darkness with his wide body blocking the opening.

She would not panic. He was right here with her.

His hand came back and touched her arm. Just enough to comfort her in the middle of racing from danger.

She fell a little in love with him right then.

Footsteps crunched on ice-crusted snow.

Her heart stampeded in her chest. But she had faith in Hunter, knew he would do whatever it took to keep them safe.

The sound of someone walking faded slowly until it disappeared. Hunter didn't move for another five minutes.

Then he hoisted the backpack on his shoulders and pulled her forward. When she stepped out of the opening she could barely see. She patted his hand to let him know she was okay.

He'd produced a monocle type of eyepiece she assumed was for night vision, which he'd need very soon. He nodded at her, his eyes taking in everything around them constantly. Hooking her hand, he took off again.

She worked up a sweat trying to make sure she followed exactly in his footsteps, more by feel than sight.

Ten minutes later the most god-awful racket came from high above them. Where the cabin was. She jerked around. That was gunfire. Automatic weapons ripping something to pieces.

Hunter's house.

He tugged on her arm, not slowing. In fact, his pace picked up again. Did he think now that the intruders had reached an empty house they were going to head back down the mountain after her and Hunter?

She kept up with him, staying right behind, stumbling on occasion and wheezing air. He was always able to grab her before she fell. The men at his cabin were moving solo, not burdened with a woman.

One who was not in shape to do this much hiking at this pace. If it hadn't been a downhill run, she'd have keeled over by now.

He slowed, so she tugged on his hand.

When he paused, she made the hand motion for talking, hoping he could see it with his monocle.

He drew her close to him. "What?"

"Can you hide me somewhere? You'd have a better chance of escaping then you could come get me later." Please tell her he could hide her safe enough those guys wouldn't find her.

He made a disgusted sound, as if she'd insulted him. "No."

"You can't find a spot or you can't escape faster alone?"

"Not leaving you anywhere. End of discussion." He tugged her forward, muttering something under his breath for three steps, then went dead silent again. Another fifty feet downhill he made a hard turn right, pushing his way through snow piling around their boots. He stopped and flicked on a tiny LED light he shined on a pile of branches barely visible from the layer of snow coating them. He handed the light to her. "Point it there."

She held the light where he told her.

He started tossing branches to the side, revealing the opening to a black hole. A cave? Not much of one.

Maybe he'd changed his mind about hiding her, but she hadn't considered being alone in a dark cave.

"Stand right here and don't move." He moved her to a spot to the left of the cave's entrance.

Like any good soldier, she followed his orders.

He let her keep the light and disappeared inside.

She mentally counted seconds to keep from thinking about what she'd do if someone jumped out of the weeds with a machine gun. A motor growled to life inside the cave.

The sound became high-pitched, then Hunter emerged on a motorcycle. She shined her bright light over the dark bike. It reminded her of motocross bikes, but this one looked street legal with the headlight and taillights.

His backpack was strapped onto the rear and he wore a black helmet. He handed her a gray helmet and gloves that were large but would keep her hands warm. "Ready to ride?"

She'd never wanted to ride a motorcycle. They were dangerous. But considering her other option was facing men with guns, this one immediately earned her safety rating. She pulled the helmet over her head, flipping up the face shield. Hunter looped her chinstrap and locked it, then he climbed on the bike.

He showed her where to step to hoist herself behind him, then he revved the motor and took off.

The rest of the way down was not as steep as what they'd covered on foot, but the jarring ride scared her. Still, she had to give Hunter credit for his skill in handling the bike with a full load and over rough ground.

When he turned onto a dirt road, her heart was thumping wildly and she had no idea where they were going, but she smiled in relief and leaned down to hug her arms around his waist. Her fingers bumped the metal loop dangling from his jeans. That karabiner. She hesitated to move her hands.

He covered her fingers and pulled both hands in front of him. The only thing she could see was whatever the headlight shined on.

Besides, Hunter would figure it out if anyone followed.

He slowed when the dirt road intersected with a highway, then swung left and rolled on the accelerator, tearing along the pavement. Icy wind buffeted her legs, but she could stand the ride in the down jacket and hugged against his body.

He had to be cold. No way to tell. He never complained about anything.

Two hours later, she'd figured out Hunter's cabin was in Montana, based on road signs, but had no idea where he was heading now. Her adrenaline kick had slowed to a dribble. She sat up to let the cold air slap her in the face.

He patted her hand as if to say, "Hang in there." She patted his side to let him know she was fine.

Another hour later, he'd taken turns in several small towns in Wyoming. Every time he passed a hotel she'd sigh.

When he flipped on his turn signal a block before a single-level motor court in Buffalo, Wyoming, advertising a vacancy, she wanted to cheer. He parked on the side of the brightly lit office that could have once been a small residence. She sent him in without her so she could stretch her spongy legs.

He returned in a couple minutes with a room key and she climbed back onto the motorcycle behind him. He drove past two cabins with assorted Harleys lined up in front of the units and turned left by the third cabin, parking at the door.

"Thank God." She pulled off her helmet, climbed down from the bike, and stretched her legs. "What kind of bike is that?"

Hunter had his helmet and gloves off. "BMW R 1200 GS Adventure."

"What does all that mean?" She used the key to open the door and stepped inside, where the smell of disinfectant cleaner and lemon furniture polish filled the air. The lamp on the nightstand lit up when she flipped the wall switch.

"It's a dual sport that can go on the highway or off-road." Hunter tossed his helmet and gloves on the first of two beds.

The pine-paneled room was old but clean, and the large space included a small kitchenette area.

"Hold the door," he called out softly.

She held it open while he carried in his backpack and threw that on the bed, too. "Pull the curtains closed."

"Where's Borys?" she asked while she closed the curtains.

"Safe. We always have an exit plan." He started unpacking clothes and dark plastic packages from his backpack.

She noticed he didn't share any details, but she mentally shrugged off his obviously limited sense of trust. She could understand his reticence to say much in his line of work. "What about everything in your house?"

Hunter shrugged again. "Nothing there that matters. Borys activated a program that destroyed the electronics we left behind. Sounded like the intruders took care of the rest."

Her mouth was gaping. She couldn't believe what she heard.

He acted as though it was no big deal to lose what had to be hundreds of thousands of dollars. "Doesn't that bother you?"

"What?"

"It sounded like they destroyed your house and probably stole anything of value. Losing all that doesn't upset you?"

All the intensity she'd seen winding through his movements for the past few hours seeped out in one long sigh. He walked over to her, his hair smashed down and sweaty from the helmet. Dirt streaked his face and weariness lined his eyes.

He placed his palm against the side of her face. "The only thing that would have bothered me was if anything had happened to you."

CHAPTER TWENTY-EIGHT

Jackson Chameleon surveyed the destruction of the home in Montana, satisfied.

"That enough or you want more, boss?" Bulked up from hard labor, Freddie was the superior of the seven men Jackson had hired for this expedition. Ragged whiskers poked out above his stained teeth. Freddie ran weapons and drugs between two Middle Eastern countries and South America and the U.S.

Four men were taken out by booby traps on the mountain Jackson had anticipated. Those four had cleared the way for Jackson and these three.

"Boss?" Freddie repeated.

Boss. An amusing term.

"That will be sufficient." Jackson cast a quiet gaze at the next man, a North American Indian in worn jeans and a moss-gray chamois shirt who could track the path of a lizard on a bald mountain. "You're *sure* no one could follow our trails?"

The tracker dipped his head in abrupt acknowledgment.

"Good." Jackson ignored the third man, who had lowered his automatic weapon, waiting on instructions.

Freddie had cut the deal for the men and organized the assault while Jackson waited on his Fratelli superior to pull the flight records on the private jet that had transported Abigail. That led him to the helicopter that had transported her next. If not for Fratelli connections within the FAA and FBI he might have hit a dead end there.

Arresting the helicopter pilot and convincing him he was part of a murder investigation to do with the woman he'd transported hadn't paid off.

Abigail's rescuer had deep pockets and power.

The helicopter pilot stonewalled them.

But Jackson had a man extract past coordinates out of the helicopter's navigation system while the pilot was being interrogated. The pilot had made multiple stops that night at equally remote locations.

Jackson had to admire Abigail's rescuer for his ability to disappear and to keep his identity hidden. But he'd eventually find that, too.

Entangling the pilot with the FAA had allowed Jackson the time he needed to unleash his team before the pilot could possibly send a warning to his wealthy client.

"A job well done." Jackson applauded his three men. "Now you have a choice to make."

Freddie frowned. The Native American tracker's black eyes thinned to evil slits. The third guy—what was his name?—moved his finger to the trigger of his weapon.

Jackson enjoyed this part. "The offer still stands, but it gets better. I only need one of you after today. So you can all take your fifty thousand apiece or you can show me who's the best among all of you and that person will make a half million on the next job."

Men who lived and died by their reflexes weren't slow to make a decision.

The third guy had his finger ready but hadn't anticipated how fast the tracker could whip a Bowie knife around and shove it into the guy's heart, then twist.

Number three slid to the floor, pulling away from the knife the tracker wiped on the dead guy's shirt.

Freddie had his Glock 9mm leveled on his only competition when the tracker stood up and faced him. "Thanks, chief. That made it easy."

"If you kill me, you won't live to enj—" A bullet struck the tracker between his eyes.

Freddie sighed heavily. "Hate that. He was a helluva tracker." He lowered his weapon and faced Jackson. "Guess that makes me your man."

"I'm not surprised," Jackson said, congratulating himself on predicting the correct outcome again. He had something special planned for Freddie. Freddie had enemies, including a really nasty one who was not happy about having his drug-running territory poached. "You're ambitious, right?"

"Abso-fucking-lutely." Freddie holstered his weapon and dusted off his hands.

"As soon as we get down from here, I have a load of cocaine for you to move." This plan lacked true challenge, but Jackson couldn't waste much time in ridding himself of Freddie.

By tonight, Freddie's enemy would have a free shipment of cocaine and Freddie would be in multiple pieces.

With no unnecessary killing performed by Jackson's hand.

The Fratelli would find no fault with his work.

"What about the bodies?" Freddie followed him outside.

"Leave them. Hand me one of the branches you cut." Jackson took it and erased his footprints leading back the way he'd come up the mountain. Freddie did the same even though his prints had approached from a different direction, but by the time the authorities identified Freddie his prints wouldn't matter.

Jackson took one last look at the razed house.

This should show the man with Abigail Blanton that she had nowhere to hide and he couldn't protect her.

Not from the Jackson Chameleon.

Chapter Twenty-nine

Hunter. Wet and naked.

Just the way Abbie wanted him.

But he was standing on the hot-water side of the flowery plastic shower curtain.

Without her.

She sat on the closed seat cover of the commode, finishing her MRE, or Meal, Ready to Eat. Nourishing and not awful, but also not the nice dinner—pizza would have been fine—she'd hoped to eat before finding out what Hunter looked like naked.

He vetoed food delivery or leaving the motor court for any reason short of a life-threatening injury.

Did getting her heart broken rate as life threatening?

As if giving her that mind-blowing orgasm hadn't raised her libido from the dead, that ride through hell had supercharged it.

She'd thought the minute he got inside this cabin he'd pick up where he'd left off after taking her through an out-of-body experience.

He hadn't so much as kissed her since then.

He *had* curled her heart into one big gooey glob when he told her he didn't care about losing a house that had to cost a fortune, but he *would* have been bothered if anything had happened to her.

She'd been speechless . . . then leaned foward to kiss him.

He'd backed up and set about putting the room in order, right down to cleaning off the second bed.

Big message there.

He had to be rethinking what happened now that they were on the run. Had to be his agency. Hunter said they'd come after him. So now he'd changed his mind about touching her.

She wanted to act like sex was just sex. To tell him with all sorts of sexual maturity that she was really okay with their using each other to forget about the danger they were in, but that wouldn't be the truth. She still remembered the guy who had touched her heart six years ago.

She wanted that Samson guy she'd first met *and* she wanted the new Hunter she now knew.

Could any woman be this stupid twice in her life?

She wanted a man who didn't exist in the real world. So what? Why couldn't she have him now? A night, or hopefully two, with Hunter would be worth more than years with another man. She'd told him she knew how precarious their time was, but he'd obviously had a change of heart since then.

The shower raged on with sounds of body scrubbing that had her painting a mental picture of water rushing over his lean and cut body.

She had to get out of this bathroom. She wiped her hands on a damp washrag and tossed the last of her MRE into the wastebasket. A cloud of steam hovered in the small room even though she'd left the door open to the bedroom, as per Hunter's instruction.

He'd been efficient about every aspect of locking them in tight for the night. That's when she'd noticed the room had no desk phone. She'd asked to use his cell phone. No cell towers. He promised they'd call in the morning. She hadn't given him grief since he was trying to keep them safe.

He finished securing the room, not missing a detail, except for how her self-confidence had slowly dissolved.

She hadn't thought she could embarrass herself any more with Hunter than she had the first time they met, but having him act as if nothing had happened at the cabin after the intimacy she'd shared was tearing her insides to pieces.

She'd had about enough of sitting in this sauna.

Water dripped off a ringlet of hair stuck to her shoulder and streaked down to where Hunter's oversized T-shirt covered her breasts. Her too-sensitive nipples brushed the soft material every time she moved.

Her entire body was too sensitive with him so close.

Worse, her emotions clung by nervous fingers.

She hated to feel insecure.

Hated trying to figure out what went on inside a man's mind. She hadn't had this problem in six years.

Not since she'd made up her mind men were not to be trusted. Hunter was the first one to come along who challenged that belief.

She trusted him with her life.

Her heart was the part in danger.

The shower stopped running.

"Go to the bedroom now that I can hear you," Hunter said.

She stuck her tongue out at the still-closed shower curtain, sighed, and walked out to the bedroom, where the temperature dropped ten degrees. Goose bumps prickled her skin.

"Leave the lights off," he called just before she reached for the lamp.

Fine. She pulled the covers back on one bed, climbed in, and covered up. The sheets were like ice. She kicked her feet to warm them and hugged her body. The window unit was silent. Had he set the heat at all?

She wasn't getting up to check. *He* could deal with that since the wall unit was on *his* side of the room, next to the other bed.

The bathroom door closed partway, leaving a six-inch gap where she could see a sliver of mirror.

The urge to check out his reflection in the mirror showing through the crack in the door proved too great to ignore.

She leaned to her right. Reflections of his masculine upper body blinked across the mirror. She propped her head on her elbow.

Why not enjoy the show?

Hunter flipped the towel out of view and crossed his arms behind his head, flexing left, then right.

God, what a body. Even that tasty little view.

Muscles rippled in his chest and abdomen. A true eight-pack. Narrow hips.

If the mirror was just a little lower . . . she'd get the full Monty. He bumped the door with his hip and she lost all her view but an inch.

Abbie rolled over and punched the pillow, then plopped down on her stomach.

Her teeth chattered. She reached for the other half of the bedspread and flipped it over to double up her covers. Once her body heat warmed the sheets, she started drifting to sleep with one thought.

Be a cold day in hell before he ever gets to touch me again.

She dreamed of men in the dark and automatic weapons and motorcycles screaming through the night . . . but the wind didn't chill her this time. The air was hot.

Fire burned across her skin sensually.

Her nipples hardened with need.

She moaned at the ache building between her legs.

Abbie came awake, her heart pounding from the most erotic dream she'd ever had—

A finger brushed her beaded nipple.

—that was still going on. She shivered in delight.

"Miss me?" Hunter whispered next to her ear.

Wait a minute. Did he think he could just climb into bed and rub that . . . uh, hmm, hot piece of male against her . . . and not explain why . . .

She was on her left side, facing away from him. He was holding her against his heat, touching her from top to bottom.

Every hard inch of him touching her.

"You smell delicious." He kissed her neck and rubbed his erection along her bottom. His fingers were busy with her breasts again, teasing her mindless.

She opened her eyes to a dark room. Not being able to see heightened her sensitivity. Turning her to face him, he brushed his lips over hers. A potent kiss that worked to persuade her hormones to give him a chance to dispel her concerns.

Cold air rushed across her heat-flushed skin. Nothing that could douse the flame building inside her.

His exploring tongue shut down communication with her brain.

He *felt* delicious.

She rolled over for better access. He slowed the sweet assault, drawing out the pleasure. She'd never considered kissing to be so sensual.

He nipped at her bottom lip.

She wanted him to keep going, but not at the cost of another bout of embarrassment later. She put a hand on his chest and pressed. No more kissing until she found out what the devil was going on with him being hot one minute, ignoring her the next, then hot again.

He curled his hand around her wrist, one finger grazing her skin in a lazy motion. "What, sweetheart?"

Her heart wavered again at the endearment, pleading with her to let him continue. To cheer him on. But her pride couldn't take another beating if he blew her off once more after this. "Why are you . . . I thought . . ."

His forehead touched her shoulder. Skilled lips moved over her neck. "Is this going to take a long time? Not sure I can wait much longer."

She growled at him and felt him chuckle against her neck. "Why'd you act so distant when we got here if you wanted to do this?" His answer would be the difference between "Go ahead, lover" and "Go sleep in the other bed." She might regret missing this chance with him, but she didn't want to be handy sex.

Hunter kissed her eyebrows, her nose and lips. Affectionate little love pats that mushed her brain. He explained, "If I'd touched you when we walked in here, I wouldn't have secured the room and you wouldn't have gotten a shower or food."

"Oh. Okay." She smiled, ready to turn him loose.

Hunter took that as a definite "go ahead," but her moment of hesitation woke his conscience. He had to be completely honest with her. "All I can give you is right now, Abbie. I don't even know where we'll both be at this time tomorrow."

If she asked him to stop now he'd sleep in the other bed.

Miserably. But he'd go.

Her fingers started moving on his chest, playing hesitantly. What did that mean? Time for a yes or no.

Her hand left his chest and wrapped around his erection.

Hunter sucked in at the unexpected action. When she stroked him once, he croaked, "Guess that's a yes?"

She laughed, sweet music filling the darkness. "If you promise not to stop this time."

"I swear it." He leaned down, taking possession of her mouth with his. He loved how she opened for him. Her tongue delved in to meet his. Her passion was unlike anything he'd held in his arms before.

He broke away to move down her. He wanted to feel her tremble again, clinging to the edge of reality before she climaxed. She moaned in complaint when he settled between her legs and her hand came up empty. "Hey, I can't reach—"

When he suckled her full nipple the tip beaded happily. That ended her grousing.

Hunter smiled, looking forward to the challenge of

taking her to the edge, then holding her there. Licking her nipple, he caressed her other breast with his fingers.

She clutched his shoulders, her fingers shaking the longer he paid intense attention to her breasts. He drew her nipple in and swirled his tongue around and across the tip.

She reached for his shoulders, her nails digging in. Her leg came up, rubbing against his erection.

Spending an hour on her might have to wait for round two.

Abandoning her breast, he licked and teased his way lower until he kissed the warm skin inside her thigh. He plundered the sensitive area until shivers raced over her skin. She was so responsive, so open and sensual, he couldn't wait longer. He turned his head, using his tongue to stroke the tender bud between her legs.

Her nails dug in, clinging to him.

Holding her back from release would have been impossible. In just seconds, she arched, quivering, her legs tight with strain. She cried out, her body taut as a bow stretching, stretching, then she groaned and shuddered, collapsing with a whimpered sound of surrender.

He shook from just feeling the power of her release.

Her strained breaths echoed in the darkness. He leaned over and snagged one of the condoms he'd dumped on the nightstand. Ripping it open with his teeth, he sheathed himself and settled over her from head to toe, kissing her damp face, then her lips.

She lay spent and lethargic at first, but passion caught fire once again when he rubbed his open palm over the tip of her breast. He was amazed at how quickly she came to life.

Her hands clutched his head, tugging him closer. She plunged into the kiss.

She lifted her hips and rubbed against his erection, urgent, demanding.

Not a problem. He entered her slowly, feeding his length until she stretched, taking all of him.

He'd never had a problem going on and on, distancing himself from the woman in his bed. Keeping himself removed from more than sex with the jaded women he'd brought home before.

But Abbie was like the first breath of spring on the heels of a bitter cold winter.

"You feel so damn good," he whispered, and moved inside her.

"Good? I don't think so," she muttered.

"What?" He stopped.

"I was thinking amazing . . . if you'd put a little more enthusiasm behind it." She kissed him, smiling against his lips.

He touched his forehead to hers. "See what I can do, hellion."

Lifting her hips, he pushed deep into her and clenched his teeth against the urge to find his own release.

Driving into her was pure ecstasy.

Her nails curled, biting his skin. "More."

Holding back slid farther from his grasp with each stroke, but if she wanted more . . . he grabbed her hips, pounding, relentless, driving past all thought.

Wait. He could hold on longer . . .

She locked her legs around his waist. Her heat tightened around him. She squeezed. *"Now."*

Game over.

Muscles clenched, locking across his body, then snapped free, shooting stars past his eyes with the mind-numbing release.

Seconds turned into minutes until he realized he'd lost track of time.

Unheard of. He never lost track of his surroundings. Ever.

But a minute ago he'd been on top of her pounding and now he held her in his arms, lying on his side.

He reached over and pulled the covers over them both, mainly so she didn't get chilled. His body still roared hot as a furnace.

When he was able to move again, he told her, "I'll be right back." Lumbering into the bathroom, he navigated by a light on the bottom of the wall-mounted hair dryer. He cleaned himself up and returned with a warm washcloth, but when he reached the bed she took the cloth from him.

How could she be self-conscious about anything now? He smiled but didn't tease her. For all Abbie's bravado she had moments of insecurity. Some idiot male had yanked the legs from under her confidence. By the time Hunter had discarded her washcloth in the bathroom even he was feeling the chill. He climbed back into bed and snaked an arm around her waist, drawing her tight against him.

He inhaled deeply, enjoying the musky scent of their lovemaking.

She shuddered out a long sigh. Her fingers wrapped around the arm he held her with. She made a little shift with her body and settled down as though ready to sleep.

No such luck for him.

Not after she'd wiggled her backside against him. He was getting hard again.

Four more condoms called to him from where he'd tossed them on the nightstand, but Abbie was out stone cold in the next minute. She had complete faith in his ability to keep her safe, hadn't even questioned if anyone would find them here.

She'd obviously left her future in his hands.

The weight of that trust pressed on his chest.

He'd lived for years without anyone depending on him or caring about him. Had to so he could function at his highest level, especially after losing Eliot. Even Borys knew how to take care of himself for the next week until Hunter had a chance to find him a new place to hide. He couldn't have kept the cabin in Montana once Abbie left since he'd never risk anyone walking around with knowledge of his personal safe house.

But he hated to lose that place because of all the memories he had of Eliot's visits. And Eliot had been the only person he'd ever trusted to know the location.

Abbie sighed in her sleep.

Hunter realized he'd been brushing a hand softly over her hair. He kissed the top of her head. She was sweet and had no reason to tell anyone about the cabin, but leaving himself vulnerable to *any* security leak went against his discipline.

He hadn't understood Eliot taking that risk with Cynthia, even if he did love her. His friend had placed a hell of a lot more faith in love than Hunter would.

He curled Abbie closer, trying to quiet the voice inside him arguing in her defense that she was different from all the other women. That Abbie would love deeply and never break a trust.

But his father had probably thought the same thing about Hunter's mother, who had sworn her love in front of the world and tossed that word around with little care for the meaning in the dictionary.

Look at Todd. He and Pia had said they loved each other. That love had ended in divorce court and his brother hitting the bottle as he never had before.

There was a limit to how far Hunter would ever invest himself.

Better to be cautious than dead because of misplaced faith.

Like the way he'd trusted Joe to be good for his word. Joe had agreed to Hunter's plan to access the Kore database.

With so little time left and the threat of bombings, why had Joe sent a team to Montana? Why not wait to see if Hunter came through with the records from Kore?

How had BAD found his Montana location?

The pilot of his brother's jet from Chicago would have known only about the helicopter Hunter and Abbie transferred to at a small airfield in Wyoming, not their final destination. Hunter had the helicopter pilot make a total of six stops at coordinates of remote locations, dropping them along the way near Beartooth Pass in Montana.

He'd known the pilot from his days with the CIA when the pilot was sent in to extract an agent in Uruguay and got captured. Hunter had led a team to rescue the pilot and the agent. That pilot wouldn't have given up a thing even if he was locked up somewhere with a trumped-up charge.

A very likely scenario.

Didn't matter. Hunter had known Joe would come after him at some point, just hadn't expected it to be now.

A complication. Not one that would stop him once he figured out what to do with Abbie.

Nothing would prevent him from finding Eliot's killer, but he also had a duty to protect Abbie and to help BAD and his country even if Joe did want to hang him right now. Hunter *would* retrieve the information BAD needed before he went to ground. He didn't hold a grudge against Joe for sending a team to bring him in. He'd known for four years this time would come. He just had to be careful not to make a mistake.

Like the one he was holding in his arms.

Abbie had stumbled into his life a second time and he shouldn't have touched her. He tried to tell himself he'd made love to her because he had to finish what he'd started at the cabin and because she needed comfort and because . . . just excuses he'd dug up to ignore the truth.

He wanted Abbie.

Still did. Didn't want to give her up.

But he'd never make the mistake Eliot had made.

Hunter would never let Abbie know how much he'd like to keep her, and he sure as hell wouldn't risk her getting pregnant.

Besides, she'd hate him once he got the information from Kore, because he'd use that to trade with BAD for

Abbie's safety. If he had a choice he'd keep her with him where he could protect her himself.

Joe had unleashed the hounds last night. If they found the cabin that fast, they wouldn't be far behind him.

Once he handed over what BAD needed from Kore, the most dangerous place for Abbie would be at his side.

CHAPTER THIRTY

"**H**ave you discussed the documents I gave you on this mission with anyone?" Vestavia asked Linette as she prepared to depart his office after their meeting. He studied every aspect of her response, from physical to verbal.

She stood next to the chair facing his desk, a file folder tucked against the front of her knee-length orange dress and open jacket. "Of course not, Fra."

He listened with an objective ear for any flutter in her voice but heard nothing suspicious. The mole hadn't made a move yet. If Vestavia couldn't prevent the destruction of a major U.S. city, at a minimum he would use this opportunity to find the person behind the leaks. Linette didn't concern him. Not that women weren't capable of subterfuge.

Josie could have pulled off being a double agent, but Linette wasn't Josie and had never been given any freedom.

Josie had traveled at will. He'd never find another woman like her.

He'd chosen Linette for this mission *because* of her lack of field experience. And because the old prick who'd abused her since she was a teen had broken her spirit. She'd tell him if anyone tried to pry information out of her.

He intended to give her the final location when he got the information from Bardaric.

Then he'd make sure everyone involved with this operation knew she was the only person privy to the bomb location other than Vestavia.

Linette stood as poised as a mannequin, awaiting his instructions. No nervous twitch or babbling.

His desk phone lit with an incoming call on his secure line. "That'll be all, Linette."

She nodded and walked gracefully to the door, shutting it quietly behind her.

He pressed a button that activated the caller ID display programmed to show only a numeric code. He lifted the receiver. "Do we have a location?"

"Not yet," Ostrovsky answered. "I wish to know your plan for detonating the bomb."

"Hadn't given it that much thought since I don't have the location. Why?" He'd spent hours trying to come up with a viable delay plan but wasn't sharing a thing with anyone yet.

"I am of the mind that Bardaric is becoming major problem. One the Council will have to face soon."

Vestavia wanted to reach through the phone and choke the Russian. "Then why in hell didn't you bring that up during our meeting?"

"Because the others will be more receptive to discussing Bardaric once you carry out this mission and dismiss any suspicions *they* may have."

Vestavia knew where this was leading but had to play along. Ostrovsky was too diplomatic to be in charge of a continent that included Russia and China, but a powerful organization run by alpha males needed someone with a cool head on occasion. "What suspicions?"

"That you might have personal ambitions in conflict with the Council's."

That just pissed him off. His voice dropped low and tight with anger. "Think I would have killed Josie if I wasn't a hundred percent committed to our plans for the Renaissance?"

"I have no question about where your allegiance lies," Ostrovsky assured him quickly, always the diplomat. "But Bardaric works hard to prove otherwise. I think he spins his deceit to draw attention away from his own ambitions, as in a sleight-of-hand trick."

"Why'd you support Bardaric when we voted? You know better than anyone what he's capable of." Accusing an Angeli of working outside the trust of the Council was dangerous, but since Ostrovsky was speaking openly so would Vestavia. "You have to know Bardaric financed the 9/11 attack that backfired. He thought the U.S. would shake in their boots. Look at the mess he's made of the Middle East. That was *not* part of the long-term plan."

"I am not without eyes and ears in these situations, which is why I called you. I believe Bardaric has another plan under way. The timing to initiate this mission is suspect."

Vestavia hit his desktop with his fist but stopped short of belaboring how Ostrovsky could also have delayed the urgent timing of the attack. He needed to know what was behind this phone call. "What're you getting at?"

"If Bardaric is behind the three killings on your continent in the past seven months—"

"*If?* How can anyone on the council believe that I sanctioned those?"

"I don't think they do, but your silence on them means you have failed to produce evidence of Bardaric's involvement."

"Not from lack of effort," Vestavia grumbled.

"Then beat him at his own game and acquire your evidence. He has contacted me several times, trying to convince me to push the council to allow him to coordinate the detonation. I believe Bardaric wishes to add one more component to this bombing."

"Such as?"

"Killing a political leader at the same time as the bombing would only multiply your problems."

Vestavia could see the direction of Ostrovsky's thinking, but weakening the U.S. would work in the Russian's favor as much as that of the other Angeli. "Why would you *not* support a plan to further undermine this country?"

"You may not have succeeded in placing a Fratelli in the White House last year, but unlike Bardaric I see how the missions you execute manage to move us toward our goal efficiently while keeping a lower profile." Ostrovsky paused.

"You think Bardaric'll take out the head of our country?"

"Why should he kill your president when that will only unite the Americans?"

Vestavia shifted, leaning his elbow on the chair to support his chin. "You think he'll go after the prime minister?"

"Why not? Then he would point the finger at you, claiming you sanctioned the hit to retaliate."

Ostrovsky was right. "Hadn't considered that. What do you suggest?"

"That if Bardaric is behind the killings he is not using a Fratelli sniper, which means his person is contract. Someone loyal only to money. Are you not capable of outbidding him?"

Vestavia had thought the sniper was a Fratelli asset. That would have allowed Bardaric to claim someone else in the UK Fratelli had been behind any unsanctioned acts if the Angeli found evidence confirming the hits were tied to the Fratelli. The Angeli wouldn't expect Bardaric to challenge any of the Fratelli unless the killings created a major problem for them. But using a mercenary made more sense.

That would eliminate the worry of a Fratelli sniper being pulled in and questioned. Paying for services motivated the contractor to keep his client's name protected.

But Vestavia still questioned Ostrovsky's taking a side when the mediator had managed to stay out of conflict with everyone on the council for so many years. "Why now, Ostrovsky?"

"Because I'm holding a folder with photos of four kills that have an unusual stamp on them. A skull with dark eyeglasses and a lizard. One photo is of a young woman who worked for me inside the British embassy. The images are . . . brutal. She was my niece."

Finally, something Vestavia could accept. "I need help getting word out quickly without Bardaric knowing it's me shopping for his sniper."

"My network is at your service."

"I'll also have to relinquish control over the timing of the detonation to Bardaric in a way that won't make him or the Council suspicious."

"I will contact Bardaric to let him know I've requested a Council meeting in two hours. They will not question this if he drives the vote and you argue at first, then reluctantly agree."

"I can do that, but when this is over I want the Council to sanction him." The kind of sanction Vestavia had in mind involved blood. "I want your support when they do."

"Get your evidence and I will back you."

He considered the gamble he was making by handing over the control to Bardaric, but he'd amend the terms before they voted. Bardaric would have to commit to a date and time for the bombing right away, plus inform Vestavia of the bomb location no later than two hours in advance, with a guarantee of taking full responsibility for any premature detonation.

Bardaric would balk at that, but the council would not.

Just in case he couldn't locate Bardaric's killer in time, Vestavia had a backup plan. He'd activate the new guy on his team. The one with the scar on his face who came so highly recommended by six Fratelli from the U.S. and Peter Wentworth.

Vestavia pressed a button on his phone. When Linette answered, he told her, "Find Cayle Seabrooke."

CHAPTER THIRTY-ONE

Abbie woke slowly in the dark room and yawned. Exhausted, but in a nice way.

Three-times-last-night kind of tired. Hunter was amazing, relentless . . . sweet. Had she really walked away from this man six years ago? No, she'd run.

"Morning." His deep and rusty voice warmed her. He moved his hand from where his fingers spanned her stomach and toyed with her nipple.

That responded as if he'd trained it to pucker upon command.

She put her hand over his to stop him. If not for worry over her mother, she'd spend a week in this cozy little room, allowing Hunter to have his way with every inch of her body. "What are we doing today? I have to talk to Dr. Tatum."

"The fog's still heavy from last night. We'll leave in about an hour."

The curtains were closed. How often had he gotten up during the night to look outside? "Then what?"

"We go to Gillette. Next town east of here. I have identification, credit cards, cash . . . things in a bank vault. We'll fly from there to Chicago."

"You have an airplane waiting there?" she teased.

"Not until I get a new cell phone and new credit

cards." He was dead serious. She couldn't imagine living this way all the time. Never knowing when he had to disappear or escape someone trying to kill him. Had to be a lonely existence. She rubbed his hand. "Can we go to the medical center when we get to Chicago?"

"Ask me in Chicago."

"What kind of answer is that?"

"The best one I have. Would you rather I lie to you?"

No, she couldn't fault him for that. His fingers started moving beneath her hand, massaging her breast.

"Sweet," he whispered, then nuzzled her ear. "And sexy."

"Don't even think about starting something if you expect me to walk out of here under my own power."

He chuckled. "Thought you realized by now I'm willing to carry you."

"Not again. You'll strain your back."

He was quiet for a minute, then said, "Don't say things like that. You were pretty when I met you six years ago, but I like you better this way. I'm not much for skin-and-bones thin."

Her stomach flipped. She'd starved herself and worked out like a fiend just to be thin for the jerk she'd been engaged to and *he'd* never said anything so sweet to her back then. "Wish I'd known you before I tortured my body to fit someone else's idea of attractive."

Hunter moved his hand to her face and rubbed his knuckles along her cheek. "That why you came strutting into that bar with payback on your mind when I first met you?"

"Was I that obvious?" Her face flamed at how transparent she'd been. "Pathetic, huh?"

"It was *obvious* someone had hurt you." He leaned over and kissed her forehead tenderly. "What happened?"

She wouldn't have told him a couple days ago, but she wanted to now. "The night before I met you I came home to find the pig I was engaged to in bed with another woman, one who came without pesky morals. How clichéd is that?"

"He was a fool to have lost you."

Okay, that earned Hunter saint level in her book. "My father would have told me he got what he deserved since he married the shrew."

"Would have?"

"He died when I was eighteen."

"That's a tough age to lose your dad."

Not as tough as feeling responsible for her adoptive father's death. She'd never know for sure, but the guilt lingered like an unwelcome guest. She'd started researching her birth father one week. Her adoptive father had drowned the next week, the death ruled a suicide, which she'd never believe. Following his funeral, her mother ordered Abbie to stop hunting for her biological father. Said he was a dangerous man.

Abbie hadn't told anyone she was searching for him and her mother refused to tell her how she knew, but the warning came through loud and clear.

"True, but plenty of other people had their fathers for less time. I'm thankful for what I did have and that he loved me."

"Why wouldn't he love you?"

"I'm a bastard. Or I was, until Raymond married my mother after she had me out of wedlock."

"What happened to your real father?"

"My *biological* father?" she corrected. "Don't know. My *real* father is the one who raised me and gave me his name when he adopted me. In my mind, a parent is more than DNA. It's the person who's there when you learn how to ride a bike and helps blow out birthday candles and listens to your problems. A parent is the person who cares about you."

Hunter didn't comment. His fingers feathered across her stomach in gentle caresses.

She felt the steady rise and fall of his chest against her back. "What about your family? Ever see them?"

"Saw Todd the other night."

"That's your brother? Now that I think about it, he does favor you." A few more mental gears shifted. "I still don't even know your last name."

"Thornton-Payne."

She'd heard that name bandied around the television station by financial and political analysts. "Is your family involved in—"

"So many things it would take too long to list them," Hunter finished. "Todd and my dad run everything. I have no claim to their success."

Hunter wasn't just wealthy. He came from a dynasty with Fort Knox credit rating. And great genetics to boot. "Which one of your parents do you favor?"

"Physically, I favor my mother. My dad's short and unattractive, but he's a decent man."

Investigating people had taught Abbie to listen to what wasn't said. "What is your mother like?"

"Was. Mercenary. She made out like a jewel thief handed the keys to Tiffany."

She wanted to keep him talking but wasn't sure how far to prod. His voice dipped so heavily with disgust she would have missed the pain riding his words if she hadn't been listening intently. "Ugly divorce? No prenuptial?"

"No battle. She had a generous prenuptial, but that wasn't enough." His hand had curled into a fist while he spoke.

"She wanted custody?" Abbie stroked her fingers along his arm.

Slow to answer, he said, "Only as a negotiating point."

Getting a bone out of a starving dog's mouth was easier than dragging anything out of Hunter about himself. "I don't understand."

"She thought she had a gold-lined womb and my brother and I were fatted calves. She wasn't keen on raising kids, one reason they argued a lot. When she demanded a divorce she threatened to fight for custody. He traveled a lot and knew she had grounds to pull it off even though she couldn't stand us."

She couldn't stand us. Abbie couldn't imagine feeling that way about her mother, but her father must not have liked her from birth to have turned his back on her. "So why did she want custody?"

"Quickest way to add another couple million to her settlement. She told my dad he could pay enough in the divorce for her to hire someone to take care of their two 'pain in the asses' or he could have us for a million each. She sold us in the divorce."

Hunter had told that as if reporting on an enemy.

She asked, "Your dad told you about all that?"

"Didn't have to. Todd and I watched that last fight from the top of the stairs. I was almost seven and he was five."

Good God. No wonder Hunter could be so cold at times. Something had died inside him as a child. She had no words to express her anger at a mother who could do that to her children. "Did your father remarry?"

His hand unclenched and started caressing the sensitive skin along her stomach again. "Three years later, but wife number two had heard about the first one through the tabloids. She built a bonus clause into her prenup for any children. She put on a good show of pretend Mom for about six months, but our mother screwed up Todd so badly he had a violent temper. My dad traveled a lot with business. While Dad was out of town, wife number two convinced him to ship me and Todd off to boarding schools. I wouldn't have hated her for that, but she had us separated. She thought I'd interfere with Todd's discipline because I kept him out of her reach when he pissed her off."

Abbie closed her eyes, trying not to picture Hunter shielding his brother from a second woman. She hated both women who had married their father. Hadn't the second one realized how much those two boys needed a mother? "Why did your dad agree?"

"He'd gotten sucked into believing this woman might really love him. But eight months later she popped up all excited and told Dad she was pregnant. Way I heard it, he asked how that was possible since he'd had a vasectomy before they married. He ran her off and brought us home. Never married again. Can't blame him."

What man would ever trust a woman again after experiecing all that?

A grim thought followed close on the tail of that one.

Hunter might one day love, but would he ever trust a woman?

Clearly not interested in discussing families anymore, he moved his hand down. Nerves prickled every place he touched along her abdomen, then he slipped his hand soundlessly between her legs. That wiped her mind blank of everything except the exquisite yearning he started again.

"I'm ready," she urged.

"Not yet." He nibbled on her neck. His finger pressed inside her.

She hissed. "Yes. I. Am. Ready."

She would not beg. Much.

Hunter laughed. An honest-to-God true laugh. Her heart somersaulted at the rich sound. "Gotta love a woman who demands service."

Her heart tripped at the word *love,* just hearing it from his lips, but he hadn't meant anything by it. He *had* held her all night as if afraid something might tear her from his arms and made her feel cared for.

He'd churned up emotions she'd never thought she'd feel again.

His finger was making her tremble. Her thigh muscles would be jelly by the time they left this room.

"I can't . . . do this." She squirmed, her body pleading for him to take her over the edge.

"We'll see."

A man not to be challenged, he got busy proving her wrong.

His finger danced over her wet folds and teased circles until her body turned on her, demanding she do something.

If only.

He drove her toward that blinding light and dove a finger inside her. She wanted to scream. He kept up the torture, driving his finger deep, then sliding it out on a wet path and brushing across the nub of coiled nerves. The delicate abrasion inched her to the edge every time.

He stopped.

She clawed at the sheets, lifting off the bed, twisting, a coiled ball of need, waiting to spring. "Hunter . . . please . . ."

He repeated the motion . . . not stopping this time.

Light exploded behind her eyes. She shook with the orgasm that went on and on.

He wouldn't let up until every muscle quivered in defeat.

She lay limp, spent. "You're going to kill me."

He rolled her beneath him. "You're perfect. Never doubt it."

Her mind cleared and heard that. She also heard the door to her heart open and let Hunter all the way in.

She never thought she'd meet someone who made her feel cherished, as though she was safe within his arms. He'd accepted her story about why she'd gone to meet Gwen when someone else might have questioned its validity after Gwen got shot. Might have suspected she was involved somehow. He'd protected her from dangerous threats and hadn't demanded the final key to accessing the Kore Women's Center.

He hadn't let anyone put her where she couldn't get to her mother.

Hunter might not ever let a woman inside his heart, but he'd climbed inside hers and was there to stay.

CHAPTER THIRTY-TWO

Sullen gray skies hung low over O'Hare airport in Chicago when Hunter helped Abbie into the backseat of a black corporate sedan identical to the next ten picking up passengers. Thanks to his brother's assistant, the car was waiting when the flight Hunter had chartered under the last name Johnson landed at noon.

"Give me a minute," he told Abbie, who nodded before he closed the door and stepped away after instructing the driver to start the car.

Hunter pressed the number in his new cell phone for his brother, sure by now he'd raised more than a few concerns. The pilot of the jet Hunter had taken the night he and Abbie fled Chicago had very likely relayed a bizarre story to Todd by now.

The call went through and his brother picked up. Hunter said, "I owe you a lot of answers I can't give right now."

A few seconds ticked off while he waited for a reply.

Todd sighed heavily. "Are you okay?"

"I'm fine."

"What about that girl?"

Hunter had to be careful about what he said since Todd's phone wasn't secure. "Everyone's fine. Just

wanted to say thanks and I'll swing by soon as I can."
That might be a very long time, but he did mean it.

"You're always welcome, but I'm not in my apartment right now."

"Where are you?"

"In Pia's place downtown on Wacker. Before you say
anything, listen to me."

Good advice if Hunter could follow it, because anything he said right now would probably piss off Todd.

"The divorce was *both* of our faults. We were hot to
trot for each other, made a baby and got hitched, then
found out it takes more than sex to make a marriage."

"How can you trust her? She got pregnant." Hunter
couldn't hold back. Todd knew how women used children against their husbands and Hunter didn't want to
watch his brother gutted a second time.

"That wasn't her fault." Todd heaved another long
breath. "Not entirely. I didn't use a condom a couple
times, but I was crazy about her . . . the bottom line is
that I really love her and she really loves me. She has no
reason to trust me either. I acted like an ass after we di-
vorced. Not like you and I had much for a marriage role
model. Pia and I just didn't know how to be married,
and my temper didn't help, then Barrett came along.
We're both spoiled to some degree, but we're learning
how to compromise."

"Sure you want to go through this again?" Hunter
heard the sincerity in Todd's voice, but was Pia truly
committed to making this work?

"If you mean having my heart shredded, no." Todd's
good-natured laugh was something Hunter hadn't
heard in a while. "But neither does Pia. She's gone

through hell with this and loves me. I found out from a good friend Pia only pretended to be happy when she was out in public so she wouldn't look like the pathetic loser still in love with her ex-husband. She hasn't seen anyone else since we broke up. Me either. We're going to make this work. We're talking like we never did before and, hell, I'm just so damned happy to be with both of them again."

Hunter finally accepted the contentment and peace he heard in his brother's voice. Todd had been thrilled when he got married, but the divorce had soured him to the point Hunter hated to even hear Pia's name.

He might have misjudged her. He'd never heard Todd speak so passionately about anyone or anything he'd wanted. But his brother clearly wanted his family.

To his credit, he went after them.

"I admire you," Hunter said quietly. What he didn't say was that he envied his brother for carving out a slice of normal life in spite of being a screwed-up Thornton-Payne. Good for Todd.

"Thanks. You need anything else?"

"Nope. I *will* catch up with you, but I've got to take care of some things first." Hunter started to hang up and paused. "Tell Pia I'm happy for both of you."

When Todd hung up, Hunter contacted Gotthard next, but this call would be secure on both ends.

Gotthard answered his cell phone with a cautious, "Yes?"

"It's me. New phone." Hunter put his back to a concrete wall in the parking deck and kept an eye on foot traffic as people dragged carry-on luggage nearby.

"You have trouble?"

Hunter ignored the irritable reply. Gotthard might have had another bad night with his wife. That relationship was tanking fast. "Did Joe send someone to meet me early?"

Gotthard would understand that he was asking if Joe had sent a team to bring Hunter in. "No. He needs you to finish this job." Meaning Joe still wanted Hunter to insert into Kore. "You still good?"

"Sure." If Joe hadn't sent a team, then who had come up Hunter's mountain? "What'd Joe decide? Am I handling all of this or is he inserting a female agent?"

"He said it's your show. You've got eighteen hours. Don't waste it."

Less time than Hunter had hoped for, but he let out a breath he was holding. Joe was leaving the plan for accessing Kore's files in Hunter's hands. "I hear you."

"By oh six hundred. Sooner would be in your favor," Gotthard warned in a clipped tone.

Hunter realized he was hearing more than Gotthard's usual grumpiness. Something to do with this mission bothered the big guy. "We got a problem?"

"Maybe. Our contact hasn't checked in since sending the last missive yesterday. I'm . . . concerned someone might have discovered the connection."

That would suck in more ways than Hunter could count and explained why Joe was letting him enter Kore solo. Hunter was expendable. If Linette got burned as the mole she'd probably face hideous consequences. The minute she gave up her method of contacting Gotthard the Fratelli would use her to track and expose BAD.

"That may not be the case." Hunter hoped he was right. "If the contact is involved in the current

Fratelli operation the contact won't be as free to access a computer if others are around. Just have to be patient."

And hope like hell Linette hadn't been found out.

"That could be." Gotthard still sounded as though he'd been hit in the gut with a telephone pole, but he shifted back to business. "Why'd you ask if Joe sent a team? You have unexpected visitors?"

"Yeah."

"Got an idea who?"

"The list is too long." Hunter joked wryly rather than mention the JC killer since he hadn't told BAD that JC was the attacker he'd confronted at Abbie's. "We'll kick around possibilities later. Gotta roll right now."

"One more thing. We checked out Tatum, that doctor taking care of the Blanton woman's mother. He died early yesterday morning. Police are calling it suicide."

Shit. Couldn't there be one bit of good news for Abbie? "How'd he do it?"

"Looks like drugs. The autopsy will tell, but no note. Tatum lost his wife five months ago and was devoted to raising his two small girls. No suicidal tendencies, no note, but the police found a spoon stuck in the body. It's the JC killer's.

Police don't know what they have. We found a spoon at Abigail Blanton's apartment, too."

"Our boy is getting around."

"Abigail's neck-deep in all this."

Hunter understood the warning from Gotthard—don't get tangled up with Abbie—but he couldn't admit to anyone he was shielding her from BAD as well as the killer. "I'll keep that in mind. Be in touch."

He pocketed the cell phone and climbed in the car next to Abbie. She had on a new pair of jeans and a pink knit top from the several outfits he'd bought her in Gillette, Wyoming, before they took off for Chicago. She'd stuffed her clothes plus a few toiletries in an oversized black canvas shoulder bag.

"Where are we going?" she asked.

He gave her credit for not hounding him all the way there. He'd put in a call to her mom's medical center when they reached Gillette, but her mother had been out of the room having tests. Abbie had deflated at missing the chance to talk to even her sister Hannah. She'd mentioned a second sister, Casey, but just said they weren't on speaking terms.

He'd told her she could try again in Chicago. The police had to be searching for Abbie by now and BAD would have both the medical center and Kore Women's Center under surveillance. If he exposed that he had Abbie, he'd have no chance at catching Eliot's killer or getting into Kore to gain a bargaining chip with Joe. Not if they locked him up. All his training warred against what he'd already put into motion, but every minute they spent on the run could be the last one of Abbie's freedom. "We're going to the medical center to see your mother."

The smile she gave him lit up her whole body. "Thank you."

"But we can't go in through the front doors." Joe's people would grab her the minute they saw her. When she nodded her compliance, Hunter instructed the driver to head to the Oakbrook Shopping Center west of downtown Chicago, where an associate from

Hunter's CIA days waited. Their sedan arrived at the parking area for the mall close to two o'clock.

He directed the driver to park next to an ambulance sitting by itself, then told him, "If we're not back by five return to the office." That gave Hunter three hours. If he and Abbie hadn't returned by then he wouldn't be coming back. Plus, he had a meeting with Kore's senior vice president at four o'clock.

A wiry guy in his thirties with sharp eyes and quick movements climbed down from the ambulance driver's seat and shook hands with Hunter. "Everything's in the back."

"Thanks, Ned." Hunter rushed Abbie and her purse from the sedan to the rear of the ambulance, then Ned shut the doors.

She sat on the gurney and looked around. "We're going in as an emergency? Won't that be a bit high pro-file?" The vehicle started moving. She fell sideways.

"Not going to the emergency entrance." Hunter caught her by the shoulders, righting her, and sat down on the gurney. He leaned down and dug through a duffel, pulling out a maternity top. "Put this on."

"I'm pretending to be *pregnant*?" She eyed him. "What about you?"

"I'm your doctor." He discarded his jeans and the faded green T-shirt came off next, exchanging them for a dark suit hanging on the wall of the truck. The white doctor's coat went on next.

By the time the vehicle parked at the rear of the medical center, he had an ID clipped in place. Abbie had pulled a sleeveless pale yellow maternity top sprinkled with daisies over a long-sleeved white T-shirt that hid a half-round foam piece.

She looked up at him, smiling. His breath caught. She'd make a beautiful mother.

Had Eliot looked at Cynthia and thought that?

Ned opened the back doors, jostling Hunter's thoughts. "Wheelchair's inside."

Hunter jumped down and lifted Abbie to the ground. A short guy with a receding hairline and stained scrubs opened the back entrance for them. For as nonthreatening as the guy appeared, Hunter knew he was not medical personnel but one of Ned's men who had reconned the facility.

Ned gave Hunter directions to the floor for Abbie's mother, then said, "You've got twenty minutes."

"Got it." Hunter ushered Abbie to the wheelchair.

At her mother's room, she pulled the foam piece from under her blouse, dropping it on the chair, then opened the door.

Where the halls had smelled antiseptic, this room reeked of sickness. Her mother had a semiprivate room, but the second bed was currently empty.

Abbie paused. Hunter looked down to find the misery she'd been holding in check clouding her face. They couldn't stay long so he gently pushed her forward. "Go see your mother."

She took a tentative step, then rushed over and carefully hugged her mother, whose eyes didn't open. Tubes ran everywhere and her breathing was shallow. By the yellow tinge of her skin Hunter assumed her liver was still deteriorating.

He hadn't told Abbie about Dr. Tatum's suicide . . . murder. Hadn't wanted her distracted while they got inside.

"Where've *you* been?" a female voice demanded.

He turned toward the doorway, where a woman stood, wearing black pants and a wrinkled cotton shirt a darker brown than her straight hair. Similar to the skinny-looking Abbie he'd orignally met.

"I've been trying to find out what's wrong with Mom, Hannah," Abbie answered.

"Where, pray tell, have you been doing that?" Hannah carried a cup of hospital coffee to a side table and sat it down. "And who's this? He's not Mom's doctor."

"He's *just* a friend. He's helping me," Abbie answered in as snippy a tone as her sister's. "I can't tell you what I'm doing or where I've been, or where I'm going when I leave here, but I *am* working on something that might help Mom."

"Oh, I see, you're doing something investigative and important." Hannah's sarcasm whipped across the room to slap Abbie.

Hunter started to step in, but Abbie pushed past him. "Will you give me a break for once? I probably don't even have a job anymore."

"You don't. I tried calling your office to find you and they said you were terminated." Hannah enjoyed sharing that too much. "If I *could* have found you, it would have been nice to have some help getting Mom a doctor. The new one's so young I'm not sure the ink's dry on his diploma."

Abbie backed up, stunned. "New doctor? What do you mean?"

"Tatum. He committed suicide."

"Oh, my God." Abbie reached for the chair next to her and sat down. "Dear God."

"Yeah, it's the pits," Hannah agreed. "His little girls have lost their mama *and* daddy in the same year." She took a sip, eyeing Hunter. She put the cup down, discarding it along with her catty snarl. "I can't do this alone, Abbie."

"I don't mean for you to, but you have to believe me when I say I'm really close to finding something that might help." Abbie got up and walked over to Hannah. She put her hand on her sister's shoulder. "Can you trust me for once and just believe me? I'll worry about my job once we get Mom turned around. But I need you to stay with her while I'm doing this. I'll come back as soon as I can."

Hannah didn't look convinced. "Where are you going?"

"To see someone Dr. Tatum told me about. Please don't ask, because I don't want to involve you if what I'm doing goes really bad."

Hannah nodded. Her eyes teared up. "They said you were with that Wentworth woman when she got shot."

Abbie swallowed. "Yeah. Is Gwen still alive?"

"Aren't you watching the news?"

"Not really. I've been on the road."

"She's hanging on, stable. Oh, and the police stopped by looking for you. They weren't happy I didn't know where you were. I gave them the message some guy left with the nurses about you traveling." Hannah slashed a glance at Hunter that should have left a mark, then her eyes lit with a sudden revelation. "A guy came here looking for you."

Hunter checked his watch. They had to go, but Hannah had raised his interest. "Who?"

Her sister glared silently until Abbie told her it was okay to tell him. "He didn't leave his name. Said he was a friend of Abbie's from the television station and wanted to get in touch, but he didn't even have a card. Wore sunshades he wouldn't take off. I hate to talk to anyone when I can't see their eyes. He said he couldn't go without glasses. He had a blood birthmark right here." She pointed above her right eye at her forehead. "Ring any bells?"

"No." Abbie looked at Hunter, who told Hannah, "The less you say about Abbie being here the safer it is for her."

That alarmed her sister. "Is she in danger?"

Hunter hated to pull Abbie away, but they had to go. "Abbie, it's time."

"For what?" Hannah said, and stepped up beside Abbie, putting her arm protectively around her.

Abbie hugged her sister. "I'm okay, but he's right. Keep a lid on my visit. He's helping me get what we need. I hope to find out something today or tomorrow."

Hannah hugged her sister back, then Abbie went over and kissed her mother's cheek before reaching Hunter's side. Pain and worry wicked through her gaze, but she soldiered up, ready to go.

He turned her toward the door as it opened. A half-put-together-looking young woman with long wavy brown hair and pudgy cheeks entered wearing burgundy corduroy pants and a gray sweatshirt. She stopped the minute she saw Abbie. "You finally managed to fit Mom into your busy schedule?"

"Get out of my way, Casey."

This had to be the younger sister. She gave Hunter an up-and-down perusal. "He's not Mom's new physician, so what's going on? You using this place for hunting grounds?" Her lips twisted in a sour frown; she was clearly trying to embarrass Abbie.

Hunter considered several ways to put this mean-hearted sibling in her place. That would only undermine Abbie, whose shoulders slumped, but her voice didn't waver when she replied.

"How's the pig, Casey? Caught him sleeping with any relatives lately?"

Hunter put everything together when she referenced the "pig" who she'd indicated had thought he was trading up to a newer model "without pesky morals." Abbie had caught her fiancé sleeping with her *sister*.

Not so clichéd as she'd joked bitterly this morning.

They had to go and he was damned tired of seeing Abbie attacked. He put his arm around her. "Ready, sweetheart?"

Casey's mouth fell open at the endearment.

He kissed the top of Abbie's head and led her out. She didn't say a word all the way to the ambulance. Once they were inside the vehicle again and moving, Hunter's cell phone buzzed. No one should have had this number, but he wasn't overly surprised to find Gotthard on the other end when he answered.

"Got something you need to hear before you go into Kore," Gotthard started in. "Tatum took a drug that induces cardiac arrest. The police now question Tatum's suicide and are trying to figure out what the killer's spoon means. They've tied the spoon to the ones found at Gwen's home and the Blanton woman's apartment. The only common thread is Abigail. The authorities haven't gone public with anything but the FBI is avidly searching for her."

Hunter closed his eyes. Fuck.

CHAPTER THIRTY-THREE

"Hunter, you getting all this?" Gotthard snapped. "Abigail is a suspect in Gwen's shooting. We *have* to talk to her first."

"I hear you." Hunter moved over to the end of the gurney so Abbie wouldn't hear much above the rumble of the ambulance motor. "What else do they have?"

"That Gwen's security saw Abigail upset Gwen enough for her to leave the party, and one of them overheard Abigail tell Gwen she would *only* talk outdoors, somewhere private. Gwen's patio was an obvious location. The shooter had to know she'd be there and in position for that shot."

"That's not definitive," Hunter argued, sounding too defensive of Abbie. But something that had been said in Abbie's apartment after the shooting started making noises in the back of his mind.

The killer told Abbie she'd been most helpful.

"There's more. Abigail works for a television station in Chicago. The station manager said she blackmailed him into letting her replace the female journalist assigned to the Wentworth party. That was *after* he'd offered her a promotion as his assistant and a raise."

Everything Gotthard said slammed up against Hunter's image of Abbie as anything but a conniving female with an agenda. He looked at her leaned back on the gurney, lost in sad thoughts. She couldn't be playing him. Something would have given her away by now. "We know anything about her boss?"

"He's not well liked by some at the station, but he is dating a board member's granddaughter, who confirmed she gave up the ticket and went to New York with him."

"That all the police have?"

"No. Remember the accidental deaths from the files our contact sent about women with rare blood who did not enter the Kore center? Abigail's stepfather, who adopted her, died eleven years ago. She went to see her father just before he died. He drowned in a lake on his farm with no history of mental problems and in perfect health. It was listed as a suicide, but our people reviewed the autopsy report and aren't buying that."

"Why?" Hunter squeezed his fingers around the frame of the gurney next to his leg.

"Her adoptive father had been on a high school swim team. He broke a state record for swimming a mile. No history of depression. He had a pig farm and everyone who came in contact with him the week before his death said he was excited his daughter was coming to visit. That fits the type of peculiar accidental deaths in the file we're building on the women with rare blood." Typing pecked through the phone speaker when Gotthard paused, then he said, "Here's a side note. She was living just a couple miles from the area where you and I dealt with that little problem six years ago."

The night before Hunter met Abbie, when six men died, not one of them worth mourning. "Really?"

Gotthard paused, waited on something, then continued. "Abigail's the only one who can answer some of these questions. Gwen can't be interrogated. She's under lockdown inside the Kore Center. Supposedly, she hasn't regained consciousness."

"Could be a lie to keep Gwen from talking to anyone."

Abbie glanced over at Hunter at the mention of Gwen, then turned away to stare at nothing.

"Could be." In classic Gotthard mode, he jumped to a new topic. "The prime minister's arriving Saturday in Denver and is speaking at a university there on Monday, then he meets the president in DC on Tuesday. If we haven't figured this out by Monday afternoon, Joe will be forced to alert the president of a possible assassination attempt. We have to plan for a bombing as well, based on what our contact has been sending us."

"Hard to pull off an attack of that magnitude in DC," Hunter interjected. "Not with that much security climbing all over the place. But we can't rule out the possibility."

"True. The last thing we can afford is for the prime minister to be harmed while he's here with the bad blood that has grown between him and the president. The best lead we have right now on finding the JC killer is inside the Kore center."

Getting to the records without being spotted was going to be a Houdini act, but Hunter had no other options.

Gotthard added, "Got another hit on the JC spoon. New location."

"Where?"

"Home in the mountain range between Montana and Wyoming. Looked like an army with automatic weapons turned it into Swiss cheese. Know anything about that?"

"Why would I?" Hunter answered noncommittally.

Gotthard held his reply for a few seconds, no doubt getting his answer from Hunter's lack of one. "Sure you know what you're doing?"

"Yes." He lied to himself as much as Gotthard with that one.

"Trusting the wrong person right now could put you so far outside our reach we wouldn't be able to help you, or it might force Joe to . . . it could get you killed."

"Just doing my job," Hunter said. Admit nothing.

Gotthard chuckled wryly. "Right. For the record, you don't look any more like a doctor than Mako does, but he has the MD to go with the white coat."

Busted. "Guess I should have been surprised at *not* seeing familiar faces today." As in BAD agents around the medical center.

"Joe wants a good reason not to snatch her from you."

"She's the only way into the Kore records," Hunter whispered. He had no intention of putting Abbie in the middle of all this, but he'd just given Joe a valid reason to stay out of Hunter's way until he got the data they needed.

"I should have given you more credit," Gotthard said, indicating he now thought Hunter was using Abbie.

Of course the people who had known him the longest believed he would put a woman at risk to find this killer and get the data. They thought he'd cut Eliot's climbing rope.

He glanced at Abbie, who must have felt his eyes. She smiled at him and his heart swelled. She hadn't told him everything. Was there any way the killer was manipulating her?

Gotthard continued. "We need every bit of intel we can get our hands on before Saturday. Joe needs your skills, but this operation requires everyone working like a team."

"I'm doing my part getting inside Kore."

"Keeping Blanton away from us isn't team thinking. Careful who you stake your life—and national security—on. Women have exploited men for centuries. Arrogance is our biggest weakness. Well, that and our cocks."

Hunter had never allowed a woman to fool him on an operation. Was Abbie that good? Had he been so sure of his skill at reading people he'd let her convince him she needed protecting and that she'd wanted him last night as much as he wanted her?

Still wanted her. Wrong brain talking again.

Gotthard had a point and Eliot would have agreed, based on the evidence presented, then told Hunter to flip it around and use cold objectivity. Had getting involved with Abbie caused him to overlook a potential threat?

"Don't make a mistake," Gotthard emphasized. "You'll only get one."

"I figured as much." Hunter ended the call, but he couldn't ignore a new question Gotthard's call had raised. The JC killer had taken a team up the mountain to Hunter's cabin. Had the killer placed a tracking device on Abbie? She was wearing all new clothes by the time she reached the cabin. Except for her underwear—and Hunter could personally attest to the fact that nothing was hidden on either of those slim pieces of material—which she'd left at the cabin.

When he'd heard her talking in her apartment before the confrontation with the intruder, he'd thought she'd been on the phone with someone at first or just talking to herself. Back when they first met, she'd told him how she talked to her plants but they still die on her. He tried to take a step back now and review everything that had happed with unbiased eyes. Play the devil's advocate.

Abbie had been surprised when she found the transmitter Hunter stuck on her dress before she entered her apartment building, but what if she'd actually found it while talking to the JC killer and switched gears to put on a show by acting terrified? If so, she would have had the tracking device on her at the point Hunter had carried her out of the apartment. Where would she have hidden a transmitter . . .

Son of a bitch. He hadn't done a cavity search, but he'd had no reason to do so and a woman had the perfect place to slide a transmitter the size of a small tube up inside her.

His gut argued none of that fit Abbie, that she couldn't be an operative, but as Gotthard had pointed out Hunter was putting a lot of lives on the line based solely on what she'd told him.

He worked with some of the best female agents on the planet. But what about their meeting six years ago?

No, that had been entirely by accident because he'd completed a mission so close to where she lived.

His forte was making logical decisions on a second's notice and executing with brutal efficiency. No hesitation.

In his line of work, hesitation got people killed.

If Abbie was innocent she should have straight answers.

If not? He'd depend on his training to guide his decisions at that point and not allow some undefined emotion that was turning his gut inside out to influence him.

He looked over at her. "We need to talk."

Abbie barely heard Hunter over the rumble of the ambulance. She stopped worrying about her mother and started worrying about his lifeless tone. What had his phone call been about? She sat up. "Okay."

His face gave away nothing, but she could feel the vast space opening up between them. "You told me a friend got you into the Wentworth event as a favor. Who?"

She glanced away, then realized how telling that would be and met his gaze. "Just a girl from work."

"You didn't blackmail your boss to get inside the fund-raiser?"

Crud. What had Stuart told the police? "What are you getting at?"

"The truth. Did you or did you not blackmail your boss to get that invitation?"

"Okay, fine. Stuart Trout is a dirtbag. He wouldn't do me one simple favor. I told him getting into the Wentworth event was very important to me."

"This same dirtbag had just offered you a better position and more money, right?"

"Yes, but what's that got to do with anything?"

"Just confirming details."

Hunter's guarded attitude surprised her. "I told you everything about that night. I had to pressure Stuart or I wouldn't have gotten to talk to Gwen."

"You threatened to tell his girlfriend he'd been involved with you?"

"No, I threatened to tell Brittany he made a pass at me if he didn't help. He's a slimeball I wouldn't let touch my dead philodendron."

The oddest moment of relief filtered through the suspicion holding his gaze hostage and gave her hope until Hunter asked, "How'd your father die?"

She flinched at the unexpected change of topic. "He drowned. Suicide."

"But he was an excellent swimmer, right?"

"Yes." What had Hunter found out about her father's death?

"Doesn't that sound suspicious?"

Yes. She'd spent many sleepless nights wondering if she was at fault for Raymond's death. She had no idea why Hunter was acting as though they were on opposite sides of a wall all of a sudden. "I questioned everything about his death from the beginning, but everyone said I was looking for a way to justify an accident. I harangued the police for over a year, but they all blew me off, accusing me of being in denial. That's the reason I got into investigative reporting, but nothing ever came of all my efforts to prove he hadn't killed himself. His life insurance company had no investment in helping. No one did. The only reason I finally left it alone was because his death had devastated my family and I kept reopening the wound."

Hunter stopped there, staring at her as if he tried to decide if he knew her. That hurt much more than she could have imagined. She asked, "What's going on with you?"

"How did the guy in your apartment know your name?"

"I told you, I don't know. Before you got there he said I did a good job. I don't know what he was talking about. Do you?"

"I can't say."

"You mean you won't say. I've told you everything—"

"Except for the final key to accessing the Kore database."

"So now you're going to strongarm me into this by acting suspicious of . . . what exactly are you suspicious about?"

This time Hunter was the one who looked away while he thought on something. When he lifted his head his eyes were filled with an emotion she couldn't pinpoint. "You have to understand, Abbie. A lot of lives depend on how well I do my job. I can't let anything but facts influence my decisions."

"What do you think I'm guilty of?"

"I'm not accusing you—"

"Just tell me what's going on, dammit." She was reaching the end of her frayed emotional rope.

"I can't. Not yet."

There it was. She ran headfirst against that steel-wall gaze born of a distrust that had started in childhood. She understood why, really, she did, but that didn't change how much it cut for him to draw an invisible line between them. He probably didn't like standing all alone on the other side of that line, but that might be the only safe haven he'd come to trust.

She wanted him to know he could depend on her.

Screaming in frustration probably wouldn't get that message across, but her insides were on a rampage.

Abbie drew up her knees and leaned forward, propping her head on her crossed arms. "You're making it sound like forcing my slimy boss to help me get into the Wentworths' was a felony, that I had something to do with my father's death, and that I know the crazy guy in my apartment."

He seemed content to hear her out, so she continued. "Here's the truth. If my mother hadn't been ill I wouldn't have risked my career by threatening my boss for an invitation to the event or badgering a Wentworth on her own property. If you hadn't been there snooping around, you wouldn't have gotten involved in Gwen's shooting. If you hadn't driven me home and broken into my apartment you wouldn't have known about the intruder, but I *will* be eternally grateful that you did come back. I don't know what's going on or why people are chasing us or why that guy knew my name. All I know is that my mother is dying and I need your help. I'm going to give you all the access information for the database. Not because I feel threatened, but because I believe in you. I trust you. What are you going to do?"

Hunter's stone face had given nothing away while she spoke. She knew he was inside that protective shell and that this might be her only chance to reach him.

He scratched his nose, a ploy to allow him another minute to think. "I'm offering the Kore center a substantial donation based on a tour I'll take at four today. If I get into the files, I'll download everything on your mother. And arrange for a medical team to treat her, too."

She wished that was all it would take to make everything in her world right, but Hunter had been talking to someone about her and she was pretty sure it had to do with the police. "And you'll let me go to my mother once you have the files, right?"

His elbows were propped on his knees. He dropped his chin down on his clasped hands and wouldn't look at her. "I can't."

"Why?"

"Lot of questions need answering first."

"I see." Not really, but if she said more right now her voice might break. He was going to hand her off to strangers after all.

"We're running out of time. Tell me what I need for the code. I'll put you somewhere safe while I'm inside."

He isn't going to like this. "To access a family file the patient must be hooked to a unit that takes an immediate fingerprint and pricks the skin for a blood sample within one minute of entering the patient and a staff code to access the database. You can't get into anything without *me*."

CHAPTER THIRTY-FOUR

Hunter waited inside the sedan, watching Abbie walk into the front doors of the Kore Women's Center in southwest Chicago. Once she convinced him there was no way to breach the computer system without her, he'd called Kore an hour ago and let Abbie speak to the staff to arrange for her admission.

Simpler than ordering a hamburger at McDonald's for a woman with a rare blood type who was already in Kore's files and willing to donate blood.

"Park across the street at that pharmacy and angle the car so I can watch the entrance to Kore," Hunter told the driver, a longtime Thornton-Payne employee who chauffeured for Hunter's father and Todd. One of the two drivers who could be trusted not to speak of anything that went on during a drive.

Hunter kept an eye on the entrance, fighting to stay in the car and not rush inside to keep Abbie in sight.

He thought he might never get over the look of shock on her face when he questioned her. She couldn't have been more hurt if he'd backhanded her.

Her answers could be construed as suspicious if he wanted to lump Abbie in with all the women he'd known.

She was in a category all her own. His gut told him so.

What was he going to do with her after he got the files out of Kore?

Gotthard's warnings pounded in the silence, but Hunter couldn't make himself believe she was involved with the killer. He should have told her so before she stepped out of the car, should have kissed her to let her know the last thing he wanted to do was hurt her.

Instead, he'd sat unmovable as a rock, unable to give her words of comfort. Gotthard's intel had clouded his ability to see beyond the mission.

Abbie had pulled back after the questions, unwilling to let him touch her in any way, not even to help her from the ambulance to the sedan when they reached the parking lot. He'd refused to consider her suggestion that she pretend to be ill so he could stay once she was admitted. He'd been too angry at the idea of having to let her enter unprotected to realize he was slamming door after door between them.

Her silence should have been warning enough. She finally just listened to his instructions on how to contact him if she had any problem, nodding in reply. He'd kept up a steady monologue, trying not to let his face show how the pain scarring her eyes shredded his insides.

He avoided the topic humming between them like an angry wasp with no place to land.

She had trusted him not to hand her over to strangers and he'd wrecked that trust when he told her she couldn't go to her mother after they left Kore. God knows he didn't want to hand her over.

He'd never wanted to keep anything more than he wanted to keep Abbie, but more than that he didn't want her harmed.

Which was why he hadn't wanted her inside Kore tonight, but she'd trumped his moves with needing her blood to access the database. She'd pressed her point by reminding him she'd be safe with Kore's tight security.

Abbie would walk into a burning building if that's what it took to keep someone dear to her alive.

She loved without restraint.

What would it feel like to be loved that way?

Was that what Eliot had felt for Cynthia? Cynthia hadn't dated since Eliot died, living quietly with her son.

Had she loved Eliot just as fiercely?

Hunter scrubbed his hand over his face, wiping away things he couldn't be cluttering his mind with right now. His eyes strayed to his watch, which refused to help by moving any quicker. Three more minutes until he could walk into Kore.

Abbie was safe in there. No men walked around.

No windows on the first floor. The closest buildings were two-story office complexes.

Where was that killer? Hunter had decided Abbie was telling the truth. She didn't know this psycho, which was why he had to figure out how the killer knew her. The JC killer had left his mark at four places tied to Abbie now that the Montana cabin had been added to the list. How had the killer found Hunter's place that fast?

He needed Gotthard's computer skills and Rae Graham's puzzle-solving ability. If he hadn't gone off the reservation hunting this killer he'd have their help and the full power of BAD behind him.

His watch alarm beeped. Hunter told the driver, "Drive me to the door."

When the car reached the curb, Hunter straightened his jacket and stepped out, pausing long enough to tell the driver, "That's all I need for tonight."

He didn't know how he was going to stay inside Kore all night to watch over her and access the computer system, but he was not leaving Abbie until they released her tomorrow morning.

CHAPTER THIRTY-FIVE

Jackson finished carving another titanium spoon with a laser cutter and eyed the piece for any flaws.

None. Testing the needle-sharp point of the three horns on the Jackson's Chameleon head at the end of the spoon handle was tempting, but that would be dangerous.

He put the spoon down, lifted a terry cloth to wipe his hands, and walked upstairs in the temporary apartment in downtown Chicago he'd taken for a month. He walked past the windows of the luxury unit facing Wacker Drive and eyed boat traffic moving along the Chicago River twelve stories down. Jackson consulted his watch. Closing in on seven. The city would hum with nightlife soon.

Sitting down at his laptop, he clicked on the website he checked twice daily for a new image. When he'd viewed the site this morning it had still displayed sixteen photos of the Brown family in Austin. Snapshots of kids, dogs, and parties in suburbia. The bogus Brown family.

The photo of a rabbit running around a toy-decorated lawn had been added since this morning.

A new image loaded up, signaled that an electronic file had been added to the backside of the website.

Jackson opened the secret file with instructions for him to be in Boulder, Colorado this weekend to receive instructions on a hit that would start a chain reaction of bomb detonations. He scanned quickly and slowed at the side note reminding him what he was to do if caught. To take extreme measures before subjecting himself to interrogation.

He shook his head at the insult. Caught?

If that happened he had a plan. He lifted a pinky into view, eyeing how the nail was an eighth of an inch longer than the others and sharp as a razor. The metal implant had been painted to look as natural as the others.

He had only to slice his wrist.

Reading further through his instructions, he located authorization for each necessary death, a Fratelli reference. He could understand why the Fratelli had such limiting rules when it came to dealing with an organization made up of humans who couldn't be left to their own decision-making.

But Jackson didn't care for limitations on a job.

No matter what, he'd fulfill his duty.

He smiled over being green-lighted to terminate Abbie, then frowned at the reminder that he could not terminate the operative protecting her.

The Fratelli wanted to first find out who the operative was working for.

Why did it matter?

Jackson smoothed his hand over the slick skin on his head. His Chinese masters had removed every hair from his body, creating a perfect killing machine that left no DNA. The Fratelli should trust his training. Why would the identity of the operative shielding Abigail matter? CIA, FBI, Homeland Security, mercenary contractor . . . the list could go on and on. Did the

Fratelli expect to identify every undercover operator?

Termination prevented problems created by loose ends.

Jackson could *not* allow Abbie's protector to live. Survival depended on never leaving a loose end and he never brought anyone in alive. That created complications no one wanted.

Jackson had not been trained for intelligence gathering.

He'd been trained since birth to kill.

Had taken a baby spoon from his chest of possessions before he turned eight, sharpened the handle, and performed his first kill—an instructor who had bested Jackson in an exercise.

The satisfaction of proving himself with the unnecessary kill had been worth the discipline he received—a painful beating, though it did not break his skin—but he never broke the rules again.

The other nine boys who trained with him fell into line much more quickly. Jackson understood the need for order. Without discipline there was chaos. What the other nine did not figure out was how to function within the scope of Fratelli rules.

His superior never questioned an accidental death, because Jackson was a strategist as much as a killer. He knew the goal for each mission and made sure any deaths—sanctioned or accidental—supported the plan.

He would deliver the necessary deaths.

As for those not authorized?

If someone were to choose death over life to protect another person, who was Jackson to stand in his way?

Time to visit the Kore Women's Center.

CHAPTER THIRTY-SIX

~~

Abbie tried to think about anything but the blood running out of her arm. She swore she could smell her blood.

Focus on the landscape print hanging on the wall. Not on how much she wished Hunter was here. She wished she could smell him when she closed her eyes. But she was the one who had said she felt safe enough inside the Kore Women's Center.

She hoped Hunter figured out how to stay inside tonight, hoped the police didn't put a notice out on the news that would alert someone here, hoped they could break into the files . . . the list grew hourly.

More than anything, she hoped Hunter would find a way to believe in her. The drive over to the Kore center had been private with the security glass up, but she and Hunter might as well have been two strangers talking. She could let a lot of things pass and assign his cautious behavior to being some kind of undercover agent, but she still had a hard time getting past the feeling of betrayal. He was going to hand her off to his people or law enforcement.

Still, she didn't want to leave things the way they were when she walked away from him.

"All done." The ID badge on the nurse working on

her left for the past hour said Leigh something. Leigh pulled the needle from Abbie's arm and covered the hole with cotton and a Band-Aid.

"What time is it?" Had to be dark by now, but Abbie had lost track of time since entering this windowless building.

"Just about eight." Leigh moved efficiently, polyvinyl gloves on her long fingers. Her white turtleneck and peach-colored scrubs were crisp and neat. Much like her perfect shoulder-length auburn hair and straight bangs. Not a voluptuous female, but she'd been kind and hadn't hurt Abbie when she stuck her. "I'll give you crackers and juice. When you think you can eat more I'll order your dinner."

Would the Kore center's food be any better than that at her mother's medical center? Abbie bet Hunter wasn't eating in the cafeteria. He was supposed to have toured the facility with a senior vice president, then discussed the donation over dinner.

She didn't care what he ate and shouldn't be missing him after the way he'd questioned her, but she did miss him.

"Here's your apple juice and crackers." Leigh placed both on the tray, then stayed busy tidying the room. "I'm leaving soon to meet with my knitting group. We make blankets for the Kore's nursery center."

She chattered on in her high-pitched voice while Abbie crunched crackers and drank juice from a plastic cup. Pale skin along Leigh's arm peeked out between the long sleeve of her scrub top and the polyvinyl gloves on her hands. Her face looked narrow behind funky oversized eyeglasses tinted a dark shade.

Donating blood after two extremely stressful days was hammering Abbie. She blinked against a wave of dizziness. Exhaustion pulled at her. She drank the rest of her juice.

"We go on yarn-buying trips." Leigh continued in a monotone, then looked over at Abbie and smiled. "You're looking wrung out. Let me ease your bed back so you can rest. You'll feel better soon."

Abbie tried to focus on the woman's mouth, because Leigh had a quirky smile she tried to place. Abbie's eyes drooped. She wasn't sleepy so much as lethargic. Her muscles didn't want to listen to her brain telling them to hold the cup. Her head ached. The cup slipped from her fingers.

Leigh's smile reminded her of . . .

Abbie heard the plastic bounce against the floor from a distance . . . couldn't hold on . . . had to go to sleep.

"We don't normally allow patients who come in for routine tests and blood donation to have visitors, Mr. Thornton-Payne," Dr. Lewis Hart, the senior vice president in charge of funding for the Kore Women's Center, explained.

Hunter didn't slow his pace, forcing Hart to continue toward Abbie's room. The damn dinner had taken longer than he'd intended. Abbie had been here for over four hours and he wanted to see her now. "I realize that, Dr. Hart, but I'm considering another donation as well."

Dr. Hart looked over with subdued interest. "Oh?"

"I didn't want to mention this yet until I had a chance to share what I've learned about your facility with my family, but I'm considering a trust fund for your prenatal area. To help with high-risk births."

"What a splendid idea!"

"I have to admit some curiosity though. I understand the point of this being a women's center, but you have the premier research facility for rare blood types. I'm surprised you don't also treat male children with rare blood types. Don't you run across those?"

"Absolutely. We have a small wing for the few males we bring in to study and those who store blood, especially if their blood matches their mother's. But that area is separate from the central building. We feel it's a more comfortable arrangement for our female patients." Hart guided Hunter around a corner. "Ms. Blanton is down this hall, but please stay no more than a half hour."

"Sure." Hunter would figure out what to do in a half hour.

The sound of clipped footsteps approaching from the opposite end of the hallway drew his attention.

A doctor led the stampede of medical personnel rushing forward.

Dr. Hart mumbled, "Must be an emergency."

That's when Hunter heard a high-pitched alarm. Abbie. He started running toward the staff, who turned into a room.

"Mr. Thornton-Payne, stay back," Hart called from behind.

Hunter shoved the door open behind the emergency team.

Abbie lay still as death with a bloodless face.

His eyes shot to the machines that monitored the patient's vital signs. The universal bouncing EKG line that indicated if someone was dead or alive had slowed to a tiny bounce, losing strength with each weak beat.

The world closed in on him until he heard nothing but a nurse's shout. "She's coding!"

CHAPTER THIRTY-SEVEN

Hunter paced the hall outside Abbie's room, waiting for the doctor to come out and give him her status. No one had come up with why she'd coded. Yet.

The only reason he wasn't in her room right now was to avoid distraction from saving her. Chaos had erupted when he started roaring at everyone to do something right that fucking minute.

Kore Women's Center's security had shown up.

Dr. Hart intervened to allow Hunter to remain in the hallway. Good thing or Hart would have needed two more beds for the pair of security guards.

Hart stood to one side, blanched with shock, no doubt believing he was watching the generous Thornton-Payne donation offered at dinner disintegrate with each pound of Hunter's boot heels against the polished tile.

Hunter scrubbed his hand through his hair, tense as a tiger stalking prey. His palms were never sweaty like this. Only one time before.

When Eliot dangled from a rope with a knife in his hand.

Hunter closed his eyes for a minute, then blinked, clearing that image so he could focus on Abbie. He'd let her come in here to help him access the database. He'd allowed his anger and suspicion to blind him to danger and let her walk in here thinking she'd somehow failed him.

That was wrong. He'd failed her. If he got her out of here alive he wouldn't let her down again.

And if this bunch saved her he'd build them a new wing. When would the doctor come out? They'd had enough time.

Hunter turned toward the door.

Hart tensed. Kore better send the best security they had and plenty of them. Hunter was going into Abbie's room.

The door opened and a haggard-looking doctor with gray hair and a slender build came out, face strained from the battle he'd fought. Hunter's chest constricted, steel bands tightening with each breath.

"She's stable," the doctor said. "She flatlined, but we got her back. Took a little longer to bring her blood pressure up to an acceptable level."

She flatlined. She died. Good God.

"Why? What happened to her?"

"We don't know yet."

"I need to see her." Hunter didn't give a damn how raw his voice sounded.

The doctor looked over at Hart, who nodded. "Of course."

Two more technicians came out. One wheeled a cart filled with equipment out the door, then Hunter entered.

A plump blond-haired woman in scrubs and thick nurse shoes wrote notes on a clipboard. She swung around at his entrance. "She's not awake yet."

He nodded but didn't move.

Hard to tell which was whiter, Abbie's face or the pillow under her head and the sheet covering her. He wanted to hold her, to feel life moving through her. The machines taking her vital signs beeped happily with a steady rhythm, but he needed to touch her to convince himself she was going to be okay.

His heart beat out of control. He'd almost lost her. Almost lost the one thing that meant more than life to him. She'd started climbing inside him the first time her laugh snuck past his barriers to touch him. Somehow she'd breached his best defense and wrapped her fingers around his heart.

He couldn't imagine living without her.

What a time to figure that out.

"Let me finish up, then you can come over here," the nurse told him. She turned to a lightweight laptop unit set up next to Abbie's bed.

He took in a deep breath and ran a hand over his hair. He could handle waiting a few more minutes now that Abbie was breathing and her heart beat at a stable pace.

No database information was worth losing her.

The nurse's typing jarred his thoughts, reminding him why Abbie had taken this risk. She expected him to get her mother's records. He shook himself mentally. Don't let her down now. If he left with nothing else, he was getting her mother's medical records. Easing the small computer shaped to resemble an iPhone from his pocket, he pulled up a program that would lift everything the nurse was typing on her laptop.

Like her staff access code.

And he wanted to find out if a treatment had induced Abbie's near death.

"That should do it." The nurse gave the machines registering Abbie's vitals stern scrutiny, nodded to herself, and walked over to where Hunter stood. "I'll be back to check on her, but if you need anything just press that red button on the control box by her bed. Dr. Hart sent an electronic directive that you not be bothered other than visual checks. Ms. Blanton's vital registration is set on high alert for any significant change."

Hunter nodded and pulled his hand from his pocket, where he'd deposited the miniature computer before she turned around. Once the nurse left, he moved to the side of Abbie's bed and reached his hand to her face. His fingers shook.

She'd died an hour ago.

He smoothed his hand over her skin, which was warm and soft. The ache in his chest eased. He could breathe again.

"Mr. Thornton-Payne—" It was Hart.

Hunter didn't turn around. "As soon as Abbie can be moved, she's going to a facility where I can be with her. I'm *not* leaving until then."

"That's not necessary. You're welcome to stay as long as you wish. Just let us know if you need anything. I assure you she'll receive the best medical care here—"

Hunter lifted his hand to silence Hart's rambling.

The door swept open and closed.

He eased his hip onto the bed, needing to be closer to her. To do a better job of protecting her.

Had someone at Kore given Abbie a treatment that caused this? That made no sense unless the person who did so had no idea Hunter was coming to see Abbie before he left. Why take that risk here? Did this have something to do with Gwen?

What if no one was responsible . . . except Abbie?

She'd suggested she fake a sickness to see if he'd be allowed to stay. Had she tried something that got out of control?

She hadn't faked coding.

Her color improved as her blood pressure continued to rise. He breathed in her soft fragrance. She smelled . . . alive.

Lifting her hand in his, he held her cool fingers, willing her to come back to him.

⸻

Abbie woke up slowly in a queasy drugged state she couldn't place the reason for feeling. Her chest ached as if someone had used her for a war drum. The inside of her mouth tasted like cardboard.

She squinted against the light until her eyes focused.

Hunter came into view. He held her hand sandwiched between his.

Her heart wiggled in a happy dance until she took in the faraway look on his face. She wanted to hug him and wipe away the sadness curving his shoulders. Why did her mind pick this moment to throw up warnings? Hunter had questioned what she'd told him. He planned to hand her over to strangers.

So why the downcast eyes? Was he putting on a show of concern for the medical staff?

Wait. How could he be here, without any doctors or nurses?

She mumbled, "Thought they wouldn't let you stay."

Hunter's eyes shot to her with a sudden flash of relief. "How you doing?" He leaned down and kissed her lips so sweetly she was in heaven, happy for those few seconds until he moved away to kiss her forehead.

Tears welled up at his tenderness, but she would not show that weakness. Not to someone she shouldn't trust as much as she did.

When he lifted his head, he stared at her as if he couldn't get enough in one look.

She wanted to believe that, but . . .

"I'm tired," she said. "Don't know why when I just woke up." Her throat was dry. She coughed. "Can I have—"

He was up grabbing a glass of water before she finished. "I'll help you." He raised the bed so she could sip.

When she finished, he put the cup aside and sat down facing her, taking her hand again. Her heart fluttered blissfully at the contact, but she wasn't going to rush down that road a second time and have a head-on collision with his distrust. "So how'd you get in here?"

"I changed their minds, or rather you did."

"Me? What'd I do?"

"You don't remember your blood pressure dropping?"

She lifted her hand and rubbed her head, reorienting herself. "I gave blood, then the nurse gave me crackers and juice . . . that's all I remember."

Hunter studied her a minute. "I toured the facility with Dr. Hart, then went to dinner. By the time I finally got him to bring me back I convinced him to let me say hello to you. We were coming down the hall when the medical team rushed into your room."

"Why?"

Hunter's throat moved with a swallow. "Your blood pressure dropped until you flatlined."

Oh, shit. "You're kidding." She'd been touched at seeing the flash of worry in his face, but now his flinty eyes hardened.

"No. I'm not kidding." His gaze wavered with something dark and frightening when he spoke just above a whisper. "I'm getting you out of here. Now."

"No!" She started to talk, then glanced around, up at the ceiling, then at him.

He nodded, catching her concern about being heard, and swung around beside her. She scooted over to make room. Before he sat back, he lifted her into his arms, careful of the wire running to the machine.

Her head spun at the change, but she gripped his muscled arms for stability. She wanted to sink into his warmth, to savor the way he held her close, but he'd set the rules for this engagement before they entered Kore.

Hunter didn't trust her. At all.

She was determined to earn that trust, but carefully.

Leaning toward him, she kept her voice down to shield what she said. "They haven't run any tests on me yet so we still have time. You might be able to forget about what you need from Kore, but I'm not leaving until I have my mother's records. We had an agreement."

He put his hand on the back of her head and held her closer, cheek to cheek. "Not if you're in danger. I never meant for you to be harmed."

Warmth curled in her heart at that, but he hadn't

said he believed her innocent of any wrongdoing. He hadn't said she mattered, only that he felt guilty over what happened to her.

Suffering guilt did not equal caring for her.

Or trusting her.

Hunter wouldn't intentionally hurt a woman, but he'd made it clear she was on her own once this was over. His tune hadn't changed. She'd maintain a working relationship with him and ensure he followed through on his part. "This is our only chance at this database, so let's stick to our deal."

He held her a minute, then sighed. "Let's make this fast."

"How are we going to access their system?"

"I saw how to do it after watching them work on you earlier. Before you almost . . . before they threw me out."

His hands had tightened on her waist when he'd said "work on you earlier." She dug back into her memory and stalled again at the juice and crackers. Had something in the juice made her sick?

Had someone tried to kill her? That scared her to her toes, but she was too close to leave without her mother's information.

"What about a computer?" she whispered, and inhaled the scent of warm male. She'd have known his scent if she was blindfolded and had to pick him out of a hundred men. If she closed her eyes she could shut out the world and still smell the lingering scent of their intimacy from this morning.

She already missed that intimacy. How had things gone so incredibly bad in a few hours?

"I've got a computer," he whispered. "There's a port next to your bed they used to access your files when you got sick. I haven't found anything to indicate there's a video feed from this room so if we keep our voices down we should be fine." Lowering her gently to the pillow, he pulled out the black unit that looked like an iPhone.

His thumbs moved as fast as a sewing machine needle running wide open, tapping the face of his gadget. From a pocket inside his suit, he produced a thin wire with an odd three-sided plug like some sort of universal attachment, which he used to connect his black electronic unit to the wall port.

When he leaned down toward her face, she had the quick hope he was going to kiss her.

But he moved his mouth to her ear. "I lifted the nurse's entry code with this unit when she hooked up a mobile computer to access the database." Pausing, he reached over to a unit that reminded her of the finger probe the medical staff used on her mother they had told Abbie was a pulse oximeter. Hunter explained, "When I put your finger in this sleeve, I'll click an activation button on the program that tells this unit to take your fingerprint and prick the tip for a blood sample. I'll use a different finger. Took like thirty seconds to get your records when she did it."

"Wow, that's quick."

"Good thing, or—" His jaw flexed. He pressed his forehead softly against hers as if he needed a minute, then drew a deep breath and continued typing.

She felt a tiny prick at the tip of her finger.

He studied the small monitor, then said, "We're in."

"Can you—"

He nodded. "Your mom first. I have her name and social."

"How?"

"Got it at the medical center today."

While she'd been wrapped up in family issues, Hunter had been doing his covert thing. But then he'd been trained by someone to do this kind of work. Snooping and suspicion was part of him, something he couldn't turn off.

He read silently, thumbing the display. His mouth pulled to one side in thought. "There's nothing here but just what Kore told you originally. Standard testing, blood donations." He looked at her. "No treatments."

"Can I see?" She expected him to deny her request based on their lack of time.

He handed her his electronic unit. "It's a touch screen."

Just when she was afraid he'd snuff out the smoldering embers of affection in her heart before this was over, he stoked the heat into a dancing flame again. "Thanks."

She fumbled with the touch screen at first, noticing how he patiently waited without trying to hurry her along. Didn't take long to see that he'd told her the truth. She searched the file tabs and opened the one for family history.

She found a subfile listed as Genetic Extensions and clicked on it, reading quickly. She stopped. "No way."

"What's wrong?" He put his arm around her and leaned close. The motion was so filled with concern she forgave him some of the pain he'd caused her.

"My biological father is listed," she told him quietly.

"You didn't know who he was?"

"No. And I didn't know I had a brother either." She glanced at Hunter, sure he saw the shock and disappointment she reeled from. Why hadn't her mother mentioned an older brother?

Hunter reached up and traced a finger along her face. "When your mother's better she'll explain."

Abbie nodded and forced the knot in her throat down so she could talk. "Her son, I mean my brother, has Mom's same blood type, right down to being RH negative. Mine is RH positive. Dr. Tatum said if he could find a larger supply of blood than what Kore banked of my mother's he could replace hers with clean blood over several treatments, but she might still need a liver transplant if we didn't figure this out soon enough. Her son could be her savior."

But what about the other hundred questions to do with a brother Abbie had never known about? Had her mother given up that child? Had her mother seen her son since giving birth two years before Abbie was born? Had her biological father been so dangerous he wouldn't allow his child's own mother to see him?

"Let me download all her files and you can read them at length later on," Hunter suggested.

Good Lord. She was wasting time. She handed him the computer and he did his magic finger act, tapping, waiting, tapping, then he was silent for several minutes.

"Gwen's condition is stable but not encouraging," he murmured. "She had extensive surgery and is in ICU. Probably under heavy guard so no chance to talk to her." He typed for another fifteen or so minutes, then shut down his unit and shoved it into an inside pocket on his suit jacket. He turned to disconnect the wire lead into the wall port beside her bed.

Someone tapped at the door.

She froze.

Hunter shoved the wire on the bed next to her and swung around to sit facing her. He leaned down and kissed her so passionately she forgot her reservations and reached up to clasp his shoulders. His hands wrapped her waist, holding her in his power as much as his mouth did.

Someone near the door cleared his throat.

Hunter broke away, heat blazing through his gaze. "What?" He asked that as if the wrong answer would earn someone a beheading.

"Just wanted to check on Ms. Blanton."

When Hunter shifted around, the man at the door said, "Hello, Abigail. I'm Dr. Hart."

She smiled politely, unsure what to say.

"How are you feeling?" Dr. Hart asked.

She'd been feeling no pain right before he interrupted that kiss. "Better, thank you." They needed to get rid of this guy. "But I'm very tired."

"Get some rest. Please excuse me." The doctor walked out.

Abbie hissed, "Think he suspects anything?"

"Maybe. Scoot over. I'm staying close enough to know if anyone breathes near you." Hunter swung around again and scooped her into his lap, then pulled the cover up around her shoulders.

He acted as if he'd fight the world for her.

Thinking that way would leave her vulnerable to

more heartache tomorrow if Hunter handed her over to his people. She had no reason to think he'd do otherwise.

If he expected her to go willingly, he was wrong.

She would fight anyone, including Hunter, who tried to stop her from finding her brother and convincing him to save their mother.

CHAPTER THIRTY-EIGHT

Sixty minutes to decide a person's fate.

Hunter had decided the fate of some in mere seconds, but those had been trying to kill him.

Abbie just wanted to save her mother.

He sat in an unusually comfortable side chair for a hospital environment, but Kore was first-rate.

The bathroom door opened and Abbie emerged, freshly showered. She'd changed into another pair of jeans and a wheat-colored sweatshirt, looking a hell of a lot better at five in the morning than she had at nine o'clock last night.

"You ready to go?" he asked.

"Can I get out before seven? They told me that's when they release patients in the morning."

"I called Dr. Hart and requested your release." Hunter said *requested* as if it had been an order. "He's on the way."

"Do we, uh, have everything?" She lifted her eyebrows and cut her eyes at the computer port.

"Yes." Of the patient files he'd downloaded last night, less than 1 percent were for males. He'd searched the files he downloaded while she slept and came up with a section entirely in code he would bet were the male patients, possibly the ten men bred to be killers.

He did find a few male cases listed in family histories the way Abbie had located her brother, but in each of those cases the boys disappeared from family records within six months.

His gaze strayed to Abbie when she moved nervously around the room, hands behind her back as though every piece of equipment intrigued her.

She was avoiding him. Had been withdrawn since she woke in his arms this morning. When he'd leaned down to kiss her she'd excused herself to go to the bathroom and rushed from the bed.

He deserved that and more after putting her on the defensive yesterday. She was right to back away from him. The farther she got, the safer she'd be.

He'd gotten her the information she needed. Finding a brother offered hope for her mother.

She wouldn't let that slip through her fingers.

One problem possibly solved.

But he had a new problem—the "we need to talk immediately" text from Eliot's widow in reply to Hunter sending her a new cell phone number. Could it have come at a worse time? Had to be important for her to even contact him since she could barely tolerate speaking to the man she blamed for losing Eliot. Hunter accepted her loathing as well deserved.

Regardless, he intended to watch over her and Theo for the rest of their lives. That was the least he owed Eliot.

The door to Abbie's room opened and Dr. Hart entered. In contrast to his freshly pressed suit and combed short hair, his eyes were swollen from sleep as though he'd just jumped out of bed. "Are you sure you're ready to go, Ms. Blanton? I'd like to run some more tests—"

"No." Hunter stood, towering over Hart.

The doctor nodded and took a step back. "I see."

"You'll hear from my people in the next two weeks about the donation."

Hart's face catapulted from disappointed to excitement. "Wonderful. I'll be available at any time for questions. I took care of Abigail's paperwork on the way up. Can I do anything else for you?"

Hunter extended his hand to Abbie. "Ready?"

She nodded and put her hand in his. He closed his fingers, wanting to hold that slender hand forever. Impossible. But he had her for now, which would only be another hour with BAD waiting for him, unless he got lucky. He turned to Hart. "You *could* do something for us. Where do you keep your corporate fleet?"

"In our private parking level downstairs."

"We need a car."

⸺∞⸺

Abbie rode silently in the limousine Hunter had finagled from the Kore center. He must have been concerned about someone *not* connected to Kore following them to make this tactical maneuver, but she kept silent. He wouldn't want to talk until they ditched the car.

Funny how she was starting to anticipate how he thought. He had the driver drop them at O'Hare airport, where he towed her quickly through the terminal, bypassing the ticket counter. In less than three minutes, he strolled with her through baggage claim and walked up to a limo driver holding up a sign for Johnson, who smiled and led them to the limousine corral.

Just like that, they were off again, and Hunter pressed a button on the panel at his armrest to engage the privacy glass.

She turned, ready to start in on him.

Hunter rubbed his eyes with the heels of his palms and let a yawn escape. Had he stayed up all night watching over her and making car arrangements? He must have felt her eyes and swept his bloodshot orbs her way. "Now we can talk."

"I have to find my brother." She didn't demand, just stated that with certainty.

"I know. I spent some time last night searching records for him. I found a home address not far from downtown Chicago and a phone number. He appears to be some kind of consultant for the health care industry. Based on his website, he works out of his home."

She managed not to let her jaw drop. "You have a phone number?"

He stifled another yawn and fished the electronic unit and his cell phone from his jacket, handing both to her. "Everything's in a file set up for you on my desktop. The only number listed is a business line, which is probably a cell phone or a home line that doubles as a business phone. We're going to Bloomington first—"

"Why?"

"Because I have to do something that will take ten minutes tops." He hadn't barked at her, but he was getting irritable. "Call your brother. We'll go there next."

She hoped he wasn't lying to her, that he really would help her meet her brother. Handling the computer phone device carefully, she clicked the file with her name, which opened, then tried a couple other files that refused to open. She tried her brother's phone number. After two rings, she got his voice mail.

Abbie ended the connection and handed Hunter his phone. "His voice mail says he'll be in meetings until two today. I knew you wouldn't want me to leave a message so I just hung up. Sorry I snapped at you about going to Bloomington. Didn't mean to sound so self-centered."

Hunter put his hand over hers and rubbed his thumb lightly across her skin. "I know you're anxious about your mother."

If he kept being nice to her she was going to lose this battle to hold a part of herself back from him. She changed the subject. "What about the information *you* were looking for?"

"Got everything I could find and sent it to my people."

"How long's the drive to Bloomington?"

Hunter propped his head in his hand, elbow on the door panel. "Two hours each way."

"You're not handing me over to someone, are you?"

"No." He hadn't said "not yet," which she'd find encouraging if he'd explain what he planned to do with her. And he clearly wasn't sharing where they were going or why.

She should slide farther away to her side of the seat and keep a distance between them. But his thumb was still rubbing across her hand, soothing her.

Trust took time and someone had to try first.

She lifted his hand to her shoulder and snuggled against his side.

Hunter turned his head and stared at her, his eyes

asking a question she couldn't read. He kissed her forehead and tucked her close. She laid her head on his chest and hugged an arm around his waist, content to ride quietly, though not at peace.

She still had no idea where they were going or when he would deliver her to a bunch of strangers . . . or law enforcement.

———— ∞ ————

Hunter came awake the minute Abbie touched his face. He took in the surroundings beyond the limo they traveled in.

"We're in Bloomington," she informed him.

He sat up and ran a hand over his face and hair, forcing the spiked ends to lie down.

She handed him a T-shirt from her shoulder bag and one of the waters from the side service console. "You can wash and dry your face with this."

"Thanks." He used a splash of water to wash up, then killed the balance of the bottle in one long swallow. He caught a street sign. The driver was heading east from the interstate and turned south on Center Street.

Evergreen Memorial Cemetery would be just down the road.

He handed Abbie the empty water bottle she put in the ice bucket, then told her, "When we stop, you stay in the car."

She gave him her not-happy look. "Why? Where are you going?"

"Have to talk to someone alone, but I'll have the driver keep the doors locked and you'll be in my sight the whole time."

She pushed away from him over to her door and looked out, not saying another word.

The car turned between stone columns on each side of the entrance to Evergreen Memorial Cemetery.

Hunter curled his fingers tight to keep from reaching for her. He'd slept hard with her in his arms, his body content when she was close by. The couple feet now separating them might as well be miles. He hated even the small distance, but she wasn't his and he couldn't keep her. Trying to stay free long enough to reach her brother would be a challenge and might very well lose him the small window he'd need to elude BAD, but he couldn't turn his back on her.

He could tell himself he was sticking this out because they'd cut a deal, but that would be a lie. He couldn't let her down. Or hurt her again the way his suspicions had slapped her emotionally.

God, he couldn't stand thinking of how she'd been hurt.

She'd practically given her life last night. If he could fix things with BAD right now he'd do it just so he could stay with Abbie. But he'd forced Joe's hand when he snuck her out of the Kore center. Joe had to be furious even after receiving the files Hunter downloaded into the online vault.

If he could believe Joe would continue to use him on the mission and not trick him into being caught, Hunter would do whatever BAD needed to prevent the anticipated bomb attack.

But he wouldn't willingly give Abbie to them.

That meant he had to figure out what to do with her while he evaded BAD.

No call from Gotthard in the last hour meant Joe had probably unleashed a team.

When the car parked near the David Davis memorial inside the cemetery grounds, Hunter said, "Be right back."

She lifted a hand in dismissal, face still turned to gaze out the window.

Hunter got out and told the driver, "Lock the doors."

"Yes, sir."

He walked around the front of the car, welcoming the cool breeze that woke him fully. Fresh air untainted by disappointment and suspicion filled his next breath. He glanced down at his wrinkled clothes and brushed at his jacket to no avail. When he reached the memorial, he moved around the far side and stopped where he could face the car.

A slender female, average height, in black pants and a gray hooded jacket approached from his left, walking through the historical markers splattered with sunlight slicing through the naked hardwoods.

As he always requested, Cynthia left her hood in place. Blond hairs escaped and flew around her face, which didn't harbor venomous eyes for once. "I would have spoken over the phone if this was inconvenient."

Her voice flowed gentle as the wind this time, not harshly like the last time.

"Not a problem." He'd told her not to leave voice mails and only to speak by phone in an emergency since he couldn't always ensure they were both on secure lines. He set up an e-mail and text program just for her to contact him and instructed her to send messages from somewhere other than home. Had to admit that she never scoffed at his security measures, just nodded and said Eliot had given her the same instructions.

"I'm moving to St. Louis," she told him in her usual get-to-the-point manner, which he did appreciate about her. "I have a new position there." She handed him a piece of paper. "This is the address where I'm moving."

He took the paper, which was another reason this had to be in person. He wanted no electronic trail to her. "I need some time to recon your new location."

"No, you've done enough. I can do this on my own."

He didn't want the irritation rising inside him to reach his voice, but he was too tired and had too little time to battle over this. "Eliot wouldn't want you to move without me checking it out."

She didn't flinch at hearing her dead husband's name, as she had before, and calmly replied, "Eliot would know that I'm capable of taking a new job, moving my home, and raising his son on my own. We discussed this when he found out I was pregnant. You're the one who feels like you have to do this, the one who can't get past his death."

That verbal backhand stung.

"Guess you've gotten over his death then." Hunter wanted to give himself a knuckle sandwich the minute he said the words. He hadn't meant to strike out at her, but she'd hit a nerve by telling him to get over Eliot's death.

He'd waited four years to find Eliot's killer, only to meet the bastard, then let him escape.

She grumbled something low, shook her head, and looked at Hunter with steel in her gray eyes. "Eliot told me once that you can be the biggest asshole when you're watching over the people you care about. I don't know where I rank on your care meter, but I'll let that slide." She shoved her hands in the pockets of her jacket. "You've always been polite, but I knew you were angry with me. News flash: I was angry with you for a long time, too. I blamed you for his death."

"I know. You have every right to blame me."

"No, I don't. I insult Eliot by thinking he'd have worked that closely with anyone he didn't trust with his life. And *you're* insulting Eliot by assuming I trapped him into marriage when I got pregnant. Think about it. Would the calculating and precise Eliot we both knew leave anything to chance?"

Hunter considered what she was saying and couldn't argue her point. Eliot might have acted goofy when he wanted to make you laugh, but he was careful and meticulous with anything important. And having a baby would have been important to him. "Eliot *intentionally* got you pregnant?"

She nodded slowly. "We talked about it. He told me you handled all the danger but said everything in life came with risks. When I came to terms with how precarious his life could be, I finally agreed. I told him I was willing to have a baby with him, so we stopped using protection. The next time he came home I was pregnant. He couldn't have been happier." Her eyes glistened. "Couldn't wait to get married."

"Eliot shouldn't have done this." Hunter argued, but he shouldn't have blamed Cynthia. He'd jumped to the conclusion she'd trapped Eliot, needing a target for his anger over losing his best friend. Cynthia had been too handy, just as Hunter had been too handy for her. Now he was irritated at what Eliot had done. "Bad enough to marry you and leave you, but to leave a child—"

"See, that's where we differ, Leroy, or whatever your real name is, because I seriously doubt you're a Leroy." Her voice held no recriminations or undercurrent of hate any longer. She sounded sad and wistful. "I thank Eliot every day that he left a piece of himself with me. I love our son and I'm a good mother raising him. He'll be four in a few months. I didn't want to move him when he was so small, but I want to get him settled now before kindergarten."

"Why move? Is someone bothering you here, or do you need a better place to live, or . . ." His natural instinct to protect surged to the surface.

She smiled. "I can't stay here. I need to move away from the grocery store where I shopped with Eliot and the restaurants where we ate and the house that's too quiet without him. I need to be somewhere it won't break my heart to wake up every day in the room we shared so much in. Eliot will always own a place in my heart. It's just too painful to look for him around every corner or to think I hear his footsteps on the carpet. If I had it to do over I'd still have spent that time with him and had our son, because I'd rather have had those two years with Eliot than have never met him. Life has no guarantees. He could have been killed in a traffic accident or I could have died from an unexpected illness. We accepted the risk of loving each other."

Hunter had no argument for that. He'd spent as little time as possible in Montana over the past four years because he missed Eliot so badly when he visited the cabin. This time he pressed in a gentler tone, "I still want to check over your new location before you move."

"Can you do that in the next three days?"

"No, I—" His gaze strolled over to the limo, where more problems waited. "I'm a little pressed for time this week."

"I'm moving Monday." She held up a hand when he started to say more. "I don't need you to recon my neighborhood. It's a nice, safe place to live. I want you to come meet your godson."

Hunter lifted the paper she'd given him and memorized the address since he planned to destroy the paper immediately. "Be careful and stay close to home once you're settled. I'll let you know when I've been there."

She sighed. "You're welcome to stop in whenever you want. *You* be careful with whatever you're doing. You may not be ready to forgive me, but I've forgiven you. I want you to be part of Theo's life, to help him know who his father was." Cynthia leaned forward and kissed Hunter's cheek, then turned away.

He fought a lump in his throat as Cynthia strolled through the markers and disappeared in the direction of Eliot's grave. She had a core of iron and had held nothing back in loving his friend. He was starting to understand how easy it would be for a man to lose his head over a woman like Cynthia.

The way he'd lost his head over Abbie.

Turning away from the memorial, Hunter started back to the limo that held the one person who'd made him feel anything since meeting Eliot.

But Hunter couldn't be as cavalier about life when

it came to Abbie even if there was no chance of seeing her again.

After telling the driver to find a restaurant, Hunter slid onto the backseat.

"Old nuisance?" Abbie asked casually, but she was annoyed.

"No. Wife of a friend of mine."

"Does he mind you seeing her now?" she asked tartly.

He shouldn't enjoy the jealous sting in her voice, not when he would lose her all too soon. "She's his widow. He expects me to keep an eye on her. She was only kissing my cheek."

"Oh, well, shoot. Sorry. How was I supposed to know?" she mumbled. "Not like you introduced us. But that makes sense because you don't trust me, right?"

"I don't trust anyone to know her identity or location."

Abbie closed her eyes. "You'll never trust anyone period."

He hadn't thought he could feel worse than he had after he'd left her unprotected at Kore and she'd almost died, but hearing her disappointment cut deep.

She cared for him.

Hell, he cared for her. Talk about stupid on his part.

But her disappointment in him would make leaving him easier for her when they separated.

Not for him.

The day she walked away she'd take a piece of him with her he'd never replace.

His cell phone buzzed. It could only be Gotthard. Hunter answered, "You get the files?"

"Yes. Where are you?"

"Why?"

"Joe wants you to come in."

"I'm following a lead on something from the Kore center."

Gotthard sounded whipped. "It isn't a request."

"I know. Thanks for the heads-up." Hunter disconnected the call.

The hunt was on.

CHAPTER THIRTY-NINE

Who would have thought riding around in a limousine would become tiresome, but Abbie was over touring through Illinois. "When will we get to Chicago?"

"By two o'clock. About twenty minutes," Hunter answered politely. He'd been nothing but accommodating since leaving the cemetery. She didn't think he cared much for her "You'll never trust anyone" comment, but if he wouldn't let her meet his friend's widow Hunter clearly would *never* trust anyone.

Including her.

"Can I call my brother again?" she asked.

"It's not quite two o'clock yet." Hunter handed over his phone.

He had a point. "I'll call Hannah to see how Mom's doing then."

"Go ahead."

She wanted to shake him out of his granite-tough reserve and see something alive in his eyes again. But she had the feeling that one call he'd taken on the way out of the cemetery hadn't gone well. Hunter had told the caller he was tracking down a lead from the Kore center, not that he was playing keep away with his people to give Abbie a chance to find her brother.

How much trouble was Hunter getting into by not bringing her in and not going to meet with his people? She didn't know and he wasn't going to confide in her.

Not in a prisoner.

No matter how he might color it, she was headed for some form of incarceration. She had to make the most of her mobility while she could. Punching the speed-dial number he'd programmed in for the medical center, she kept pushing buttons until she reached her mother's room.

A woman who had been moved into her mother's room answered the phone.

"May I speak to Mrs. Blanton?" Abbie asked.

"She's gone."

"Where?"

"To ICU. She's not doing so good," the lady told her.

"What happened?" Abbie clutched her throat.

"I don't know. Your mama was gone when I came back from having an X-ray. Nurse just said she had a bad spell." Abbie thanked her and hung up, then called the ICU desk. She inquired about her mother and found out Hannah was in with her.

When she ended the call, Hunter asked, "What's happened?"

"Mom's heart is beating irregularly. Her liver hasn't gotten worse, but it's not improving either. She had a bad night and ended up in the ICU." Abbie lifted the phone and pressed the buttons for her brother, waiting through two rings.

This time someone answered before the third ring. A shallow male voice said, "Hello?"

"Hi." She was so unprepared to hear a voice she didn't know what to say. "Is your last name Royce?"

"Yes. Can I help you?"

That encouraged her. "I'm Abigail Blanton. I, uh, am calling because we're related. We have the same mother."

"Really?" He sounded surprised and curious but pleasant.

"Do you *know* who your mother is?"

"Sort of. I have photos. She died when I was born."

He'd been as lied to as Abbie had. Was their biological father some kind of heartless bastard or what? He might be worse than she suspected. "Your mother's *not* dead." *Yet.*

When her brother didn't speak, Abbie rushed on. "None of us knew you existed. I just found records of your birth. You and I were born—"

Hunter touched her arm. She understood the warning to share as little as possible and nodded before going on. But she was desperate. "We were born at the same place. I never met our father. Did you?" She still didn't hear her brother. "Are you still there?"

"I'm sorry. I'm just in shock. No, I never met my father. I was told my mother died in childbirth so I ended up in an orphanage."

All she'd learned about her biological father from the Kore files was that his initials were S. J., but she didn't need records to figure out she'd been lucky not to know him. That didn't erase a bazillion questions she had for her mother. "I'm so sorry. You have family, more than you realize, and—"

"I hate to cut you off, because I'd really like to talk to you more, but I'm due to take a conference call in a few minutes. I work out of my home. I'll be around this afternoon. If you'll give me your number I'll call you back."

"Are you in Chicago at . . ." She gave him the street address Hunter showed her on the handheld computer.

"Yes . . . how did you know that and how did you find my phone number?"

"It's a long story and I'll be happy to answer questions if you'll let me come by to see you." *Please say yes.*

"You don't have a cold or anything, do you? My resistance to germs is not the best, which is why I work out of my home. I have weak lungs and have to be careful not to expose myself to a lot of people."

"No, I'm perfectly healthy." She tried not to sound like a panicked stalker, but she had to see him today. "I can be there in thirty minutes. Just a short visit, okay?"

"I suppose that will be all right. Call when you get downstairs and I'll clear the security so you can come up."

Abbie hung up feeling like a huge weight was beginning to lift from her chest. Hope was taking the place of fear. She handed the phone to Hunter, so excited she wanted to hug him and hating the fact that she hesitated. "You heard. He's going to see me when I get there."

Hunter pocketed his phone. "I hope he agrees to help your mother."

She knew the word "today" was at the end of that sentence in Hunter's mind. She understood that he had an important job of some sort to do, but she had to get her brother to help.

No matter what it took to convince him.

CHAPTER FORTY

Linette had six more steps until she could get inside her office and shut the door.

She'd been given the time for the bombing. Saturday—tomorrow—at 2200. She'd asked if that was Eastern Standard Time and Vestavia said he'd been told it was, but he hadn't sounded convinced.

No information on the city yet, but Vestavia expected to have that in time to get his people on the ground at the bomb site. What did Vestavia want his people to do once they arrived on-site if the bombs were already set?

Would his people detonate the bombs?

Vestavia always made her feel like she had to check to see where she stepped. He kept her on edge, particularly with this project. Might just be feeling jumpy because she'd never been included at this level.

Inside her office, she locked the door and sat down at her desk, excited and terrified. She wanted to share as much as possible with her online contact, whose group had proven they put her information to good use. But if Vestavia was telling the truth, that he was only sharing certain details with each of his three lieutenants, would he be able to figure out that the information passed along had came from her?

Or would he think someone connected to Bardaric had tipped off the FBI or a domestic defense organization?

She lifted her hands to the keyboard. A movement stopped her. The doorknob turned slowly, then the door opened.

Basil walked in grinning. One cheek pooched out with the caramel candy he sucked on. "Ready to buddy up some? I'm the one in the know."

"No thanks."

He closed the door, then sidled across the room and leaned two hands down on her desk. His sickeningly sweet breath breezed across the short distance separating them to nauseate her. "I don't think you realize just how unforgiving Vestavia is," Basil said.

"I believe I know the Fra just fine."

"I don't think so, little girl. You've never *seen* what he's capable of."

She had the urge to tell Basil stories of her time with the older Fra she'd bet would turn even a strong stomach, but she sat still with her robotic mask in place, though nothing deterred him.

"When I first came into the Fratelli with eight other guys, one of them showed up a minute late for our first exercise in fieldwork. Vestavia wanted to make an example of him. The kid couldn't have been more than twenty-two. He was stripped and stretched spread eagle over a metal grate out in the woods. Vestavia had us build a fire under the kid. He'd been gagged. I swear his eyeballs popped out of his head when we lit the flame. Not a big fire that would engulf him. No, this was a roasting pit, and he was the main dish. We had to stand back a ways when the smell got bad. He lived most of the day until it rained. Buzzards showed up and started ripping into him. He finally died, but it took a while."

"Your point?" she asked in a nonchalant voice. Eating any cooked meat would be difficult for a while.

"Just want you to know what you're risking if you fail him." Basil chuckled and stood up. "I heard worse was done when he was banging Josie. That was one mean bitch."

"I do not wish to discuss the Fra or his associates and suggest you take care what you say."

"Boss is across town at a party schmoozing city officials who think he's their most upstanding citizen. Why'd you think I came by now?"

Her skin quivered with a touch of fear. "Please leave."

"Sure thing. See me to the door." He crossed his arms, declaring he was content to wait.

Linette gritted her teeth and stood up, walking around her desk.

He lunged and caught her arm, yanking her against him.

She shoved her fist between them. "Don't be stupid!"

"Been called a lot of things, babe, but not stupid. Especially since we both know they only promote someone with a genius IQ to lieutenant."

She had no one to back her in a dispute, but he'd been right about her intelligence. She'd figure out a way to stop him from playing with her as if she were a puppet. Or a blow-up doll in his case. "Leave now or you'll regret this."

"Only thing I'll regret is not having planned enough time to take you right here in the office." He reached up and fondled her breast.

She stood perfectly still, not fighting him. "You should take care not to risk angering Fra Vestavia," she warned.

"You wouldn't dare say a word to Vestavia. You complain and he'll yank you off the team and give you to me for sure. The Fratelli would suspect a woman of flaunting herself, even you."

She didn't say a word. Basil was right.

And he was going to be a problem whether the mission succeeded or failed.

CHAPTER FORTY-ONE

Hunter left the limousine parked a quarter-mile from the address north of downtown Chicago. Abbie had jumped out, raring to go meet her brother. He hoped she could convince her brother to help her.

If not, Hunter had to find her somewhere safe to hide soon.

Things would turn ugly when he encountered BAD.

She wore a suede coat he'd picked up for her in Bloomington, where he'd changed into jeans and a black turtleneck pullover. The down vest he wore was all he needed with the late-afternoon temperatures hovering in the low fifties.

She surprised him by taking his hand when he reached for hers. They walked along at a quick pace, dodging a woman with a little white dog and another lady with a stroller. When Hunter located her brother's six-story building, Abbie used the phone on the wall next to the entrance to his apartment to call him so he could key the security code to unlock the door.

Hunter kept an eye on the area, but nothing out of the ordinary moved around the quiet neighborhood.

"Hi, it's me." Abbie listened and raised her head to face a security camera, then nodded at Hunter and said, "He's a friend of mine and he's healthy, too."

She frowned, listened, and rubbed her head. She'd had a headache on the way back, but this seemed to be a new headache. "Uhm, let me find out." She covered the phone and turned to Hunter. "He doesn't want anyone else up there but me."

"That's a negative." Hunter eyed the camera, not caring if the guy didn't like what he saw.

"He's sickly. I read in the file he's a hemophiliac," she explained. "I'm just going to go up for maybe ten minutes and come right back down."

"Tell him I'll stand outside the door." That was more ground than Hunter would normally give.

She told her brother, then covered the phone again. "He said he has elderly residents nearby who get upset if anyone lingers in the hallway."

"I'm not letting—"

She cut him off. "I know you've been holding off all day to turn me over to somebody and I do appreciate the trouble this is causing you. I have to talk to my brother now, because the minute you hand me off my mother's dead if I don't make this work. I can't live with missing this chance for her. If you aren't going to let me go up there to see my brother then just kill me now because I will fight *everyone* to the death who tries to stop me. I need ten, maybe fifteen minutes. If I'm not back down by then, come and get me." She lowered her voice. "I know you can get inside this building."

He wanted to ask her to trust him to know what was best, but she'd throw back in his face that he didn't trust her. The longer they stood outside, the higher their chance of being seen, especially if Gotthard had found the time to search Abbie's file further and find the connection to her brother. "Okay, you go up, but do not go anywhere except up there and don't leave his apartment unless I'm outside the door when he opens it."

"You think I'll *run* the minute I get up there?"

"No, Abbie. I know you're going to try to convince your brother to go to the medical center right now. If you manage to do that, I don't want you to leave with him because you think I'm going to hand you over to someone. Trust me when I say I'll tell you before that happens."

She didn't say a word.

Hunter put a hand on her shoulder, wanting to keep her right here with him. "Stop looking at me as if I've treated you like that pig did. I just want you safe. I'm not turning my back on you. Dammit. If I could make it happen, I'd take you away with me somewhere I could spend hours showing you how much you do matter."

Her bottom lip quivered. "You have the worst timing."

"I know. I just need you to be careful . . . for me." He kissed her and thought about shooting his finger at the damn camera, but he didn't. He ended the kiss and whispered, "Hurry up and remember to wait for me to reach his floor before you leave. I'll be standing within ten feet of his door in ten minutes or less."

She looked torn in half, unsure what to do, but she said, "Thank you," then spoke into the phone. "I'm coming up alone."

The minute the door closed and she stepped onto the elevator, Hunter backed away and walked calmly to the end of the building, out of sight of the security camera. When he turned the corner, he ran.

———∞∞∞———

Abbie stepped off the elevator, wrinkling her nose at the suffocating mildew smell. This building had appeared old downstairs, but not this dilapidated. Spiderwebs climbed the wall and trash littered the carpeted hallway.

Couldn't her brother afford a better place? Especially with his illnesses?

She found his door ajar with a note stuck on it that read:

———∞∞∞———

Come on in and walk to my library on your right. Walking strains my asthma.

———∞∞∞———

She pushed the door open and squinted at the dark living room that smelled like the hallway, but a light shined from a room fifteen feet to her right. "It's me, Abbie."

When she'd taken two steps inside the living room, the front door shut as though kicked and someone strong grabbed her arms, twisting them behind her.

"What are you doing?" she yelled.

One hand held both her wrists. Cold fingers wrapped her neck. "Hello, sister."

She tried to think past the slamming of her heart. "You're scaring me." Was her brother some kind of freak?

He didn't say anything.

Why hadn't she insisted on bringing up Hunter? "Who are you?"

"The only person who can save your mother."

"She's your mother, too." Abbie's words tripped over her tongue on shaky breaths.

"Details, details. I'm only interested in negotiating."

"You *know* about her . . . that she's sick? So you know who I am?"

"Of course I do, *sister.*"

She cringed at the sound of the word sister coming out in a taunting voice. "What do you want?"

He ran the back of his hand along her cheek and down across her breast.

Please don't let him want that.

He whispered, "I'm going to let you choose."

"Between what?"

"Who lives and who dies."

<hr>

Hunter needed tools, something he could use to activate the power-operated lock on the gate constructed of crisscrossed metal. Abbie's brother had picked an apartment with decent security, but nothing really challenging . . . *if* Hunter had tools.

His phone buzzed and he considered not answering, but Gotthard was the only one helping him right now. He pulled his phone out in one hand and kept searching for a way into the parking garage while he spoke quietly. "Yes."

"Still working through all the records, but Rae broke the coded file with the ten males that were designated for training. I've cross-referenced everything I've got so far."

Someone cranked a car engine on the bottom garage level.

Hunter squeezed between a hedge and the concrete wall that surrounded the parking area. "What'd you get?"

Gotthard said, "We ran the data on all ten boys and found a Kore file showing updates every two years. The nine students who died have been noted as deceased. The last one is still counted as living. That's our JC killer."

The car inside the garage drove to the exit, activating the electric gate, then passing through and speeding away. Hunter shot out from where he hid and jogged toward an exit door marking the stairwell.

"Joe's using this new information to find out if the JC killer was with MI6 or still is. While we're waiting on that, I ran his profile through our computer and got a hit . . . from the rest of the Kore files."

"Makes sense he'd be in the test files." Hunter opened the door to the stairs carefully.

"Not what I mean. I found a family tie to him. His name in the secret files is Royce Jack."

Hunter had started quietly up the stairs and froze.

Abbie's brother's was J. Royce. *No. Can't be.*

"He's got the exact blood type and matching physical characteristics as a male child by the same woman who birthed Abigail Blanton. Her brother is the JC killer."

And Abbie was in her brother's hands.

Hunter took the stairs two at a time.

"We went through Abigail's records from Kore."

"She's not fucking involved," Hunter said in sharp whisper even though he was now banging steps to get to her as fast as he could. He'd made it up two floors. Three to go. Abbie needed her brother for her mother, but Hunter wanted the bastard's blood.

Shouldn't take long to get it from a hemophiliac.

"What I'm talking about is Abigail's medical file from yesterday and last night. I'm going to assume you know she coded at Kore."

Hunter grunted rather than waste breath he needed to race up two more flights of stairs. He would catch that bastard and hand him over to Joe in trade for clearing Abbie out of this mess.

Gotthard continued. "That's because Abbie's white-cell count dropped severely after giving blood. We compared it to her mother's medical files and there are similarities."

"Tell me all this later. He's a hemophiliac. Going to be tough to take him down without making him bleed, but I'll do it." Hunter stuffed the phone in his jeans pocket, freeing his hands as he reached the top floor.

He thundered down the hallway.

Why worry about noise? The prick had to know he was coming. Hell, the door was ajar.

Hunter burst into the room. "Where is she?"

No one answered . . . because the apartment was vacant.

CHAPTER FORTY-TWO

Hunter exited the elevator that had dropped two levels below ground into BAD's mission headquarters beneath downtown Nashville. He followed Korbin, his silent escort, who led him to the mission room.

Gotthard, Rae, Carlos, and Retter stood or sat around a black acrylic conference table.

"Told you I was coming in. Think you needed all these to lock me up?" Hunter asked Retter.

"No," Retter said, beefed-up arms crossed over his black T-shirt and long black hair pulled back in a pony-tail. "I could handle bringing you in on my own. You did save me the trouble of hunting you. So I'm going to give you a choice."

Hunter quelled his normal reflex to slam anyone who thought they could actually outmaneuver him in the field. He had one concern and that was getting Abbie back. "What's my choice?"

"We can put you in lockdown right now or you can help with this mission."

"Easy choice."

"Not through." Retter continued. "When we finish this mission, you come in without any trouble to meet with Joe and Tee. Up to them what they want to do with a renegade."

"Renegade?" Hunter scoffed. "You guys not allowed to say *asshole* anymore?"

Gotthard's eyes twinkled, but he didn't smile.

Rae and Carlos kept their reactions contained. No surprise there.

Korbin didn't hold back his black glare.

"If you don't come in without trouble," Retter went on, "we'll lock up Blanton forever, then we'll find that snitch Borys you keep hidden and hand him over to the CIA."

Hunter knew coming in that all his moves were gone. "Agreed."

"Gotthard and Korbin will fill you in." Retter turned to walk away.

Hunter's phone buzzed. BAD had installed relays for underground access to cell and satellite links, but only two people should have this number. Hunter read the display. Wasn't Cynthia, and he was looking at Gotthard, whose bark-brown eyebrows lifted in question.

Hunter answered the phone. "Yes."

Rae walked out and came back with Retter.

"Now the fun begins," a smooth male voice said into Hunter's ear.

"Who's this?"

"Abigail's brother, but you can call me Jackson since you know who I am by now."

Using hand signals, Hunter let everyone know who had called. Gotthard swung around to key a trace, but this prick would not be located that easily. "What do you want?"

"To make my next task a little challenging. I'm going to Colorado for a small job. If you figure out where I am before I complete my job and leave I'll tell you where Abigail is. I couldn't harm her the last time we met because she had not been authorized. But, good news, she was included in my new list of necessary kills as of yesterday."

That's why the bastard had tried to kill her last night at the Kore center. "Where in Colorado?"

"Be serious. *You* have to have some challenge, too. Don't drag your feet. I gave Abigail a cocktail at Kore. Not the same one I gave her mother, but similar. She's starting to have headaches, like her mother had in the beginning. I altered the files at Kore a long time ago. Abbie and her mother have identical blood to mine so she needs my blood, too." The phone disconnected.

Hunter was going to kill that man. Not until Abbie was safe and healthy, but one second afterward. If his guess was right about this wacko, Jackson wouldn't hurt Abbie until the time came to meet. The question was, what did Jackson have planned then? Jackson wanted a game in play, which meant everyone had to be alive until the point when *he* decided they died.

"What'd he say?" Gotthard asked.

"He told me he's going to Colorado. If we find him before he finishes his task and leaves, he'll tell us where Abbie is."

"We have a time that may or may not be for an attack in Colorado," Rae shared. "The contact inside Fratelli said there would be a bombing at 2200 EST tomorrow, but the contact has warned us not to trust that time. We don't have a lot else, so we'll add Colorado to the mix."

"Anything significant happening in Colorado?" Hunter asked.

Korbin's iron-hard glare hadn't let up since Hunter walked in. He said, "Guess you've been too busy to keep up with world events. UK's prime minister is coming into Denver on Saturday to see a friend, then speaking at a college there on Monday. Then he heads to DC to meet with the president on Tuesday."

Hunter scratched his two-day start on a beard. "If the killer is after the prime minister it would be easier to take him out in Colorado before he meets with the president."

"Could be," Retter said. "But why's he leading you to him? Why not just tap the prime minister and not play this game?"

"Remember the Fratelli code about 'no unnecessary kills'?" When the agents nodded, Hunter said, "Killer calls himself Jackson and talks as though he holds to the Fratelli rules of no unauthorized kills. Makes sense. If not, he'd have shot me when I found him at Abbie's apartment."

Korbin scowled. "Knew you had her the whole time."

"Her mother's dying," Hunter explained for the benefit of some in BAD. Korbin's opinion didn't count. "Abbie went to the Wentworth event to talk to Gwen about finding out what happened to her mother, because her mother had been healthy when she visited Kore almost two weeks ago. Jackson just told me he gave her mother a cocktail of some sort and gave Abbie something similar last night before she coded."

Rae uncrossed her arms and leaned forward. "Is *that* how you got the data?"

"Not the way I wanted to, but yes," Hunter said. "We had to have Abbie's fingerprint and her blood sample taken through their machines at the same minute we accessed the Kore computer systems. So if we get her out of this we all owe her for those records."

Rae smiled slightly.

"About the killer," Gotthard said, pressing him. "Finish explaining why he wants to play this game."

Hunter walked over and leaned against the door frame. "Jackson sounds like a bored killer, handcuffed by too many Fratelli rules. He wants a challenge. Like Dr. Tatum. Jackson must have put him in a no-win situation and threatened to harm his children if Tatum didn't take the pills and commit suicide. Jackson gets his rocks off by watching people make life-and-death decisions. I've thought back on the mission in Kauai four years ago. Jackson wouldn't consider Eliot's death a kill since he shot Eliot in the shoulder, which wouldn't have necessarily been life threatening. Jackson knew there was no way for someone with a blown shoulder to get down. That bastard laughed after Eliot cut the rope."

"Eliot?"

Hunter tensed, taking in the faces in the room. "Yes. Those of you who were here then know the intel had changed by the time Eliot and I inserted into the Brugmann house. Once we found the CIA list and plans for a terrorist attack in the UK, we had to fight our way out. We'd just started rappelling when the estate went silent too soon for the FBI to have arrived. Eliot knew something had gone very wrong and that we might be the only two who knew about the terrorist attack if someone got to Brugmann's before the FBI. Eliot's leg was broken, too. When he realized he couldn't get down, he wanted to make sure one of us could prevent the attack planned for the hospital in Britain the next day. He cut his rope so I could get down."

"Fuck." Korbin summed up the room's reaction.

"Jackson was the shooter." Hunter could hear the laugh echoing in the back of his skull. "He wounded me to toy with me, to let me know he could have killed me, but I must not have been part of the sanctioned hits. It's as if he couldn't give me too mortal a wound to climb down or he'd have broken his oath to the Fratelli."

"You went to the Wentworth party looking for him." Rae had spoken her thoughts out loud.

Hunter had nothing left to shield from these agents. "Yes, but I had no idea he'd try to make a hit on Gwen. After dropping Abbie at her apartment with a transmitter I'd planted on her, I drove away, parked down the street, and doubled back. I was inside the building when I heard Jackson grab her. He wanted to see my face, but he didn't kill either of us. He popped a flash bomb and released a tear-gas canister. I carried her out and took her with me." He looked at Retter and said, "I *was* bringing her here that night until she told me about her mother dying. In hindsight, I should have put Abbie in protective custody and dealt with the guilt of pulling her away from her mother, because now he's got her."

Hunter turned to Rae in the silence. "That's why I

didn't want you to be connected to me at the Wentworth party. I had no doubt of your ability to pull off being my companion. I was putting the mission first, but if the opportunity presented itself I was not going to pass up a chance to take down Eliot's killer. I didn't want you or anyone else hurt because of me."

Rae gave Hunter a look he hadn't expected. Her eyes softened with understanding.

Korbin said nothing, but the glare subsided.

"Abbie was in play before she met you," Gotthard said.

"Why do you say that?" Hunter crossed his arms. Felt damn good to utilize the expertise of this group to find Abbie. Gotthard had tried to get him to realize they were greater as a team than as individuals. Too bad Hunter hadn't accepted that sooner.

"Rae figured out the Jackson Chameleon puzzle," Gotthard said. "Jackson disappeared from the U.S. at three years old, but Abbie's mother had to donate blood for him five years later. I searched customs for that period of time and found clearance within a couple hours after she'd donated. The blood was delivered to a hospital in Shanghai for a child with the last name Jack."

Rae picked up the thread. "In the Asian culture a male child is called Son of, as in Jackson, meaning Son of Jack."

"So what did that give us?" Hunter asked.

"That opened up a world of information on one Sigmund Jack who lived in the United States at the right time to have gotten Abbie's mother pregnant."

"Where is he now?"

Gotthard took over. "Dead. We traced his son's life until Jackson went into MI6 in his early twenties then disappeared two years ago. Joe tapped his UK contacts to find out MI6 is after Jackson, too. They think Jackson is behind the death of two powerful supporters of the former prime minister and possibly behind the former prime minister's death."

"So why would Jackson kill the current one, who basically opposes so many things the prior prime minister supported?" Hunter wondered aloud.

"Only the Fratelli can answer that one," Rae said.

"Then we have to find him." Hunter stood away from the desk. "He wants me there for some reason. I'm going." He looked at Retter to let him know he wouldn't be stopped.

"We'll let you go," Retter countered. "But I'm telling you now if you make any move that doesn't put the security of this nation first I'll take you out myself."

"Done. I'll leave for Colorado tonight."

Retter added, "You're not going anywhere alone."

Hunter started to argue, then realized he needed someone with him. One agent in particular. "Do I get to pick who goes with me?"

Korbin looked at Rae, then at the others. No one spoke up.

Retter said, "That'll be up to the agent."

CHAPTER FORTY-THREE

H unter stopped hiking within a stand of bare aspens protected from the wintry winds by a snow-capped granite ridge rising on his left. A single mountain chalet straight ahead sparkled bright as a spotlighted diamond in a dark room. The helicopter had deposited him and Brendan "Mako" Masterson two miles away, where they'd donned winter gear. The temperature plunged into the thirties, mild for nighttime in the Rocky Mountains in spring.

He studied the brightly lit trilevel lodge positioned innocently in a dip in the mountains north of Idaho Springs, Colorado.

A perfect spot for a private party to celebrate the visit of an international dignitary.

A perfect spot for an assassination attempt.

Mako dropped his pack alongside Hunter's, white puffs striking the cold air when he breathed. He read his watch and quietly said, "Time: twenty-one oh two, sixteen seconds."

"Check," Hunter answered.

Fifty-eight minutes until someone died.

He considered where the sniper might choose to position himself along the ridge west of the house. Tall windows stood around the curved third floor, which faced west, toward the spectacular sunsets. "Shooter could be anywhere from one hundred feet to three hundred feet up there." He nodded, indicating the obvious location for the closest shot through the glass windows. "I'll determine the prime minister's position in the building. You cover the grounds and see if the shooter's got any eyes down here. Once we split up, stay far enough off me that he doesn't see you or he'll change the game."

"Got it." Armed heavily and dressed in a pewter-gray arctic suit just like Hunter's, Mako's wide frame melded into the night when he moved away.

Hunter owed him for agreeing to be his backup. No one volunteered, that's for sure. With a little luck, he'd figured Jackson's intentions correctly.

If not, Abbie would pay for his mistake.

Bile stung his throat at the thought of her out here terrified, because Jackson would have to keep her close enough to play out his next move.

Thinking about that instead of the mission was fruitless and dangerous. He had to focus to have any hope of getting her back alive.

Hunter moved around to the left, lifting his binoculars to study the quiet cocktail mixer going on. All activity appeared to be contained on the third level of the seven-thousand-square-foot vacation home belonging to British friends of the prime minister.

The UK leader came into view among a group of men, allowing no clear shot . . . yet. Hunter's radio clicked once.

Mako had detected someone on the grounds.

Hunter lowered his binoculars, searching for . . .

there. A tall man with a thick build moved carefully from the building to vehicles strewn across rutted, snow-covered ground to . . .

Hunter focused in on the man's right cheek . . . a scar.

Fuck a duck. There was the guy who had been in Brugmann's compound in Kauai *and* at the Wentworth party.

"Need a location, Gotthard," Joe said, striding across the research analyst's area in BAD's underground operation center.

Gotthard hit the refresh button on the chat board where he and Linette left posts on Saturdays. They used a different site for every day of the week and the seven chat boards changed monthly. "Everyone set?"

Joe paused. "Yes. Twenty teams spread across the country, ready to contact bomb squads and emergency warning systems in every city. Plus our five best bomb specialists. If the detonation time for the bomb *was* twenty-two hundred Eastern Standard Time it would have happened already. Must be tied to the Colorado event if it's really going down tonight."

"Too bad we don't have twenty demolition experts as good as Korbin."

"No shit."

Gotthard hit the refresh button and Linette's message appeared. "Got something." He decoded as he copied her text. "She sent coordinates. Strike is in Chicago in twenty-three minutes."

Joe stabbed the air with his fist. "Fucking A! Retter

and Korbin are in Chicago. Get the coordinates to Retter and I'll contact local authorities for emergency management in Chicago."

Gotthard picked up his phone, hoping Linette had covered her ass with the Fratelli. She was obviously involved up to her neck.

Retter straddled a Suzuki GSX-R motorcycle, studying the traffic rolling past Chicago's courthouse. Citizens unaware their city might be scheduled in some terrorist's Day-Timer for tonight. He glanced around at his team, who were on identical black Jixers.

Korbin, their demolitions expert, had a backpack full of any tools he needed. He was armed with a 9mm in a shoulder holster, but Rae, Jeremy Sunn, Nathan Drake, and Retter would cover his ass if Korbin had to disarm a bomb.

Drake's beefed-up body dwarfed the bike. His weathered look had been earned in the big house when he took his twin brother's place in prison after his sibling was conned by a drug lord. That had been on the heels of Drake's tour of duty as a Special Forces soldier. Sunn had spent his share of time in lockup, but mostly under orders, though he'd come to BAD with his own rap sheet. His blond hair stuck out haphazardly when he removed his helmet that was now hooked on a handlebar.

Rae hadn't twitched a muscle in a while, her helmet on and latched, backpack slung across her shoulders. Tall, toned, and tough, she wore a thin all-weather suit in black like the other agents.

Retter's phone beeped through his Bluetooth. He pressed the button. "Go ahead."

Gotthard said, "Got a location. Chicago. Clark Street Bridge and Lower Wacker. Bomb detonates in twenty-one minutes."

Ending the call, Retter spoke into his transmitter, passing the information to his team. "Take off, Korbin. We're right behind you."

Korbin flipped his face shield down and rolled on his throttle, squealing rubber in a streak as he left.

Retter took off right behind him. Korbin wove between cars then cut over after a truck to take a fast right turn. Retter followed around the same curve, pressing hard and leaning close to knee dragging the pavement. He straightened up quickly before plowing between traffic cluttering every lane ahead.

Korbin sliced over to the sidewalk, which had little foot traffic. Some guy jogging in sweats flew up a set of steps. Korbin zigged and zagged, blaring his horn and missing anyone in the way. The pedestrians he passed had vacated the sidewalk by the time Retter and the other three bikes roared down.

Retter slid around the corner when Wacker Drive turned right. He faced a wall of people running away from the Clark Street Bridge. Gotthard and Joe had contacted local police by now, under the guise of being with the FBI, ordering the police to put out announcements for evacuation of vehicle traffic and pedestrians anywhere near that bridge. Joe would have informed Chicago PD an FBI bomb squad was heading to the scene on motorcycles, which gave Retter and his team a half hour before the PD showed up. Maybe.

If the time for the detonation was accurate a half hour would be plenty of time. Unless they didn't disarm the bomb.

Retter slammed on his brakes, his back tire coming off the ground, then dropping down. He kicked the stand down and climbed off the bike, pulling out his FBI windbreaker. Rae parked and pulled her matching jacket on, then shouldered a high-powered LaRue Tactical OBR rifle. All four of them plowed through the crowd.

"I'm at the base of the bridge," Korbin's voice said calmly in Retter's earpiece.

He hated fucking bombs.

"Got it," Korbin muttered, indicating he'd found the bomb. "Still scanning . . . shit . . . see a second one."

Retter stopped at the top of the bridge on the south side, sending Sunn and Drake across to cover the north bank of the river. Rae didn't slow until she reached the park area below and to the southeast side of the bridge. She had the best vantage point to keep an eye on Korbin's movement and any unexpected activity beneath the bridge.

"Goddammit," Korbin said.

Retter said, "What's wrong?" He leaned over to see Korbin swinging under the bridge, using his hands to carry his weight and the backpack.

"Five, repeat, five bombs." He was breathing faster with the exertion. "Let me get a look." Silence for a few seconds, then, "Material appears possibly uranium based, but not a large amount."

Retter had seen Korbin teaching Rae how to disarm minimally complex bombs in seconds. Let this be quick and simple. "How much time will each one take to disarm?"

"First one might take five minutes. Next ones will be faster." But Korbin didn't say how much faster.

Not encouraging.

Retter scanned the mass of panicked people moving away from the bridge and flooding out of the buildings, adding to the chaos. Korbin was one of the very best. Since the bombs didn't contain much uranium, maybe the team would get lucky and the bombs would turn out to be duds. But amateurs didn't normally use uranium.

His phone buzzed again. When Gotthard's voice came through, Retter jumped to the point. "We got five bombs—"

"I know," Gotthard said. "Our contact sent additional information. Five bombs, and the sniper in Colorado controls the detonation somehow."

Hunter better find that bastard, and quick. "You have anything else?"

"Yes. Unusual uranium in bombs. Destruction estimate for simultaneous detonation of all five bombs will result in leveling nine square blocks."

Tens of thousands would die.

—∞—

Hunter sent a set of confirmation clicks on his radio to let Mako know he'd located the man prowling the grounds around the lodge. The mystery guy with the scar was connected to too many events not to be playing a role in the shooting tonight. When the guy hiked up the mountain ridge on the west side,

Hunter sent another message through clicks to let Mako know he was following.

The mystery guy was headed right where Hunter expected Jackson to set up a sniper rifle to shoot the prime minister.

From now on, he'd have to trust that Mako would keep up and shadow Hunter since any radio contact was out.

The mystery guy had no sniper rifle with him, but he moved like he was on the hunt. Was he watching the shooter's back, searching for Hunter since Jackson was expecting him? By the time Hunter closed in on him two hundred feet up the ridge, he had to make a choice.

He was running out of time.

Nineteen minutes until the hit, and he had no idea where Abbie or the sniper was.

He couldn't covertly follow this mystery guy any longer. Hunter palmed his 9mm and moved in fast.

The mystery guy swung around a step before Hunter attacked. They went down, hitting rocks and snow. Neither made a sound beyond grunts and the thud of fists hitting bodies. Hunter took a blow to the jaw, ducked, and flipped his weapon in his hand, slamming the guy in the head, sending him to the ground.

He jumped on him before the guy caught his wind and bent a knee into his back. Hunter shoved his weapon inside his waistband and wrenched the guy's hands behind to bind them with plastic cuffs. He bound his legs next, then flipped him over. "Who are you?"

The guy groaned. "You just fucked up royally."

"Guess it's all a matter of perspective. I'm the one with the gun. You're the one tied up."

"We're after the same sniper. You're letting him take the kill shot."

What the hell? "Start talking."

"You've got maybe ten minutes to find his location. I scoped the property earlier. The Jackson Chameleon has to be up this ridge another twenty yards. There's a perfect spot to take his shot when the prime minister starts playing the piano. He'll be sitting with his back to the windows. The guests were told he'd play at ten o'clock."

"Why should I believe you?"

"Don't. Blood'll be on your hands."

"Who're you working with?"

"No one. I'm on my own team."

Hunter had used that line with teammates from BAD. No wonder they looked at him with the same disgust he fumed with as he looked down at this worthless speck of humanity. He didn't have time to find Mako. If this guy *was* telling the truth, the killer would take that shot soon. "Why would you tell me any of this?"

"Because you stopped me from getting to him before he makes the hit. He's the trigger for a bombing tonight."

Who the fuck was this scar-faced guy?

"Longer you talk to me the less time you have to find him."

Hunter had no time to deal with him. He yanked off the guy's tie and used it as a gag, then shoved him over to the side of the path and raced up the incline.

When he reached the high spot, he used a small handheld infrared device Gotthard had given him to search the area for a heat signature in a prone position . . . and found it. He couldn't even send a click to Mako at this point without alerting Jackson too soon. When Hunter got within twenty feet of the shooter he'd lost any chance of approaching silently with so little time. Besides, Jackson was expecting him.

Hunter walked up with his 9mm in hand.

"Got here sooner than I anticipated." Covered in a white ghillie suit and white knit skullcap, Jackson turned on his side to face Hunter. His index finger remained curled around the trigger of an Accuracy International .300 Win Mag sniper rifle.

"Where's Abbie?"

"Close. And alive for now." Jackson looked more ghost than man with his pale face inside all that white clothing. The only color visible was the tip of a blood-birthmark that dripped down the right side of his forehead as if he'd been shot.

I should be so lucky. "What do you want?"

"Aren't you interested in who's in my crosshairs?" Jackson asked in the tenor voice of a school bully.

"Prime minister." Hunter had never wanted to kill anyone as much as he did now. His fingers tensed with the need to choke the life from this one.

"Ah, you did figure out something on your own. I can see the effort it's taking to restrain yourself, but if you kill me, Abbie dies. You have to know by now that I'm a hemophiliac. Wound me and you lose her, plus anything else you hope to gain from me."

Hunter had to think like the BAD agent he'd been trained to be and not a man ready to kill this psycho who dared to harm Abbie. "We have agents all over this place. You won't get out alive. You want to show some good faith, my people will work with you if you have something on the Fratelli to trade and give me the co-ordinates on the bombing."

"I didn't mean I'd *surrender* to you." He snorted at that. "And if another agent shows up, I'll pull this trigger immediately. Besides, your people couldn't keep me alive long enough to get any information."

"Yes, we can."

The sniper checked his watch, then looked back at Hunter. "Like Josephine Silversteen? You must be part of the group that captured her last year. She didn't even make it to jail before her head exploded like a smashed pumpkin."

"Wouldn't take you to jail." Hunter would enjoy handing this prick over to Joe and Tee. Tee was a tiny, frighteningly beautiful demon when it came to getting information out of a captive. "What Fratelli group are you with?"

"Should be obvious. The UK. That's not why you're here."

"Why am I here?"

"To make a choice, of course." Jackson pulled his thin lips up to one side, not resembling Abbie in the smallest way. "I'm curious how you'll negotiate your way out of this tangle."

"We don't negotiate, so there are no choices."

That made Jackson grin. "You should hear me out before you decide. If I kill the prime minister and send confirmation of that in the next twelve minutes then only *one* city in the United States will suffer, keeping the loss of life down to maybe a few thousand. That would be considered an encore after killing the prime minister, both events of which will result in destroying the fragile communication in progress between the U.S. and UK right now. Your president needs the UK prime minister to vote with the U.S. at the upcoming UN meeting."

When the shooter paused to check his watch again, Hunter's skin tightened. He wondered what Jackson was planning besides the shooting. If the sniper's finger hadn't been locked around the trigger and the rifle pointed at a room full of innocent people, Hunter would attack. The longer he kept Jackson talking the more time BAD had to get to the bomb if Linette managed to send location coordinates. This prick was sharing nothing.

"If I *don't* kill the prime minister," Jackson continued, looking up again, "then *three* American cities will be hit, each with more severity than the last, bringing the death toll up over a hundred thousand. Subsequent bombings would come with a message that any other countries willing to support the U.S. would do so at risk of the same fate."

"Why are you willing to put our country into political and possibly armed conflict with your country?"

"I don't actually have a country. I just perform a duty."

"You want me to choose between killing an innocent man and destroying three cities? How about maiming you as an option?"

"There is that, but if you so much as cut me I'll bleed out. I'm a type-B hemophiliac, the most prolific of free bleeders." Jackson enjoyed showing off his perfectly white teeth again. "Speaking of blood, if you win our game without killing me, you'll be able to save Abbie and her mother."

"Your mother, too."

"Genetic semantics."

Hunter wanted to hurt this Jackson for so many reasons, Eliot and Abbie topping the list. But unsuspecting civilians would die by the thousands if he made a wrong decision. He had to find out why the shooter had brought him to this spot. "Are you through laying out the rules?"

The killer consulted his watch again, then cocked his head at Hunter. "Wait, it only gets better. You can go save Abbie or you can stop me from killing the prime minister, at which point only one city will be sacrificed when five compact bombs with a new strain of uranium detonate. Bombs capable of taking down nine square blocks in . . . Chicago, Chicago." He sang the name of the city like the words from the musical. "The explosion will detonate at the Clark Street Bridge and shake the foundation of your ex-sister-in-law's condominium building on Wacker. Now, who are you willing to save and who do you sacrifice?"

Todd, Pia, and baby Barrett would be home at Pia's place.

Hunter struggled to breathe. His heart hammered his chest, threatening to burst from the blood surging through his body.

He had to get word on the bomb location to BAD.

"Abbie," Jackson said, drawing Hunter back to him, "is hanging off a cliff exactly one hundred feet from here, but you don't know the direction yet, so don't get excited. And if you don't leave in"—the killer glanced at his watch again and looked up—"twenty-six seconds you won't reach her before the small bomb attached to the tension anchor snaps her connection to the wall. What's it going to be?"

"You fucking bastard!"

"If you read the hidden files, you know I'm not a bastard. Twenty-one seconds."

"Where is she?"

"Not yet . . . fifteen, fourteen, thirteen." He looked up. "There's a path six feet above you. At that point go twenty-two yards, then veer directly left and keep going until you reach the ridge." He grinned at Hunter and counted down. "Six, five."

Jackson's finger relaxed from the trigger.

Time for a leap of faith that Mako was now in position.

A gunshot exploded from behind Hunter. The bullet hit the backside of the trigger guard and shattered Jackson's fingers.

The killer howled in pain. He jerked his hand up in horror, blood spewing out of his ragged fingers.

Hunter kicked Jackson backward, away from the rifle.

Mako burst out of the dark and dove on Jackson, yelling, "We know about Chicago. More agents on the way. Get Abbie."

Hunter had already taken off running. Joe had sent extra agents. Not that much of a surprise since Hunter hadn't expected to get out of this clean. Mako had explained during the helicopter flight that if they had to wound Jackson, he'd use a tourniquet to stop the bleeding. Mako would inject a clotting agent into Jackson and had no problem tightening the tourniquet to the point of the sniper losing a limb.

Mako had shot "Expert" in the Marine Corps, and was capable of blowing a hole in the enemy with skill that equalled his ability to sew one up in someone he wanted to save.

He'd do whatever it took to keep Jackson alive.

That miserable piece of shit had better survive.

After counting twenty-two yards with running strides, Hunter swung left. He shoved branches out of his way and stumbled over rocks and burst into a clearing at a cliff.

A rope was tied to a tree six feet back from the edge of a cliff. The face fell off for days. He hurried to grab the rope that was slack, which meant the killer had climbed back up from wherever he'd left Abbie hanging.

Hunter looked over the edge into a black abyss.

His heart dropped faster than the blood pressure of a dying man at the sight of her body in a snowsuit dangling in the wind.

Her sobs echoed against the stone.

"Hang on, baby, I'm coming!"

All Hunter had was Eliot's beat-up karabiner. He hooked the rope through it and looped the tail of the rope around his back in a makeshift rappelling tension, then swung over the side, easing himself down.

"Don't come down," she cried. "There's a . . . a bomb . . . it's—"

"Stay still."

"Hunter, stop!" she screamed. "You'll die. Go back."

He dropped fast, sick with fear he'd reach her too

late. When he reached the tension anchor holding her rope sling he spotted the bomb device. It had enough C-4 to start an avalanche. And there was no way to remove the bomb without removing the anchor.

The timer ticked down. Sixty-four seconds, sixty-three . . .

She begged him between sobs. "Please go back."

He lowered himself. "I'm not losing you." When he dropped down beside her he only had another six feet of rope trailing from his waist. Her hands had been tied in front of her.

"We don't both have to die."

"We're not going to." He hoped. He looped a quick knot at the karabiner, not even sure if the battered piece would still hold, then used his knife to free her wrists. Pulling up the tail of his rope, he threaded it under the rope tied around her waist and made two quick figure-eight knots.

Waves of tremors shook off her, but he couldn't comfort her yet with seconds flying away. "Hold this rope. Brace your feet apart and keep them against the wall," he ordered and climbed back up, hand over hand, feeding the rope through his karabiner.

"He told me you'd die trying to save me," she yelled in a stronger voice, determined to negotiate. "He said—"

"Forget him. Do what I say." Keeping her alive was not negotiable. He walked his feet against the wall, stopping next to the bomb, and tied off with what slack rope he could pull up. "Look straight ahead," he ordered.

Twelve . . . eleven seconds. Disarming the device would be easy. If he had tools.

He reached for his knife. "Abbie, get ready."

"For what?"

Ten . . . nine.

"To fall." He cut the rope sling holding her and grabbed the anchor attached to the bomb as her weight yanked him back.

She screamed when she fell.

His hand slipped off the anchor.

Six seconds . . . five.

Lunging up against the dead weight towing him down, his fingers hooked on metal. He released the tension clip and yanked the bomb and anchor free, flinging the deadly pair away. *"Cover your ears!"*

The bomb detonated. Compression and heat boiled off the explosion, but far away from Abbie. "Baby, you okay?"

He didn't hear anything. "Abbie, goddammit, talk to me."

"I'm okay," she yelled.

He started breathing again and almost laughed at her angry tone until she got quiet again.

"But . . . you can't get back up with me," she said in a small voice. Her terror traveled easily in the empty night air, but it didn't stop her. "He told me . . . how your friend died. That I had to—"

"Abbie, stop."

"—untie my rope . . ."

"Don't you fucking do that!" Hunter couldn't live through this again. "Don't . . . baby, please, oh, God, please trust me. I can get us both out of here."

She was wheezing, close to hyperventilating. "How?"

"Just give me a minute. Don't quit on me now." His

voice shook, the words coming out in a rough croak. Something sure and strong blazed in his mind. She needed to know why she could trust him. "I love you. I can't lose you."

But had the bastard jury-rigged the rope sling so that the loops around her waist would come loose? Hunter couldn't think that way.

"Hunter—"

"Please . . . don't leave me."

"I don't want to lose you either."

He dropped his head against the rope, getting his breath back. "Then hold on. My team will get us out of here."

Reaching around, he got his hands on the trailing rope and pulled with everything he had, lifting her slowly to him.

When she got closer, he called out in a voice thick with worry, "Give me your hand."

He pulled up another foot of rope, and another.

Her fingertips touched his arm. He grabbed her arm, hauling her up to him with a burst of adrenaline. She was sobbing and terrified and alive.

He had her wrapped in his arms and wasn't letting go.

Mako and the other two agents weren't really his team, but Joe and Tee expected—no, demanded—all their agents to work as a unit of one in any situation. Hunter could now see how much space Joe and Retter had allowed him to prove he could be a team player for the past four years.

He'd failed miserably. And going rogue to find the killer had sealed his fate.

Joe wouldn't suffer that with any agent.

Once Hunter got off this mountain, he'd find out the extent of his penalties and pay them without a word of complaint.

"It's okay, baby. They're coming," Hunter assured her, even though Mako's first duty was to secure the prisoner. Might be another half hour, but he'd talk her through this.

"Ready to come up, *asshole*?" someone shouted from the top. Lights appeared overhead and Mako peered down at him, his big grin in place. He had extra rope looped over his arm.

Being called *asshole* had never sounded so good.

But what about Todd and his family in Chicago?

CHAPTER FORTY-FOUR

R etter kept checking his watch, willing it to slow
down and help Korbin, who had gained a slight
edge from the learning curve after disarming the first
bomb. He'd just called an all-clear on the third bomb
in less than two minutes, but the first one had cost
nine.

People had scattered faster than ants from a disturbed anthill from the Clark Street Bridge, but thousands were clogging downtown Chicago in a mad dash
to exit. The roar of voices competed with sirens coming
from all directions.

Korbin could do this. Had to come through.

When Joe had brought the cocky demolitions expert into BAD two years back, Retter withheld his
opinion of the former stunt professional until he'd had
a chance to observe Korbin in action during a mission
in Chechnya.

Korbin ran so cool when he worked he could freeze
lava.

Gotthard had joked that Korbin lived on a diet of ice
water and available women.

One female might be too available. Retter hadn't
determined if Korbin and Rae had hooked up or not.
Something he'd deal with later.

The ping of a bullet striking metal sounded clearly at the same time as Korbin's yell. "Incoming fire."

A second shot rang out.

"Shooter low on the north side," Rae called, already racing along the parking area below the south side of the bridge. She wheeled and shot out lights along the bridge to give Korbin the cover of darkness first, then she took out the lights above her.

"Find him, Drake." Retter issued the order, then ran down the drive from the bridge and joined Rae in the parking zone to better cover Korbin.

With so many civilians around, no agent could return fire unless he or she had a clear shot.

"I'm at number four," Korbin said.

Retter used his thermal imaging scope to sweep over the north bank, looking for a heat signature from the next flash. He told Rae, "You keep watch for the flash; I'm going to take a look at Korbin's position."

"I'm on it." She swept her rifle systematically across the opposite bank.

"Number four disarmed," Korbin said a minute later, calm and controlled.

Retter watched Korbin's heat signature swing toward the last bomb, his body fully exposed.

A shot pierced the night.

Rae called into the headset, "Second floor, two o'clock from the bridge."

Korbin's body jerked. He cursed. The bullet had hit him.

"How bad are you?" Retter called.

"I'll make it," Korbin ground out.

Rae held her weapon steady, watching.

The next shot hit a steel beam on the bridge, then she fired and cursed. "He moved. Drake, you got him?"

Shots echoed, striking metal . . . then no ping against metal.

Korbin cursed, livid. He'd been hit again, but there was nothing any of them could do except find the shooter.

A shot exploded from the other bank. "Got the fucker," Drake called out. "Terminated."

Korbin stopped moving forward on the bridge. He was at the last bomb. Retter checked his watch. Seventy seconds until 10:00 PM. If the bullet wounds hadn't incapacitated Korbin, Retter estimated he could disarm the last bomb in sixty seconds, maybe less—

"Last one's activating," Korbin yelled. "Get away from the bridge."

Rae swung around and ran *toward* the damn bridge.

Retter ran after her, yelling, *"Rae!"*

She looked back at Retter. The explosion threw her off her feet sideways.

Retter stumbled, watching in disbelief. The far end of the bridge shot up in the air, twisting, powerful steel sections wrenching and screeching. Windows of towering buildings on that side of the river blew into the offices. The smell of chemicals and sulfur stung the air. Concrete foundation buckled on the north side of the bridge.

The mangled half of the bridge that had lifted up hung suspended for an eerie second, then crashed downward, slamming the Chicago River.

Displaced water exploded upward, a violent wave busting over the bank.

Silence followed so suddenly it was jarring.

Rae jumped up from where she'd fallen, screaming, *"Korbin!"* She started running for the bridge. *"Korbin!"*

Retter dove and tackled her to the ground. "Stop, dammit."

"What happened to Korbin?" She rolled over, fought him, beating his arms away, but Retter wouldn't let go.

"We've got agents on the other side, Rae."

She finally stopped fighting him. Her breaths came out ragged in the grip of agony, but she nodded. "Right. Call 'em."

Retter let her up and jumped to his feet. She'd lost her earpiece when she went down. He spoke into the mic and had to cup his ear to hear. "North bank report. Where are you?" He listened, then slowly turned to look across the river.

Rae stepped forward, eyes tracking toward the same spot as if she could will the answer she wanted.

Sunn flicked a light on and off to pinpoint his position on the north bank.

She grabbed Retter's arm. "What about—"

"Where's Korbin?" Retter listened. His mouth dried out. He pulled his hand down from his ear and looked at her. "Rae—"

She swung a look at him that started out hopeful, then reflected the horror he felt.

"He didn't make it off the bridge," Retter said, repeating what he'd been told. "Jeremy saw Korbin swinging up to the last bomb, then the shooter . . . we'll get divers—"

"No! Get rescue. He. Is. Not. Dead!" she yelled.

"It's not possible that he could have survived—"

She turned her weapon on him. "Get the goddamn helicopters and water rescue now!"

He grabbed her, stripping her weapon away only because she was too wrapped up in shock over Korbin's death to be a threat right then. She fought him, screaming to let her go find Korbin. She wanted blood.

So did Retter. He understood the blinding pain of loss.

He could knock her out, but he wouldn't do that to Rae in front of agents she'd still have to work with. What he did next would cause her almost as much humiliation, but he had no choice.

Folding her arms in front of her, he wrapped her up in his, holding her tight. He felt the minute she broke.

Not big sobbing tears, just a hard shuddering.

Korbin had saved thousands. But he couldn't have survived.

BAD would make someone pay for taking one of their own.

———◦◦◦———

Hunter accepted the hand Mako offered him and climbed up over the edge of the cliff, then took five steps. "Where is she?"

Abbie shot out of the darkness. "Are you okay?" She launched into Hunter's arms, trembling.

"I'm fine." He hugged her close, amazed at the feeling. He wanted this. Wanted her, but he'd screwed up so badly Joe and Tee might bury him.

"She's gotta go now, Hunter," Mako said. "Got a helicopter landing to pick up her and Jackson. I slowed the blood flow, but he's thready. Might not make it to the medical center."

"He talking at all?" Hunter asked, loath to release Abbie, though he knew he had to in order to have any hope of saving her and her mother.

"Talking his head off in trade for pain medicine, especially after I cut the circulation off to his hand." A sound came out of Mako's throat that reverberated with disgust. "Not so dangerous when you take his rifle away."

Hunter wanted to know one thing. "He tell you what he gave Abbie and her mother?"

"Not yet."

Abbie shook from shock and cold.

Hunter hugged her, turning her toward the helicopter.

"Sorry, Hunter. Joe said you had to stay with me."

Abbie looked up at Hunter. "Who are these people and why can't you come with me?"

He gripped her hand for an extra second, then pulled her into his arms and kissed her. This might be his last chance. When he broke the kiss, he cupped her face. "I can't tell you—"

"Dammit," she shouted, and backed out of his arms as though he had leprosy. "I *trusted* you! With my life. With my mother's life. And you can't trust me with *anything*?"

"Abbie, you don't understand."

"You're right, I don't. You said you—" She shook her head, refusing to repeat his words.

He'd told her he loved her. He did.

She looked over at Stoner, one of the two extra agents Joe had sent. "Are you taking me back?"

"Yes, ma'am."

She nodded and walked over to Stoner.

Hunter cursed himself a thousand times over for letting things get so out of shape with Joe that he couldn't leave with Abbie, because Mako would use his weapon if necessary. "Abbie, wait."

She swung around, eyes fiery with a level of disappointment he'd never expected. "I'm through waiting. I've waited and waited for you to give me an inch. Love is important, but it's nothing without trust." She glanced at Mako. "I appreciate every one of you helping to get that genetic mistake to the medical center for my mother, but I'm done with *all* this."

Looking back one last time at Hunter, she added, "Go back to your secret life. I can't live that way."

His insides withered at the finality in her voice. She was done with him and he couldn't blame her. His lack of trust had smacked her every time she'd offered her trust in return. If he hadn't alienated his team she wouldn't have walked into the lair of an assassin and ended up dangling off the side of a mountain.

With a ticking bomb.

Abbie disappeared into the darkness with Stoner.

"How'd you find JC?" Mako asked Hunter once Abbie and Stoner were out of earshot.

Talking would be easier without a knot of disappointment in his throat. Hunter coughed to clear his voice. "The guy with the scar." He stopped and wheeled on Mako. "Did you find him on your way up the path, about halfway?"

"No. Show me."

Hunter guided Mako to the spot where he'd left the mystery guy. Two cut plastic handcuffs dangled from a limb.

He shook his head. "How could he have gotten out of that?"

Mako lifted both pieces with a pen and slipped them into a plastic bag he produced from a jacket pocket.

"Bet the only prints are mine," Hunter told him.

"I wouldn't take that bet." Mako's phone buzzed. He answered it, then listened a minute and hung up. "Jackson is stable. A Dr. Murphy from Johns Hopkins is reviewing the files on Abbie's mother and waiting to see Abbie. Says he knows what's wrong with her mother."

Hunter had lined up Murphy for her mother, but now he was doubly thankful since Abbie needed the doctor as well. "Can he cure them?"

"Possibly. Murphy said Abbie's mother was given a synthetic disease that attacks the spleen. He believes he can stop the disease and maybe reverse the damage with a treatment that includes a transfusion loaded with the same white cells as her natural blood. If Jackson makes it to the medical center alive, she may live."

"Jackson gave Abbie something, too," Hunter said.

"Murphy won't know what Abbie's diagnosis is until he runs tests on her."

Hunter considered overpowering Mako to get to Abbie, but Retter had made it clear what he'd do to Abbie and Borys if Hunter gave them any trouble. He had to tell himself that Abbie was safe for now and finish this op to have any chance of making peace with Joe and Tee. Hunter doubted that was possible, but he wouldn't screw the only chance he had to show he could work with the team.

But what about Todd and his family? "You get the bomb location to Joe?"

Mako nodded. "Retter's there already."

That didn't meant they knew everything. "It's a bridge—"

"With five bombs."

"Have they disarmed them yet?"

"Korbin got four before the last one detonated. Damage is minimal compared to what it could have been."

"No buildings came down?" Hunter was trying to read Mako's reaction.

"So far, only one casualty. Korbin."

Chapter Forty-five

"It sounds as though the damage was not as extensive as anticipated," Ostrovsky said, opening the conference-call meeting with five members of the council of Angeli. He'd placed the call the minute he'd received word of the bombings. Vestavia had called him immediately to share his good news about Bardaric's failure. "The prime minister surviving is good, yes?"

"What the hell happened?" Chike demanded.

"Bardaric has been running his own operation for a while," Vestavia answered. "He lied about delivering materials for three bombing. We've found his people who were involved with the Chicago bombing. They're all squealing and said Bardaric only delivered enough for one bombing."

Renaldo interjected, "I, for one, think he got better than he deserved. MI6 was much nicer, with a bullet between his eyes, than I would have been, given the opportunity. We must replace him and take care we do not allow this to happen again."

"Anyone know where he was keeping this apparently bogus supply of UX, just in case it exists?" Vestavia asked.

Ostrovsky addressed his question. "I did some checking and believe the 'accidental' bombing in a small Ukrainian town a month ago was the test for Bardaric's bomb. I don't know that the bomb material is going to be our issue. My sources tell me Bardaric's sniper told the U.S. authorities where to find Bardaric and where he hid his research facilities. I would say if we wait a week or two, our contacts within the intelligence organizations will be able to confirm if Bardaric's UX reserves were located."

Ostrovsky waited until everyone agreed, then added, "We're fortunate the MI6-turned-assassin working for Bardaric was stopped. Our intention was never to start World War Three."

"Not at this time," Vestavia joked, clearly happy now that his nemesis had been neutralized. "Let's get back on track and continue dismantling each continent in an orderly way."

"Speaking of getting back on track, what has become of Peter Wentworth and his daughter?" Derain asked, his tone bulging with suspicion.

Ostrovsky had been waiting on Stoke to ask that so he didn't have to, but Derain was even better.

"Peter and Gwen disappeared, along with all of his Fratelli staff, before Bardaric's assassin was caught," Vestavia answered, clearly not happy to be put on the spot. "I have no idea. The secret wing in Kore burned to the ground, damaging part of the public area of the women's center. All records relating to the Fratelli were removed. Bardaric might even have them stashed somewhere, if they're still alive. He was hell-bent on ensuring I would have no allies here, but if he thought removing Wentworth would cripple me he underestimated me and the extent of my resources."

"Speaking of which, have you located your mole, Vestavia?" Stoke asked.

"Yes. I'm taking care of that as soon as we finish here."

Ostrovsky finished up the meeting and ended the call. He sat back in his overstuffed office chair, contemplating the sun burning off the fog in downtown Boston outside his living room window.

The Denver mission was not an entirely successful operation but was also not a complete loss since Jackson had pinned the whole mess on Bardaric, right down to the attempt on the prime minister's life.

Jackson had told the authorities Bardaric had been the person directing him. Yes, Jackson would have told the FBI and anyone else that he'd been a paid killer for some crazy guy who believed he supported a cause. The name Fratelli never came up in the report Ostrovsky had gotten his hands on.

He'd chosen well twenty-seven years ago when he killed Jackson's father and became the boy's benefactor, guiding his education and destiny.

The greatest casualty in all of this was Jackson.

He'd served Ostrovsky exceptionally by convincing Vestavia that Bardaric had been behind the unauthorized killings in the U.S.

Jackson was loyal to the end, sending the U.S. after Bardaric, which took care of Ostrovsky's problems. Then Jackson ended his own life, as they'd always discussed. He'd used one of his small fingernails to slice his wrist.

Vestavia had been right to worry about Bardaric being the most dangerous of the seven on their Angeli council . . . until now.

None of the other five had considered who the second-most dangerous one might be. Ostrovsky pressed the speed dial on his cell phone and waited until the clicking finished so he could speak over a secure line.

When his Asian contact answered, Ostrovsky told him, "We will have a new UK representative soon. How is my project coming?"

———

Linette walked into the reception area outside Vestavia's office, where Basil and Frederick waited. She took stock of her counterparts and the past twenty-four hours.

The mission had failed according to Fratelli terms. She and the other two had to answer for their parts.

She'd worn a windbreaker over her blouse and slacks. Vestavia had called her twenty minutes ago and ordered her to his office. Bed heads and casual clothes on the other two meant they'd also received little notice. She'd grabbed the first thing she could find that would hide any trembling.

Basil looked grim, but when he caught her eye he shrugged, as if to say "Some things are out of our control."

Not true. She'd been in full control of sending the bomb locations the minute she could. If she'd been able to leave Vestavia faster once she had the information she might have gotten it to them in time to disarm all five bombs. One had gone off, but there had been only one casualty. Not thousands.

Still, someone had died because she couldn't give them five or ten more minutes' notice.

Vestavia would not be forgiving.

Her conscience would have been less forgiving if she'd allowed thousands of innocent people to die. She steeled herself to face her punishment for failure and prayed he hadn't discovered that she'd leaked the information.

Basil lifted his eyebrows suggestively and winked. So sure of winning something—her—out of this mission.

She ignored him.

Vestavia opened the door and walked away—their sign to enter.

Linette tried to breathe normally but all she could manage were painful little drags of air through her constricted throat. She took her usual position next to the brass statue, standing with straight posture, eyes staring dead ahead.

Basil and Frederick filed in behind her, closing the door, then standing next to her. Three lieutenants in a line.

"Fra, I know there were problems—" Basil started.

Vestavia held up his hand, which brought immediate silence. "Actually, this project went better than I anticipated."

Linette blinked twice quickly but maintained her stance.

Vestavia went to his desk and lifted a file. "Yes, in spite of the underwhelming results of the Chicago bombing, I did get something I've been searching for."

Basil and Frederick relaxed immediately.

Linette had worked with Vestavia long enough to understand the meaning of his deceptively happy voice. He was anything but.

"I've kept close tabs on all of you." He strolled along in front of them, holding the file behind him in the image of Hitler addressing his men. "One of you has been a very busy person."

Frederick's skin seemed to shrink and lose color.

Linette's hands were icy and damp. Had Vestavia found a second ghost on the computers? She'd been forced to wait until the very last minute to send her on-line contact the coordinates, and routing the post had taken extra time.

She'd been careful, but maybe not careful enough.

Vestavia smiled at Basil. "I've seen you here late at night putting in overtime. Long hours every day."

Basil's cheeks puckered, but he didn't smile, though she could feel how much he wanted to gloat at what he clearly perceived as a compliment.

"You've certainly worked hard to show me how bright and dedicated you are." Vestavia's voice lightened, as if he were happy about something. "I have to admit, I'm impressed."

"Thank you, Fra," Basil said.

When Vestavia turned to stroll back the other way, Basil sent Linette a confident leer.

And here she'd been worried about getting caught by Vestavia. That disgusting toad Basil was making mental plans for how he'd abuse her. She could see it in the liquid slime gleaming in his eyes.

No, not again. Never again would she let some animal use her. The last one had been too old to hurt her more than three or four times a week.

The animal standing at her elbow would hurt her that many times a night.

Vestavia stopped and wheeled back around. "You covered many parts of this mission, didn't you, Basil?"

Basil was stunned. He licked his lips, unable to answer.

"It's okay, Basil. You earned the credit. Why not take it?"

The sound of pressure releasing slipped past Basil's lips. He gave a fair impression of looking humble. "Just checking on the whole team, Fra. I knew this was important to you."

"Yes, this mission was important, but for more than just wrecking a city. We can do that any time we want."

Basil's next facial impression was that of a confused mutt.

Vestavia opened the file and glanced at the notes. "I need good people, dependable people, trustworthy people. I reward those who show me more than simple commitment."

Linette noticed Vestavia left out the part about what he did to those he couldn't trust.

"I've been looking for a mole in our organization for a while now, and I've found that person."

Linette kept staring straight ahead. Panic would be a dead giveaway. If he'd caught her, she'd—

"You're brilliant, Linette." He started walking toward her. "You're the epitome of dedication and follow instructions to a T."

Basil gaped at her.

She slid her eyes horizontally, refusing to take the bait. She had no other plan than denial.

"That's why I picked you." Vestavia stepped past her. "What I'm wondering is why I ever allowed someone like Basil to infiltrate my operation." He turned on Basil. "I found the ghost trail on your computer where *you* sent the coordinates to a chat room."

Basil's face looked as though he was already dead.

He would be soon.

Vestavia snapped his fingers and guards burst into the room. Basil finally caught on. He looked from Vestavia to the guards in horror. "No, I didn't betray you."

When one guard grabbed Basil, he screamed, "Noooo!" The second guard slapped a piece of duct tape over his mouth.

Linette should feel some guilt over leaving her files in her office for Basil to break in and read them, or for routing the post with the bomb location to the chat room through Basil's computer, using his ID code in a buried signature.

To be honest, she felt relief.

Vestavia dismissed Frederick, then told Linette, "Sorry I couldn't give you time to shower. We've got a busy day. Meet me back here in an hour."

"Absolutely, Fra." She nodded and walked out on weak legs, but she'd taken one animal out of the game.

CHAPTER FORTY-SIX

Hunter walked into the offices in the Bat Tower overlooking downtown Nashville that housed the BAD agency.

He doubted this meeting would be casual considering Tee was joining Joe to give Hunter their decision on his future.

"Joe and Tee are waiting," Danya said when he stepped through the doors into the reception area. He'd heard about a new hire for the offices. Average-looking except for the spiked red hair and blaring yellow skirt with a black sweater, she sat behind a desk tapping at a computer.

"Thanks. Gotthard here, too?"

"In the back conference room with Rae, uh, working on the memorial," Danya answered, a halfhearted smile on her lips. The quick downcast of her eyes back to whatever she was working on reflected the general mood after they'd lost one of their own.

Korbin had died saving the lives of thousands of people.

Including Todd, Pia, and Barrett.

Hunter thanked him daily for their lives. He'd never be able to repay that debt. He *would* keep an eye out for Rae and watch her back if he gained his freedom again.

He was glad to have cleared the air with Korbin before this happened, but that didn't make his loss any easier.

Pushing forward, he turned down the hall to Joe's office, which connected with Tee's.

Rae came around the corner at the other end, barreling forward on long sweeping strides, head down. She must have sensed him when he stopped walking. She looked up and slowed a step, then picked up speed.

"Rae, I'm sorry about—"

"Save it." She only glanced at him for a microsecond. Long enough for him to see that nothing would repair the damage inside her. Losing Korbin had torn her in ways Hunter understood, but she wouldn't want to hear it.

Not right now and not from him.

He reached Joe's office door and entered.

Tee stood behind Joe's desk. The glance of acknowledgment she gave him reminded Hunter of an executioner sizing up a condemned man's neck. "Joe was called away."

Most people might foolishly think having only Tee, a petite Vietnamese woman with fine features and gorgeous eyes, would play into Hunter's favor.

Those would be the people who had no inkling of Tee's background or abilities. Those who were deceived by a woman in four-inch heels who just reached his shoulders and turned the electric-blue skirt suit she wore into an erotic statement.

She could handle a man twice her size and kill with the paper clip she held in her delicate fingers.

"Still want to talk?" Hunter knew the answer, but someone had to make the next move.

"Of course." She finished clipping the document and placed it carefully on the corner of Joe's desk. Everything about her was careful, calculated, and controlled.

"Have a seat," she said, moving to the front of Joe's desk, where she leaned a hip.

That had not been a suggestion but an order.

"Didn't think this would take that long." He sat down in the office chair facing her.

"You in a hurry?" she asked.

"Depends on what you and Joe have decided."

"We haven't."

Ah, hell. They were going to lock him up and make him sweat out their decision. If he tried to disappear, they'd simply go get Abbie, who couldn't leave her mother's bedside now that she was improving. They both were.

Hunter owed a few more thanks, like to Dr. Murphy from Johns Hopkins, who'd determined Abbie hadn't been given anything really harmful. Jackson had lied. Big surprise.

Abbie had gone home with her mother. Hunter wanted to see her so much his body ached from missing her.

He'd never been passive in his life and wasn't starting now. "Why haven't you made a decision yet?"

"We can't agree."

He leaned forward. "On?"

"I was ready to take you out of the field."

She hadn't said "permanently," but this was Tee, so that was a given. He had no idea what he could say to sway her, so he waited for her to continue.

"Joe and Retter understand why you did what you

did. It's not that I don't understand. It's that I don't care. I only care about our missions and our agents."

He had nothing to gain by trying to bullshit her. "You're right. No one should take the autonomy I did."

She angled her head a fraction and raised one fine black eyebrow. "Why didn't you realize that before now?"

"I wanted to kill the person who had taken Eliot from me." He hadn't expected to be talking about this, but he owed Joe and Retter for blowing the chance they'd given him to prove he could be a part of the team. If Joe was willing to speak up for him then Hunter could tell Tee the truth. "That was rage speaking. Eliot would have been pissed if he'd known. He wouldn't care about stopping one assassin for payback. He worked for BAD to stop groups like the Fratelli, to make this country safe for the people he loved. I've finally realized I was actually doing a disservice to him and what he lived for by going after one assassin. If he was standing here today he'd kick my ass across this building and back for losing sight of the big picture."

She didn't speak, just kept piercing him with a stiletto-pointed gaze, so he continued.

"Regardless of what you decide, I'd like to attend Korbin's memorial. I don't know if he's got any family, but I'm in if we're doing something for them." He wasn't going to flaunt his money and say he'd cover it all. That would insult the rest of the team. He'd pay his share. That's what a team member would do.

"I wouldn't have believed it," she murmured.

"What? That I could be honest?"

"No, that you could change my mind." Her lips

curved softly into a smile with only a hint of evil hiding. "You're back on the team, but what about this Abbie? She's in the media. Not our favorite people."

"She lost her job with the media."

"Make sure she doesn't get another one."

"How do you expect me to do that?"

"I don't care how you do it." Tee got up and walked around the desk, then leaned forward with her hands supporting her. "She knows about you and what you do."

"She's not going to say anything," Hunter argued. "She doesn't know anything about this location, the name of our organization, nothing that she could tell anyone, even if she would, which she won't."

"You sound pretty certain."

"I *am* certain. I trust her with my—"

"Life?" Tee smirked.

Hunter didn't have to think before answering this time. "Yes."

"Really." Tee straightened away from the desk and crossed her arms. "Did you get a new safe house?"

"Yes."

"Going to share that location with us?"

"Not unless you want to be tied to the fallout if the CIA ever finds out about my houseguest."

"No, we don't, which is why we never pressed you before. Anyone else know about the location?"

"No."

"But Eliot knew, didn't he?"

Hunter shrugged. "Yes. What's your point?"

"You don't trust Abbie, so I don't trust her. How do you plan to assure us she isn't going to be a threat to our security?"

"You need plenty of fluids." Abbie held the cup so her mother could take a sip of vitamin-infused water. Dr. Murphy had released her mother two days ago to come home.

Abbie's apartment still stank of tear gas, which reminded her of the deep fear she'd lived through. She'd packed a bag of clothes she washed as soon as she reached her mother's house.

Her mother took the cup from her hand. "Don't ignore me, Abigail. This is the first chance we've had to talk without Hannah in the room. What happened? Why did you lose your job?"

"Because the station is still spinning this to fix the backlash from me being involved when Gwen Wentworth was shot. They gave me a chance to save my name if I'd write an exclusive on my ordeal. I refused. When I started, I thought I'd like working for television, but I don't want to share intimate details of what happened to me, so I can't see myself asking someone else to do that. My reputation is shot in television."

"I'm sorry, honey."

"The only upside is that I hated working for a scumbag." She smiled at her mother. "But I did hear some good news. Brittany's grandfather fired Stuey. And I did get an offer from a regional magazine to report on Chicago's who's who in business and where they're seen around town. They seem to think since I was seen with a Thornton-Payne I must be 'in the know.'" She did the air quotes with her fingers. Filming documentaries might not happen in this lifetime with the dark cloud hanging over her television career.

"Oh."

"Why do you sound disappointed, Mom?" Not that Abbie was doing backflips over this job offer or that she believed anyone in the Thornton-Payne league would ever speak to her, but it was a paying gig if she got it and meant reporting on the cream of the corporate world.

She might run into a Thorton-Payne, as in Todd, but not Hunter. The tug of pain caught her by surprise again.

"What about that idea you had to film children at different times in their lives for a couple—"

"No." Abbie had once thought about creating video scrapbooks for parents. She'd saved the idea to start with her own family, because filming documentaries had always been her true passion. What was the chance she'd ever have little ones of her own? Zilch if she couldn't have a family with the man she loved.

Falling for Hunter proved trust and love didn't go hand in hand as she'd always believed.

Worse, she still loved that bastard.

He'd said he loved her, but he hadn't trusted her.

She couldn't accept one without the other and Hunter lived a life that didn't allow for opening himself up totally to a woman.

"You're awake." Hannah strolled into the bedroom eating a dish of ice cream and carrying a second one she handed to her mother.

"I don't get one?" Abbie asked, annoyed.

"You've got laundry to do." Hannah shoved another spoonful in her mouth and moaned.

"I thought you wanted to stay a size six." Abbie grabbed for the bowl. Hannah stuck it high in the air.

"Plumping up a few curves didn't hurt you. I'll take someone like that Hunter guy you were running around with anytime."

Over my dead body. Abbie clamped her lips shut to keep from speaking her thoughts.

"Besides, Dr. Murphy said to be careful what you ate for a few days." Hannah stepped back and lowered the bowl to mouth level, watching Abbie for any sudden moves.

"I'm fine. I didn't get the crap Mom had. Dr. Murphy meant I shouldn't eat anything abrasive to my stomach." She glared at Hannah.

"Okay, all right. I'll get you a bowl." Hannah left.

Thin fingers touched Abbie's hand. She turned to her mother, whose eyes were watery. "I'm sorry you were hurt—"

"Mom, you didn't do anything wrong. You only gave birth to him. You didn't raise Royce to be a killer. Sigmund Jack did that to him and he put you in danger. You were set up from the beginning." Abbie would have nightmares forever about thinking she was going to die with no way to stop the killer or save her mother. "I was more scared for you. I still shake when I think about how close we came to losing you. If they hadn't sedated Royce so heavily, he'd have committed suicide *before* Dr. Murphy had a chance to do the transfusion."

"I would have done anything to keep you safe," her mother said. "Sigmund threatened the one thing that would keep me from ever telling about him or my son when he said he'd kill you if I did. Or if I pointed a finger at the Kore Women's Center."

Abbie couldn't imagine being given that choice. She'd have fought the world to protect a child . . . which she'd never have to worry about since she was never getting married.

"Abbie, uh . . ." Hannah called from the bedroom door.

"I don't see a bowl of ice cream in your hand," Abbie pointed out, though she laughed to lighten her accusation.

"Yeah, well, you might not have time to eat it."

"Why?"

"There's a man at the door asking for you. When I wouldn't let him talk to you unless he told me what he wanted, he said there's a private jet waiting on you at Midway Airport. He's driving a stretch, and I mean *stretch*, limousine. He has a sealed envelope for you."

———∞———

Hunter paced the tarmac at Lambert-St. Louis airport. He'd never been nervous in his life, but he was damned nervous now.

The limo driver stood at the ready next to the rear door of the black limousine.

The jet Hunter had sent for Abbie was finally taxiing in his direction. He'd debated meeting her at her mother's house to fly with her. But that would have allowed Abbie to dig in her heels at her mother's house or at Midway airport.

Nothing but the note he sent would have gotten her this far. He'd written that he'd share the story behind the karabiner he carried if she'd come to St. Louis to hear it.

He had the karabiner with him, hanging from his belt loop, where he'd clipped it the night he pulled Eliot's climbing gear off his body.

What he hadn't told Abbie was that she'd have to hear the story while she was riding in a car.

When the jet Todd loaned him, again, finally stopped and the steps were lowered, Hunter had to force himself to wait by the car and not go to her. He hadn't seen Abbie in five days.

He'd never realized how long five days could be.

When she emerged from the airplane and started down the steps he just stared, soaking her up from head to toe. She wore jeans and a turquoise sweater. Her eyes were bluer than her sweater. Black boots padded down the steps. Her hair was free, curling to her shoulders.

The only thing missing was her smile.

When she reached him she said, "I'm here because I'm naturally curious. Not because I'm willing to compromise."

"I understand and won't ask you to change the way you feel."

Her gaze faltered, as if she might have wanted him to at least try. "Glad you understand. What's with the car?"

"I thought we could take a drive while I told you the story."

She considered it slowly, her eyes going from him to the car. "Okay, but do not take me out of St. Louis or this state or the country."

"I won't take you anywhere you aren't willing to go."

Again, she gave him a curious look. The wind lifted her hair and floated her scent over to him. Hunter couldn't imagine not feeling her in his hands again or waking up next to her to make love. But she'd made her position clear when she said she would not stay with someone who didn't trust her.

Just saying he trusted her would never work with Abbie.

She walked to the car and climbed into the backseat. When Hunter slid in, she moved to the seat across from him. "Start talking."

When the car motored away, Hunter said, "I met Eliot in college." He told her about things he and Eliot had done and how his friend had died, leaving out classified details, but sharing that Eliot had entrusted Hunter with protecting Cynthia and little Theo. That Cynthia was the person Hunter went to see in at the cemetery.

"I can understand your caution with Cynthia's identity, especially given the responsibility Eliot left in your hands," Abbie said. "I'm sorry about him. I can't imagine losing someone the way you lost him."

She'd been clutching the side of the seat and lifted her hand. He thought she might reach for him in a gesture of comfort, but the limo pulled to the curb in front of a brick home at that moment and she pulled her fingers back.

He hid the twist of misery he felt over her withdrawal again, but he had brought her here for a reason and would not let her reticence stop him now. "I want you to meet someone."

Abbie looked around but made no comment on the

quiet neighborhood with sidewalks and trees in the front yards. Children played next door.

Hunter got out of the car and stood in sunshine that warmed the air to the mid-sixties. He offered Abbie his hand. She hesitated, then put her hand in his. Touching her again struck him like a lightning bolt. He wanted to feel her in his arms but would take what she gave him. When he turned her toward the ranch-style brick house, the front door opened and Cynthia stepped out onto the small porch. She smiled at him, expecting them since Hunter had called in advance.

When he walked Abbie to the house, he said, "This is Cynthia, Eliot's wife."

Abbie's mouth opened. She couldn't believe he was bringing her here, but she was at the steps and meeting Cynthia before she could put her thoughts in words.

"It's so nice to meet you, Abbie," Cynthia said, stepping back so they could enter.

"You too," Abbie mumbled. Hunter had explained how important it was to protect this woman's identity. What was he thinking? When she remembered her manners, she said, "Your home is beautiful." The toasty smell of baked cookies filled the house.

"Thank you. I'd love for you to come back when you can stay longer, but I understand you're on a tight schedule today," Cynthia said, turning to lead the way.

Abbie followed her through rooms decorated in down-to-earth chic. They walked through a kitchen in white and blue, then outside to a back screened porch, where a beautiful little boy played with plastic building blocks.

Hunter stepped up next to Abbie. His gaze was fixed on the little cherub with blond hair.

"Theo?" Cynthia said.

Her son raised powder-blue eyes and smiled at her.

"There's someone here to see you, Theo."

He stood up and walked to his mother, who said, "This is Abbie." Theo shook Abbie's hand like a little gentleman.

"And this is Hunter, your godfather."

Abbie couldn't speak. Hunter had clearly not met this child before today. She held her breath as Hunter walked over and dropped down on his knees, closer to eye level with Theo.

Hunter smiled at Theo. "Your daddy was a great man and he was my best friend. When you're older, I'll tell you stories about your dad, but you only need to know two things. Your daddy loved you very much . . ." He paused, his throat working as he swallowed, then added quietly, "And he was a hero."

Abbie's heart thumped wildly.

"This belonged to him," Hunter said, unhooking the carabiner from where it hung on his belt loop. "It's yours now."

Theo touched the karabiner with his little hands, then he looked up at Hunter with wonder in his eyes. He leaned forward, arms wide. Hunter lifted him into his arms, hugging the tiny boy.

Abbie's heart was breaking over the loss these three had shared, but she had a feeling Hunter hadn't healed at all from that awful night on the cliff.

He was healing now with Eliot's child in his arms. Hunter sat Theo back on his feet, then hooked the karabiner through a loop in Theo's jeans. The little boy's smile filled the room like bottled sunshine. Being a tiny person who didn't understand everything, he sat down to play again.

When Hunter stood his eyes were different, not so filled with dark shadows. He hugged Cynthia and said, "I'll call when I get some time. You call if you need anything."

Cynthia kissed his cheek. "Thank you." She didn't seem able to say anything else but walked them back out to the front porch and hugged Abbie good-bye.

Abbie was trying to assess everything that had happened, to figure out why Hunter had brought her here.

He walked over to the car and said something to the driver, who nodded, then drove away.

"How are we getting back to the airport?" Abbie asked.

"He's not going far," Hunter answered. "Take a walk with me to a park about a block away? Please?"

She put her hand in his. When they were out of sight of the house, she asked, "What's this really about, Hunter?"

"You haven't asked about Borys," he said, blatantly dodging her question.

"Okay, I'll play. How's Borys?"

"He's good. Sends his love. Says he'd like to see you. Don't you want to know where he is?"

"No. I really understand your need to be careful."

"He's in Wyoming at a new location. Pretty place up in the mountains I'd like to show you."

Abbie stopped and turned to him, but he held on to her hand. "Why are you telling me this?"

Hunter lifted his free hand and held her cheek. "Because I love you and I trust you. I've never told anyone about Cynthia, not even Borys. There are some things in my work I won't be able to tell you, because it's classified and this is what I do. But I trust you with my life and my love."

A tear leaked and ran down her face. He really did trust her. "How do you do that?"

"What, sweetheart?"

"Make me crazy to beat you one minute and crazy to love you the next."

He pulled her to him and kissed her. She gave up trying to figure out anything except how she could keep her hands on this incredible man forever. "I love you," she murmured between kisses, then pulled back. "What about your people or agency or whatever?"

"They aren't crazy about me being with someone connected to the media, but . . . I'm willing to leave the agency if reporting is what you want to do."

"I couldn't do that to the man I love," she whispered.

"Baby, you have no idea how much I love you or what I'm willing to do to keep you." He looked down at her. "I want you in my life more than anyone or anything else. Marry me."

She smiled and lifted her hand to trace his lips. He kissed her fingertips. "The good news is that I hate working in television news. Hate dealing with scum. I want to film documentaries."

"I'll buy you anything you need—"

"You can buy me camera equipment, but I want to make my own contacts and build a name again for myself in the business."

"Whatever you say as long as I get to hire a security team to protect you when I'm not around to do it myself."

Her heart thumped. He'd be a possessive and protective husband. She could live with that. "How about a deal?"

Hunter stared at her a minute, then said, "Sounds like something that requires hours and hours of negotiating."

"One thing isn't negotiable," she said, and smiled when he didn't look so sure of himself.

"What?"

"That I love you and always will."